5F (Yost)
4/03

THE FAIRY TALE SERIES
CREATED BY TERRI WINDLING

ONCE UPON A TIME...

. . . fairy tales were written for young and old
alike. It is only in the last century that they
have been deemed fit only for children
and stripped of much of their original
complexity, sensuality, and power
to frighten and delight.

Tor Books is proud to present the latest
offering in the Fairy Tale Series—a
growing library of beautifully designed
original novels by acclaimed writers of
fantasy and horror, each retelling a classic
tale such as Snow White and Rose Red,
Briar Rose, Tam Lin, and others in interesting—often startling—new ways.

Fitcher's Brides

GREGORY FROST

THE FAIRY TALE SERIES
CREATED BY TERRI WINDLING

A TOM DOHERTY ASSOCIATES BOOK
NEW YORK

FITCHER'S BRIDES

Copyright © 2002 by Gregory Frost

Introduction copyright © 2002 by Terri Windling

This book is printed on acid-free paper.

Edited by Terri Windling

A Tor Book
Published by Tom Doherty Associates, LLC
175 Fifth Avenue
New York, NY 10010

www.tor.com

Tor® is a registered trademark of Tom Doherty Associates, LLC.

Library of Congress Cataloging-in-Publication Data

Frost, Gregory.
    Fitcher's brides / Gregory Frost.—1st ed.
        p. cm.
    "A Tom Doherty Associates book."
    ISBN 0-765-30194-6 (acid-free paper)
        1. Finger Lakes Region (N.Y.)—Fiction.   2. Religious communities—Fiction.
3. Spouses of clergy—Fiction.   4. Remarried people—Fiction.   5. Stepmothers—
Fiction.   6. Sisters—Fiction.   7. Clergy—Fiction.   I. Title.
PS3556.R59815 F58 2002
813'.6—dc21

                                                                                2002028583

First Edition: December 2002

Printed in the United States of America

0   9   8   7   6   5   4   3   2   1

For Jeanne,
and all the other women who've eluded
their Bluebeards

I would like to thank first and foremost Kelly Link and Karen Joy Fowler for their incredible insights into the text in all its forms. You two made things crackle. Also my thanks to Natalie Anderson and the 2001 Sycamore Hill Writers' Workshop for further inestimable feedback; Rose and Roman at Gothic Eve's Bed and Breakfast of Trumansburg, New York, for providing both significant historical details and a lovely place to stay; Kelly, Gavin, and Deerfields, for the perfect retreat (and an incomparable wedding); Midori, Kerrie, and everyone else on the SurLaLune Fairy Tales site for the discussion on glass and other fairy-tale topics; Bala Cynwyd Library for material on candles; Barbara for putting up with the slight obsession this project became; Terri Windling for making the offer and then letting it run; Tom Canty for his artistry; Patrick Nielsen Hayden; and especially my agent, Martha Millard, for handling all those pesky little details.

*T*hese things saith the first and the last, which was dead, and is alive;

—Revelation 2:8

... the villains are those who use words intentionally to exploit, control, transfix, incarcerate and destroy for their benefit.

—JACK ZIPES, "Spells of Enchantment,"
When Dreams Came True

Once upon a time fairy tales were told to audiences of young and old alike. It is only in the last century that such tales were deemed fit only for small children, stripped of much of their original complexity, sensuality, and power to frighten and delight. In the Fairy Tale Series, some of the finest writers working today are going back to the older versions of tales and reclaiming them for adult readers, reworking their themes into original, highly unusual fantasy novels.

This series began many years ago when artist Thomas Canty and I asked some of our favorite writers if they would create new novels based on old tales, each one to be published with Tom's distinctive, Pre-Raphaelite-inspired cover art. The writers were free to approach the tales in any way they liked; and so some recast the stories in modern settings, while others used historical landscapes or created enchanted imaginary worlds. The first three volumes in the series (original published by Ace Books) were *The Sun, the Moon, and the Stars* by Steven Brust, *Jack the Giant-Killer* (now expanded into *Jack of Kinrowan*) by Charles de Lint, and *The Nightingale* by Kara Dalkey. The series then moved to its present home at Tor Books, where we published three more vol-

umes: *Snow White and Rose Red* by Patricia C. Wrede, *Tam Lin* by
Pamela Dean, and *Briar Rose* by Jane Yolen. After this, the Fairy
Tales Series was put on hold while Ellen Datlow, Tom Canty,
and I worked on a related project: the World Fantasy Award-
winning "Snow White, Blood Red" series (six volumes of original
short stories based on traditional tales). When this was complete,
the Fairy Tales Series resumed with the publication of Tanith
Lee's *White as Snow*, a dark, mythic version of the Snow White
fairy tale, followed by the book you now hold in your hands:
Fitcher's Brides by Gregory Frost.

Greg is the author of several previous novels, including *Lyrec*,
Tain, and *Remscela* (the latter two based on Irish myth). But to
fairy-tale aficionados he is best known as the author of "The Root
of the Matter"—a dark, sensual re-telling of the Grimms' fairy
tale Rapunzel (*Snow White, Blood Red*)—and "Sparks"—a modern
re-telling of Hans Christian Andersen's The Tinder Box (*Black
Swan, White Raven*). His haunting version of the Celtic ballad
Cruel Sister is forthcoming in *My Swan Sister and Other Re-told
Fairy Tales*. On the strength of these fine stories, I asked Greg if
he would create a novel-length fairy tale to publish in this series,
and he kindly agreed, choosing the old tale of Bluebeard for in-
spiration.

Though based on older folk tales of demon lovers and devilish
bridegrooms, the story of Bluebeard, as we know it today, is the
creation of French writer Charles Perrault—first published in
1697 in his collection *Histoires ou contes du temps passé* (*Stories or
Tales of Past Times*). Perrault was one of a group of writers who
socialized in the literary salons of Paris, creating among them a
vogue for literature inspired by peasant folk tales. These new
stories were called *contes des feés*, from which our modern term
"fairy tales" derives—but the *contes des feés* of the French salons
were intended for adult readers.[1]

[1]Perrault's collection was originally published under the name of his son, and presented
itself as a book of bedtime tales from "Old Mother Goose"—but a "faux naif" style was

Bluebeard, for example, has little to recommend it as a children's story. Rather, it's a gruesome cautionary tale about the dangers of marriage (on the one hand) and the perils of greed and curiosity (on the other)—more akin, in our modern culture, to horror films than to Disney cartoons. The story as Perrault tells it is this: A wealthy man, wishing to wed, turns his attention to the two beautiful young daughters of his neighbor, a widow. Neither girl wants to marry the man because of his ugly blue beard—until he invites the girls and their mother to a party at his country estate. Seduced by luxurious living, the youngest daughter agrees to accept Bluebeard's hand. The two are promptly wed and the girl becomes mistress of his great household. Soon after, Bluebeard tells his wife that business calls him to make a long journey. He leaves her behind with all the keys to his house, his strongboxes, his caskets of jewels, telling her she may do as she likes with them and to "make good cheer." There is only one key that she may not use, to a tiny closet at the end of the hall. That alone is forbidden, he tells her, "and if you happen to open it, you may expect my just anger and resentment."

Of course, the very first thing the young wife does is to run to the forbidden door "with such excessive haste that she nearly fell and broke her neck." She has promised obedience to her husband, but a combination of greed and curiosity (the text implies) propels her to the fatal door the minute his back is turned. She opens it and finds a shuttered room, its floor awash in blood, containing the murdered corpses of Bluebeard's previous young wives. Horrified, the young wife drops the key into a puddle of blood. Retrieving it, she locks the room and runs back to her own chamber. Now she attempts to wash the key so that her transgression will not be revealed—but no matter how long and hard she scrubs it, the bloodstain will not come off. That very night, her husband returns—his business has been suddenly concluded. Trembling, she pretends that nothing has happened and wel-

---

often adopted by the salon writers, who nonetheless intended their work for an audience of fellow *salonnières* and other aristocratic, educated adults. Embedded within the tales were sly, pointed critiques of life under Louis XIV.

comes him back. In the morning, however, he demands the return of the keys and examines them carefully. "Why is there
blood on the smallest key?" he asks her craftily. Bluebeard's wife
protests that she does not know how it came to be there. "You
do not know?" he roars. "But I know, madam. You opened the
forbidden door. Very well. You must now go back and take your
place among my other wives." Tearfully, she delays her death by
asking for time to say her prayers—for her brothers are due to
visit that day, her only hope of salvation. She calls three times to
her sister Anne in the tower room at the top of the house ("Sister
Anne, Sister Anne, do you see anyone coming?"). And at last they
come, just as Bluebeard raises a sword to chop off her head. The
murderous husband is dispatched, his wealth disbursed among
the family, and the young wife is married again, Perrault tells us,
to "a very worthy gentleman who made her forget the ill time
she had passed with Bluebeard."

This bloodthirsty tale is quite different in tone from the other
tales in Perrault's *Histoires* (the courtly confections of Sleeping
Beauty, Cinderella, etc.), and its history has been a source of
debate among fairy-tale scholars. Some assert that Perrault was
inspired by the historical figure of Gilles de Rais, a fifteenth-
century Marshal of France and companion at arms to Joan of Arc.
After driving the English out of France, this martial hero returned
to his Breton estate where, a law unto himself, he practiced al-
chemy and dark magic while young peasant boys began to disappear across his lands. Rumors swirled around de Rais and when,
at last, the Duke of Brittany intervened and investigated, the
remains of over fifty boys were dug up in de Rais's castle. He
later confessed to sodomizing and killing one hundred and forty
boys, although the actual number may be closer to three hundred.
De Rais was simultaneously hanged and burned alive for these
crimes in 1440.

There is another old Breton tale, however, which relates more
closely to the Bluebeard story: that of Cunmar the Accursed, who
beheaded a succession of wives, one after the other, when they
became pregnant. Cunmar was a historical figure, the ruler of
Brittany in the mid-sixth century, but the legend attached to him

has its roots in folk tales, not history. The story concerns a nobleman's daughter, Triphine, the last of Cunmar's wives. Heavily
pregnant with his son, she enters Cunmar's ancestral chapel
where she is warned of her fate by the bloodstained ghosts of his
previous wives. She flees to the woods, but her husband pursues
her, cuts off her head, and leaves her to die. Her body is found
by Gildas, the abbot of Rhuys, who is destined to be a saint.
Miraculously, he reattaches the head and brings her back to life.
The pair follow Cunmar back to his castle, where Gildas causes
the walls themselves to crash down on the murderer. Triphine's
son is safely delivered, given to Gildas and the church, and Triphine devotes the rest of her life to prayer and performing good
works. Eventually, she too is sainted (depicted in religious statues
and paintings as carrying her own severed head)—while the ghost
of Cunmar continues to haunt the country in the form of a were-
wolf. The Bluebeard parallel becomes stronger yet when one
considers a series of frescoes depicting Triphine's story in the
Breton church St. Nicholas des Eaux. One panel of these medieval paintings shows Cunmar handing a key to his young bride,
while another shows her entering the chamber where his previous
wives are hanging.

It's possible that Charles Perrault knew the story of Cunmar
the Accursed, using details from it to color his own. Or it may
simply be that he knew other similar stories from French and
Italian peasant lore, with their wide range of "monstrous bridegroom" and "murderous stranger" motifs. Indeed, these motifs
are ones we find in folk traditions around the world. But in
marked contrast to Perrault's Bluebeard (the best known of such
tales today), in the old peasant stories the heroine does not weep
and wait for her brothers' rescue—rather, she's a cunning, clever
girl fully capable of rescuing herself.

In the Italian tale Silvernose (as compiled by Italo Calvino
from three regional variants[2]), the devil, disguised as a nobleman,
visits a widowed washerwoman and asks for her eldest daughter
to come and work in his fine house. The widow distrusts the

---

[2]*Italian Folktales*, Italo Calvino (1956).

man's strange nose but her daughter agrees to go nonetheless, bored as she is with life at home and looking for an adventure. She follows Silvernose to his palace, where she's given keys to all the fine rooms. He gives her the run of the place—except for one door that she may not unlock. That night, Silvernose enters her room and leaves a rose in her hair as she sleeps. In the morning, he rides off on business, leaving his young servant behind. Immediately she opens the forbidden door. Inside, she finds hell itself—a fiery room where the souls of the damned writhe in eternal torment. The horrified girl swiftly slams the door shut, but the flower in her hair has been singed. When Silvernose returns, the flower is proof of her transgression. "So that's how you obey me!" he cries, opening the door and tossing her in. He then returns to the washerwoman, and asks for the second daughter. The middle girl meets her sister's fate. But the youngest daughter, Lucia, is cunning. She too follows Silvernose to his palace, she too is given the forbidden key, she too has a flower placed in her hair as she lies asleep. But she notices the flower and puts it safely away in a jar of water. Then she opens the door, pulls her sisters out of the flames, and plots their escape. When Silvernose comes home, the flower is back in her hair, as fresh as ever. The devil is pleased. Here's a servant at last who will bind herself to his will. Lucia prevails upon him then to carry some laundry back to her mother. Her eldest sister is hidden inside the bag, which is very heavy. "You must take it straight to my mother," she says, "for I have a special ability to see from great distances, and if you stop to rest and put that bag down, I will surely know." The devil starts upon his trip, grows tired, and begins to put the bag down. "I see you, I see you!" the eldest sister cries from inside the laundry bag; and thinking it's Lucia's voice, Silvernose hurries on. Lucia repeats this ruse for the middle sister. Then she hides in the third bag herself, along with a store of gold pilfered from the devil's treasury. Reunited with their mother (and wealthy now besides), the sisters plant a cross in the yard and the devil keeps his distance.

The Italian story Silvernose is similar to an old German tale called Fitcher's Bird, collected by the Brothers Grimm and pub-

lished in *Kinder- und Hausmärchen*. In this story, the Bluebeard
figure is a mysterious wizard disguised as a beggar. The wizard
appears at the door of a household with three beautiful unmarried
daughters. He asks the eldest for something to eat, and just as
she hands the beggar some bread he touches her, which causes
her to jump in the basket he carries. He spirits the girl away to
his splendid house and gives her keys to its rooms, but forbids
her, under penalty of death, to use the smallest key. The next
day he sets off on a journey, but before he leaves he gives her
an egg, instructing the girl to carry the egg with her everywhere
she goes. As soon as he leaves she explores the house, and although she tries to ignore the last key, curiosity gets the better
of her and she opens the final door. Inside she finds an ax and a
basin filled with blood and body parts. In shock, she drops the
egg in the blood, and then cannot wipe off the stain. When
the wizard comes home, he demands the return of the keys and
the egg, and discovers her deed. "You entered the chamber
against my wishes, now you will go back in against yours. Your
life is over," he cries, and cuts her into little pieces. This sequence of events is repeated with the second daughter, and then
with the third. But the youngest girl is the clever one. She puts
the egg carefully away before she enters the forbidden chamber,
determined to rescue her sisters. Inside, she finds her sisters
chopped up into pieces. She promptly gets to work reassembling
the body parts, piece by bloody piece. When her sisters' limbs
are all in place, the pieces knit themselves back together and the
two elder girls come back to life with cries of joy. Then they
must hide as the wizard returns. He calls for the youngest and
asks for the egg. She hands it over, and he can find no stain or
blemish on it. "You have passed the test," he informs her, "so
tomorrow you shall be my bride." The girl agrees that she will
wed the wizard, under this condition: "First take a basket of gold
to my father. You must promise to carry it on your back, and you
mustn't stop along the way. I'll be watching you from the window." The two elder girls are hidden inside the basket, beneath
a king's ransom in gold. The wizard picks it up and stumbles off,
sweating under his burden. Yet every time he stops to rest, he

hears one of the sisters say: "I see you, I see you! Don't put the basket down! Keep moving!" Thinking it's the voice of his bride, the wizard continues on his way—while the youngest girl invites the wizard's friends to a wedding feast. She takes a skull from the bloody room, crowns it with garlands of flowers and jewels, and sets it in the attic window, facing the road below. Then she crawls into a barrel of honey, cuts open a featherbed, and rolls in the feathers until she's completely disguised as a strange white bird. As she leaves the house, she meets the wizard's equally evil friends coming toward it. They say to her:

> "Oh, Fitcher's bird, where are you from?"
> "From feathered Fitcher's house I've come."
> "The young bride there, what has she done?"
> "She's cleaned and swept the house all through;
> she's in the window looking at you."[3]

She then meets the wizard himself on the road, and these questions are repeated. The wizard looks up, he sees the skull in the window, and hurries home to his bride. But by now, the brothers and relatives of the three young girls are waiting for him. They lock the door, then burn the house down with all the sorcerers inside.

The Robber Bridegroom is another classic fairy tale about a murderous stranger. It too can be found in the Grimms' collection, and in variants around the world. One of the most evocative of these variants is the English version of the story, in which the Bluebeard figure is know as Mr. Fox (or Reynardine). A girl is courted by a handsome russet-haired man who appears to have great wealth. He is charming, well mannered, well groomed, but his origins are mysterious. As the wedding day grows near, it troubles the girl that she's never seen his home—so she takes

---

[3]The unexplained name Fitcher, according to Marina Warner, "derives from the Icelandic *fitfugl*, meaning 'web-footed bird,' so there may well be a buried memory here of those bird-women who rule narrative enchantments." (Marina Warner, *From the Beast to the Blonde*, 1994).

matters into her own hands and sets off through the woods to seek it. In the dark of the woods, she finds a high wall and a gate. Over the gate it says: "Be bold." She enters, and finds a large, dilapidated mansion inside. Over the door it says: "Be bold, be bold." She enters a gloomy hall. Over the stairs it says: "Be bold, be bold, but not too bold." She climbs the stairs to a gallery, over which she finds the words: "Be bold, be bold, but not too bold, lest your heart's blood should run cold." The gallery is filled with the body parts of murdered women. She turns to flee, just as Mr. Fox comes in, dragging a new victim. She hides and watches, horrified, as the girl is chopped to bits. A severed hand flies close to her hiding place, a diamond ring on one finger. She takes the hand, creeps out the door, and runs home just as fast as she can. The next day there's a feast for the wedding couple, and Mr. Fox appears, looking as handsome as ever. He comments, "How pale you are, my love!"

"Last night I had a terrible dream," she says. "I dreamed I entered the woods and found a high wall and a gate. Over the gate it said: Be bold." She proceeds to tell him, and the assembled guests, just what she found inside.

"It is not so, no, it was not so, and God forbid it should be so," said Mr. Fox.[4]

"But it is so, and it was so, and here's the hand and the ring I have to show!" She pulls the severed hand from her dress and flings it into her bridegroom's lap. The wedding guests rise up to cut Mr. Fox into a thousand pieces.

An Indian version of the tale has the daughter of respectable Brahmans courted by a man who is actually a tiger in disguise, anxious to procure a wife who can cook the curry dishes he loves. It is only when the girl is married and on her way to her husband's house that she learns the truth and finds herself wife and servant to a ferocious beast. She bears him a child, a tiger cub, before she finally makes her escape. As she leaves, she tears the cub in two and hangs it over the flames so that her husband will smell the roasting meat and think that she's still inside. It's an odd little

---

[4]These words are repeated by Shakespeare in *Much Ado About Nothing.*

tale, in which one feels sneaking sympathy for the tiger.

In various "demon lover" ballads found in the Celtic folk tradition, the Bluebeard figure is the devil in disguise, or else a treacherous elfin knight, or a murderous ghost, or a false lover with rape or robbery on his mind. In "May Colvin," False Sir John rides off with a nobleman's daughter he's promised to marry—but when they reach the sea, he orders the maiden to climb down from her horse, to take off her fine wedding clothes, and to hand over her dowry. "Here I have drowned seven ladies," says he, "and you shall be the eighth." May begs him, for the sake of modesty, to turn as she disrobes. And then she promptly pushes him in the water to his death.

In a Scandinavian version of this ballad, a nobleman's daughter is courted by a handsome, honey-tongued, false suitor who promises to take her to the fair if she meets him in the woods. Her father will not let her go, her mother will not let her go, her brothers will not let her go, but her confessor gives permission, provided she keeps hold of her virtue. She finds her suitor in the woods busy at work digging a grave. He says the grave is for his dog; but she protests that it is too long. He says the grave is for his horse; she says it is too small. He tells her the grave is meant for her, unless she consents to lie with him. Eight maidens has he killed before, and she shall be the ninth. Now the choice is hers—she must lose her virtue or her life. She chooses death, but advises her false suitor to remove his coat, lest her heart's blood spatter the fine cloth and ruin it. As he takes it off, she grabs the sword and strikes his head off "like a man." The head then speaks, instructing her to fetch a salve to heal the wound. Three times the girl refuses to do the bidding of a murderer. She takes the head, she takes his horse, she takes his dog, and rides back home—but as she goes, she encounters her suitor's mother, his sisters, his brothers. Each time they ask, "Where is thy true love?" Each time she answers, "Lying in the grass, and bloody is his bridal bed." (In some versions, the entire family is made up of robbers and she must kill them, too.) She then returns to her father's court, receiving a hero's welcome there. But in other "murderous lover" ballads, the heroines are not so lucky. Some meet with graves at the bottom of the sea, others in cold rivers, leaving ghosts behind to sing the sorrowful song of their tragic end.

Charles Perrault drew a number of elements from folk tales and ballads like these when he created the story of the urbane, murderous Bluebeard and his bloody chamber. Like Silvernose, Bluebeard is marked by a physical disfigurement—the beard that "made him so frightfully ugly that all the women and girls run away from him." Like Mr. Fox, his wealth and his charm serve to overcome the natural suspicions aroused by his mysterious past and the rumors of missing wives. Like the false suitors, he seduces his victims with courtly manners, presents, and flattery, all the while tenderly preparing the grave that will soon receive them. Perrault parts with these older tales, however, by apportioning blame to the maiden herself. He portrays her quite unsympathetically as a woman who marries solely from greed, and who calls Bluebeard's wrath upon herself with her act of disobedience. This is absent in the older tales, where curiosity and disobedience, combined with cunning and courage, are precisely what saves the heroine from marriage to a monster, death at a robber's hands, or servitude to the devil. Perrault presents his Bluebeard as a well-mannered, even generous man who makes only one demand of his wife, marrying again and again as woman after woman betrays this trust. Only at the end of the tale, as the bridegroom stands revealed as a monster, does Perrault shift his sympathy to the bride, and Bluebeard is dispatched. Perrault ends the tale with a moral that stresses the heroine's transgressions and not her husband's, warning maidens that "curiosity, in spite of its appeal, often leads to deep regret." In a second moral, Perrault remarks that the story took place long ago, modern husbands are not such "jealous malcontents." Jealous malcontent? "Homicidal maniac" would be a better description. Again Perrault's words imply that despicable as Bluebeard's actions are, they are actions in response to the provocation of his wife's behavior.

Another departure from the older folk tales is that Bluebeard's wife (like the other fairy-tale heroines in his *Histoires ou contes du temps passé*) is a remarkably helpless creature. She does not outwit Bluebeard herself, she weeps and trembles and waits for her brothers—unlike the folklore heroines who, even when calling brothers to their aid, have first proven themselves to be quick-witted, courageous, and pro-active. As Maria Tatar has pointed out (in her book *The Classic Fairy Tales*), "Perrault's story, by underscoring the heroine's kinship with certain literary, biblical, and mythical figures (most notably Psyche, Eve, and Pandora), gives us a tale that willfully undermines a robust folkloric tradition in which the heroine is a resourceful agent of her own salvation."

This difference is particularly evident when we compare Perrault's passive heroine with those created by other fairy-tale writers in the French salons—the majority of them women writers, whose works were quite popular in their day. Perrault's niece, Marie-Jeanne L'Héritier, was also the author of fairy tales; her story "The Subtle Prince," published three years before Perrault's *Histoires*, drew on some of the same folklore motifs as the story of Bluebeard. In L'Héritier's tale, a king has three daughters, two of them foolish, the youngest one clever. When the king journeys away from home, he gives each of his girls a magical distaff made of glass that will shatter if the girl loses her virtue. (The telltale key in "murderous bridegroom" tales is often also made of glass.) The wicked prince of a neighboring kingdom enters the castle disguised as a beggar, then seduces each elder sister in turn—marrying, bedding, and abandoning them. The youngest sister sees through his charms, whereupon he tries to take her by force. No wilting flower, she hoists an ax and threatens to chop him into pieces. The story goes on, with more attempts on the life and honor of the Subtle Princess, but she turns the tables on the wicked prince, kills him in a trap he's set for her, and goes on to marry his gentle, civil, kindhearted younger brother. The Subtle Princess has no brothers of her own to come rushing to her aid, nor does she need them. She manages matters very well for herself, thank you.

In the following century, as women lost the social gains they'd made in the heady days of the salons, tales by L'Héritier and other women (D'Aulnoy, Murat, Bernard, etc.) fell out of fashion, while those by Perrault—with their simpler prose style, their moral endings, their meek and mild princesses—continued to be reprinted and recounted year after year. As the eighteenth and nineteenth centuries progressed, re-tellings of Bluebeard increasingly emphasized the "sin" of disobedience as central to the story—a subsequent version was titled *Bluebeard, or The Effects of Female Curiosity.* As fairy tales became an area of scholarly inquiry in the nineteenth and twentieth centuries, folklorists pounced upon this theme in their analysis of the tale—and took it one step further, suggesting that Bluebeard's wife's disobedience was sexual in nature, the bloodstained key symbolizing the act of infidelity. (Never mind the fact that there are no other men in the whole of Perrault's tale until those convenient brothers come thundering out of nowhere to save her.) Psychologist Bruno Bettelheim was one of the critics who read Bluebeard as a tale of infidelity. In his flawed but influential book of the 1970s, *The Uses of Enchantment,* he pronounced Bluebeard "a cautionary tale which warns: Women, don't give in to your sexual curiosity; men, don't permit yourself to be carried away by your anger at being sexually betrayed." But as novelist Lydia Millet has pointed out in her essay "The Wife Killer"[5]: "Blue Beard wanted his new wife to find the corpses of his former wives. He *wanted* the new bride to discover their mutilated corpses; he *wanted* her disobedience. Otherwise, he wouldn't have given her the key to the forbidden closet; he wouldn't have left town on his so-called business trip; and he wouldn't have stashed the dead Mrs. Blue Beards in the closet in the first place. Transparently, this was a set-up." Fairy-tale scholar Maria Tartar comments: "Bloody key as a sign of disobedience—this is the motif folklorists consistently read as the defining moment of the tale. The bloodstained key points to a double transgression, one that is at once moral and sexual. For one critic, it becomes a sign of 'marital infidelity'; for another it marks the heroine's 'irreversible loss of her virginity';

[5]Published in *Mirror, Mirror on the Wall: Women Writers Explore Their Favorite Fairy Tales,* edited by Kate Bernheimer, 1998.

for a third, it stands for 'defloration.' If we recall that the bloody chamber in Bluebeard's castle is strewn with the corpses of previous wives, this reading of the bloodstained key as a marker of sexual infidelity becomes willfully wrongheaded in its effort to vilify Bluebeard's wife."

Marina Warner, in her excellent fairy-tale study *From the Beast to the Blonde*, suggests another way to read the tale: as an expression of young girls' fears about marriage. Perrault was writing at a time, and in a social class, when arranged marriages were commonplace, and divorce out of the question. A young woman could easily find herself married off to an old man without her consent—or to a monster: a drunkard, a libertine, or an abusive spouse.[6] Further, the mortality rate of women in childbirth was frighteningly high. Remarriage was commonplace for men who'd lost a wife (or wives) in this fashion, and ghosts from previous marriages hung over many a young bride's wedding.

An aspect of the Bluebeard tale that we see emphasized in later re-tellings is xenophobia, with the bridegroom betrayed as an Oriental. There is nothing in the text of Perrault's tale (except that extraordinary beard) to indicate that Bluebeard is anything but a wealthy, if eccentric, French nobleman—yet illustrations to the story, from eighteenth century woodcuts to the famous Victorian illustrations of Edmund Dulac—depict Bluebeard in Turkish garb, threatening his bride with a scimitar. It must be remembered that "Arabian Nights" style fairy tales were enormously popular in Europe from the eighteenth century onward, yet none of the other tales in Perrault's collection *Histoires ou contes du temps passé* were given this Oriental gloss as persistently as Bluebeard. Both monstrous and sensual (all those wives!),

---

[6]Arranged marriages to monstrous men had blighted the lives of several women in Perrault's salon circle. The fairy-tale writer Madame D'Aulnoy, for example, was pulled out of a convent at age fifteen and married off by her father to a wealthy brute thirty years her senior. After a series of rather scandalous adventures, she managed to establish a separate household in Paris, where she ran a fashionable salon that Perrault and his niece, L'Héritier, both frequented. Perrault, like his fellow *salonnières*, was firmly against arranged marriages.

Bluebeard is perhaps a more comfortable figure when he is the Other, the Outsider, the Foreigner, and not one of us. And yet, it's the fact that he *is* one of us—the polite, well-mannered gentleman next door—that makes the story so very chilling to this day. While tales like Beauty and the Beast serve to remind us that a monstrous visage can hide the heart of a truly good man, Bluebeard shows us the reverse: a man's fine facade might hide a monster.[7]

Bluebeard remained well known throughout Europe right up to the twentieth century, inspiring new tales in its turn, as well as dramas, operettas, and countless pantomimes. William Makepeace Thackeray published a parody of Bluebeard called *Bluebeard's Ghost* in 1843 that chronicled the further romantic adventures of Bluebeard's widow. Jacques Offenbach wrote a rather burlesque operetta titled *Barbe-bleu* in 1866. In 1899, the Belgian symbolist Maurice Maeterlinck wrote a libretto entitled *Ariane et Barbe-Bleu*, set to music by Paul Dukas and performed in Paris in 1907. Maeterlinck's version, written with the aid of his lover, the singer Georgette Leblanc, combined the Bluebeard story with elements from the myth of Ariadne, Theseus, and the Minotaur. In this sad, fatalistic version of the tale, Ariane, the last of Bluebeard's brides, attempts to rescue his previous wives and finds them bound by chains of their own making to Bluebeard's castle. *The Seven Wives of Bluebeard* by Anatole France, published in 1903, re-told Perrault's story from Bluebeard's point of view, portraying the man as a good-hearted (if somewhat simpleminded) nobleman whose reputation has been sullied by the duplicitous women he's married. Bela Bartok's opera *Duke Bluebeard's Castle* (1911), libretto by Bela Balasz, presented a brooding, philosophical Bluebeard, reflecting on the impossibility of lasting love between men and women.

[7]For an interesting look at orientalism and Bluebeard, particularly as it relates to Angela Carter's rendition of the tale, see Danielle M. Roemer's article "The Contextualization of the Marquis in Angela Carter's 'The Bloody Chamber,' " which can be found in the special Angela Carter issue of *Marvels and Tales: Journal of Fairy-tale Studies*, Vol. 12, #1, 1998.

   As fairy tales were relegated to the nursery in the twentieth century, Bluebeard was seldom included (for obvious reasons) in collections aimed at children. And yet the story did not disappear from popular culture; it moved from the printed page to film. As early as 1901, George Méliès directed a silent film version titled *Barbe-bleue* that manages, despite cinematic limitations, to be both comic and horrific. Other film treatments over the years included *Bluebeard's Eighth Wife* directed by Ernst Lubitsch, starring Gary Cooper and Claudette Colbert (1938); *Bluebeard* directed by Edgar G. Ulmer, starring John Carradine (1944); *Bluebeard* directed by Edward Dmytryk, starring Richard Burton (1972); and *Bluebeard's Castle*, a film version of Bartok's opera, directed by Sir Georg Solti (1981). In addition to these direct interpretations of the Bluebeard legend, Maria Tatar makes a case that Bluebeard is a precursor of cinematic horror. "In 'Bluebeard,' as in cinematic horror," she writes, "we have not only a killer who is propelled by psychotic rage, but also the abject victims of his serial murders, along with a 'final girl' (Bluebeard's wife), who either saves herself or arranges her own rescue. The 'terrible place' of horror, a dark, tomblike site that harbors grisly evidence of the killer's derangement, manifests itself as Bluebeard's castle."[8] Marina Warner concurs. "Bluebeard," she notes, "has entered secular mythology alongside Cinderella and Snow White. But his story possesses a characteristic with particular affinity to the present day: seriality. Whereas the violence in the heroines' lives is considered suitable for children, the ogre has metamorphosed in popular culture for adults, into mass murderer, the kidnapper, the serial killer: a collector, as in John Fowles's novel, an obsessive, like Hannibal Lecter in *The Silence of the Lambs*. Though cruel women, human or fairy, dominate children's stories with their powers, the Bluebeard figure, as a generic type of male murderer, has gradually entered material requiring restricted ratings as well. (As patriarch, he remains at ease in the nursery.) There are several pornographic film titles which use the name Bluebeard; more surprisingly, perhaps, the story has appealed to women writers like

---

[8]*The Classic Fairy Tales*, Maria Tatar (1999).

Margaret Atwood and Angela Carter, both of whom have produced contemporary treatments."[9]

Indeed, for modern prose versions of Bluebeard we must go not to the children's fairy-tale shelves, as we do for other stories by Perrault. We must go to the shelves of adult literature, where we find a number of interesting re-tellings. Foremost among them is Angela Carter's splendid story "The Bloody Chamber," published in her short story collection of the same name, in which the author gives full rein to the tale's inherent sensuality, and expands the role of the bride's mother to wonderful effect. *Bluebeard's Daughter* by Sylvia Townsend Warner is a wry, sly, elegant tale about the daughter of Bluebeard's third wife, with her own abiding interest in the locked room of her father's castle. Margaret Atwood's fine story *Bluebeard's Egg*, published in her collection of that name, is a contemporary, purely realist tale of marriage and infidelity that draws its symbolism from both Bluebeard and Fitcher's Bird. *Bluebeard* by Kurt Vonnegut and *The Blue Diary* by Alice Hoffman are both contemporary novels that make use of symbolism from the fairy tale in intriguing ways. Vonnegut's book is the tale of an artist with a secret in his potato barn; Hoffman's novel is the study of a seemingly perfect man with a mysterious past. "Bones" by Francesca Lia Block is a brief but thoroughly chilling take on the Bluebeard story, concerning a lonely girl and a wealthy young man in the L.A. hills. It was first published in her fairy-tale collection *The Rose and the Beast* (2000). Neil Gaiman draws upon Robber Bridegroom legends and the English tale of Mr. Fox in his haunting prose-poem "The White Road," first published in the fairy-tale anthology *Ruby Slippers, Golden Tears* (Datlow & Windling, eds., 1996). Bluebeard poetry ranges from Edna St. Vincent Millay's "Bluebeard" (*Renascence and Other Poems*, 1917) to Anne Sexton's "The Gold Key" (*Transformations*, 1971) to Gwen Strauss's "Bluebeard" (*Trail of Stones*, 1990).

In "The Wife Killer," Lydia Millet reflects on Bluebeard's potent, enduring allure. "Blue Beard retains his charm," she writes, "by being what most men and women feel they cannot

[9]*From the Beast to the Blonde*, Marina Warner (1994).

be: an overt articulator of the private fantasy of egomania. At first glance he is simultaneously what we can never be and what we long to be; by implication a sadistic killer, by extension a sexual hedonist, and at the least a particularly earnest misogynist, he is the subject that takes itself for a god. He is omnipotent because he accepts no social compromise; he acts solely in the pursuit of his own satisfaction." She goes on to remind us that "between an egotist with high expectations and a sociopath stretches only the fine thread of empathy and identification."

Her words apply to the Bluebeard at the heart of Gregory Frost's new novel: the controlling, calculating, charismatic Reverend Fitcher, ruling over his flock of true believers in nineteenth-century New York State.[10] The author draws upon Fitcher's Bird, The Robber Bridegroom, and other related "murderous stranger" tales to spin a story in which faith (like curiosity) is a two-edged sword. Like Bluebeard, the story that follows is about illusion, transgression, and carnal appetites. Like Fitcher's Bird, it features a traditional fairy-tale heroine: the third and youngest daughter, clever, disobedient, and courageous. Like The Robber Bridegroom and Mr. Fox, it warns us: Be bold, be bold, but not too bold, lest your life's blood should run cold. Beware of strangers in the wood . . . and of gentlemen in the front parlor.

We hope you'll enjoy this latest edition in the Fairy Tales Series. With the help of the good folks at Tor Books, we have more Fairy Tales novels in store for you. (Publication information will be posted on the Tor Books Web site: www.tor.com, and on my own Web site: www.endicott-studio.com.) To learn more about Blue-

---

[10]Historically, this was time when religious fervor, doomsday cults, and experimental utopian communities were widespread in the area—as well as quasi-scientific ideas like mesmerism, which Gregory Frost makes use of in *Fitcher's Brides*. Oddly enough, mesmerism grew out of the same French salons that fostered the creation of fairy tales like Bluebeard. You can read Gregory Frost's article on the subject on the Endicott Studio Web site: www.endicott-studio.com/formsmr.html.

beard and other tales, and to see classic Bluebeard illustrations, visit the SurLaLune Fairy Tale Pages Web site edited by Heidi Anne Heiner: www.surlalunefairytales.com. For further reading on the subject, I recommend the following books: *From the Beast to the Blonde: On Fairy Tales and Their Tellers* by Marina Warner, *Spells of Enchantment* edited by Jack Zipes, and *The Classic Fairy Tales* edited by Maria Tatar.

TERRI WINDLING
The Endicott Studio for Mythic Arts
Tucson, Arizona, and Devon, England

looks and smiles tenderly to each of her daughters as she buries the handkerchief beneath her where they won't see, so they won't know.

Crack! Crack!

It's only a game. It's only for show. No one is hurt.

She peeks again at the stripe on her mother's chin.

Three months hence her mother will lie in a casket on a bier, her hands folded. Her father will sit beside her as if the bones have been torn out of his body. Outside the black-draped parlor, the world she knew will have stopped.

Crack!

Fitcher's Brides

CRACK! GOES THE WHIP. SHE flinches at the sound.

Crack! and the animal jumps. *Crack!* The lion leaps to a perch. *Crack!* The lioness paws at the air.

The tamer wears jodhpurs and thigh-high boots that fold at the top. She has never seen boots like that before and wants a pair of her own, but she does not like what he does with that whip and would snatch it from him if he came near.

Her mother is there beside her, saying "ooh" and "aah" with the crowd, and also at her as if to say, "It's a trick, dear, a game. It doesn't hurt the animals."

This is the last time her mother will be able to go anywhere with them. Even now she gives a little cough and clutches the handkerchief in a ball against her mouth. The cough is inaudible over the noises of the crowd; the lurch of her shoulders gives her away.

When her mother slides the handkerchief down, it leaves a smear on her face, like bright clown makeup wet and shiny from her lip to her jaw. Mother doesn't know it's there because she

One

*T*HEY CLIMBED THE GANGPLANK to the steamboat, the three Charter sisters. As the eldest, Vernelia led them, followed by Amy, and finally Kate, the youngest at sixteen. The plank was wet but someone had thrown a layer of grist onto it so that feet could find purchase in the climb.

In the middle, halfway between land and lake and part of neither, Kate stopped and turned for a final look at the town of Geneva.

The wharf and streets teemed with people, more than the girls had ever seen gathered in a single place, even on the commons in Boston on the Fourth of July. Certainly all of the people below had not come down the Cayuga & Seneca Canal with the girls, their father and stepmother: No canal boat could have held so many. Even the steamboat that would carry them to the southern tip of Seneca Lake could not have held this many.

Spencer coats and shawl collars bumped up against buckskins, carriage dresses, cloaks, and bustles; polished beaver and stovepipe hats, gipsys, capotes, and lace cornettes flow around bales and boxes, wagons and valises. The girls' journey across the wharf had been a clumsy, dodging stumble behind their father and stepmother; yet from the higher vantage there was a liquidity of purpose, as pockets of activity swirled like eddies in the bend of some greater human river. They had spent but a day in this town, knew nothing of its secrets, but Kate was compelled to unriddle the place in a final glance, and she might have done if Amy hadn't grabbed hold of her from above and hissed, "Kate, you're holding everyone up!"

Indeed, below her everyone was staring, and reluctantly she continued her climb.

Vern had already stepped off. Amy reached the top, then clumsily descended as if she might topple; but a hand caught her elbow and steadied her.

A young gentleman in a sharp blue coat stood on deck and, taking Kate's hand, helped her climb down on three boxes. "Mademoiselle," he said. "Welcome aboard the *Fidelio*, the finest steamboat in New York State." He couldn't have been much older than Vern—nineteen or twenty perhaps, and his French accent was not very believable. He had a little strip of a mustache on his lip that looked more like a line of ash than hair, but Kate was too polite to let her opinion show. She smiled demurely and thanked him for his assistance, calling him "Monsieur."

He bowed, the gallant knight, and answered, "Charity never faileth." Amy stood tugging at her green wool pelisse, but she looked up from beneath her bonnet and blushed as he spoke, as if the comment had been directed at her. Then she said, "Come now, sister," and took Kate by the elbow. The young man had already returned to his duty at the head of the gangplank.

It was the early spring of 1843, and much of New England was on the move. People headed west in droves, into new territories, some running to keep ahead of civilization, others intending to drag civilization into the wilderness. Still others had been swept up in one or more of the religious frenzies that had burned across New York State, one upon the other, for over half a century—one of which had dislocated the lives of the Charter sisters.

The two girls meandered across the deck, past bales of cotton and wool, and trunks and bags toted by servants, and families gathered around their belongings, and even at one point three men kneeling in an open passage and playing at dice. Amy averted her eyes but Kate watched shamelessly until she was pulled away. "It's not ladylike to stare that way," Amy instructed.

"But—"

"Just wait till I tell Vern."

By then they had spotted their elder sister. She stood beside their father and stepmother just ahead, at the rail. Mr. Charter stared out across the lake at the crisp blue sky.

Vern saw her sisters and called out, "I swear I cannot turn my back a moment. If you two should ever get lost, what *would* I do?"

Lavinia, their stepmother, pushed forward like some black-garbed ghoul, blocked Vern with her body, and spoke over the girl's words: "Young ladies do *not* mill about! How is it that from dockside to ship you could not keep up with your own *kin*?"

Vern stared daggers at the back of Lavinia's head but said nothing, leaving it to Amy to account for herself; but the middle sister had never been able to express what she felt to her step-mother, and barely to her older sister, who had acted as mother to the two younger girls for most of the past six years.

In the silence into which no one could insert a response, their father turned finally from the rail. His heavy-lidded eyes ex-pressed a rooted weariness until his gaze settled upon his three girls, and then his face composed a smile, though the eyes some-how did not participate—eyes that had borne such iniquities, such calamities, as the girls had no appreciation for.

Mr. Charter had lost his savings in the financial panic of '37, and it was Lavinia's money which now, six years later, kept the family afloat. Lavinia was paying for their relocation to Jekyll's Glen from Boston. Lavinia had secured Mr. Charter's new posi-tion. When the girls married, it would be up to Lavinia to provide them with a dowry. They didn't believe she ever would, just as they had come to accept, in traveling here, that they were prob-ably *never* going to marry. Nevertheless, the girls maintained a polite if chilly truce with this stepmother none of them had ever desired.

If Lavinia had made their father happy, they might have rejoiced, or at least accepted her. Instead, she had stolen him from them as surely as if she'd replaced him with a changeling. It was Lavinia who had led Mr. Charter to the tent of Elias Fitcher, where his brain began to burn with the twin lights of judgment and salvation. It was she who had brought the end of the world into their house. And it was she who, by manipulating their father, now brought their household to the end of the world.

The three girls leaned on the rail and watched the blue waters of the lake slide swiftly by. The shoreline moved slower at a distance. The smell of pine rode the blustery wind across Seneca Lake from the trees that hemmed it in all around. The hills above had been cleared for farming, and even now tiny figures were visible there, though the ground couldn't be much past spring thaw.

Beneath their feet the deck thrummed with the chugging engine, vibrating up their legs. Behind them various people strolled the boards, and snippets of conversations flitted by.

"A sick philosopher is incurable—"

"I hear'ed news of a gold strike a'way out west in Ohio."

"And will you be goin' there yourself?"

"He is among us even now, I tell you. Cast about you . . ."

"Landed gentry? Why, how can we be when we're on water here."

Sometimes they glanced back, if the voice was pleasant and sounded young enough that a handsome man might be at the end of it. Often they played a game of imagining who they would marry, how life would be, how many perfect children they would bear. "It has to be a tall man," Amy would say. "He must be clean, too, well groomed," Kate would throw in. Then they'd both look at Vern until she put in something of her own: "And we'll have six children, all girls." From there they would refine the description, change the number of children or detail the color of the phantom husband's hair, or else pick a city to live in and describe the house they would manage. They had played the

game back home in Boston and to pass the time on the slow
canal boats that had brought them across the state to Geneva,
and the lake, and their advancing destination. Their fancies flew
in the face of the very reason for their journey, which made the
need to pretend all the more poignant.

Then abruptly as the *Fidelio* crossed the middle of the lake,
the breeze blew colder, as if they had passed into some deep
moist cavern of air. The two oldest girls stood in the partial
shadow of the pilothouse and stack, and they drew their cloaks
and shawls tighter around their shoulders. All three trembled for
a moment, glanced at each other to see if the sensation was
shared, and discovering that it was, traded their uneasiness.
Then, as if each had heard her name called, they turned slowly
about.

A man stood a few feet away, considering them. The girls
squinted and shielded their eyes to see him, but he'd chosen to
stand so that the morning sun seemed to ride upon his shoulder.
Its rays flared across him, blinding them to all but his general
shape.

He wore a long gray coat, and a white cravat. He was tall and
rail-thin, and his hands at his sides curled and uncurled slowly.
Beyond that the girls couldn't make out more than the shadows
of his features.

While she shaded her eyes, Vern said, "Sir, is there something
you wish of us?"

Vern's stance spoke more defiance than her tone, while Amy,
true to her nature, blushed and glanced down at her feet. The
two of them held hands in mutual support. The wind blew Kate's
fair hair into her eyes. She tucked it back under her silk bonnet
and continued to squint at the interloper.

"Oh, no, young miss, not the slightest." His voice was dark
and smooth as syrup, delicious, as if Kate could taste it. "But you
are all such beautiful creatures, aren't you, that one has to stop
and take you in. I simply cannot help myself, as what man could?
You must pardon me." He bowed, and this afforded Kate a mo-
mentary glimpse below the dazzle of the sun, of a long, severe
face and blue eyes as cold as stars. He continued. "Pardon me as

I have beheld the fruit of the garden and found it delectable. But is it wise for three such as yourselves to travel into this undiscovered country unchaperoned?"

"Our . . . father," Vern began, "is just across there."

The stranger did not turn his head to where she pointed, but asked, "You are none of you married, then? Are the men of this world so blind?"

Now Vern blushed.

"I will see you again, I hope. In this life surely before the next." He bowed slightly again, then turned and walked off.

They watched him weave through the crowd, and it wasn't until he was out of sight around the far side of the pilothouse that they found the sense to react. Amy pleaded, "Kate, let us move down so that we're in the sunlight with you. We're *freezing.*" They shuffled along toward the nose of the boat, clinging to the rail as if they couldn't stand without it. The sunlight was reinvigorating.

"Who *was* he?" Kate asked.

"He was dreadfully forward," replied Amy, "whoever he was."

"I think I've never met anyone like that in my life," said Vern, and the tone of her comment—as if made in private—caused her sisters to glance her way in alarm, for she sounded as if she had enjoyed him. She laughed when she saw their looks. "You don't know, my dears, but you will one day, what it is that we women need in men."

Amy stood dumb, uncomprehending.

Kate shook her head, dismissing the avowal in a gesture. She focused her attention across the deck, after the stranger.

She had acted her eldest sister's confidante many times—a role that Amy was ill-equipped to handle—and she was fully informed of Vern's notions of womanhood, of sundry insubstantial claims, but mostly of Vern's one great indiscretion, after which the pretense of sagacity had given way to blind panic until, after some delay, Vern's monthly flow had arrived. She loved her eldest sister dearly, but found the wisdom dispensed on the strength of one hasty and ill-chosen congress most absurd. Who was she acting the queen for then—Amy? Still, there had been about the stranger something beguiling, Kate admitted. His voice had shaken her as well.

She determined that she wanted a better look at him. She excused herself then and headed for the pilothouse. Vern called after her but Kate didn't acknowledge that she heard. She pushed past men and women in their travel clothes, saw her stepmother look up and nearly catch her eye, and ducked her head and drove quickly through the crush, into pockets of odor, of bodies that had traveled long in the same clothes, of cigars, of pine tar, of water-soaked wood, past the moist spray and hiss of the turning wheel. She came up for air far enough away that Lavinia would not see her, then strolled ahead with purpose. She could not find him. Then, as she approached the back of the pilothouse and stepped through a gap between two crates, she brushed up against the young man who had helped her onto the boat deck.

He regarded her with shy amusement, head turned slightly down as if he knew he'd been forward earlier and now must account for himself. But Kate didn't care about that. "You—why, you helped everyone on board today, did you not?"

It certainly wasn't the question he'd expected, or perhaps hoped for, and he hesitated a moment before answering almost in defense, "It's my job."

"No, I mean—there's a man on board here who has accosted my sisters and myself, but now I can't find him."

"Oh, well," he said, and puffed up, "*I* am the person you need. I know 'em all."

"You've lost your French," she replied, a small tease, then went on to describe the man in gray.

She'd hardly begun when the young steward said, "Why, I know him, sure. He's over this a'way." He led her through the throng. "There you go," he said, and pointed.

The man stood with one foot up on the lower rail, at the stern of the boat, the tail of his coat hanging straight to his knee, and as if sensing their interest glanced over his shoulder at them. He was not so tall nor as thin, and sported a short red beard.

"Ma'am?" he asked, and the voice was one she'd never heard.

"No," she told her guide, "that isn't he. This man was much taller, thin as a sapling, and his eyes . . ." She could not find words to describe them. "He'd a wide white cravat at his throat, like a preacher might."

"Oh." He scratched his head, then pushed back his cap. "No, I surely don't recollect such a gentleman, and the way you set him, I think I surely would."

"Yes."

"I'm sorry. But, that is, I might not have seen *every*one who boarded?" He smiled sheepishly. "I did sort of concentrate my efforts on you ladies."

She couldn't help but laugh. He was very sweet. "Thank you for your kindness, sir," she told him, and he tipped his cap and returned, fairly glowing, to his work.

Kate circled the rest of the way around the pilothouse. She scanned this way and that but saw no one resembling her stranger, and by the time she reached her sisters again she had concluded in some ineffable way that the man in gray had never been among them at all.

Two

*J*EKYLL'S GLEN WAS THE *FIDE-lio*'s last stop on the southern leg of its journey. Some passengers had disembarked at Lodi. Others would continue on to Dresden or, if they were aboard for a day's excursion, ride all the way back to Geneva by day's end.

Amy was disappointed in her expectations of this new home. She'd anticipated something akin to Geneva or at least to the towns that had lined the Cayuga & Seneca, where the towns came right up against the canal. The town of Jekyll's Glen was nowhere to be seen. The boat pulled in at a broad dock. Beyond it a dirt path curved around the shore and up a slope to the west. Where, she wondered, was the town?

The only obvious signs of life were an overturned dugout that had been dragged out of the water and leaned against the base of the hillside, a flat ark anchored in the shallows, and the three carts waiting at the end of the dock. Three carts, three stevedores. Mr. Charter managed to secure the services of one of them.

The stevedore loaded their trunks, two crates, and one of the dressers onto his cart. He could not haul all their belongings in one trip and would in fact need help to move the furniture, most of which belonged to Lavinia. She then insisted that she and Mr. Charter remain with her belongings at the dock while the girls went ahead with the first cartload and prepared the house to receive them.

There was no room for them to ride on the overburdened cart, for which the stevedore apologized. He was about to remove some of the trunks, but Vern stopped him. "We shall walk," she told him. He then explained that they could walk along with him, but the path was muddy in places—a fact borne out by the dirt clumped on his boots—or they could climb up. He pointed, and they saw that a narrow line of steps had been cut into the hillside beyond the dock. A small post had been hammered into the ground at the bottom. An arrow was painted on it, pointing up the steps. The hill was steep but the way much shorter. He would meet them, he said, at "the crossroads of the churches."

Vern opted for the hillside. No one asked Amy, who would have been more than happy to replace a trunk on the cart.

Trees grew thickly up the hill. There were birch and beech here and there, but mostly pine. The hill was steeper than it looked, and the steps turned out to be flat stones of varying sizes. There wasn't so much as a rope to use as a handrail. At first they climbed happily enough, with Vern and Kate commenting on the passengers ahead of them, naming trees and remarking on the spicy scent of the pines—how fresh and invigorating to be out in nature—but by midpoint they'd stopped talking to conserve their breath, and plodded up each step. Amy, who hadn't taken part in the conversation, noticed the change in atmosphere first.

She stopped climbing suddenly and said, "Listen." The word seemed to die just beyond her lips, but her sisters heard her and paused in their ascent. The air seemed utterly lifeless. No birds twittered and nothing moved anywhere beneath the trees.

Kate replied, "I don't hear anything." Her voice was dull, muffled.

"No, that's it. There's nothing, nothing at all," said Amy. "No sound." She looked down at the lake, at the edge of the dock, at the smooth water. If this was wilderness, Amy thought, then wilderness was like being trapped inside a painting. "How do we know there's a town anywhere?"

Then somewhere overhead a branch cracked and a breeze from off the lake rushed upon them, so strong that they had to clamp their arms to their thighs to keep their skirts down.

Vern smiled as if reassured. She turned and continued the climb. The cold breeze pushed them along.

By the time they reached the crest, they were flushed and puffing, but no more than the other travelers ahead of them, some of whom leaned against trees and mopped at their faces with kerchiefs. Kate looked up at the sky and walked in a circle with her hands pressed into the small of her back. Vern fanned herself. Amy leaned forward, hands on knees, as much as her corset would allow, but if anything this made breathing more difficult, and soon enough she was imitating Kate.

Some distance away she spotted two cabins that could not have been bigger than two rooms each. In one of them someone was cooking up bacon and the smell of it was almost sinful. Except for a biscuit that morning, they hadn't eaten at all. The smell triggered a desperate longing in Amy for the home they'd given up, for life as it had been before—even life under Lavinia's rule. Why did she have to be here? It wasn't fair at all.

Other than the cabins, there was no habitation in sight. What if Jekyll's Glen turned out to be nothing but two tiny cabins in a dead forest?

The people who'd preceded them soon set off on the path, and Vern gathered herself up and said, "This way, then." She pointed to another arrow that was nailed in the side of one of the trees. Amy abandoned her fit of despair and fell in behind Kate.

After a few more minutes, the trees thinned ahead. To the right in the distance, sharp edges of shadow appeared—corners and slats and window frames. Up ahead a horse went by, and then another hauling a curtained dearborn. The wheels knocked along a rutted dirt road.

The trees ended abruptly, and they arrived at the edge of the road. To the left it ran straight as far as Amy could see, vanishing finally into forest gloom. To the right it led within a hundred yards to the houses that had appeared through the woods.

They were clapboards, on the far side of a big whitewashed sign displaying the name JEKYLL'S GLEN. Beyond the sign the road curved away out of sight. With great relief, Amy saw that a graded and lightly graveled walk led past the houses, paralleling the road, to accommodate all the foot traffic from the steamboats.

The sisters headed toward the sign. Not until they came around the bend did they finally, and with great relief, see the town.

More houses around the bend gave way quickly to a main street of storefronts, but not many. Another wagon rolled past, the driver lean and scruffy, with a dirty child by his side. The child stared at them balefully. His father ignored them altogether.

The first establishment was a tavern. Some of the men ahead had turned from the path already and gone in. Vern pretended it didn't interest her, while Kate tried to peer inside the door. Amy scrupulously avoided looking. Taverns were sinful places, and this one gave off a sour smell.

The town proved to be so awfully small that they could count the different businesses on both hands. There was a carriage maker and wheelwright's across the road; the wide doors were open and the frame of a wagon like a spidery skeleton squatted inside. An apothecary and botanical medical shop was followed by another tavern. There were two general stores, facing each other across the street. A sign in the window of one announced FRESH EGGS. The other had its own sign, which read WE SELL WATKINS MILL FLOUR. Then came a blacksmith's beside a saddler and shoemaker, an unnamed shop with bow saws hanging on the wall, a cooper's, and a tiny house with a physician's sign hanging from a post in front of it. Finally, where a narrower road cut across the main one, two churches stood on opposite corners: a Methodist of stone on the left, and a shining white Presbyterian on the right. The latter had its own sign planted in the middle of the path leading to its double doors, proclaiming one word: TEM-

PERANCE! The road sign there identified the crossroad as MILL
CREEK ROAD. Arrows below pointed the way south to the Watkins
flour mill and to an unnamed grist mill.

To the north, traffic moved along the Mill Creek Road—
wagons and pedestrians, some of whom they recognized from the
steamboat. A large black dog dashed into view from behind one
of the wagons. Its breath steamed out of its nostrils and it ran
across the main road as if in pursuit of something, disappearing
within moments into the woods.

They'd only been there a few minutes before their own cart
appeared. The stevedore, walking beside his mule, tipped his cap
as he reached them. "And where is it you ladies want your belongings took?" he asked as if only a moment had passed since
they'd spoken.

Amy thought it queer that her father or Lavinia hadn't told
him, although it might have been one of Lavinia's tests, to see
if the girls were paying attention. Vern at least had. She answered,
"Our house is on the Gorge Road. It's called the Pulaski house,
I believe."

"*That's* your residence?"

"Why, yes."

He shifted his stance from side to side as if making up his
mind how to proceed. Then with a solemn shake of his head he
prodded the mule and headed farther out the main road. The
girls followed close behind. A carriage raced around them. Its rear
wheel hit a rock and jumped it precariously onto two wheels for
a moment before it bounced down onto all four rims again. The
stevedore muttered, "That fool's breakin' the speed limit. Somebody oughta 'rest 'im."

The graveled sidewalk ended just beyond the churches, but
there was little traffic, and the girls flanked the cart—its wheels
flung off bits of mud, and they quickly learned not to follow in
its path. A few people rode by on horseback, heading toward
Jekyll's Glen. They looked the girls over, and the contents of the
cart, but there was nothing welcoming in their faces. Amy looked

at them with the foolish notion that she might spy someone she knew. Sometimes strangers could look familiar.

They walked another half mile on the main road, which the stevedore informed them was the Catskill Turnpike. Already the town was lost behind them.

The Gorge Road branched sharply off to the south. They passed only three houses on it, all of which sat well back from the road. As much as a half mile separated each from the other. Then there were no more houses and the cleared land was swallowed up in woods, and Amy began to wonder if the stevedore knew where he was going. Trees overhung the road, and though there was hardly a breeze now, the air took on a chill. Sunlight spackled them through the almost leafless branches, lacking any warmth. One wheel of the cart rolled through a hole, and it cracked a thin layer of ice so that the hole spat brown water. The girls shivered and pulled their cloaks more tightly around them. The civilized world had become a myth, a remembered story, and they'd been lost in wilderness their whole lives.

Then, up ahead, a horizontal line emerged out of the dimness—a long, straight pole supported by two posts, one on either side of the road. To the right a kind of sentry box stood next to the pole. Amy expected at any moment someone was going to emerge from the sentry box to demand a payment from them. That was how it was on turnpike roads, and they hadn't brought any money with them, at least she didn't think so. But no one came to take their toll.

A clearing came into view as they neared the pike. A house sat in the middle of it.

The stevedore abruptly switched the mule, and drove the cart off the road and across the dirt lawn, right up to the flagstones surrounding the front door of the house.

"What's this?" Vern asked.

"This would be the place called the Pulaski house," he announced, "only the Pulaskis is not among us anymore, nor 'n' those before them."

It was a catslide house, a two-story clapboard with a long sloping rear roof, double chimneys in the middle, and windows all around. Bare bushes showing their buds were planted to either side of the front door. On the southern side, dozens of trees had been cut to stumps to let sunlight reach the house. To Vern there was something ugly and dismembered about so many stumps, which tainted the house. Kate looked through the windows at the empty rooms and thought only that it was an unknown quantity, a question that couldn't yet be answered. The air smelled of spring forest, wet and on the cusp of new possibilities. A breeze stirred the tops of the trees, and birds twittered and darted overhead. Amy was relieved that there was a house at all: a house where they might be happy if only they could forget that happiness would not be theirs for long.

A hallway ran from the front foyer to the back of the house—or so it seemed at first. Further investigation proved that the door at the back let onto a kitchen that extended across the entire rear, like the top of a "T." On each side of the hall was a single large room—one would serve as a parlor and the other, with its own door to the kitchen, would be a dining room.

The cooking hearth in the kitchen was broad and deep, and though it still contained a pivoting crane for hanging pots over a fire—the way people had cooked for centuries—the lower half of the hearth was filled by a fine cast-iron stove, the sight of which put Amy at some ease. She had dreaded the idea of cooking like some old fairy-tale witch.

Three lard-oil lamps stood on the mantel, and two half-used candles lay beside them. A door at the back of the kitchen opened onto a narrow spring room containing a pump. They would at least have water for baths, even in the cold. Outside the spring-room door was piled a full two cords of split wood.

A rough-hewn wooden table stood opposite the hearth, its thick top scarred with cuts. An envelope lay there with their father's name written on it in a long, sharp, masculine hand. They left it alone and continued to explore the house.

The stevedore had piled their belongings in the foyer and pushed some into the dining room, as if he hadn't wanted to come any farther than necessary into the house. Exiting the kitchen through the empty dining room, the girls had to shove the trunks aside to get into the hall again. The stevedore and his cart were gone.

The stairway to the second floor began just past the doorway into the dining room. It took up half the width of the hallway, and led to a small triangular landing and three more steps up to the second floor. The second floor was divided into two long rooms separated by another hall. Each room contained a small fireplace near the back, where the ceiling sloped. One of these would become the girls' room, but they must wait upon their father's choice.

While the first floor had been empty, the second floor conveyed the feeling of a house abandoned in haste. In one room two narrow beds stood at angles in the middle. There was a third bed in the opposite room, and all three had been stripped of bedclothes. Amy idly plumped up one of the mattresses, exploding dust into the air. She squeezed it and the mattress crackled. She decided it must be stuffed with barley straw—hardly the most comfortable of choices.

Farther along in the second-floor hallway, a Hitchcock rocking chair with cane seat lay overturned as if it had skittered and fallen when its occupant jumped up. A layer of dust edged the legs and rungs, and light cobwebs were strung between the stenciled rails of the back. The girls left it where it lay.

At the bottom of a narrow stairwell to the third floor Vern paused. She made no move to go up. A trapdoor at the top was closed. She tilted her head as though listening to something, which drew Amy's attention. She stood beside her sister and listened too but heard nothing. Her younger sister ignored their reluctance, pushed between them, and climbed right up the steps. She lifted the trapdoor and it fell back with a report so loud that Amy jumped.

"Katie," Vern started, "I swear one day, you're going to poke your nose in someplace it doesn't belong and get it cut right off." She glanced at Amy as if for confirmation of this, and Amy nodded. But by then she was looking up Kate's skirts as her sister stepped out of view. Her footsteps echoed down from the empty room—emptiness so much more noticeable when it was a different room than you were in, thought Amy.

"Amelia, go see to her," Vern instructed.

"Me?" Her eyes cast to the ceiling just as a loud screech issued from above—not the sound of a voice, but of something being dragged on the floor. "I've *no* interest in going up there. It's trespassing."

Vern sighed. "No, it isn't. It's our house, stupid girl. Lavinia's anyway." She climbed the steps far enough to stick her head through the opening. "Kate, what are you doing? Oh. Oh, my goodness," and she climbed the rest of the way up.

Amy had an active fear of being left alone, a complementary fear to her resentment at being left out of things, which manifested as suspicion whenever she found the other two girls conferring without her. They had secrets, and she knew it, even though they denied this and always provided an explanation for whatever they'd been doing. Her fear and suspicion compelled her up the tight stairwell after them. If they had entered some cursed chamber, she would go to her death alongside them rather than let them discuss her secretly in the afterlife.

Amy had thought that what the house lacked so far was mostly character: The walls were bare, the floors bare, the rooms stripped of any hint of the former occupants. Now she discovered that its character had been put into storage in the cramped little attic.

The low ceiling sloped sharply toward the rear, ending perhaps two feet above the floor. The bricks of the fireplace chimneys intruded into the middle. To either side of them, all manner of furnishings had been crammed. Kate and Vern were seated on a big mahogany sofa with a serpentine back, which had been dragged out from under the low ceiling. There were more stenciled Hitchcock chairs identical in design to the one below, a shell cabinet, cast-iron fenders for one of the hearths, lamps, a mahogany dresser with lots of scroll and foliage work carved into it and a swivel mirror on side pins at the back, and another chair that she quickly identified as a Boston rocker. On the dresser stood

an eight-day clock. Her sisters held a frame between them and
were looking at it. As Amy stepped from the stairs, Vern turned
it around to show her. She said, "Oh, my," and drew closer, finally
taking her place on the sofa beside her sisters. "Is that one of
those—"

"Daguerreotypes. Yes, it is," said Vern.

They had seen a few of these in Boston, but never expected
to encounter something so novel here. Daguerreotypes had only
existed for a few years, and almost the only people who had them
were well-to-do. At one time or another they had all wished they
had a family portrait of their own like this, one that included
their mother.

The young couple in this one looked stiff and nervous, intim-
idated no doubt by the camera itself if not by the interminable
time they had to sit rigid in their finery. The man wore a tight-
fitting tweed suit. His dark hair was slicked down and one front
lock curved across his forehead; his short beard had been
trimmed and waxed, his great mustaches sweeping like steer
horns to either side of his mouth. He sat upon one of the chairs
stored here. He was looking toward his wife. She stood beside
him, in a half profile as if her attention had been distracted by
something off to the side. Her hair was coiled about her head
with little sausage curls in the front. Her dress had puffed sleeves
with frilled epaulettes. The only flaw in the picture was a blur
at the bottom of the woman's skirt, as if she had shifted her feet,
although fortunately the rest of her body hadn't moved. Amy
wondered, was that even possible? Could *she* move her feet and
hold her body still? She wasn't too sure. "Were they the Pulaskis,
do you s'pose?" she asked.

"No way to tell, there's nothing written on the back. Unless
maybe that stevedore would know 'em. But when do you think
this was taken? I can't believe they can have these a way out
here."

"Vern, you cap the climax," Kate observed of her sister's
snobbery, and getting up from the sofa, she walked around the
furniture. "We'll have plenty of things to *sit* on, least ways."

"Are we going to entertain?"

"We won't find any husbands if we don't," Kate replied, but idly, as if it really didn't concern her—which was probably true, Amy thought, seeing as how Kate was third in line for marriage, and only sixteen. What could the notion of marriage mean to her? Amy had no clear sense of it herself, except that she was supposed to want it, it was what everything came to, what duty to her father and family was supposed to require. Still, she couldn't imagine the three of them ever being separated. They never had been. They were a family and this was to be their family home. Besides, there likely wouldn't be time for them to marry now. Not before the world came to its appointed end. Even if they met someone tomorrow, there wouldn't be enough time for them to have a baby or make a new home before they were judged.

"We'll be going to Harbinger House," announced Vern, "as soon as everything is arrived and uncrated. Papa says we're not an hour from it on foot."

"He's going to be in charge of the pike, isn't he?" said Amy. "That's why we're in this house. I wonder what's in that letter."

"I expect the letter's from the Reverend Fitcher, probably our invitation to Harbinger, to meet them," Vern answered.

But Amy had fixed upon the notion of Judgment Day and could not be directed to another topic. "When the seals are broken and the skies roll back," she recited, "the Lord God will come to judge us all."

Vern nodded. "And it'll be those who stand with the Reverend Fitcher who are preserved and made glorious in Heaven."

Kate looked on in silence. Something in her attitude led Amy to the conclusion that she secretly discredited these words. She said, "You don't want to be cast into the pit, do you, Kate?"

Amy's obsession included the more infernal images of Judgment: seven-eyed beasts with seven heads, plagues, locusts, the demons of Abaddon. Despite repeated assurances from her father and sisters, she doubted her worthiness to enter Heaven, suspecting that some corruption lurked in the depths of her soul. Even if *she* couldn't identify it, certainly God would.

"No, I don't," Kate replied, as though it wasn't a possibility and thus of no concern.

Amy turned to her older sister. "But how will I be any different at Harbinger than I am here, Vern? When the day comes— in the eyes of God I'm me wherever I am."

Vern sighed. It was an old conversation. "The Reverend Fitcher will advocate for you, for all of us, dear sister. You'll be of his flock, so you'll be saved and your sins forgiven, so it won't matter that you're the same. That's what Papa says and that's why we're all here now. All that we've given up, we give in order to free ourselves of earthly ties, bindings to others"—and here her voice went tight—"others who'd keep us from our destiny." Quickly she added, "You'd do well to begin believing it, too. You must prepare your heart for the end time that's coming. What's in your heart is what matters, Amelia. You don't want to be corrupt in your *heart*—"

"Oh, Vern, you're scaring her to death," Kate said. "And you sound just like Lavinia."

Angrily, Vern answered, "And should I lie, then?" She looked around to find her sister watching her with tilted head, like a cat, in the swivel mirror.

Kate observed flatly, "The world hasn't begun to end yet. Why hurry it up?"

It was at that moment the clock on the dresser chimed. All three girls stared at it. Kate, who was closest, leaned forward and said, "Why, it's keeping time."

"That's impossible," Vern replied.

"Maybe so. But it's doing it all the same."

And it was.

Three

Dear Mr. Charter,

My apologies for not meeting you upon your arrival. Alas, duty to our community will keep me from you for some few days. Please do not enter Harbinger on your own but wait for my appearance, when I shall meet your family properly and accompany you across the gorge.

You are our gatekeeper, Mr. Charter. Many who are sick or ill-formed will arrive, craving entry, and these people *should* gain entrance, provided their need and belief are real, of which you act as sole judge, sir. There are others who, knowing me by reputation only, will petition for entry into our utopia. Some, gathered from our campaigns, will be deserving of it. As the Day draws nigh, their numbers will increase, but also shall those whose hearts are not ours, who come finally out of fear rather than reverence, and you must decide their worth. You must separate wheat from chaff. It's a great burden I place upon you, our Minos, but one I know you to be capable of bearing. My agents tell me this.

We will have no circuit riders, nor peddlers or drummers.

The price to cross the gorge is one half dollar. I feel it is a
small price to pay for the promise of salvation in the Next Life.
Why, it's no more than the price of a pair of woolen stockings.
We shall meet by and by to discuss all matters and details.
My future happiness rests with you.

                                                  Elias Fitcher

"What an odd thing to say," Kate commented when her father
had finished reading the letter to them.

He folded it up neatly. "He will be coming here," he said.
"We must make our house presentable." As if they might not
unpack otherwise.

By the time the last of their belongings had been delivered
and Mr. Charter arrived from the dock, dusk had fallen and
they'd been too exhausted to do more than make up beds and
retire for the night.

During that previous afternoon Lavinia had assigned the
rooms, choosing the slightly larger one for herself and Mr. Charter, directed the stevedores to carry her bed frame up to that
room and assemble it, and made the girls drag the two old beds
already there into the other second-floor room for themselves. In
the assigning of rooms and shuffling of furniture, they had forgotten all about the letter by the hearth. Amy, preparing to make
some biscuits for breakfast, had discovered it again.

The foyer and dining room were now filled with crates of
silver and chinaware, chairs and rolled-up carpets, lamps, brass
fenders for two fireplaces, Mr. Charter's double-door oak cabinet-
on-stand, his Federal-style worktable, drop-leaf dining table,
corner cabinet, and their three bureaus. The girls had had to
pile items up or move them aside to clear a path from stairs to
kitchen.

Mr. Charter, contemplating their collected belongings, muttered, "We don't have enough chairs for company."

The girls wanted to haul down the sofa and chairs from the
attic room, which would make a very presentable parlor, one with
enough seating for family and guests, but they met with immediate opposition. Lavinia insisted the furniture belonged to some-

one else and should be kept stored in case the owners returned. It wouldn't do to have them arrive and find the family using the belongings as their own, she said, and so for the time being the attic furnishings were left alone. The one overturned chair in the second-floor hall the girls captured and took into their room.

With the letter rediscovered and read, they still hadn't had breakfast. Amy and Lavinia returned to the kitchen, and the other two girls assisted their father in distributing the furnishings and boxes around the house. They soon discovered that his work-table had been damaged in transit. One leg was split. Mr. Charter patted the table as if it were an old dog and said, "We'll have to take it into the village and find some local craftsman to repair it. There'll be someone who can work wood."

They set the table aside then, and decided they should start by carrying the larger pieces up the stairs, notably Lavinia's black walnut bureau. Amy wanted to know why Lavinia hadn't had the stevedores do it the night before, but she knew better than to ask. At least after moving that, everything else would seem easier. Even before they'd cleared a path wide enough to carry it to the stairs, a voice called from outside: "Halloo! Is there someone who can move this for me?"

Mr. Charter turned immediately and went out. Kate and Vern wrapped themselves in shawls and followed after him.

A small wagon sat before the pole blocking the road. The driver wore a large floppy hat. He was mud-stained and unshaven, his eyes red with exhaustion. The team of two horses looked as if they had been run nearly to death. Their nostrils smoked in the air. In the back of the wagon lay a woman. She stared up in their direction with sunken eyes dulled by illness, and seemed to see nothing. Her hands, which gripped a blanket up to her chin, trembled. Like her face, they were thin and bony.

"I got to get her to Harbinger to be cured," the driver ex-plained. "This be the road, yes?"

"It is," said Mr. Charter.

"There's a toll, then, that I have to pay?"

"There is and I collect it *for* Harbinger."

The man sagged a little. "There are barriers everywhere, it seems," he replied.

"It's a half dollar, the toll."

"Is it so much?"

Mr. Charter replied as the Reverend Fitcher had instructed him: "Since you've come here to renounce the outside, and offering all of your worldly possessions to the community, why, it is a very small price, sir. Hardly more than a pair of socks."

The man leaned into the back of the wagon and pawed through the belongings tied up beside the woman. When he turned back he was holding a pepperbox revolver. For a moment the family stood frozen, not knowing how to respond. Then he let go of the gun so that it flipped and dangled on his finger in the trigger guard. "Here," he said, leaning toward Mr. Charter. "I've no use for it now we're this close. And it's worth far more than half a dollar."

Mr. Charter accepted the revolver. "I don't know," he said.

"Sir, we've gone day and night from Delaware to get here in time. You wouldn't hold us up so close?"

Mr. Charter shook his head. "No, I'm certain the reverend wouldn't want that." He leaned on the pole. The upright had been notched so that it could be levered easily. He kept it raised while the wagon rolled beneath.

"I'm much obliged to you, then," the man called back; then he flicked the reins and the exhausted horses lifted their heads and picked up their pace. Mr. Charter eased the pole down across the road again.

"That poor woman," said Vern. "She can't last."

"That will depend on the will of God. Reverend Fitcher has cured many with the touch of his hands. Lavinia and I've seen people made to walk who couldn't take a step, and those with the gout suddenly free in their movements, painless in their joints. And in Milford there was a deaf man that was made to hear."

"Well, I pray she'll recover," Kate said, and Mr. Charter touched her shoulder and agreed, "That's what you must do."

The three of them walked back to the house together.

In the dining room, Mr. Charter explained solemnly to his wife, "My work here has begun." He set the gun down on a crate. She looked at it as if he had placed a serpent there, took two steps back, and retreated to the kitchen.

They labored through the rest of the morning. Most of all, the girls wanted to make the house look like their old home. One by one they and their father carried the bureaus, crates, and trunks up the stairs to the second floor. The items were old. Except for Lavinia's things, all of the furniture predated the family's economic misfortunes. While most everything was still in good condition, none had the polish of their stepmother's black walnut pieces. The carpets were worse—nearly threadbare in places. Nevertheless, unrolling them made the rooms instantly familiar. They softened the coldness of the bare floors, but more than that the smell of the rugs belonged to Boston and their home. The tranquility imparted by that smell was infinitely more important than how the rugs looked.

For lunch they ate the fresh biscuits they'd planned to have for breakfast. It was their first meal in more than a day.

Afterward, Mr. Charter and Kate set off on foot for Jekyll's Glen, carrying his damaged table between them, and Vern and Lavinia went along to buy some candles and other necessities. Amy remained behind. Her father instructed her in the maneuvering of the pike on the off chance that someone passed by, and she listened while scowling at her sisters.

Save for Kate in a burgundy half-sleeve *visite*, the women wore shawls, and Mr. Charter his traveling coat. Vern had a small pagoda-style parasol and she brandished it, though there was no reason for her to bring it save for ostentation.

The table was small and not nearly as heavy as the beds and bureaus, but Kate and her father had to rest a few times on the way. Lavinia and Vern waited with them. The division of duties meant that the two girls could not separate from the adults for conversation; they might as well, thought Kate, have gone in opposite directions.

The village was bustling with activity. Even from a distance on the Catskill Turnpike they could count dozens of wagons and carts on both sides of the road, and people strolling along the gravel walks.

A hawker had set up at the corner of the Mill Creek Road with a small grinding wheel and a stool. He was calling out, "Scissors and knives, sharp for your lives!" and ringing a tiny bell at the same time. People seemed to have been expecting him. A line queued up down the walk. Some people held razors, and some knives, while others brandished all sorts of tools from axes to small scythes; and even a few scissors.

Lavinia and Vern continued on to Van Hollander's General Store, while Mr. Charter entered the first shop along the street, which happened to be the cooper's, to inquire after a woodworker. Kate remained outside with the table. She nodded and smiled to people as they passed, and most nodded in reply or said, "Good morning," even as they looked her over and tried to identify her. She watched her sister and Lavinia approach Van Hollander's. On the street in front of the two stores, people were busy loading provisions into their wagons. There were one-horse carts and larger wagons pulled by a team. One cart in particular looked small and clumsy, with no mule or horse hitched to it. The owner, a slight, bearded man, came out from the store across from Van Hollander's with a burlap bag filled with some kind of grain. He dumped the bag on top of another in the cart, then stepped in between the two shafts and began to pull it along himself. As he passed her, he smiled and said, "Good day," pleasantly, although the muscles stuck out like ropes on his neck and arms from the strain. She smiled broadly and answered him in kind, and couldn't help thinking of Jesus carrying His cruel burden through the streets, unbowed. The man shortly turned left on the Mill Creek Road.

Her father came out of the shop and they picked up the table. He led the way back to the crossroad, and took Mill Creek Road to the right down past the church in the direction from which the stevedore had come the day before. She glanced back over her shoulder at the tiny cart vanishing in the opposite direction, and could not explain even to herself the sense of longing and loss that distant, retreating figure provoked.

The woodworker's shop was a broad shed beside his small house. It looked like a one-story barn with large double doors. As they approached, the smell of fresh wood and varnish enfolded them in a cloud.

The man, a Mr. Jasper, came out and shook Mr. Charter's hand, then crouched down beside the table and ran his palm around one of the good legs as if he couldn't see it and had to touch to know what it was. His hand was large and dry and spotted with stains. He leaned his head down, and Kate could see the bald circle at the crown. "Decent work," he said. "Nice turnings. They made a good piece here. Wasn't a flaw did this. Someone got clumsy whilst moving it. I can fix you up another, cut it here, right below the knee"—he pointed at a thick spot high up on the leg—"fit a dowel and put you a new one on. I'll get the turnings to match pretty fair but the color won't be the same. Still an' all, you shouldn't note the new leg unless you're looking for it." Without moving his head, he raised his eyes. "So you're new here, then."

"Yes, just arrived yesterday," replied Mr. Charter. "We're with Fitcher."

Jasper said, "That so. Lots of folks are, here. People coming through all the time now on their way out to Harbinger. He hasn't said when yet, has he?"

"No."

"No. I expect when he does, we'll be running out of places to put everyone. The world will come pouring in, that's for certain, pouring in just to see if it all goes as he says. They'll be fighting to get in at the end, but I guess from hearing him that they're gonna be too late. That's so, yes? So, you're with him but you ain't out at Harbinger, or you'd be using them for to fix this table leg, since they got their own lathe and all out there. Their own smith, wheelwrights, their own everything. It's a little town. Yessir, got their own version of everything. Even a mill, I believe I've been told. Where are *you*, then?"

"House on the Gorge Road."

Kate chimed in, "It's called the Pulaski house." As soon as she said it, she sensed a change in Mr. Jasper. He didn't shrink from them or even bat an eye; but something stilled in him. She said, "There's something about that place, isn't there?"

Her father glanced at her. "Whatever do you mean, daughter?"

"I don't know. But the black man who carted our belongings—"

"That'd be Stephen, I expect," Jasper chimed in. "Stephen the stevedore." He was careful not to smile too much at his own joke, but gauged their reactions.

"He came over almighty strange when he learned where we were living."

"He did, I've no doubt. He moved those people in there. That place, it belonged before to another of your Fitcherites."

"Fitcherites?"

"That's the name people got for the followers of Reverend Fitcher. You'll hear it attached to yourselves before long." Then he added, "It's not in disrespect, at least not all the time—just a way to identify them as come to Harbinger. And you're right, miss, there's something about that place that sets people to talking. Pulaski and his young bride moved in there, would have been two, more like three years back. About the time your preacher started building his community out there on the far side of the gorge. I guess they were supposed to keep the unwelcome from getting past or something, which is why there's that turnpike set up there. Anyhow, something happened to her, to the wife. She just up and disappeared one night. Nobody saw her after, and there was talk that young Pulaski had kilt her and hid her body in the house, and for a time after that he didn't have many friends hereabouts. And then when *he* disappeared, well, the stories just rolled right along like wheels looking for a wagon."

Mr. Charter asked, "You mean to say, both of the people who lived in our house disappeared?"

"Yes, sir, they did. Nobody's sure what it was about. I mean, the furnishings were all left behind. You must've found 'em, as no one would claim them, and not many wanted to set foot inside anyhow and nobody wanted to buy 'em for fear there's some taint on 'em. Some fine craftsmanship there, too. Good chairs. I expect whoever sold you the house didn't breathe a word of this to you."

"My wife—that is, my wife made the arrangements, through someone known to her in Reverend Fitcher's group. I'm sure they never said . . ."

"Well, and I don't mean to trouble your mind, either. But you are going to hear some tall tales around town associated with your house. Some will let on as it's a haunted place, and some will say that something came in the night and snatched the people away. I've heard tell that some of the folks at Harbinger believe the Angel of Death dwells among them."

"And what do you say, Mr. Jasper?" Kate asked.

"Well . . . what I say really shouldn't matter, miss, since I wasn't there."

"*I'd* like to know."

"Kate, that's very forward," her father warned with unusual sharpness.

Jasper ignored him. "In that case, miss, I think there's only two ways you go down that road. One comes back here, where nobody saw either of them pass by. The other crosses over the gorge, and it ends at Harbinger. I think they fell in with your Mr. Fitcher, one after the other."

"But why would they hide? If they were already part of the community. Why would his wife not tell him where she was going?"

"I may have misspoke. They weren't part of the community. Your Mr. Fitcher didn't want his people consorting with nonbelievers or touching money, so he hired this fella to collect his tolls. I don't know as how they're hiding. Just maybe no longer caring about the things left behind in *this* world," he said. "You say you haven't been out there yet."

"Sir, we shall be going shortly," Mr. Charter replied, with inordinate anger in his voice. "We're still settling in. Our belongings just arrived, including this table."

"Well, you'll see soon enough how someone could just be swallowed up in that big place. You'll see that. And maybe you'll see Pulaski. And if you do, then we'll *all* know—"

"My *table*, then?"

Mr. Jasper brushed his hand across the top of it, almost as if he were calming it down. "The table. Well, two weeks."

"Very good. I shall return then to collect it."

Jasper nodded slowly. It seemed to Kate that her father's anger had fatigued him.

As her father turned to leave, she quickly asked, "Then you don't believe the end time is approaching?"

Jasper brushed his hand across the tabletop again and said as if to it rather than in reply, "The world will end or it won't, without my participation."

"Katherine," her father said, and she fell in obediently behind him.

"You ought not to dignify such talk by treating it seriously," said Mr. Charter to his daughter as they walked home. "That man is not saved and not planning to be. He cares nothing for the truth."

"I thought he seemed to care a good deal for it, Papa."

"Would you disagree with me, child? He said the Reverend Fitcher didn't want his people touching money—yet here am I in the very position he claims that Pulaski youth was, and am I not one of his 'Fitcherites'? I daresay, I am."

Knowing where her interests lay, she held her tongue. Her father took the silence as compliance. "He's a gossipmonger. The world is a foul place, Kate, we've all made it thus. And those who are of the world will find themselves brought down soon, and they'll beg then for God's mercy, but too late, the gates will have closed. Like Sodom and Gomorrah, they shall be expunged, their corruption erased, and then we who listened will step out upon a cleansed Earth, ready for purity."

Kate listened, less inspired than embarrassed for him. She could remember a time when he hadn't preached when he spoke. He'd been gentle with his daughters, never raised his voice, never threatened to rain down fire and brimstone upon them. "The clarity of their love" was Vern's phrase for how it had been between their father and mother, a version that seemed to have emerged out of a dream Kate had before she was ten, in which she had a mother who laughed and sang lullabies with a lovely voice, who combed and braided her hair, and who told her fairy tales at bedtime. It hadn't been so long ago—only six years, yet nothing save echoes remained.

Their financial troubles had come first. Some sort of wild speculation had caused the market to collapse—an unprecedented economic disaster. Their money—invisible though it was to the girls—had evaporated, and overnight their father had become estranged from them. Mother had shored him up for a while, but when he was gone—either looking for work or working at any task he could find just to feed them—then their mother crumbled, apologizing through her tears, trying to explain to the children that forces larger than they could understand had tried to crush the family and now they all must rally, they all must endure. She made them promise to help their father any way they could, to support him, for he was so miserable. Often he would be gone for days on end, and when he returned he was sunburned and unshaven and he smelled, and he seemed smaller, as if time and distance had wrung the blood from him. Vern had overheard her father say how he wished his daughters were all married off and gone, because now he would never be able to provide a dowry for any of them. Why, he could barely feed them.

They might have come through the hard times, but within months their mother had fallen ill, and nothing and no one seemed able to save her. Papa couldn't go for work, didn't dare leave her alone, yet not to work was to not have any money for doctors, for medicine, which forced him to take any menial job at all that might keep him nearby. Even sweeping sidewalks, cleaning gutters for a few pennies.

After her death he cut himself off from his daughters. It

wasn't much of a change. He had been distant for some time; now they simply lacked their interpreter. The very sight of the girls seemed to remind him of the ragged hole in his life.

He turned to strangers for solace.

People appeared in their home whom they'd never seen before. Some brought consolation pamphlets; others arrived with enough food for an extended siege, which should have warned the sisters that more would follow. Most of the time these people arrived early in the afternoon and set up in the parlor, where they read strange poetry about gloomy cemeteries and life in the grave, and children watching everyone from on high. They talked almost exclusively of the dead, as though the room were full of spirits and everyone aware of them. All three girls were made to attend the meetings, although unlike their father they felt no desire to prolong the pain this way, much less wallow in their mother's loss among ghoulish people who could speak of nothing else. After they'd recognized the pattern to these events, they made a point of trying to leave the house before the guests arrived—with varying success.

During one of the meetings Mr. Charter tearfully revealed that the girls had had a brother, one who'd been born before Vern, but who had died within his first month. He hadn't even a name. He'd been sickly at birth, and so Mother and Father had hesitated to give him one, circumscribing their impending loss through anonymity. It was a fearsome revelation to the girls that something so momentous had been withheld from them by both parents for so many years. Previously they'd been concerned about Papa, even frightened by the gloom he wore like a shroud. Now they had cause to distrust him.

Sometimes at the gathering of ghouls there was a lecturer; often this was someone "on the circuit"—traveling up and down the seaboard to dispense personal views on the afterlife—of which there seemed to be an endless variety. Most speakers were women who had lost someone close—a child more often than not—and who felt that their own experience could inform and guide others; they had a disagreeable tendency to clutch the nearest of the Charter girls to their bosoms during the telling. A few men turned up to speak—priests and circuit riders whose paths crossed those of the death artists. Everyone seemed to know everyone, just as they all seemed to have mapped the territory of the afterlife. Speeches and recitations often were punctuated by periods of weeping, and the girls—save for Amy, who would frequently fall in with the weeping—learned to withdraw the moment it began, else find themselves passed around like handkerchiefs among the bereaved and blubbering. Helpless to intervene, they watched their father slide into a world of constant, raw memorializing. He took up residence in the afterlife.

It was during this period that Lavinia appeared. One of the later speakers—more than a year after their mother's death—she'd proclaimed that all lost souls would be reunited on the day the heavens opened, and that Mrs. Charter had surely set up house there in anticipation of their arrival, and that the girls would meet their little brother there, too, by and by. Everyone would be reunited. And that day was coming quite soon. The Parousia—as she called it—was going to take most everyone by surprise.

Unlike the other speakers who focused upon the closeness of death, the soon-to-be-second Mrs. Charter guaranteed its delivery. It was the first time the girls had ever heard of the Reverend Fitcher—the man who knew the date of Judgment. When the time was right, he would tell everyone, giving them a chance to prepare themselves and put their lives in order. "Put your faith in *Him*," Lavinia frequently insisted, leaving the girls uncertain whether she meant God or Reverend Fitcher. She made proclamations all the time: "Forswear the false prophecies." "The Reverend Fitcher sits upon the Throne below Jesus Himself, from where he can look straight into your soul." "He will gather the good and bring them straight into Heaven."

Mr. Charter, already fully lubricated with the elixir of the afterlife, succumbed to the message immediately. Had that been the extent of his devotion, the girls might have accepted his spiritual transmission. But Papa had succumbed to the messenger as well as the message. Lavinia was the bridge between worlds for him: Her presence kept him in sight of eventual reunion. His daughters suspected her of evil powers, or casting a spell over his will, but they had no way to persuade him of this, no word the equal of hers, no promise that could soothe his soul—especially if they were right. They had known him to be a gentle man; in Lavinia's shadow, his inherent irresolution became apparent.

Their mother's piano served as final proof. Lavinia insisted it was too large for the parlor. She wanted to put other furniture in there. Over the girls' protests, Mr. Charter had done what they would never have believed him capable of—he had sold the piano. Watching the men haul it away had been like watching their mother's coffin carted to the cemetery a second time.

Thereafter they were allied against their stepmother. Kate and Vern learned quickly to mask their opinions and to protect Amy from direct interrogation because she was helpless when it came to dissembling. Invariably Papa now sided with Lavinia against them in all matters. He, who had never punished them, could now be coerced by Lavinia even to draw his belt.

Whenever Reverend Fitcher preached within a few days' journey, Mr. Charter left the girls in Vern's care to travel with his new wife to hear the prophet's words. Vern had accepted maternal duties as soon as her mother had fallen ill, and watching out for her sisters was no hardship; but now it felt provisional.

When her father returned, he was always charged with new fervor, new sureness of the world's peril. He immersed them in his belief, quoting from Reverend Fitcher's sermons or parroting the same biblical passages, crying, "God says I am with you always to the end of the world!" as if by exercising his own enthusiasm, he might persuade the girls. Rather than take them to see Reverend Fitcher, it was as if they were to be their father's flock, Lavinia's flock. As if they were being saved for some future event. Meanwhile, Lavinia wrested the role of mother back from Vern, usually by giving her orders, assigning her some task to reestablish the household hierarchy. Of all the sisters, she surely hated the woman the most. Kate merely considered herself the least persuaded of the trio.

Thus, as she followed her father up the road, she focused upon the world around her, and only paid enough attention to his preaching to know when to nod or murmur a response. There were tulip poplars, elms, and chestnut trees, bare as yet but sure to blossom. She imagined collecting the chestnuts come winter and roasting them over the kitchen hearth, as the family had done in Boston. Amy used to shriek each time one popped, certain, though it had never happened, that it was going to explode and do her harm.

Kate saw the white straight trunks of beech trees, and the hawthorn, dogwood, thimbleberries, and staghorn sumacs. It would be a beautiful place soon, and if it was not Boston, at least it offered its natural lushness as recompense.

They approached the house without passing anyone on the Gorge Road, and it was surely an illusion that tricked Kate's eye, for as she looked ahead at the turnpike, she thought she saw the pole slowly lowering onto the posts as if it had been fully raised only moments before. There was no sign of Amy, no one about at all, and she checked her father to see if he was seeing what she saw. He continued to rail against "those who would trample upon the Doctrine of God," clearly unaware of anything out of the ordinary. When she looked again, the pole was in position, motionless.

They walked across the yard, and she gave the turnpike a final, probative glance before entering the house.

Once inside, Kate knew immediately that something was wrong.

Vern caught her eye the moment no one else was watching and there was fear in her look. Kate assumed initially that Lavinia must have invoked a cruel punishment for some misbehavior during their shopping excursion, but when the stepmother entered the room, Vern hid her unease and helped with the tea that had been brewed for Papa's return. Lavinia did not seem conscious of any disturbance, and she would have been all too willing to recite Vern's transgression had there been anything to report.

Yet each glance Vern gave her was a silent tocsin, and the time they sat in the parlor seemed interminable, Amy prattling with Lavinia about the need to plant vegetables—shouldn't they do it soon, and what should they be planting this early, and could they find someone to plow up the ground for them. Amy couldn't sit still while she talked, which drew a sharp "Don't fidget so, child!" from Lavinia, but that was the equivalent of a familiar ritual, a litany between her and Amy. Amy's behavior was so typical in fact that Kate knew she was unaware of whatever troubled Vern.

Mr. Charter picked up the topic of redemption, embellishing upon what he'd said on the trek home, now that he'd had time to reflect. "Cotton Mather is right," he told Lavinia, "when he says that children are all fountains of evil. I was lax in my . . . my life before with my—our—girls." He was forever stumbling over his pronouns, and part of the reason his preaching failed to convince Kate was that he never quite seemed to know what he was about to say.

"They don't recognize their own innate sinfulness," to which Lavinia nodded, casting them all distrustful glances. "Katherine, you provoke people with your questioning and doubting." The rebuke stung her and she looked back at her father with hurtful eyes, but he didn't meet her gaze, speaking again to Lavinia. "She attempted to engage in religious discourse with a nonbeliever. I fear that for all its nearness to Harbinger, Jekyll's Glen may not be persuaded of Reverend Fitcher's rightness."

"Many will not be swayed before the day of reckoning, husband," Lavinia said. "And still others will not resign from their sinful ways even *then*. That's what He has told us, and so it's to be. Some'll wait until the sky opens to swallow them. But it'll be too late then. The door will have closed and no entreaties will persuade."

"*I'm* persuaded, ma'am," Amy said. "*I* want to be saved." She cast a trembling sidelong glance at her sisters.

Lavinia nodded solemnly. "The easiest room in hell awaits children," she said.

Amy quivered with guilt, but the other two sat stiffly, a defiant wall against these familiar words. Children could all expect to occupy that room. Children had been visited by the devil early, before their parents could intercept and protect them. The devil came into their rooms, into their cribs, to breathe his foul breath

upon them before they'd grown enough to have any will or
knowledge with which to combat his evil. He breathed sin into
them. Being the devil, he hid his intervention even from their
memories.

They knew this speech by heart, and may have believed in
their wickedness after a fashion, each with her own interpretation, her own response: Vern choosing to examine her sinfulness;
Amy accepting it all; Kate awaiting better proof. The catalogue
of sins might well drag on for hours.

Vern and Kate finished their tea and offered to clean up.
Their father smiled grimly to his wife and gestured as if to say
here was proof that his words had had an impact on their
wretched souls.

Vern soon excused herself from the kitchen and went out the
back door to the privy. Kate put away the cups and the pot, then
found her way outside as well.

Her sister awaited her in back of the privy. Immediately she
set off into the woods, keeping the shed between her and the
kitchen door, Kate following close behind her.

"If anyone asks, we decided to hunt for berries to make a
tart," she said over her shoulder.

"There aren't any berries so early," Kate replied, but she
knew her sister knew that. Finally Vern stopped and turned to
her. They stood beside a big birch tree, its roots like knuckle-
bones clutching the earth.

"What is it?" Kate asked.

Her sister glanced about, although no one could have sneaked
up on them there, not even one of Fenimore Cooper's Mohawks.
Vern's gaze was so intense that Kate was compelled to follow it
back to the house. There was nothing there she could see.

Finally, at the point where she had begun to think her sister
was stalling just to provoke her, Vern told her what had happened.

Four

NO DOUBT VERN WOULD HAVE appreciated the morning a great deal more had she not been saddled with the company of her stepmother.

They'd avoided the hawker sharpening knives on the street, crossing behind the line of customers who, sporting their various tools and blades, looked like an incipient mob.

Lavinia took quick short steps when she walked anywhere, which reminded Vern of a spider; the quick little movements let her dart past anyone who might have tried to confront or greet her, or establish a conversation. Before they could get a fix upon her she had moved and moved again. Even so, her defense failed her when, having avoided the queue, she stepped onto the walk on the far side of the road only to be confronted by a nicely dressed couple, who, passing just at that moment, wished them both a pleasant good morning. Lavinia flicked her head, a twist to the side, the slightest sign of acknowledgment. Unprepared for the inconvenience of courtesy but unable to escape, her eyes darted to their faces as her own face pinched into a wince of a smile and she dodged around them. Not bound by similar misanthropy,

Vern tilted back her parasol and with a smile replied with sincere pleasure, "Good morning." She gave the parasol a little spin. The man tipped his hat and the woman returned her smile. They were slicked up as if for going to church. Even if they were, it wouldn't be the "true church," as Lavinia would have said.

Right behind them came another man. Lavinia managed to elude his outstretched hand, but he blocked Vern's way for a moment and presented her a handbill. Then, tipping his hat, he walked on. She glanced at the bill—it was an advertisement for a demonstration of mesmerism. Looking back, she saw that the man had caught up with the couple, and was offering them a handbill, too. He had a sheaf of them pressed in one armpit.

Vern folded the handbill to carry with her. She saw Kate across the road, still waiting for their father to come out of the cooper's. Lavinia called her name impatiently. She hurried on, collapsing the parasol before she passed through the front of Van Hollander's General Store.

Lavinia's stated purpose in coming to Jekyll's Glen had been to purchase candles if any could be had. Failing that, they would have to make their own.

Back in Boston, chandlers had been plentiful and candles easy to come by, although Vern had once helped her mother make bayberry ones for some special occasion, Christmas most likely. Bayberry gave off a lovely scent, but it had been hateful work. Before adding the bayberries, her mother had melted mutton tallow, which stank so in its hot liquid state that she'd smelled its ghostly traces throughout the house for days afterward. It seemed to have bled into her skin. She hoped the store would have plenty of candles for sale.

Van Hollander didn't know them, and when they walked in, he was busy assisting some other people. Vern turned her attention to idly inspecting the dry goods he offered. He had large burlap bags of flour, cornmeal, dry beans, and of ground feed for animals and bags of potash for making soap. There were some bonnets, beside a stack of folded shirts all of simple muslin. Premade clothing was so new a product that the shirts here were all of a single size, which looked to Vern large enough to fit most men. There were bolts of calico in plain dark colors and stripes, glassware and china, jars of maple sugar and syrup and horehound candies, a small barrel of eggs in lime water, bottles of blackstrap and flax seed oil, shovels and leather fire buckets. Her foot slipped at one point, and she looked down to find that she'd stepped in someone's spit tobacco. The dusty floor everywhere seemed to be spotted with the stuff. It had been thus in Boston, too, but more on the streets than indoors. The habit disgusted her. At least her father had never taken up spitting.

While Vern made her circuit of the store, Lavinia pulled out a purse and began to count half and quarter eagles, as if to see how much she would be able to buy. She counted her money openly, making certain that Van Hollander heard the clinking and saw the coins. Vern noticed first. Lavinia seemed to the girls to have an infinite supply of money, the source of which they had thus far failed to locate.

The dour-faced Van Hollander lit up like a lantern at the sound and sight of those coins. Vern imagined that he was more often paid in less reliable currency—probably bungtown coppers and useless State Bank notes, and maybe even a pig in a place like this. He concluded his transaction with a desperate haste and fairly flung himself in Lavinia's direction. She introduced herself and Vern, and explained where they were living. If the name Pulaski meant anything to him, Van Hollander knew how to mask it. "Mrs. Lavinia," he said, immediately intimate, "what is it I can do for you today?"

"Candles. We need some candles."

He blanched. "Mrs. Lavinia, I so regret that the very first thing you ask of me I don't have. The great truth of it is, I sold the last of 'em to the folks at Harbinger yesterday late, quite unexpected. I could have some for you by Thursday if that's consolation. And it'll do you no good going across the road to Eggleston's, as they bought up all of his, too. It's a big place they have to light out there, with all them buildings and people. Are you familiar with the estate of Reverend Fitcher?"

"Yes, I am acquainted with it," she said dryly, and Vern had to restrain herself from laughing aloud at her stepmother's obfuscation. "I believe if you have spermaceti for sale, we will solve our lighting problems for now."

He nodded enthusiastically. "That I do have, in buckets. And I'll cut you the price, as I can't fulfill the other."

Lavinia nodded. "Then we'll make do. I believe we have the rest of the ingredients for candles." She cast a glance at Vern for confirmation.

"We have beeswax, yes'm. We could use alum."

Van Hollander said, "And you'll be needing wicks then?"

"Vernelia?"

"We'll need some. I don't believe we have any."

Van Hollander collected the items. As he placed the wicks on the counter he asked, "What else might I get for you?"

"Some salted pork or beef if you have it. Some butter and preserves. And can you tell me where one might purchase vegetables?"

The answer it turned out was from him. He had a back room to the store where he kept potatoes and onions, cheeses, raisins, and coffee beans along with barrels of pork and beef in brine. They bought some of most everything he had and he loaded it into a burlap bag; Lavinia even consented to bring with them a little maple sugar candy as a treat for the girls. She paid for it all with a half eagle. Van Hollander could hardly keep from trembling.

There were other customers waiting, but he took the time to usher them to the door and wish them well.

The two women lugged the spermaceti bucket between them all the way back home and never shared a word. Vern had to tuck her parasol under her arm to carry the bag as well. She dropped it twice. Lavinia gave her the standard glare of disapproval but said nothing. Vern wondered if Kate would be home first, but as it happened she wasn't.

Amy had hung out the washed clothing and was resting. When she realized that they were intending to make candles, she busied herself with the items they'd brought back rather than get drawn in. Vern could tell she was pretending not to know what to do with the food.

Lavinia studied the cast-iron pots and settled on the largest of them. "Have you the molds?" she asked. "I know they were shipped."

Vern said yes, she knew where the molds were. She hurried up the stairs into their room.

The molds were tin, a set of six tubes fixed to a flat base. The family had three of them, and even though they hadn't been used in forever, Vern had to concede the wisdom of bringing them.

She rooted through the crates they'd stacked in the corner next to Kate's bed. Naturally, the molds were in the bottom one.

She had just found them when the wall beside her head gave a loud *crack*, as if a board inside it had snapped. She jerked up in surprise. For a few moments she stared at the smooth plaster and wondered what she'd heard. She leaned forward and touched it. It was cool under her palm. Then the wall cracked again beneath her hand and she sprang back.

At that point Lavinia shouted her name. Vern glanced warily back at the wall. "Come on, girl, this is no time to be lazing!" Lavinia complained. "Get those molds down here."

She hurried from the room.

"What did you do, fall asleep up there? Well, set them down, child." Then she added, "We'll have to wait on them till tomorrow in any case now," as if by staying upstairs for more than a minute Vern had made it impossible for them to continue. "We got two up here on the mantel and the lamps are full. That'll tide us over. Right now get the stove stoked up for your father's tea. He'll be back any time."

Vern fed wood into the stove, then pumped some water into a kettle and set it on top. She found a tin of tea and shook leaves into the teapot. When the water had boiled, she removed it from the fire.

Everything had been prepared when she went out the back and walked around to the side of the house.

She gazed to where she thought the sound had come from.

The white slats were unblemished, unbroken. It was absurd any-way—the spot was more than twice her height. She looked around, nevertheless. A few old chestnuts lay scattered, but the tree they had fallen from stood far from the house. It would have taken a strong wind to fling chestnuts—a strong wind or a strong arm . . . She walked around to the front of the house and mulled over the suspicion that Amy might have thrown nuts at the out-side of the house; but even as she considered it, she admitted it was absurd. How could Amy have known Vern was in the room just then?

Vern carefully opened the front door. She could hear Lavinia in the kitchen. She crept inside, closed the door without a sound, and made her way up the stairs.

In the room it was silent and still. Dust motes floated in the sunlight spilling through the side window. She walked to Kate's bed again, and rapped her knuckles on the wall. It sounded dull and thick. Then she pressed her hands against it and pushed. It didn't flex at all. Where the sound had emerged, the wall was solid.

Half in frustration, she slapped it. The wall snapped back like an angry dog. She jerked her hands away.

After a moment, tentatively, she said, "Hello?" Nothing hap-pened. "Hello, is someone here?"

Silence, and then the *crack* repeated, softer now.

Vern threw off a shiver. "Say again."

Tap, came the noise.

"Oh, my Lord," she said, and sat on her sister's bed. Her mind whirled with implication. Among the many consolation art-ists who'd passed through their Boston home over the years had been those who described communicating with the departed as "table rapping." It was precisely thus. Even at the time the idea had excited her beyond the mere notion of contacting her mother. She'd tried once or twice, in secret, but had always felt foolish doing it, the more so for failing to get any response.

She wanted to run downstairs and call Amy, but she stopped herself, knowing that Amy was the last person she should tell.

After a while, she said, "Do you live here?"

Two taps sounded.

"Does that mean no?"

One tap.

"So one means yes and two means no? Rap once if that's right."

Tap.

"All right, you don't live here. But you *are* here. Are you passing through this house, bound for some other place?"

Two raps. *No.*

"You've come for a reason?"

Yes.

"Did you—did you die in this house? Are you here to tell me how you died?"

Two raps. *No.*

She had been so sure that was going to be the answer. Confused, she asked, "Do you know who I am?"

One. *Yes.*

"Do you know my sisters?"

Yes.

"Do you see us here?"

Yes.

She blushed with false modesty at the thought of this spirit having seen them all naked in this room. How would she ever undress again? Even as she asked it, the side of her that defied restraint and teased propriety imagined disrobing in the secret knowledge that she was doing so for an admirer. *Her* admirer.

"Am I the reason you're here?"

Yes.

Her heart trip-hammered. "Are you seeking me out?"

Yes.

A thrill ran like an electric current through her. The ghost— for it must be a ghost—was here just for *her.* "Do you have something to give me?"

Yes.

"Can I tell the others?"

No.

"Oh, my." She folded her hands, as if in prayer. "Tell me, then. What is it, what's the message?"

Silence. She had asked a question that tapping couldn't answer.

The tapping had become softer and softer with each successive question—the disembodied words "Yes" and "No" had slithered in behind and around the taps, but Vern had been too focused on counting the number of taps.

Now, unable to disengage, she repeated, "What's the message?" even as she realized that she was getting no reply because it wasn't a proper question for this mode of communication, and she muttered, "Stupid girl," and was about to frame the question another way, when into the silent interval a soft seductive voice insinuated a whispered: *"Save you."*

A tiny cry of terror barely creaked from her throat. She scrambled back off the bed, got up and ran.

Five

ATE DIDN'T BELIEVE VERN. She listened to the interminable story, and at one point while Vern was explaining the noise, she even took a few steps back toward the house to look at the side of it. As her sister said, there was nothing to mark that spot, nothing out of the ordinary. A few branches of the chestnut tree might have been close enough to drop chestnuts onto the roof, and maybe that's all it had been. Vern was scared, but Kate reasoned that she'd scared herself: She certainly had the presence of mind to tell all about Van Hollander's store and the walk back to the house.

Kate was pragmatic in a way that neither Vern nor Amy was, and no doubt it was because of her elder sisters' individual fatuities that she'd become so. She didn't think of herself as superior or smarter; only, she often found her opinion sought by both of them. Vern couldn't entrust Amy with any secrets because Amy had too often told on her, sometimes unintentionally. Amy just had no common sense when it came to knowing what you said and what you withheld. And she often explained things to Kate, the little sister, even after Vern had done so, as if feeling it essential that she be listened to, too—as if she wanted to be in Vern's place, acting the surrogate mother for the household. That, Kate suspected, was why Amy had worked so hard to learn to cook. It was something she could do better than Vern, a way she could perform as mother. Amy also approached Kate and not Vern if she thought she was being left out of something. That Vern had even for a moment attributed the noise in the wall to Amy cutting up a shine made Kate smile. Amy would never have fabricated such a tease.

Lavinia came out of the spring room and saw the two girls. She called out, "Vernelia, there is enough light left for us to make a first batch of candles today. Now, come and help."

Vern threw Kate an imploring glance and Kate said, "Don't worry, I'll go look." Then Vern ran across the yard and into the back.

Kate glanced again at the window of their shared room before following.

The salty stink of spermaceti poured out the door. Vern had set up the candle mold on the floor of the spring room. The wicks, like six worms, dangled over the sides. In the kitchen, she and Lavinia hovered over the pot, Vern with her face scrunched up. Kate walked through the dining room to the hall. She noted that Amy was out beside the road with Papa. She went quietly up the stairs.

In the doorway of the bedroom she stopped to look and listen. The room was silent, still. The beds stood where they'd been pushed into place. Amy had insisted on the area nearest the fireplace. She was always the coldest of them. Vern's bed was right here by the door. Kate, of course, had the bed beneath the noise. There was nothing different about the wall there, but she found herself viewing it edgily as if she half believed Vern's story. "Oh, my girl," she muttered, and made herself cross the room and sit on the bed.

After another minute of silence she said, "Hello?" Nothing happened. "Is anyone here?" she asked. The room remained silent. She got up and went to the window and looked out at the

bare branches of the big tree nearest. There wasn't so much as a
breeze stirring.

Kate returned to the bed. She considered the wall again for
a moment, then leaned forward and knocked on it as if on someone's door. When a full minute passed and nothing happened,
she sighed and got up. Vern was not going to like the suggestion
that she'd imagined this.

Kate was halfway to the door when the wall knocked. She
turned. Knock wasn't the right word—it sounded more like a
board had snapped in two. She expected to see a crack in the
plaster, but the wall was unblemished. *Well,* she thought, *it certainly isn't the sound of chestnuts dropping on the roof.* It also wasn't
proof of anything.

She took a step back toward her bed. "Repeat?" she asked.

The tap sounded again.

Kate stopped dead. The back of her neck prickled. "You—
you're answering me?"

Again the wall cracked.

"Oh, my Lord," said Kate. She backed away, then turned and
ran.

The tap sounded twice.

In the parlor she sat and tried to sort it out. The noise hadn't
been random. It had answered, or at least it had seemed to. But
it had taken a while to begin, as if whatever the cause was, it
had to come from somewhere, to travel to reach the wall.

Vern claimed she'd heard a voice but Kate hadn't. Of course
that didn't necessarily signify anything. So if it was a ghost, what
sort of ghost was it? And why was it in this house? She thought
about the things Mr. Jasper the carpenter had related—about the
couple who had disappeared. Might it be one of them trying to
communicate? Certainly it wasn't anything like the terrifying
ghost Mr. Irving had conjured up in Sleepy Hollow, or the more
awful one that had ridden in a coach in that novel about the monk
that Vern had read with relish at the same time as she described
it as "horrid." There was nothing ghostly about this at all, really.

And the spirit (if such it was) had told Vern it was here to protect her, so maybe it was no ghost at all. Maybe it was an angel. An angel, Kate thought, would be preferable.

The parade of consolation lecturers through their house had introduced the Charter sisters to a notion of spirits that ran counter to the spooks of gothic tales. However odious the speakers themselves, their talk had always been filled with the gentleness of the spirits, the closeness of that world to our own if only we could recognize it.

Kate recalled one man in particular who had told of his own wife's death. It had come the year after their child had succumbed to a fever. His wife in her final hours had heard their little boy laughing and playing with other children in Heaven. The closer she'd moved to death herself, the more her perceptions of him crystallized. She heard him calling to her from that distant land. Finally, she had raised her hand and her fingers had curled as if around a child's tiny hand. Kate remembered his tears as he spoke of his wife holding a hand he could not see; but he had felt it, felt the presence of the spirits come to collect her, of all of Heaven entering the room, and his anguish had been tempered by his happiness that their little son who'd gone before had eased his dear mother's translation.

After hearing him she'd thought that perhaps ghosts were not something to fear. If there was a ghost in their wall . . . well, there was certainly something in there.

She had nearly talked herself out of being afraid by the time Vern found her.

"What happened? Did it speak?" Vern asked.

"Not exactly."

"But you heard it. It was there."

"Something was, though not at first. But then it answered. It knocked on the wall when I spoke to it."

"Oh, God, Kate, how can we possibly stay in that *room*? What does it want?"

"I thought it wanted to protect you." Then Kate glimpsed the slightest secret smile from Vern, and knew at once that frightened though Vern might be, she was also secretly thrilled.

"You'll sit with me, won't you?"

"Sit?" Kate asked.

"We have to try and communicate with it. But not alone. We shouldn't be alone with it."

"No, I suppose we shouldn't." She shook her head as she heard her sister's words again: *How can we be in that room?* "After dinner, then. We'll come up and see what we can find out."

Eyes bright with excitement, Vern squeezed her hand.

Sometimes Kate felt as if she were the eldest by years.

"And you are dead?" Kate asked.

The wall cracked once.

" 'Yes,' he said 'yes,' " Vern interjected.

"I know that, I *heard* the sound, Vern. Once for yes, twice for no. You needn't answer for him."

"Oh, but, Kate, I hear his voice! I hear his words. I can't help myself." She smiled a little sheepishly, expecting her sister to be sympathetic. Kate had no trouble hearing the taps, just as before. She'd been so bold as to put her hand against the plaster to feel the vibration as the disembodied communicant knocked—just to be certain that the sound was coming from inside the wall. Each tap occurred only when a question had been asked, and only in the exterior wall. But only Vern heard a voice. Kate, though she strained for even a whisper, an echo, heard nothing. As much as she would have liked, she couldn't even make the wind outside warp into the cadences Vern described.

Her sister had gone from terror to enthusiastic defense of the ghost *as* a ghost without any prompting; Kate hadn't even mentioned her thoughts about angels. She would have been more concerned if she hadn't seen this behavior in her sister before.

The last time Vern had shared such excitement, it was over that French boy with whom she'd decided she was in love, Henri. He had been in Boston only six months when Vern met him. His parents' house stood opposite theirs and halfway up the street. Vern had been out for a stroll with her parasol when she saw him, and it had been love at first sight—or at least she'd proclaimed it so, undyingly. She'd gushed and sworn and made incredible statements about what Henri intended for the two of them, about how she would throw her heart from a cliff for him, or leap off a tower to her death if she could not have him and how they were going to run away together if Papa refused him—the more ridiculous the assertions, the more adamant the claim. Henri obviously felt something in return: He'd pledged her his heart. And, as it happened, he'd done a good deal more.

It wasn't until Vern had finally been shaken to her senses by the threat of pregnancy that her ardor cooled somewhat. By then Mr. Charter and Lavinia had determined to sell the house and come here. The timing allowed Vern to make of Henri a martyr to love. "*Mal au coeur*," she had repeated in her sulks, and whether this was a phrase Henri had said or Vern had selected it for herself, Kate never knew. Either way, it was ever so histrionic.

Kate couldn't imagine what would be necessary to shake her sister's fervor this time.

In the hour after dinner, they learned—if that was the right word for it; if Vern's claims could be trusted at all—that the spirit's name was Samuel, Samuel Verity. The full name seemed to preclude the possibility that he was a true angel. He had been dead for twenty years. He'd been a Shaker, come from Dublin, and had caught an ague and died before his nineteenth birthday. Kate received none of these details. She watched her pie-eyed sister tilt her head and then nod enthusiastically as she received each covert message, crying, "Yes, yes, I understand, did you hear, Kate, did you hear what he said?" As she did not, Kate insisted on her own method of verification, and to each question, the knocking sounded on cue.

Vern practically leaped up with glee as the spirit confirmed what she said it had said, too excited in her triumph to notice that in requiring corroboration Kate was not accepting her account. She had certainly forgotten about being afraid.

That something incredible confronted her in the room, Kate could not deny. Yet as the time went on and she became more and more the observer and not a participant in the discovery, she lost her earlier belief that what was happening here was in fact spirit communication. There was no reason for her to think this. The rapping came when it should have. The things Vern said were corroborated again and again; yet the suspicion grew that she was playing an unwitting part in some elaborate parlor trick, performed for their benefit—or at least for Vern's benefit—and that there was a great deal more devil than God in the miracle.

The sun had sunk below the trees, but the two girls carried on their interrogation even as the room darkened.

Then all at once the light from a candle threw their shadows against the wall, and they both twisted about like two children caught misbehaving.

Amy stood in the doorway, holding one of the half-burned candles from the kitchen. She took one look at them seated on Kate's bed and facing the wall and her eyes narrowed with suspicion. "Whatever are you two doing?"

While Kate tried to ease into the subject—"Amy, come sit with us and see what you make of this—" Vern blurted out, "Oh, Amy, there's a *ghost* in the wall and he's talking to me, and even Kate has heard him, you must come and listen, too, you must!"

In the face of such unprecedented behavior—even at the peak of her ecstasy over Henri, Vern would never have confided in Amy—Kate could only sit mutely dumbfounded. This sister was no one she knew.

Amy squinted at them. From where she stood, she had come upon another secret kept from her. "I suppose if I hadn't come upstairs," she complained, "you wouldn't have told me about this at all, would you?"

"Amy," Kate placated. "Don't be silly. It's just that—" She stopped, trapped by circumstance. She could not confess here that she mistrusted Vern, and couldn't deny that neither of them had spent even a second considering the exclusion of their hapless middle sister; it would have required elaborating on the ghost's having told Vern not to reveal his presence to anyone else—which of course she'd immediately violated, though without any apparent repercussions. The best Kate could muster from her cramped choices was, "We've only been listening a little while."

"Well, let's hear him then," Amy said. She set her candle down on a dresser and came around and planted herself on the bed between them. She crossed her arms. "Spirit, are you here?" she asked to the room at large. Her tone made it clear she gave no credence to the notion.

The words were barely out of her mouth when the wall snapped right in front of her. Amy's eyes rounded and her mouth hung open, but as quickly her jaw pushed out. "That's the ghost of a woodpecker you got." She would not give in easily. Kate could have predicted it.

"He says you'd do well to believe in him," Vern scolded.

"What do you mean *he* says? You got all that from one tiny little noise?"

Kate then explained that their eldest sister was the only one who heard the voice of this supposed angel. She hoped Amy would recognize that it was the two of them united against Vern, but instead of establishing any such camaraderie, the revelation made Amy *more* resentful. "It's always Vern," she whined. "Vern gets to do everything first. Vern gets to break the rules and we two have to cover for her. When she sneaks out of the house at night, we're supposed to watch to make sure she doesn't get caught. Never mind that she's gettin' away with *doing* it!"

Both her sisters stared at her in surprise. Kate answered, "Amelia! What a thing to say!"

Amy's eyes darted from one to the other, a nervous glance that made it clear she hadn't meant to reveal quite so much. Her knowledge of Vern's promiscuity was a trump card. It was power. In a moment of anger she had tossed it away. She had no choice now but to forge ahead. "You two think you're having secret conversations but sometimes you aren't so secret. I hear lots of things you think are just between you. Sometimes you think I'm asleep when I'm not. And sometimes you think you're all by yourselves but maybe there's a window open or a door. I heard Vern telling you all about that Italian boy."

"He's not Italian," Vern objected. "He's French. And he's wonderful."

Amy laughed harshly, and even Kate shook her head. "Papa'd take a strap to you till your skin came off if he knew. Probably throw you out of the house, I expect." She stuck her nose in the air and imitated her older sister: " 'Oh, you girls will find out one day what we women really need from men. When you're older and more sophisticated.' Pshaw! I don't know what sophistication's got to do with it. All I see is, they want to get your drawers off and you're helping them by going around without any on in the first place."

Vern just gaped.

Amy continued, "You always think that 'poor little Amy' is so simple and stupid that she won't realize—"

"Amy, that's not so," Kate objected, although it was and she knew it.

"Sure and it is. And probably I am stupid, but I don't care." She folded her arms, posing in a sulk.

Vern couldn't decide what to object to most—the accusations of her carelessness with Henri (even as she sat there she was reenvisioning how she lay with him and how she had to guide him into her because finally despite his boldness he knew less than she did about what they were up to), or the notion that she intentionally and cruelly kept her sister in the dark, when the truth was, she was protecting herself and wouldn't even have told Kate except that she just *had* to talk to someone about how much in love she was. She could never have made such confession to Amy, because she'd been Amy's mother for six years now and couldn't exchange her ironclad role for that of a love-struck girl. Kate, despite the fact that she was a year younger than Amy, was more grown-up about things. More to the point, Kate didn't judge her. Amy surely would, on the spot, as she was doing now. Amy, the open book, was as quick to judge as Lavinia.

While Vern and Kate sat in entangled silence, Amy kicked off her shoes and pulled her stockings down. She sat and admired her own feet, curling her toes as if she hadn't a care in the world. She idly asked, "Who is this spirit, then, hmm? Why's he in this house in particular? You say he's a Shaker, so how come he's not with them over at New Lebanon? He isn't the one who lived here before us, is he, so what's he doing in *our* house?"

Kate had wondered much the same things but had not voiced her doubts, being too curious about the phenomenon itself. She also had information about the history of the house that neither of her sisters could know. Had the former occupants met this spirit, too? Might the ghost have had something to do with their disappearance? Certainly, if it *was* a ghost, it must know what had happened. She even wondered if Vern had got the last name wrong. She could almost persuade herself that "Verity" might be "Pulaski"—she didn't know how well Vern heard the voice. Although the notion frightened her, she wanted to have a session with the rapping spirit by herself.

Amy told Vern, "I don't think I believe in your Samuel." Then she leaned over to Kate and whispered loudly, "I think Vern's having us on." She raised one foot straight out till her toes touched the wall. Then she turned her foot under and made her ankle crack as loud as the tapping within the wall. She twisted it back the other way and her ankle bones cracked again. "I do believe," she said, "I got a spirit in my *feet*."

Vern's lips pressed so tight, the color bled from around them. "I very much doubt it," she replied. She got up and stormed into the hall.

Amy giggled and cracked her ankle again.

Kate sighed. "Oh, Amelia, why do you always think we're plotting against you? When have we *ever*?" Then she stood and left the room as well.

Until that moment Amy had felt terribly clever. Now her audience had gone. She lowered her legs and crossed her arms again, pushed her lips out; but there was no one left to see her sulk.

It must have been a breeze drawn by her sisters' departing that caused the candle to gutter and go out then. The room fell dark. It became instantly sinister. Amy glanced from one end of the bed to the other. She didn't want to be alone in here with a spirit. A *spirit*—and she admitted to herself what she had refused to say to her sisters, that she did believe in ghosts and believed they must surely be hungry for the living. For her.

She stood, but stumbled over her cast-off shoes and stockings and pitched toward the wall. She slapped her palms against it to steady herself, and the wall cracked so loud it should have split in two. The vibration shot up her arms as if the thing had burst out of the plaster. She cried out and launched herself away from the wall. She stumbled again on her shoes—they seemed to be sliding around, tripping her every step. The wall cracked behind her as if it would split down the middle. She flung herself across the bed and came up running in blind panic for the door. Her bare toes struck the leg of Vern's bed, which impossibly had slid into the middle of the room. She shrieked with pain. She hopped, fumbling, clutching at her foot. Tears flooded her eyes. She ran clumsily and all but fell into her sisters' arms.

They caught her in the doorway as she wailed, arms wrapped around her leg. They sat her down in the dark hall, both at a loss how to cope with her, how to silence her. But it was too late: Amy's caterwauling brought Lavinia charging up the stairs with one of the oil lamps. Mr. Charter followed close behind her.

"What have you girls been doing?" the stepmother demanded, and, taking it all in at a glance, pronounced her sentence: "You two, torturing your poor feeble sister. You're wicked, both of you."

Amy wailed louder at being called "feeble." "It wasn't them, it was the *ghost*!" she cried. "He would've touched me, he tried to, he grabbed my arms, and he moved the bed to trap me!"

"What foolishness is this? What ghost?"

Vern and Kate glared at their sister for revealing what they'd been doing. This was precisely *why* Amy found herself excluded from their activities. She hadn't the sense to keep things to herself.

"What ghost?" Lavinia repeated precisely.

It was clear that Vern couldn't speak of it. Kate replied guardedly, "Vern was communicating with . . . with something. In the wall."

"Show me." Lavinia pointed the way back into the bedroom.

They turned, but as she passed by her stepmother, Kate glimpsed the strangest tiny smile sliding across Lavinia's lips—there and gone in an instant—as if this turn of events were delighting her. She craned her head back, but Lavinia was already herding her sisters in with her lamp.

It threw their shadows ahead as if into a hollow cavern. She lit Amy's candle from it, then walked to the far end and lit the lamp on their mantel as well. Wind whistled in the chimney. "You should have a fire in here to keep you warmer," she said, then turned around. The room was all in order. Vern's bed was not in the middle but against the inside wall where it belonged.

Amy blubbered, "It was too in the middle. This isn't fair. He's put it back."

No one much paid attention to her grievances.

"Where is this ghost?"

Kate pointed at the wall over her bed.

Lavinia marched around the bed. Mr. Charter trailed after her like a judgment.

Vern moved up beside Lavinia. With obvious reluctance, she explained, "You ask him a question."

"What question?"

"Any question."

Lavinia opened her mouth but said nothing for a moment. She faced Vern. "You ask."

Vern pressed her palm to the wall. "Spirit, are you with us?"

Nothing happened.

"Samuel?"

"Oh, has it a name, your ghost?"

"It's Samuel," she answered, her head bowed, brow creased. She stood a few more moments, then with a sigh removed her hand. "He's gone. He told me not to tell anyone, and now he's gone." She was nearly in tears.

Lavinia's look would have withered an olive tree. "Is he, now? No doubt all the ruckus here drove him away, a bunch of screaming girls carrying on like they were half their age, and causing such commotion as this house has undoubtedly never seen. Mr. Charter?" she said expectantly.

The girls stiffened. They'd heard the request in that tone many times.

Mr. Charter studied the floor and cleared his throat. "Lavinia," he said, "we've only just arrived, what possible punishment can we invent when there's no routine even established yet?" He said to his daughters, "I expect that you girls may not go into town now for some days, except as to help us carry supplies back home—"

"The *belt*, sir."

Mr. Charter stood a moment before answering. His shoulders sagged, and the girls dreaded that he would obediently retrieve the heavy belt that Lavinia wanted. For once, he chose to stand his ground. "Lavinia," he answered, staring at the floor, "I'll not take a belt to my daughters for the nothing that this nonsense is."

The stepmother's Medusa gaze swept the room. Collecting the lamp, she walked stiffly out the door, her skirts swishing like whips.

"Papa, it was—" Vern started to protest, but her father raised his hand to silence her, though his head remained bowed.

"The spirits of children are corrupt," he said, but without much conviction behind the words. "Those of us who guide them must remember they are born into it and cannot help."

"But he's *real*, Papa, the ghost—"

"Vernelia Anne!" he snapped, then more softly, "It matters little if he is or not. The penalties we all endure are the same either way. Think on that awhile, if you would, before you make your apology on the morrow." He withdrew into the dark hallway and was gone.

Amy sulked and rubbed her toes.

Kate told her, "You didn't break anything. It'll stop hurting after a bit."

"But the bed really was in the middle of the floor. How could I have run way over to *there*." She pointed.

"Oh, sister, you are cutting up the didoes with us. You provoke us that way and then you give up everything. Why couldn't you keep it to yourself for once? Why did you have to tell them when you could have just said you stubbed your toe, which is what you did?"

Amy refused to be made the villain, but could think of no adequate defense. Her soul *was* corrupt and spiteful—this she knew about herself, although knowing didn't seem to prevent her from acting that way. She supposed she should apologize to Vern, but she simply could not. *She* was the wronged party, the one left quite literally in the dark. In mute frustration she resigned from the battle. She turned away and went to her bed, where she started unbuttoning her dress.

There seemed to be nothing left to say. Kate went downstairs, out through the kitchen to the back of the house, and collected an armful of wood. When she returned to the room, Amy was in bed and Vern standing as before. Kate knelt and made a layer of crisscrossed kindling, which she lit using a lucifer match and striker from the mantel cup. She added the larger wood to the blaze. Only when there was a decent fire going did she begin undressing for bed as well.

Vern was still looking at the wall.

"You should go to bed," Kate told her.

"I cannot," she said.

"Why?"

"I can't *change* in here. He's watching me. Samuel's watching me."

Kate glanced at Amy. "Sister," she said, "if he's truly a spirit or an angel then he can watch you wherever you are. It won't make a difference what room you're in or even if you're in the house. And why should it, if he's a spirit—your body can't mean a thing to him. Besides which, he's gone away."

"I know it, but I can't. I can't." And she walked out into the hallway, closing the door after her.

Amy asked, "Now, where does she think she's gonna sleep?"

Kate hung her dress on a peg. In her chemise she sat on her bed. She was the one nearest the point of communication, closest

to the wall and the ghost. She ought to have been the one most
fearful. Yet what she felt was an unease less specific in its source
than Vern's displaced Shaker.

As she climbed into her bed, she was thinking that they had
been in this house for less than two days and already their world
had been turned upside down. The world was supposed to be
ending, Jesus awaiting, and Heaven approaching. What did ghosts
have to do with that? Were they privy to the opening of a door
between worlds? Could this be seen as a sign that Reverend
Fitcher was right? If so, then why did she harbor such undeniable
doubt?

She stared at the wall and asked quietly, "Who are you?"

The wall chose not to reply.

Six

*T*HE MAN TOOK SHAPE FROM THE words of her sisters. Vern heard Amy say, "A tall man," and Kate add, "He has to have dark hair." In her dream they were playing the game of making up a husband, but this time he appeared, coalescing into a handsome, dark-haired man who had no mouth. Then Amy and Kate were gone, and the man they'd conjured was reaching to touch her while she retreated down eerily lit hallways that seemed to unfold forever; she turned and he followed her, and behind him the view went black, as though his body cast the light by which she saw. Stranger still, though she was always moving away from him she didn't fear him; in fact she was not moving by her own volition but could not face what impelled her, what dragged her away from him. Then all at once something supple, fluttering, like live tendrils of smoke reached out of the blackness behind him, looped around his throat, and snatched him into it, and everything went dark. She cried out and awoke. She lay in her bed in the predawn grayness, listening to her sisters' steady breathing, guessing that she had made a noise only in her dream. She called out in her mind to

Samuel. Nothing answered, but when she glanced at Kate's bed, the wall above it seemed to glow with lambent fire, as though the plaster were luminous.

She stared at the glow, expecting every moment for something to emerge. Instead, the glow faded slowly away and the room darkened as if the wall were absorbing all incoming light. A shadow took form in the air beside her, a shape made from nothing. It reached toward her.

She awoke with a start.

It was morning, her sisters stirring beneath their quilts, and the air in the room crisply cold. Kate's fire had long since gone out. No shadow stood beside her. The wall above Kate's bed looked perfectly normal. Vern had dreamed that she'd awakened, that was all—one dream encapsulating another. Nothing called to her, no voice echoed upon the aether, the room was silent. If Samuel had been driven away, it was Lavinia who had done it, and not she.

As she sat up, her foot brushed the chamber pot beneath her bed. It sloshed, and she leaned down to look at it. Someone had used it during the night without waking her—one of her sisters, despite having their own pots. Probably Amy. She said nothing about it, but once dressed carried the pot out back to empty it. The ground was covered over in a rime of ice, and her breath made a mist in the air; but the sun was already blasting its rays through the trees across the road.

The breakfast that morning was boiled oatmeal and pan bread. Amy had made it, and it was quite good. Vern had to admit, Amy had the instincts of a cook, which she did not, though she still made some meals. It was something she could respect about her younger sister, and the Lord knew, sometimes Amy made that difficult to do. She silently forgave Amy for telling everyone about her ghost. It really wasn't Amy's fault that she couldn't lie. If anything it probably made her a better Christian. Better than her oldest sister, anyway. Vern just hoped that the ghost of Samuel would come back, that she hadn't lost him, too. If she had, she knew, it was not Amy's fault. She wanted to blame Lavinia, she had done, but the truth was, he'd instructed her to tell no one and she had disregarded that and told Kate, and then Amy, and then . . .

She wondered about Judgment Day, and what it truly meant. Wouldn't God be able to look into her soul and see that it was good and kind, and that what she'd done with Henri had been an expression of love? She *had* loved him. She still did, but she was resigned that she wouldn't ever see him again. He wasn't going to be let into Harbinger, wasn't going to be saved unless he changed his mind soon. She wouldn't be punished for caring for him, surely. It wasn't evil to care for someone, even if they weren't saved. Lord Jesus had cared for everyone, even prostitutes. She maintained a secret hope that she might intervene for Henri's soul when the time came—rescue him. That was a very romantic notion, but didn't it also provide proof of her purity?

She'd nearly convinced herself that she could portray her actions in the proper light if given the chance. She just didn't know how her life would be confronted, and whether she would have to look back over it as one looked back along a road one had walked down. Would she have to answer for every action, every mistake, and would they arrive finally at Henri and allow her the chance to wrap herself around him and beg for his life? She would be like Esther or Ruth. She would save somebody. Her affection for her mother lay bound up in the past, too. So much love abounded inside her, how could she be judged harshly? Not if God were fair . . .

It was then she turned to Lavinia and said, "Please forgive me, ma'am, for the events of last night, which were purely my fault and no one else's."

Everyone stopped eating, Amy with her spoon halfway to her mouth.

Lavinia flushed. She bowed her head as though to pray. After a moment, she raised her napkin to her lips and patted them dry. "Of course, child, I can grant you my forgiveness. But you require a higher power's absolution than mine for your wickedness. I believe you should stay in your room awhile once we've finished

arranging our household for company—stay there and think on
what act you must perform to be absolved of your sins. Later, I'll
call you down to make those candles that couldn't be done yesterday."

Vern licked her lips. She traded a look with Kate, and saw in
her sister's gaze a warning not to take the bait. She bit back her
outrage and said, "Yes, ma'am." Picking up her spoon, she began
to eat her food as if her entire world lay in that bowl.

The parlor had been assembled. Kate had found some way to
persuade her father to use the furniture from the third floor—at
least, the chairs: The dresser and sofa remained where they were,
which gave the small attic the look of an inhabited garret. Vern
had to admire Kate's skill in maneuvering him. Whatever Kate
had done, neither Vern nor Amy could have accomplished it. Amy
was limping around the kitchen barefoot, claiming that she
couldn't tolerate a shoe, though her toes didn't look at all swollen.
Her father made it clear that he didn't believe her, either, and
certainly she could have asked no favors from him at the moment.

Some of the rugs had been beaten, the lamps and vases and
dishes arranged, tea tables set up, the antimacassars laid over the
back of the sofa. She knew what was coming next, but rather
than have Lavinia banish her—which would surely include further upbraiding for having not governed herself—she retreated
to her room on her own.

There was nothing to do there, of course. She had no nee-
dlework at hand, and the only thing to read was a copy of *Wieland*
that had been unpacked from Amy's things. If nothing else, it
might provide a diversion to make the time go faster.

She removed her shoes and lay down on her bed, opening
the book. She read aloud, " 'Wieland, or the Transformation. An
American Tale.'

> *"From virtue's blissful paths away,*
> *The double-tongued are sure to stray;*

Good is a forth-right journey still,
And mazy paths but lead to ill."

This was followed by an advertisement by the author, who
promised that the book would address "some important branches
of the moral constitution of man." Well, Vern thought, no wonder
Amy felt compelled to read it—she was always worried about her
moral constitution and never entirely resolved that she might
have one.

All Vern had known of it was that Amy thought the book
spooky and strange, but didn't really seem to understand it.

She started to read the first chapter, but had gotten only a
few lines along—to where the narrator promised to tell of things
that had happened to his family—before her eyes were drawn
beyond it to the wall over Kate's bed. Of course it was dull and
blank. There was no glow, nor anything else that had been in her
dream.

No, she didn't want to think about it. About the voice of
Samuel.

With a furrowed brow, she plunged into the book again, trying
to absorb the full depth of what was being proposed. Something
had happened to this narrator, something to destroy his hope. She
read with growing unease, as everything he said seemed like a
description of her own state: "I have nothing more to fear. Fate
had done its worst . . . the storm that tore up our happiness . . ."
She closed the book before some detail might destroy the illusion
that this was her life, her misfortune, her own happiness torn up.
It wasn't fair that she'd been robbed of it before she was old
enough to know life, to make one of her own—a conspiracy of
fate. All of humanity doomed, and she along with it.

Sitting up, she walked over to Kate's bed and sat down. At
that point her nerve failed.

She sat without saying anything, afraid to inquire, afraid that
he wouldn't be there and that if he wasn't she would have to
admit she'd driven him away. And that would be too terrible to
bear. Everyone was driven away from her.

She wanted him to make a sign so that she wouldn't have to ask—to show that he knew where she was—but there was no tapping. No voice spoke.

She rested her chin on her fists. There was no point in going back to her bed and trying to read that book. No point in trying to do anything else. What she really wanted to do was talk to her ghost.

Finally, she said, "Samuel?" She closed her eyes and listened. "Samuel, are you there?" She thought she heard a scratching in the wall, and placed her cheek against it. "Can you hear me?"

There was not a sound, but something slid against her face, crawling caterpillarlike over her cheek where it touched the wall. She drew back in alarm.

She heard his voice then: "Vernelia." Her name spoken as though by rustling leaves or wind upon long grass. "I am here."

"Yes," she replied. Her heart opened to him with a loving tenderness that was almost painful to bear. She touched the wall and it seemed that her hand passed straight through the surface of it, as if *she* were the ghost. So close, the plaster became a mist, a fog. She let it draw her in.

This is Heaven, she thought, *I'm in the clouds.*

Nothing condensed, no form appeared, no specter. She saw no more than milky whiteness, which seemed to press itself to her, its touch bittersweet, arousing. She shifted her hips against the pressure, and a soft moan escaped her, muffled in the mist. She spoke his name again, and he answered, "I'm here, Vern," his voice coming from everywhere at once, but so close that it filled her head, leaving no room for thoughts of her own. His voice made her fingers move, her toes curl, its sound was like strings upon her; it kissed her throat with pleasure. He told her, "I'll guide you to do what you need to do. But this time you tell no one. I am the way." She could only answer that he was. Her eyes rolled up and her tongue licked the sweet air. He laughed and she pursued the sound.

*   *   *

When, an hour later, Kate entered the room, she found her sister curled up in bed with the book that Amy had been reading. The last thing Kate wanted to do was wake Vern. She would have to be very quiet, but at the same time had to try to communicate, which meant asking questions. Would a ghost hear her if she whispered?

She sat on her bed, facing the wall, then thought awhile about what she wanted to ask. She placed her palm against the wall. "Hello?" she said softly, and glanced at her sister to make sure Vern didn't stir. As she twisted, something tapped against the wall beneath her palm. She jerked her hand away, then chided herself. This was what she'd hoped for, after all. She put her hand to the wall again.

"Samuel?" she asked.

Nothing happened.

"Are you there?" Another tap.

Not Samuel, then, she concluded, and wondered, *How many ghosts are there in this house?* She spent a moment deciding if she wanted to take the time to try to identify the entity. She didn't know how long she would have, if Vern might awaken or Amy come looking for her. She didn't want a reenactment of the previous night.

"Did you know the people who lived here before?"

Tap.

"The Pulaskis."

Tap.

"What happened to—oh, wait, that's not the way to ask it. Are they—are they alive?"

Tap.

She opened her mouth to ask if they were close by when the second tap came. Did that mean "no" or was that "yes" for each of them? A "no" had been much quicker the night before, but this wasn't necessarily the same spirit, or even any spirit—after all, it hadn't said anything so far that meant anything.

"One of them left this house first. Was it Mr. Pulaski?"

Tap. Tap. Quickly this time.

"It was his wife."

Tap.

That was right, or at least it agreed with what Mr. Jasper had said.

"Did you see her go?"

Tap.

"Did she go far?"

Tap. Tap.

She wished there were a way to get other kinds of answers out of the wall, have it name things and places.

"Is she at Harbinger?"

Tap.

"Is her husband there, too?"

Tap. Tap.

"No. Where is he? I wonder. Only, you can't tell me that. So, Mrs. Pulaski is safely at Harbinger?"

Tap.

"We'll see her there?"

Tap. Louder this time.

"That means we're going there, too."

Tap.

Of course, she'd known that, too. It was why they'd come here.

"The Judgment Day—is it truly close? Are we, is our world ending soon?"

Tap.

"Oh." She withdrew her hand. She had wanted it to be a lie. Instead, here was apparent corroboration from beyond the grave of what the Reverend Fitcher preached and what her father believed. She touched the wall again. "Will we be with our mother again on that day?"

At that moment Vern muttered and rolled onto her side. Kate instinctively hunched forward, as if to conceal something; she looked back at her sister, but Vern was still asleep. Facing the wall again, she realized there had been no tap. No reply.

"Hello. Aren't you there?"

The wall remained still.

"Oh, please, don't go now. Won't we see our mother again?"

Another ten minutes she must have sat, waiting for the answer. Now and then she whispered, "Samuel?" "Spirit?" but got no reply. She tried to convince herself that, distracted at the critical moment, she had felt and heard a tap, but she knew it wasn't true. Why had the ghost left her at that moment? Why hadn't it answered? Here was the question she most wanted an answer to, and the wall, as if toying with her, withheld it. She glanced at her sister again.

Vern slept wrapped around the book. One bare leg dangled off the bed as if any moment now she was going to stand and sleepwalk out of the room.

Kate recalled what she had thought the night before: that Vern was the victim of some huge japery, some cruel trick played at her expense.

Kate knew now that it was more than a simple trick. The spirit knew things that only she and her father knew. It had revealed that much. If this was a trick, it was of a different sort—one full of treachery.

She got up and left the room.

Seven

SOMETHING WAS GOING ON BE-
tween her sisters.

Despite Vern's apology, and Kate's denials that they kept anything from her, Amy knew they were up to something. The matter of the ghost or whatever it was knocking in the walls was not done.

Lavinia had banished Vern to their room, which seemed not a very wise thing to do, given that it put her together with the ghost. After last night, Amy would never have stayed in that room by herself, even for a minute, even if it meant she had to sit on a stool in a corner, but she was sure Vern would use the opportunity to talk to the spirit.

Her resentment festered even more when Lavinia told her, "You can prepare the dinner later, right now we're going to make the candles."

"But, Vern's supposed to—"

"Vern has been sent to her room for her behavior. I've a like mind to send you, too, for your part in last night's shenanigans, but your father convinced me otherwise, and I need someone to help me haul the spermaceti from the stove to the molds out back."

"Kate isn't—"

"Young lady," Lavinia said sternly, "I have already decided who is helping me."

And that was that. For three hours, they heated the whale fat, poured molds, reheated the fat, soaked the molds to release the candles, then poured another batch. And when that was done, there was still the salted beef and onions and carrots for dinner that she had to prepare, by which time the kitchen stank something awful. Amy was furious with Lavinia, but far more so with her two sisters who didn't have to do this extra and accursed chore.

The minute the dinner was simmering, she went looking for Kate. No one was in the parlor, which looked nice all arranged. Upstairs, Vern lay asleep with the copy of *Wieland* open on her breast. Even though Amy had given up on the book she resented that Vern had simply taken it without asking.

Kate had disappeared. She might have been wandering in the woods; she might even have been sitting with their father in his sentry box beside the road. Rather than inquire, Amy decided Kate had gone to the third floor, into that tiny room where no one would think to look for her, and where Amy would not dare go by herself. Obviously she'd gone there to hide from Lavinia.

Both her sisters were angry with Amy for last night. They were so angry that they wouldn't listen to her when she said Vern's bed had moved into the middle of the room and then back again. But it had. She had the bruised foot to prove it. Letting Lavinia pile on the agony was just their way of getting their own back at her.

The rest of the time until the food was cooked, Amy spent in the parlor. She looked at the lamps, the pieces of glass on the shelves, the books of Mr. Charter's modest library, all of which had been part of their life in Boston. Amy thought she should feel homesickness, but instead as she touched the familiar things she started humming a tune under her breath, just a nonsense singsong tune that she was making up as she went. She'd felt homesick on that hill from the lake. Now she couldn't find it, as if the part of her that reacted to change had been pulled out like a baby tooth and put away in a box somewhere, still to be unpacked. Today was like yesterday, would be like tomorrow and the day after, right up until the days all stopped. And then—

What would the Next Life *really* be like? How would it be any different from this? Would she no longer be afraid of her own soul? She must know forgiveness firsthand then. She would know she was saved and taken up and wouldn't that prove she was worthy of God's love? Would they live in houses again? On Earth again? Would they have bodies? She couldn't imagine life without a body. Like Vern's ghost, who watched without eyes, spoke without lips, tapped on a wall from inside it without hands. How did he exist? Was that his soul then, and did it match the body so closely? "I bet he doesn't have to make candles," Amy muttered.

In the new life would there be chores? She could imagine being with her mother again. She could picture the world after Judgment as a paradise where the weather was always perfect and her mother was with them. But Lavinia would be with them, too. How could she have two mothers, and to whom would Papa be married then? Could he be married to both women? She didn't think her mother would much care for Lavinia. For one thing, Lavinia never laughed, and Amy could remember her mother laughing. Her mother had been happy. None of Lavinia's friends seemed to be happy, either. And Papa rarely smiled anymore. It was as if joy had been pushed aside to make room for the sermons and constant reminders of Judgment Day. As if Lavinia had moved inside him as well as into their home.

Amy looked up, and started. Lavinia's face hung before her in the shadows. It stared at her. She realized then that dusk had fallen without her noticing. Lavinia's black hair and dress blended into the encroaching dark, making her pale face a floating skull in the doorway.

"Where are your sisters?" Lavinia asked. Amy could not find

her voice. "What is the matter with you, girl. Daydreaming? There's no time for daydreaming here. There's too much work to be done. Now, come along—if we can't find your sisters, then *you'll* set table."

Amy got up, exaggerating the effort this took. As she stood, Amy saw Mr. Charter walking toward the house in the half-light like some empurpled shade himself. Kate was not with him.

She nodded to herself as she followed her stepmother. She did know where Kate had been after all.

During the meal, neither Kate nor Vern spoke much. Vern seemed to Amy to be half asleep still. She complied with every-thing Lavinia asked of her, as if she lacked the energy to argue.

Amy watched Kate watching Vern, too.

When the meal was finished, Kate and Vern cleared away the dishes and went to clean up. Amy remained seated between her father and stepmother. He read from Isaiah, loud as a preacher, so that the girls would hear in the kitchen. Lavinia nodded every so often, as if confirming the words, as if the possibility existed that he might read some false ones at some point and she would know it.

Then Vern retired. She emerged from the kitchen, wandered through the room from person to person, bidding each a good night, and went up the stairs to bed. Amy could see that her father found this odd. He stopped his recitation in midsentence, and his gaze lingered on the doorway to the hall long after Vern had gone. Lavinia paid it no mind, and finally, Mr. Charter re-turned to his reading.

Amy excused herself as if to use the privy. She found Kate in the hall doorway to the kitchen. Kate seemed to be listening to sounds from upstairs. She told Amy, "You should go to bed, too. And I'll follow momentarily."

"Come down and sit in the dust. O virgin daughter of Babylon," cried Mr. Charter.

"What?" asked Amy.

"We shouldn't leave Vern alone."

"There is no throne!"

Amy shrugged. "Why, what's the matter with her?"

"You saw her at dinner."

"She's sleepy."

"*I'm* sleepy, Amy," Kate replied. "Vern's in a daze. Remember when I was little and she used to sleepwalk around the room? She looks that way now. As if she isn't here."

"Thy nakedness shall be uncovered!"

"You think it's the ghost?"

"I think—" Kate began. "I don't know what I think. There's something going on."

"Where were you this afternoon?"

Kate said, "I went upstairs. To see if that clock was still going."

"You were gone long."

"It was warm and I fell asleep. What difference does it make? The something going on's to do with Vern."

"Sit thou silent, and get thee into darkness. O daughter . . ."

Amy asked, "What could it be more than the ghost?"

"I wish I knew." She acted like she wanted to say more, but stopped herself.

". . . Thou shalt no more be called the lady of kingdoms."

After that the dining room was silent. The two adults would be praying. They would expect the girls to be praying as well.

"All right," Amy whispered. She went out through the spring room. When she came back from the privy, Kate had gone.

She felt she couldn't leave abruptly without raising suspicion, so she returned to her chair. Both Mr. Charter and Lavinia had their heads bowed in silent prayer. Amy closed her eyes and bowed her head, too, but only seconds later Papa said, "Amen." She repeated it, though it was obvious she could not have made a prayer in so brief a moment. He and Lavinia smiled at each other with a kind of shared pride. Amy got up and exited before either of them could ask her about her sisters.

*   *   *

Somewhere in the deep of the night, she came wide awake.

The fire in the hearth had burned to hot embers and ash, and the air was cool on her face though she snuggled warmly in her blankets. There must have been a moon, because enough light entered through the window that she could make out the two other beds. She could see Kate's head, her hair spread across her pillow.

Vern's bed was empty.

Amy sat up.

They each had a chamber pot so there was no cause to leave the bedroom during the night. A few times in Boston, Vern had sneaked off at night to meet with Henri, but here they didn't know anybody. Amy thought she should probably wake Kate. Before she could move, the ceiling creaked.

She knew then where her sister was as if she could see through the beams and floorboards.

She tiptoed to Kate's bed, still amazed that Kate could sleep so close to the source of the spirit knocking. She touched her sister's shoulder.

Kate rolled onto her back. Her eyes opened, dully at first, but focusing on Amy she came alert. "Where's Vern?" she asked. Instinct told her why she'd been awakened.

"I think she's in the attic. Up there."

"Light us a candle, Amy," said Kate. She threw back the quilt.

Amy hurried to the mantel and took down the big square candle. She knelt by the hearth and blew on the embers. Small flames soon appeared. She held the candle to them until the wick lit. It dripped wax, hissing, into the ashes as she got up.

Now she and Kate could see each other in their nightclothes, and they shivered as if the light drew off all the warmth from the room.

The floorboards were cold underfoot as they crept to the door, then into the hall. They expected the boards to creak and give them away, but the floor accommodated their need for silence all the way to the cramped stairwell.

Kate reached for the candle. She whispered, "Here, let me go ahead." Amy let her take it. Kate took one step up, then stopped with a gasp. Amy leaned around her to see.

There on the third step, the candle revealed a drop of blood, gleaming darkly. Kate carefully avoided the spot, and Amy did likewise, following as close behind as if they were joined together. She dreaded falling outside the small envelope of light.

The steps creaked, almost every one, but there was nothing to be done about that. They had to go up.

The attic was colder than their room or the hall. The candlelight revealed their breaths and, at the very edge of its influence, a motionless figure in white.

"*Vern*," Kate whispered. Amy hastily climbed out of the stairwell behind her to see.

Vern stood before the mahogany dresser, facing the swivel mirror, and slowly, rhythmically, combed a hard bristle brush through her unplaited hair. She was muttering something under her breath, a wordless tune. Kate repeated her name but she didn't seem to hear.

With the chairs moved out, there was room for her sisters to crowd in beside her. The mirror was tilted, reflecting the tops of their heads. Yet Vern stared straight ahead, as if at her reflection. She didn't seem to be injured.

Kate touched her shoulder, and Vern didn't respond. She continued muttering words to her tune—words from a poem the three of them knew: " 'My love is like a red, red rose that's newly sprung in June.' " She half sang, half breathed the words. When they turned her about, she didn't resist. She continued to brush her hair for a moment, then slowly lowered her hands. Amy followed the hairbrush in its descent.

"Oh, Kate," she cried, "look!"

Kate lowered the candle. A great stain of blood was spread across Vern's nightgown. Her period had come. Her feet, and the floor where she stood, were spattered with it. It seemed like a lot—more than it should have been, as if a cycle's worth of blood had all poured out at once. Amy couldn't be sure, but she thought

Vern's period was early, too—usually it just preceded her own, and hers was at least another few days away. She wasn't even having cramps yet, and she always did.

Kate said, "We can't take her back to the room like this—she'll leave footprints all over. You stay here with her. I'll go down to the pump and get some water. And try not to make any sound."

Amy nodded, and Vern, as if movement were contagious, pensively nodded, too, singing softly, "I will love you still, my dear." Before leaving, Kate took the top off a lamp on the dresser and lit the wick from her candle. The lamp was dry, but the wick still greasy enough to flame. "It's a good thing you made these," she told Amy, and they traded a brief smile before she descended. The glow in the stairwell faded.

Amy held Vern by the arm, uncomfortable with the idea of being left here, but more uncomfortable with the idea of wandering through this ghost-plagued house in the dark by herself. It was the arm holding the hairbrush that she held. After they had stood awhile, Vern tried to raise it up again to brush her hair. Even though they weren't facing the mirror anymore, Vern tilted her head and stared as if at her image. Amy relaxed her grip. She reasoned that letting Vern draw the brush would keep her there.

Vern stopped singing and said, "I'm going to have a suitor."

Amy eyed her doubtfully and answered, "Really, Vern? That's nice." She didn't think her sister could hear her anyway.

"I'm going to have a suitor soon. I'm going to marry."

"How—how do you know this?" she asked, but Vern seemed to have finished talking. She drew her arm away to comb the hair on the other side of her head.

The stairs creaked, and Amy tensed in alarm until she saw Kate's golden head pop up. Kate had brought wet cloths and a pail. She set the candle down on the floor, knelt, and mopped at the blood smeared around her sister. She wiped Vern's ankles and feet, lifting them up to clean the blood off the bottoms of them, and raised the nightgown up to clean her calves as well. "She's just covered in it," she muttered. "Amy, she couldn't have bled this much just from her time. We have to look."

She handed the cloth to Amy, then with both hands drew up the nightgown.

Vern's legs were red above the knee, all the way to her hips. Amy remarked, "She must have done it, she must have smeared herself like that." Then she added, "But she couldn't, could she, Kate—look at her hands, there's no blood on 'em."

Kate took back the wet cloth and wiped her sister's thighs as best she could. Vern shifted as her legs were pried apart, but she said nothing and acted oblivious to the cold touch of the cloth.

"We have to take her back," Kate said, "clean her up in the room, not here."

They turned her and impelled her toward the stairs. She looked over her shoulder at the mirror, and smiled. "I know," she said. "I know he's coming, yes, I believe you."

"Who's coming?" Kate asked. She looked to Amy.

"She says she's going to have a suitor. Someone's coming to marry her."

"Where'd she get a notion like that?"

"I don't know," said Amy. "I reckon the ghost told her. I think she saw him in the mirror."

Kate went back to the dresser and blew out the lamp. Peripherally, she thought she saw movement in the mirror, but when she looked straight at it, she saw only the shapes of her sisters across the room, waiting for her. She couldn't concern herself with mirrors and ghosts now. With pail in hand, she eased down to the first step, then helped push Vern ahead of her.

They made it back to their room without incident. Vern had gone back to her song. She just repeated one line now, as if she'd lost the thread of the poem: " 'And I will love you still, my dear, and I will love you still, my dear.' "

Kate set the candle down. Then she and Amy drew off Vern's gown. Dried blood painted a swirl on her belly, and wet blood glistened in her pubic hair. Kate wiped away all that she could, until she'd satisfied herself there was no wound and that Vern was not bleeding freely.

Amy produced a menstrual rag and they wrapped it between

Vern's legs, then put a clean nightgown on her. Vern let them
raise her arms and lower them, let them lead her to her bed, and
on her own climbed into it. She closed her eyes, and her singing
stopped. She sighed once, deeply.

Amy noticed that she was still holding her hairbrush. "Was
she asleep all the while?" she asked.

"I think so. She probably won't believe us when we tell her
what she's done."

"She'll have to. With her nightgown soiled and all." She
looked at the bloodied gown and cloth, then at Kate. "You got
more blood on your hands than she did."

Kate's hands were pink with it. She rinsed the cloth, and
wiped them as best she could; but there was blood in the cuticles
of her nails.

"It's this house, isn't it?"

"I don't know, Amy. This house, this ghost she says talks to
her, having to give up Henri back in Boston—it's maybe all of
it. Something seems to be happening to Vern that's not happening to you and to me. We have to watch out for her till we know
what's what."

"Maybe," Amy said thoughtfully, "the end of the world is
starting. Maybe Vern's sensitive to it. To the wearing down of the
wall between the living and the dead. Maybe she's going to guide
us."

Kate replied only, "Maybe." She climbed into her bed. Her
fear had exhausted her.

"Shouldn't we tie her to the bed or something?" Amy asked.
"What if she goes sleepwalking again?"

"More likely, she'll wake up, find that you've tied her up,
and start screaming. You could tie a string to her toe if you want
to, but every time she rolls over she's going to jerk that string
and wake you up again."

Amy considered that. "I guess so," she said, and went back
to her bed. Vern's face had already gone slack. It didn't look as
if she would get up again tonight.

Amy got into her bed, then blew out the candle.

She lay nervously on her back, thinking that she could never go to sleep now, but soon enough her eyelids were closing, and as she drifted off, she imagined she heard a man's voice singing Vern's whispered song again. " *'And I will love you still, my dear . . .'* " It followed her down to oblivion.

Eight

*I*N THE MORNING, THE FAMILY breakfasted on batter cakes with maple syrup, and store-bought tea. Vern fried the cakes, and Kate pumped water and brewed the tea.

Before coming downstairs her sisters asked Vern what she remembered of the night's events. She denied that anything had happened and insisted she had slept soundly the whole night through—until Kate and Amy showed her that she was wearing a different nightgown and that the one she'd gone to bed in lay in a bloody heap at the foot of it. She also had a rag tied up between her thighs. She blushed, humiliated by the thought that she'd been cleaned and dressed like an infant. Angrily, she maintained nothing had happened. "You're playing some awful trick on me because of Samuel. You are, you're jealous, both of you." Her eyelids fluttered as she spoke. It was a habit of Vern's that she couldn't help, a small but significant indicator of when she was dissembling.

Kate was not willing to provoke her sister further. Sooner or later Vern would tell her everything. Not so Amy. As Vern started for the hall, Amy recited as if to herself, " 'And I will love you still, my dear.' "

In the doorway Vern froze like someone turned to stone.

"That's Robert Burns, isn't it, Vern?" Amy asked.

Without replying, Vern raised her head in a clear expression of offense and strode away.

"That was cruel," Kate told Amy, but secretly was glad of the proof it offered as she was glad it had come from her sister. *She* had to work with Vern in the kitchen all morning.

Amy was to clean up afterwards, and didn't follow them downstairs. She was the better cook, but Vern the surrogate mother had accepted the responsibility of making the meals back when the other girls were too young to cook. Over time she had relinquished most cooking duties to Amy, but there were some foods she still preferred to prepare herself, batter cakes being one of her favorites. When it was bannock cakes or oatmeal, then Amy was more than welcome to cook. When they had rye flour on hand, they took turns making Boston brown bread steamed in molasses—they all liked to make that. Such camaraderie did not flow through the kitchen on this morning. Vern had nothing to say to Kate, least of all any thanks for having looked after her while she walked in her sleep, and Kate couldn't think of a way to persuade her otherwise—in fact, was herself angry with Vern. Silence reigned between them.

It was cold throughout the house—nights would stay cold right up to summer—but the kitchen was warm from the stove, and the girls left the door to the dining room open to let the warmth flow in.

The family sat awhile after they had eaten, and sipped their strong tea without speaking. The expectation was that they should take this time to commune with God, to find their individual bearings for the day, and to reconcile what they had accomplished or failed to do the previous day. That the girls had said almost nothing during the meal seemed to have escaped the attention of their elders.

There was still much to do to make the house into a home. Curtains had to be made, and most of the household goods still remained packed. The dressers and other bedroom furniture had been dusted and polished now. The doilies had been found and placed on tea tables, and the remaining rugs beaten and laid down.

Kate excused herself from the table to go to the privy. She had been gone no more than a minute when someone knocked at the front door.

The foursome traded glances, confirming in one another's eyes that they had all heard the noise. Mr. Charter placed his napkin on the table and got up. "Must be someone needs the pike raised," he muttered as he left.

The girls remained seated with Lavinia, but strained to listen.

The front door opened. Silence hung for a moment, followed by Mr. Charter's voice crying, "Merciful Heaven." Then a low murmurous voice spoke. The shape of words evaporated but the murmur, like a tune, was hypnotic, beguiling. Their father replied, and his voice, nervously pitched, quick and excited, shattered the effect. "Please, *please* come into our humble household. Let me have your hat, sir, and your stick. Oh, I'll just set them down on the table here, we haven't placed the stand yet, I apologize, we've only just unpacked. I can offer you tea, would you care for—it's store-bought tea, no sassafras or the like—"

Closer now, the voice answered deeply, "Tea would be most welcome, and do not worry about the little niceties, Mr. Charter. They are all of the corporeal sphere, little pleasures and temptations and comforts to make us forget who and what we truly are. You are better off freed of society's tentacles. I should leave such things in their packing."

Lavinia reacted to the voice as if she'd been stuck with a fork, leaping to her feet, glancing about her at the furniture, at the girls, her face tight as if with anger, but it wasn't anger, rather some emotion more akin to ecstatic anticipation.

Mr. Charter stepped into view, his narrow shoulders high and pushed together, his head bowed so that he looked at them through the hair on his forehead. It was as if he had been squeezed inside the confines of an invisible box.

The visitor stepped through the doorway.

He stood tall and slender, with sapphire eyes beneath sharp prominent brows. He wore black boots to the knee and black trousers above them, and a deep maroon cutaway coat. The white cravat above his red vest looked more dapper than pastoral. His thick dark hair shot with gray was brushed forward into curls about his forehead. His beard, so black that it shone almost blue, was trim and sharp, giving the line of his jaw a machinelike unnaturalness, like the blade of an ax.

He focused on the girls, and his wide mouth curled up at the corners like parchment. "Good ladies, my pleasure," he said, gently bowing. He held up one hand and added, "Please do not arise from your meal," though neither of them had attempted to move. Only Lavinia was standing, and she sank back onto her chair as if pressed down by his palm, her face an adoring mask.

"Daughters," said Mr. Charter, "this is our Reverend Mr. Fitcher." To the visitor he sputtered, "I—we weren't prepared, sir. I'd hoped but didn't really expect—"

"Of course you didn't." Fitcher turned his head and his look seemed in an instant to calm their father. "I myself had no certain sense of when I would be unbound. My flock must always be shepherded, Mr. Charter, and I am close to all. I would be lax in my duties were I not to pay your family a visit at the first possible opportunity, for it's the family that will fill the kingdom one by one. The family is the basic unit on which all is constructed. But, my dear Mr. Charter, I understood you had *three* fair daughters." His look shot like a dart straight at Lavinia and then at the sisters again.

"Yes, yes, I do. My youngest is—is . . . briefly indisposed. This is my eldest, Vernelia, and her sister, Amelia."

"Ah, so *you* are the eldest, Vern," said Fitcher, and he unfurled his index finger and stabbed the air in her direction. "I see. And unmarried, all. I am so surprised. To not know such love as every woman should, before our grains of sand run out. This is tragic, I think."

"Yes, unmarried, I regret to say," Mr. Charter replied. "Not through any fault of their own of course. Events in our household . . ." and he rolled to a stop, unable to express completely the deprivations they had suffered.

"Beg pardon, sir," Amy interjected, "will it be soon, the new beginning?"

Before Fitcher could answer, Kate emerged from the kitchen. She stopped still in the doorway when she saw him.

"Why, here is my youngest girl. Katherine, this is Reverend Fitcher."

Fitcher's smile spread wider. "Ah," he said appreciatively. His gaze fastened on Kate. It was almost tactile, his look: She could feel it slipping beneath her clothes, gliding over her bare skin. She shivered and the sensation abated. A quick glance at Vern found her looking as if she'd fallen into last night's trance.

"Please join us, sir, at our table," said her father.

"Yes. A cup of tea for the reverend," Lavinia added.

"Kate, is there more hot water?" Mr. Charter asked as he ushered Fitcher to his chair at the table.

Kate nodded and withdrew. Beside the stove she leaned against the brick wall. Her legs had gone weak and trembling as if she had lost all her energy, and she closed her eyes for a moment. Then she heard the Reverend Fitcher say, "The fruits of your loins, Mr. Charter, are quite beyond compare. Many women dwell at Harbinger, but none as lovely as your three."

Her eyes went wide, and on the back of her neck the hairs bristled. She knew that honeyed voice. She'd heard it once before—on board the steamship.

Had the man they'd journeyed all this way to join shared ship's passage with them, unaware of who they were? Could that be possible?

He did travel up and down the eastern seaboard, even to the frontier of Kentucky, so her father and Lavinia said. They'd joined his entourage for a time between Boston and Providence. He would have recognized *them*; but of course they hadn't been with her and Vern and Amy when Fitcher encountered them; they'd been all the way across the deck. Fitcher and her father

could have missed each other with so many people aboard. Surely
that must be the explanation. It could be no more than a coin-
cidence—

"Kate!"

She jumped at the voice at her back. Lavinia had followed
her into the kitchen.

"Was the water not hot? What are you doing, girl?"

"I'm sorry." She quickly gathered her wits. "Yes, ma'am, it's
hot. See, it steams on the stove."

Lavinia glanced at the pot, then solicitously her way. "You
look pale, dear. Are you ill?"

Kate might have excused herself by saying so, but she didn't
want Lavinia to know anything about anything. She replied, "Not
really, ma'am."

"Well, please put in the leaves and bring it to the reverend
immediately." It was said without the sharpness that usually
edged Lavinia's commands. She thought: *My God, he's had an effect
even upon* her!

Kate's hand trembled as she carried the china cup and saucer
to their guest. He watched her approach. He was speaking, and
yet so still that he might have been a waxwork were it not for
the sense of power, of energy, that radiated from him. She tried
to set the cup on the table, but he reached out suddenly to take
it. His hands brushed her own, and she was surprised by their
warmth and smoothness. It was as if a sheet of silk had been
drawn against her skin. She released the cup and stepped back.
A scent of pomade or some perfume came from him.

"I'll be traveling again soon," he was saying to Mr. Charter,
"and would be most gratified if you would agree to accompany
me."

"I?" Mr. Charter's eyes almost flooded with tears. "I would
be so honored—"

"And Lavinia—your wife. We shall be journeying to Pittsburgh to bring more sheep into our flock before they can jump
into the wilderness and be lost. There are many there waiting to
be persuaded, as there are everywhere. And now that time is

short, we must do all we can to prepare them. It is a long journey, so do not answer lightly.

"I know your obligations. You feel of course that your duty is that which brought you here—the managing of the turnpike on this road. I would hope that your fair daughters might be persuaded to take over such duties while we travel. You'll have sufficient notice—" and here he paused and thought for a moment, sipping his tea, before continuing. "Well, there's no point in my withholding what I know from all of you any longer, as the community will soon hear the announcement and we will be preaching it as we travel even to the frontier." He set down his cup. "God has spoken at last to His servant, and I now have the date. This corporeal world is to end on October fifteenth."

"Oh," said Mrs. Charter. Mr. Charter didn't move, but the color drained from his face. Vern covered her mouth with her hand to hide her moan. Amy closed her eyes and folded her hands, bowing her head in prayer. Kate, caught standing, had to sit. "So soon?" she asked.

With the smile of one who knows that truths are not always easy, Fitcher replied, "The sooner undone, the sooner God's new plan will be revealed." He placed the empty cup and saucer on the table. "No mistake, I do know how this news affects you. It's one of the reasons I've withheld it a time. The shock is perilous to many. I, like you, Miss Kate, truly regret the speed with which all is coming about, for I wished to enter the kingdom as a husband, and I have *no* wife. It grieves us all not to have someone's hand to hold when the day arrives. You girls, I'm sure, can lay claim to this feeling. You can't help but be tormented by the thought of going into the next life alone. True, you'll have your family, which is important, but it is not the same love as one feels for a partner, for a spouse, for the perfect mate, as I'm sure your parents would tell you."

Had anyone else referred to Lavinia as their parent, the girls would have objected. Fitcher's voice made their emotions syrupy slow. Reactions thickened, clotted. Their attention fell elsewhere, to the issue of how little time they had—a fleeting wisp of time.

Time to look for love.

That message coated the reverend's words: They *must* know love before their time came. He was urging them to do so.

Kate's thoughts congealed as in a dream, the world seeming to spin down, and she wondered if the sensation was akin to what Vern experienced with the disembodied spirit in their room— Samuel, the archangel in the attic, or whatever he was—a seductive prompting to take pleasure. The spirit had promised Vern a bridegroom, but where did it expect one to show up?

Here in this wilderness there was little chance of them meeting anyone with whom they might share intimate feelings—little enough chance of meeting anyone at all. Somewhere below these dismal thoughts, the syrupy voice became a low murmur, the hard sounds of speech planed away, leaving sound to buoy every thought, and each floating in the direction of desire . . .

Kate glanced up, blinking, emerging from a fog. She checked herself against Amy, finding Amy similarly dazed. Together they glanced at Vern.

Their sister held her head slightly tilted, her lips parted, her teeth lightly gripping the bottom lip as she stared with naked infatuation at Reverend Fitcher. It was the look of someone beholding the divine.

The only thing missing, thought Kate, was her hairbrush.

"My girls," Mr. Charter said, drawing their attention to him, "must marry in proper order, though I fear no time's left for them to find eligible suitors, much less husbands. It's regrettable, but while we approach the end of days, we mustn't allow propriety to be cast to the wind."

"Oh, certainly not," replied Fitcher. "You're so right to hold to principle. And that, sir, is why I feel a man like you must accompany me. I am honor bound to bring such members as yourself, whose passions are leavened with sense and purpose, and thus can persuade others. Someone who will approach God's Judgment without doubts about duty."

Mr. Charter replied, "I'll have to go, of course. It's why we came, isn't it, Lavinia?" He clutched his wife's hands between his, and she beamed at him and at Reverend Fitcher. To Kate, she seemed in her joy to have shed years.

"Why you came," Fitcher repeated, but his eyes slid around them to focus farther down the table. "Yes. And I think you must all come with me to Harbinger today, there to meet the others saved among us, and especially, Mr. Charter, my other ambassadors, with whom you'll work closely on our travels."

"Harbinger." Mr. Charter spoke the name in awe, as if invoking a secret name of God.

Reverend Fitcher asked, "Is there more tea?"

Vern got to her feet. "I'll make it," she said. "Let me."

"Of course," said Reverend Fitcher, and held his cup out to her.

Nine

*T*HEY WALKED, THE SIX OF THEM, along the rutted road. To either side the woods engulfed them. Signs of habitation had vanished, yet they were only a few hundred yards beyond their house.

Fitcher strode along at the front of the group, swinging his black walking stick, unimpeded by the uneven road. His followers had to scurry to keep up while picking their footing carefully to avoid twisting an ankle.

It wasn't long before they arrived at the gorge that gave the road its name. A wooden trestle bridge spanned it, wide enough that two wagons could pass each other on it. They paused beside the reverend at the brink.

"Jekyll's Gorge," Fitcher announced, sweeping his arm over the railing as though creating it before their eyes. The girls moved past their father and Lavinia to see.

The gorge wasn't very wide, but the sides plunged straight down. The rock face seemed to have been chiseled with intent by nature: In places vertical columns protruded from the face of the cliff, and elsewhere similar natural processes had removed a

huge ellipse, and within it a smaller one and within that still
another like a series of doors opening onto doors, each smaller or
receding.

The formation reminded Vern uncomfortably of her dream of
unfolding hallways and the man without a mouth.

"Gorges run all through the countryside here," Fitcher was
saying. "There's another at the tip of Cayuga Lake, but nothing
to compare with this one. Shh, listen now!"

They hadn't spoken but they stilled themselves and strained
to hear. Finally, Amy said, "Something's hissing."

Fitcher smiled upon her. "Indeed, Amelia, the falls. You can't
see them from here. There's a path on the far side of our bridge,
however, that winds down to the bottom of the gorge and along
it to the base of the falls. Up that way some distance." He
pointed behind them with his stick. "It brings you right back
beneath this bridge, but down there at the bottom." He started
across the bridge, and they followed.

Halfway across, he paused again to lean over the railing. From
that vantage, the gorge curved inward on either side so that they
seemed to be heading toward a promontory, a chimney of rock.

They were all so lost in the vast beauty of the chasm below
that they didn't hear the approach of the buckboard. Abrupt
thunder shook the bridge beneath them and the family shrieked
and shouted and clutched at one another as if the world had
decided to end here and now. Reverend Fitcher turned, unruf-
fled, and watched the heavily laden wagon's approach.

The driver, a young man with scraggly chin whiskers, cast a
malevolent grin at the Charters, but his smile faded as he recognized Fitcher beyond them. He snapped the reins to speed the
horses then. Fitcher swiped his stick through the air and struck
the side of the wagon as it passed. The wagon bounced off the
end of the bridge, its contents jumping. The driver glanced back
over his shoulder once before rolling out of sight.

Fitcher walked over to the family. "I do so apologize." He
glanced after the wagon. "Young master Notaro requires some
discipline, I think. Such behavior is inexcusable in our people.
You needn't worry, though—this bridge is perfectly sound. I over-

saw its construction myself." He allowed himself a slight smile. "It wouldn't do to have my disciples falling into the pit prematurely, now would it?" Then, taking a step back, he swung around and strode on, his heels thumping on the boards.

They were so shaken that no one wondered at that moment how the wagon had gotten past the turnpike without Mr. Charter there to raise it.

On the opposite side of the gorge, they continued along the track into complete wilderness. Fitcher said nothing now, but trod steadily, solemnly, ahead. The trees here seemed to lag a few weeks behind those on the other side. There were no apparent buds on the leafless branches. Only the pines were green.

The road ran to the right around an outcropping of rock, and they looked for something to appear in that direction.

Then for a moment, through a break in the trees ahead, something flashed like a sunburst at Vern. She glanced up to see a bright geometric shape—sharp gleaming lines not of nature—in the treetops, but before she could draw anyone's attention to it, the thing vanished again behind the branches.

The serpentine track curved back to the left around a second outcrop. The two jagged hunks of rock stood like eroded monolithic gateposts bordering the track. Beyond them the path ran straight. The tree limbs hung over it, creating a long, veined tunnel, at the end of which stood a tall wrought-iron gate between two man-made gateposts. The right side of the gate hung open. Beyond it, a portion of a huge house was visible.

The house was white, set upon a rise, seeming to swell into the sky. A portico extended from the front, braced by six Corinthian columns, each two stories high. Behind the columns black shutters as tall as a man defined windows built at the level of the portico floor. Three stories of windows ascended above the portico, ending in a flat roof. Amy counted six chimneys, but there might have been more farther back. She mentioned the number to Vern, but Vern wasn't listening. She was staring up at the center of the roof where a cupola or widow's walk would have been on many houses this size. Instead, at the top of Harbinger was the shining thing she'd glimpsed through the trees: a pyramid of glass.

As they neared the gate, they could see extensions to either side of the main house; smaller two-story miniatures of it, fronted by shorter columns and each extending like wings across the yard. The sloping roofs overhung more tall black-shuttered windows. The house in its entirety had the look of some reimagined Greek temple, a Parthenon robbed of friezes and paneled over in white-washed slats, a manor, a phalanstery.

The wagon that had passed them stood to the left at the top of the rise. It had been unloaded and its maniacal driver was nowhere to be seen. An iron arch spanned the two stone columns that held the gates. On either side more wrought-iron fencing ten feet high extended in either direction. Tree branches overhung or poked through the uprights, which ended in spikes.

Fitcher pushed back one of the gates. "Welcome to Harbinger," he said. The family followed him in.

The fence stretched far to either side, vanishing behind the wings. There were no people anywhere to be seen.

"We have our own ironsmith," Fitcher said, as if a question about the fence had been asked. "And carpenters and masons besides. We've proved a refuge for the latter, who were driven out of many communities they once called home after that affair in Canandaigua. I do not care what beliefs they have professed to or rituals performed, provided they embrace our own Parousia and contribute to our society. As I know all of you shall do." He led them up the slope to the front of the house. Flagstones separated by lines of gravel composed the portico floor. "There's even a mill," he added. "If God chose to delay His descent, why, we could survive with all we have here for another century at least."

He opened the front doors. The warm scent of baking bread rolled over them.

The interior foyer was an exercise in lushness. Hardwood floors had been polished to such a high gloss that the walls and columns reflected in them as in a looking glass, making the space seem twice as vast as it was. The walls were covered in a cream-colored paper with sienna arabesques; square white pillars stretched to a ceiling three flights up.

In the middle of the space, bicameral staircases led to a single wide landing. A large clock of black walnut and with a silvery face stood on the left side of the landing like some dark inquisitor, but it was the space below that caught everyone's attention. Between the staircases an enormous weathered crucifix had been set in place on a small dais. The cross tilted forward as if it had been uprooted from Golgotha and planted here—an image reinforced by the decayed ropes that dangled near the ends of the crosspiece. Amy, as she stared at it, could almost see the phantom of Christ hanging there. An arrangement of dried flowers spotted the dais with reds, yellows, and blues; in the center of this a single Lenten rose was blooming, its ivory flower like a hallmark above them.

The slanted underbelly of a second staircase ran from the landing to a mezzanine balcony overlooking the front doors. In front of it and directly above them hung an ornate chandelier.

Dark green drapery skirted the outside of the bicameral stairway in crescents decorated with gold tassel and braid. There were chairs and deacon's benches along the walls on either side, separated by urns and small statues or busts set on pedestals, all seemingly of Greek or Roman antiquity. A gilt and ebonized girandole mirror hung on the right-hand wall above one of the benches. The tall windows to either side of the front doors were polished so clear that the glass would have been invisible had it not caused the view of the outside to ripple as one moved.

There was not a speck of dust, not a cobweb, not a smudge or finger stain to be seen anywhere. There didn't even appear to be knotholes in the woodwork.

Doorways led off the foyer on every side. One, on the left, was open, and gave onto a keeping room. They could see one end of a red Chippendale mahogany sofa with its scrolled arms, next to a Federal card table through the doorway.

There was still no sign of anyone else, but the smells of bread and rosemary and gravy filling the space painted the air with phantoms industriously at work baking and cooking somewhere near; smells of community, of family.

Fitcher led the way to double doors halfway along the right-hand wall. The family clustered behind him. He opened the doors and, like a magician, stepped back to reveal his illusion.

The room beyond was a long narrow refectory. Two central tables ran the length of it. On benches to either side of the tables sat an entire congregation, which had paused in their midday meal to look up. There must have been hundreds of faces, thought Kate. Their eyes were wide, bright, and motionless, like the eyes of mounted animal heads. Their features seemed to run together. She couldn't focus on anybody.

No one ate or even moved until Fitcher made a slight gesture with his hand. Then in unison the congregation said, "Welcome."

Mr. Charter shuffled humbly forward and replied, "Thank you," first to the group, then to Fitcher.

The congregation went back to eating, making hardly a sound with their wooden utensils and bowls, and paying no further attention to the new arrivals, even as Fitcher explained things.

"We are many hundreds in number, thus we eat in shifts in order to accommodate everyone," he said. "Our midday meals begin early, usually after a sermon or silent communing." He stepped back, closing the doors behind him.

"They don't speak?" said Kate.

"They do, in fact, quite a lot when they have something to say, Katherine. But it's a courtesy to the next group that they eat in silent contemplation, finish quickly and make way. Once the meal is over, many of them will take up kitchen duties for the next group, and so forth. Everyone participates in every duty before very long. We are all of us part of a great mechanism, you know. All of us equals. No leaders, and no governing body to intrude upon our lives. In God's eyes this is how we are, so this is how we are here. It will make the transition to the next level that much simpler." He turned. "Please," he said, indicating they should follow him again.

They crossed to the rear of the foyer and went through one of the doors there. It opened onto a narrow corridor that ran the width of the foyer. There were doors at either end of it, doors in every wall. Fitcher walked directly across to a back door that opened to the outside.

They found themselves on a broad porch at the rear, between the two wings of the house, which extended a good thirty yards farther. Along the outside edge of the porch, X-shaped uprights supported a railing. Fitcher leaned on the rail as if to survey his world a moment before leading them down the steps to the lawn.

"Our chapel," he said, gesturing to the left. The porch ran around the wing of the building, ending in more steps at the end. A row of round stained-glass windows punctuated the chapel wall at eye level. Viewers outside could peer in through the colored images.

In the center of the yard, a large bell hung on a wooden frame. A handle by which the bell could be swung extended up from the frame. Fitcher passed it by without a word. He had his sights set elsewhere.

The lawn stretched unbroken to the first of five or six rows of trees—an orchard. It served to separate Harbinger House from both the fields and the village that had been erected.

There were people in the fields, hoeing from the look of it, but too far away to be sure. Fitcher said nothing about them, either.

The buildings of the village were laid out upon a grid of narrow dirt lanes. People walked about here and there, most of them carrying something. A squealing group of small children charged momentarily into view across the nearest lane, engaged in a game of pursuit, and disappeared as quickly between two buildings. Most of the people were concentrated in or around the buildings, all busy at some task, but they paused in their work as the group approached. Their eyes, Kate noticed, followed Fitcher obsessively. The people bowed their heads in reverence before him. He strode past, giving the slightest nod to their gesture. They muttered, "Welcome," to the Charter family as those in the dining hall had done and kept their heads bowed until the group had passed. Amy glanced back to watch them return straight to their tasks.

Unlike the village of Jekyll's Glen, this one had no obvious main street. The lanes were of equal width and seemed to have been laid out based on utility. The ironsmith shared a lane with a row of carriage houses, machine shops, and wagon sheds. Animal pens, coops, and an abattoir lined another.

Fitcher led them away from the pens.

They arrived at a cluster of henhouses, and Fitcher ducked through the small door in the side of the nearest one, sweeping back toward them almost as fast, pivoting on his walking stick. He held out his hand to Vern. A brown egg rested upon his palm. Vern accepted it shyly. He said, "You shall take some eggs home with you today, as you have no chickens of your own just yet and we've many."

A third lane contained a tanner's, which stank acridly, followed by a glassblower, where the girls paused to watch the two craftsmen at work: One was blowing a long cylinder. While it was still warm, the other man slit the length of the tube and opened it out into a sheet. It looked like magic. Fitcher waited patiently behind them until the glass had been laid flat, then said quietly, "Let us see the rest now, good ladies."

They walked on, passing a furniture shop, one for broom-making, and finally a workshop for musical instruments. Through the door to that one, they could see the bellies and backs of violins dangling, slowly turning in the sunlight like hanged men. Even within the shops, the workers paused and stood as Fitcher and his group passed by, and repeated the universal welcome.

One shop, designated as the chandler's by its small hand-carved sign, was closed. Vern stared at it as they walked past. Fitcher said, "We lost our candle-makers—isn't that terrible? A husband and wife. They were very good, too. A most unfortunate accident took them and I'm afraid I've not yet assigned anyone to replace them. We must, too, and soon, as we've exhausted our supply and now deprived Jekyll's Glen of every candle it had."

Farther on they passed a laundry with sheets and clothing
hanging on dozens of lines. At the end of the village stood a huge
barn. The smell of hay and manure rode the breeze.

Fitcher skirted the barn, taking yet another lane. "Up here
are what the community calls the 'sisters' shops,'" he said, and
they shortly found themselves passing the broom-making shop
again but from a different side, though how they'd come there
they couldn't say. As open as the village was, it seemed queerly
labyrinthine, a maze constructed of buildings, folding in upon
itself.

After the shops came plots of ground for vegetables. A brown
and white dog sat, sunning itself. Fitcher said, "Behind the barn
there's a church. Even now we can't all fit in the chapel, and so
many worship in the course of their working day, that I delegate
to other preachers in our midst to sermonize here. It saves time,
which is most precious, more than the community yet realizes. It
also serves as our school, for the children. Off that way"—he
raised his stick and pointed it toward the open woods beyond
the tilled fields—"on the creek lie the grist and flour mills and
the granary. We are, as I said, self-sufficient."

"Where are all the good folk housed then?" asked Mr. Charter.

"The upper floors of the wings above the dining hall, kitchen,
bakehouse, and above the chapel itself, those are dormitories.
There are more rooms in the main house on the second and third
floors, and others used mostly for . . . special members of the
group."

The way he emphasized "special" made Kate glance his way.
He was already looking at her, as if he had known his remark
would catch her attention of all of them. He smiled before turning to lead them back to the house.

"This is Harbinger, my friends. Our grand utopian experiment here on Earth as it is in Heaven, and hence our name. This
is where we shall experience the Next Life. Now, you will stay
awhile? For a meal, and the afternoon sermon?"

"Of course," Mr. Charter answered.

"Excellent. I'm sure the walk has given you an appetite as it has me. We'll eat with the next group, and then attend to matters of employment."

He turned and stepped between Amy and Vern, throwing an arm around each of them. Beside Vern he held his walking stick by the shaft. She could see the silver knob on it clearly for the first time. It was in the shape of a woman's head with scooped-out eyes and an open mouth that seemed to be shaping a cry; the strands of hair were oddly thick and dotted as if with tiny eyes. They lay so that the fingers of his hand could fit between them. Fitcher told her, "It's the head of Medusa. But don't worry, I'll protect you from her glare." His voice was light and carefree, his encompassing arms warm and avuncular, as if he were the greatest friend she could imagine.

"Ah, but I didn't show you our flower garden, now, did I?" And as he spoke, he steered both the elder sisters around the back of the shops. The other three followed after, Lavinia and Mr. Charter arm in arm, and Kate on her own, an afterthought to the entourage.

The garden comprised row upon row of flowerbeds. There were plants with buds but no flowers to be seen. A thin trellis ran up one side, supporting the bare stems of roses. Then Fitcher pointed with his stick again, and they saw, right in the middle of the trellis and utterly out of season, a single red blossom. The reverend stepped between the girls and plucked it. He held it before him as if observing a miracle, then with a flourish presented it to Vern.

" 'My love is like a red, red rose,' " he quoted as she took it. Beside her, Amy gasped. The Reverend Fitcher remarked, "A perfect flower. That is a rare thing indeed. I don't know that I have ever met one." Blushing, Vern held out her hand to take the rose. A drop of blood fell into her palm. Fitcher released the flower into her hand and spread wide his fingers. Blood shone on the tip of his index finger. "Mmm, a thorn," he remarked, then put the finger to his lips to suck the blood away. He'd stepped back between them, and to suck on his finger he snaked his arm around Amy's throat, which drew her against him.

He let his hand fall across her shoulder again for a second.

His touch was as soothing as his voice. Amy stared at his long, thin fingers. The hand abruptly snaked away behind her. "And now," Fitcher said, "please allow me to lead you all to dine. This way." He fell back and took Mr. Charter by the arm as he might have guided an old compatriot, adding, "I have another matter to discuss with you, sir, away from here."

Lavinia released her husband as Fitcher drew him ahead, and her walking slowed as though she had been dismissed. A moment later Kate caught up and took her arm. The gesture of kindness seemed to dismay her stepmother even more. Kate was no less surprised herself. She'd acted upon instinct, without thinking, and had chosen compassion. She couldn't think why. Nevertheless, linked, the two of them walked together through the orchard and back toward the massive edifice of Harbinger above them on its rise.

The meal was a wholesome if meatless stew, and bread. The stew had cooked so long that the carrots in it had turned to mush. Everyone drank water. As Fitcher had said, nobody spoke. The fifty or so Fitcherites in the hall ate eagerly, but encapsulated as if no one else shared the space with them.

Even Fitcher, who had seemed so animated a few minutes before entering, ate silently once he had blessed the meal.

Those who finished their food first waited contemplatively for the rest to catch up. Only when everyone had set down their utensils and taken a last drink of water, did the group rise as one. Those next to the family reached over and gathered their bowls and cups to carry away with their own.

Fitcher explained, "This is the last group for dinner. Normally, you would all be expected to contribute to the washing up and cleaning, or preparing the supper—different tasks on different days. As you're guests, that isn't your concern. And now I must speak with Mr. Charter privately. You may bide your time in the chapel if you like. We'll have a small service there in a while."

They went across the main foyer, which was still empty. On

the far side, the reverend threw open a set of double doors. "Our Hall of Worship," he said.

Where the refectory stood on the opposite side, a brief corridor led to an open archway, which opened onto the Hall of Worship proper. Tall windows like those at the front of the house lined the left side of the hall, and a red runner defined a central aisle between rows of high-backed pews.

The hall dwarfed every other room they'd seen. Even the elaborate foyer did not seem as impressive. The Hall of Worship was as broad across as the dining hall had been, but where the other side of Harbinger House had been broken up into smaller areas—into dining room, kitchen, and bakery, this hall ran the entire length of the left wing. The runner ended, in the distance, before a pulpit. To the left of that, on a dais, stood a small pipe organ.

The pews were dark, stained almost black. Candles on metal tripods lined the outside aisles. It was easy to see how the congregation had needed all the candles Jekyll's Glen had to offer: Just to light the hall at night would have taken thirty or more.

The inside wall, the one across from the tall curtained windows, glowed with the dozen small stained-glass windows they had first viewed from outside. Dark beams sectioned the ceiling. In awe of the space, the sisters almost crept along down the center.

At the far end of the runner, two steps led up to a raised altar beneath the pulpit. The arrangement was a strange affair. The pulpit, rising above the altar, also projected toward the pews like a ship's figurehead. It looked as if it should have fallen forward. It was rosewood, with darker strips of wood on the corners, between which were panels inlaid with bone. The bone described swirls and scrolls and tiny figures. The center panel might have represented Adam and Eve on each side of either a tree or an immense snake; or maybe it was the snake wrapped around the tree. Small bone crosses adorned the upper lip of the pulpit. The stone altar below sat on four pedestal feet, also decorated with filigree bone. The altar table was slightly convex and rough-hewn. Dried cornstalks, squashes, gourds, and multicolored ears of corn had been arranged over it. Resting in the center of these like a part of the harvest was the strangest element of all.

It was a skull of milky glass or quartz. Light played on its features, defining it in bright splashes and stripes. Above the brow a crown of thorns had been carved, two intertwined strands circling the skull. The thorns stood out sharply. The head was human-sized. It was as though the skull of Jesus had crystallized in the tomb. The light playing around the orbits made the skull seem to have huge eyes with dark dilated pupils.

Reverend Fitcher ushered them to a front pew—all save Mr. Charter. "Others will be here soon," he told the women, "and we shan't be long, ourselves."

He led Mr. Charter around the pulpit and out a door beyond the pipe organ. The sound of it closing echoed around the hall. The three girls sat beside Lavinia in envelopes of silent contemplation. They weren't alone more than ten minutes before members of Harbinger began filing in. As with dinner, there was no discussion, no talking. Footsteps clumped along the aisle, some coming right up beside them. People sat directly across from them—three men and two women, all solemn, simply dressed, and perspiring, as though they'd come there straight from the distant fields. The odor of sweat, of human bodies, enshrouded them.

Sound muffled as the room filled with people. There was something discomforting about having an entire speechless room gazing upon them. They could feel hundreds of eyes. The oft-repeated "Welcome" did not color the sensation this time. Someone crossed behind the pulpit and seated himself at the organ, then began to play an unfamiliar hymn.

When finally Fitcher and their father returned, the sensation of being on view abated. But then Mr. Charter was staring with an indescribable look at Vern in particular, as though he were watching her transform before his eyes into something not altogether wholesome. She and Kate exchanged glances—both had seen his expression but neither could account for it.

He took his place beside Lavinia.

The Reverend Fitcher ascended the steps in back of the pulpit. He immediately gripped the sides hard, as though he expected to be tossed off it. After a moment, he raised his hands, palms outward, revealing the shapes of crosses pressed into his skin. The crowd shifted in their seats and a few voices moaned, as if he'd performed a miracle in imprinting his flesh.

He lowered his hands and began to recite: " 'Love not the world, neither the things *that are* in the world. If any man love the world, the love of the Father is not in him. For all that *is* in the world, the lust of the flesh, and the lust of the eyes, and the pride of life, is not of the Father, but is of the world. And the world passeth away, and the lust thereof; but he that doeth the will of God abideth forever.'

"John's words, from his epistles, but he might well have been speaking directly to us of our own endeavor here. He might have been directing us in our preparations for the Advent and days to come. I say to you now: That time *has* been decided. The date of our departure from the world and it from us has been fixed. There can be no doubt of it, for the angel of the Lord has imparted His decision to me. I've *been* with that angel. We can see the end of things now, and we know that we have just eight months left to make ourselves fit to answer God's call."

He paused. The hall was as still as death. The power his voice evinced when soft became the crack of lightning at volume. They all felt its charge. It rang out to the back of the hall and, returning, it drew people forward in their pews, physically propelled them toward him. In the front row, they could not look away, and Kate thought, *This is what Papa has felt and tried to imitate. This is his power.*

"The pride of life is what plagues our world. The living feel by the very fact that they live, they are somehow privileged, and full of pride at the special position they occupy. They do not *hear* God's words. They haven't *listened* to John's warnings, or Matthew, or Moses. The rutting, slavering hordes manifest their lust everywhere, on every street, in every dark closet of their malformed souls. They experiment in His name—those ultraists who think the sex act to be communal, those lustful experimenters in

Oneida, in Brimfield, who argue that to give in to sin is to wash it away. They sin and think that God will not see the sin or will forgive them in their ignorance for having committed it. Because they deceive themselves, they believe they surely will be able to deceive God.

"They—are—*wrong*!

"God does not hear excuses. He cares nothing for experiments. He knows only true actions. The ways of the flesh should offer no allure to the one who is prepared in his heart for the ascension with our Lord. So I ask: Are *you* ready?"

The room rumbled with the answer: "I am ready, O Lord!"

"Are you ready to taste the divine fruit, to sample the *wine* of Heaven?"

"I am ready, O Lord," replied the crowd. Amy and Vern had joined Mr. Charter and Lavinia in the chanted response. Kate was aware that her own lips moved, too—moved as if willful.

"Are *we* ready to cast off our earthly shells and step into our new and ever*last*ing bodies—bodies not of the flesh but of the spirit?"

"We are ready, O Lord."

"*Yes*. We are ready," he agreed, and his smile might have devoured them all. "Those who are not, who deceive themselves and us even now—and they are among us even now, make no mistake of it—they shall be *known*. We will know them when the time comes, as God will know them. Some of them may be our friends now, but they will speak with the voice of the snake. Their words will worm through your soul, tearing at the divinity in you. They will ask you to taste the fruits before the Day. They will bundle you into their beds, promising purity but delivering wantonness. Do not listen to them. Listen to *my* words and we shall all arrive on that fateful shore together."

He paused again, this time casting his glance over the three sisters, as if ensuring that they especially took his words to heart.

"There is one holy estate," he said now much more softly, "a holy estate where those same sins of the flesh become blessed acts. Where impure thoughts are made pure, and where life acknowledges purpose. It is an estate known to many here, and in which they may take solace as they face their Judgment, knowing that they come before God together.

"I, being a weak man of the flesh, have looked upon you with envy. I've sensed the bond between you and thirsted for it myself. Though I bless your union and give it shape, I remain separate from it, and envious. I confess this sin, that of a weak man who wants what others have found. Why, many times I've stood here and said to you all that there is no better way to approach God than hand in hand, man and wife. To know you will enter the Kingdom of Heaven together, ah, that is the most blessed thing, and I have yearned for it. You know I have. A perfect partner who cannot be persuaded, misguided, misdirected—how rare is this gift.

"Well, today, I have found such a one."

He sprang down the steps of the pulpit and came around the altar.

At the same time, Mr. Charter rose to his feet and stepped around Lavinia. "Vern, my girl," he began, but Fitcher interrupted him, interjecting, "My dear, dear Vernelia, it comes as a shock to you, I know, but I have petitioned your father just now, and he is wholeheartedly behind a union between us. If"—he dropped to one knee before her—"if you will consent to marry me."

Vern stared at him as if he'd spoken in tongues and the meaning of it all had slipped past her. She looked at her sisters, first Kate and then Amy, as if they might explain it to her. "My suitor," she said, hardly louder than a whisper. "He told me there was a suitor and I was to wed. Didn't he?" she asked Kate, who could only, if reluctantly, nod.

A slow smile spread across Vern's face, a strange detached smile, as though invisible fingers stretched her lips. "I must, of course. I must. It's ordained. Prophesied." Then, rising, to Fitcher: "Here's the proof of it then." Her gaze swept across her entire family before resting on him again. "I must consent."

The reverend arose before her. Kate could only see him over her sister's shoulder. From that vantage, with his head bowed he looked like a mantis about to devour its prey, and she lowered her eyes rather than see him thus. There, directly in front of her, Vern's hand was balled into a fist, and through her fingers crushed petals of the miraculous rose leaked like blisters of blood.

Ten

SHE MIGHT HAVE BEEN STAND-
ing inside a bell, his voice ringing
the metal, his captured speech in
a tight spiral around her until the clapper struck and pitched her
out into space, and everything she had been and known fell away.

Abruptly, her sisters were holding her up. She didn't remember swooning. She remembered that she'd said *yes*. Yes to a husband, to a suitor, to the man who had caused her to be here. Her
father wanted this for her. He had struck a bargain for no other
reason than her happiness surely, but he had done so without
asking. She wanted to say she was alarmed, but felt nothing that
could be called alarm exactly; more a sharp knot of anticipation.
Not only was she to marry, but she was to marry the man who
would lead them all into the glory of God. He was like an angel
himself, so tall and thin, so gentle and concerned. And his touch,
when he'd put his arm around her in the garden, had been like
fire, like ice so cold that it burned. She would never have shared
this observation with her sisters for fear they would admit having
sensed it, too; it was a sensation that had spread down between
her legs, an urge to lust more potent than anything she'd ever

felt for Henri, whom she'd loved. What word, then, could describe that flow of fire that Fitcher kindled?

The rest of the day whirled about her, as though she stood in place and everything else spun in orbits.

Fitcher and her father went off to meet with the other ambassadors of The Word. Some members of the congregation came up to her and offered brief congratulations. Yet none of them seemed truly happy for her, as if they resented her being thrust into this union, almost as if she'd connived for it somehow.

Amy hugged her. Lavinia looked lost. And Kate, though smiling as she embraced her, had pinched lines of concern in her brow. Vern thought dreamily that Kate was not terribly good at hiding her worry. She was such a worrier, too, and had been for the longest time. She'd worried while Mother wasted away, never letting on directly how she felt, but clearly fretting. She remembered once saying, "Kate, you think about things too much." *Poor dear.*

Preparing to leave them, Vern could think only charitable thoughts about her family. Even Lavinia, whom she'd never liked, but who said not a word to any of them after the proposal and acceptance, not even on the ride back to their house, for Reverend Fitcher said he wouldn't hear of them going back on foot, though it was a short walk, less than an hour, hadn't it been? Mr. Notaro, the same wild driver who'd wickedly whipped his team across the gorge a few hours before to startle them, was called upon to drive the family back—most politely and carefully—across the gorge. At the pike he drew up, climbed down, and unloaded the straw-stuffed crate full of eggs that Fitcher made them take with them.

It was while they stood collecting themselves and young Mr. Notaro was driving away that Kate suddenly asked, "How did he get past here earlier?" Everyone stared at her—no one understood the comment. "I mean," Kate said, "we were all on the bridge. There wasn't anyone here to lift the pike for him. How did he get around it in a wagon?" No one had an answer, of course, and Vern shook her head, musing, "Yes, here's my sister again, thinking too hard about nothing, worrying every event as

if to pull some secret truth from it." Kate gestured to show them
how no wagon could have driven around the pike because of the
stumps in the yard, but nobody was paying her much attention.
Vern suspected it was Kate's way of grabbing some of the attention away from her on this momentous day, but she was so warmly
happy that she didn't mind. Instead she thought of how unpre-
dictable life could be. She'd come from a home in Boston, from
a lovely but shy and irresolute suitor, from a world she thought
had made her happy, and arrived at a new place that had looked
so disappointing and hopeless only a day ago. Now she was about
to forge a new life that no one could have predicted even this
morning—except for Samuel, her angel. He had known what was
going to occur as surely as if he had looked into the future, which
of course must be what he'd done. Spirits could see in all directions, couldn't they?

The girls sat in the parlor with nothing to say to each other
at first. Then Amy piped up, "We'll have to make you a gown,
won't we?"

Vern nodded. "Yes, we will, and soon. We'll have to go into
town today—I remember that Van Hollander had some nice material in his store."

"Do you think they'll let you go?" Kate asked.

"Why not?"

"We're supposed to be kept from town as punishment, remember?"

"But everything is changed now. I'm to be a wife. I can't be
treated like a little *girl* now." She got a sharp look from Kate, and
Amy blushed. She realized what she'd said. "Oh, I don't mean
that you're both children. In fact, just the opposite. If I'm married, then you no longer have to wait. Why, you might truly find
someone now. You have half a year."

"Do you really think so?" asked Amy.

"I don't see why not. There were many men out there at
Harbinger, weren't there? That young Mr. Notaro—well, perhaps
not a soaplock like *him*. But there are bound to be others who
don't have wives, and Reverend Fitcher puts such stock in entering the new kingdom in conjugal bliss."

"We sound like mail-order brides the way you tell it," Kate remarked.

"*I* want to get married," Amy stated, as if Kate had objected to the concept itself. "I want to be married when the time comes, when we meet Jesus."

Mr. Charter walked in on them then. Amy turned to him and said, "Vern's going to have to have a dress, Papa."

"Yes, she is. Reverend Fitcher wishes to marry you on Saturday, child. The Lord's Day."

"We can't have a new dress ready by then!"

"No, no, that's true enough," answered her father. "But you might not have to." He sat on one of the cane-seat chairs. "Though I didn't keep the piano—and I know that upset you all, and I'm sorry it couldn't be done—I did keep your mother's wedding dress. It's folded up in my cedar chest upstairs. I couldn't even say why I did at the time, though your stepmother urged me to keep it, which I then thought peculiar, but now I see that God was directing me to bring it along for this occasion. Vern, I think, you might only have to fix it a little to make it fit—you're much like she was in shape and size, you know. A little taller mayhap."

"Oh, Papa," Vern said. She could see his eyes going shiny, filling with the memory of her mother on their wedding day, and she crossed to him, sat beside and hugged him. The other two girls came and wrapped arms around both of them.

Mr. Charter finally drew back. He took a handkerchief out and dabbed at his eyes, then blew his nose. "Your mother would be so proud to see you in that dress. Any of you." All his daughters smiled to him. "You're all such fine girls, though you're every bit as headstrong as she was. Do you know, she chose me, not the other way about. She cared nothing for how things must go. Propriety did not keep her from anything. Well." He tucked the cloth back up his sleeve, then slapped his knees in feigned good spirits. "Now, you must go try on the dress, see how it is, and then tomorrow you'll go into Jekyll's Glen and get whatever you need to finish it. And by Saturday we'll have a trousseau all prepared for you."

He stood as if to leave, and it was at that point that Lavinia came into the parlor, carrying a tray with cups and the china teapot on it. To the girls' surprise, she set it on the tea table nearest the window and said, "I thought we might like a cup of tea, so I made a pot for us all. It's getting chilly, don't you think? We'll need a fire tonight, Mr. Charter." An awkward moment followed where it seemed she didn't know what more to say or do. Suddenly she marched over to Vern, and stiffly embraced and kissed her. "Oh, my dear, I am so happy for you. Truly happy. And I know your father is, too. It's all he's hoped for."

Vern said, "Yes, I know he has. I—" She shook off whatever she'd begun to say and instead replied, "Thank you, Lavinia. And for the tea."

"Yes," agreed Kate. "Thank you."

Vern lifted her mother's carefully folded wedding dress out of the cedar chest at the foot of her father's bed. When she opened it up, a handkerchief trimmed in lace and a pair of gloves fell out. She knelt and gathered them up.

She had never seen the dress before. It was a white batiste with puffed sleeves. The bodice tied with a ribbon sash beneath the breasts; a sheet of Point de France lace was stitched onto the front beneath the sash, falling straight to the hem. There was no discernible waist. The same lace circled the hem of the full train in back. She held the dress to herself, imagining her mother wearing it twenty years earlier, and wondering if she would truly be able to fit into it. The style was out-of-date—had she been making a new dress, it would have had a narrower waist and fuller skirt—but it meant she didn't have to concern herself with her waist. She wouldn't need a tight corset, nor was there a need to let the dress out. She closed the chest and carried the dress across the hall. Her sisters, in the parlor with Lavinia, had set up a dressmaker's dummy, but they had to see it on Vern first to know what had to be done with it.

In her room she undressed. As she stepped out of her skirts, she couldn't help sneaking a glance at the wall, imagining him there in the plaster, watching her—her angel.

"Samuel," she whispered. There was no response.

She stepped barefoot into her mother's dress and pulled it up over her chemise, putting her arms through the short, puffy sleeves. They tied with tiny ribbons at the bicep. The bodice fit snugly. Her mother had obviously had a smaller bust. The tied sash pushed her breasts up and together, rounding them conspicuously. The skirt rustled and swooshed when she swung about. The train wound about her like a great tail. She looked at her toes protruding from beneath the lace. It probably wasn't too short, though she would have to see it over petticoats to be sure.

She glanced at the wall again, secretively. How long would they wait downstairs for her to appear before someone came up to find her?

She gathered up her train and went over to Kate's bed where she sat down. Placing her hand against the wall, she said, "Spirit, can you hear me?"

The lightest tap answered, weaker or possibly more distant than before—barely sensible through her hand. She heard no voice at all.

"Oh, spirit." She leaned her face to the wall. It was cold and felt soothing against her forehead. "Everything you told me is coming to pass. Not only a suitor, but a husband."

One tap answered. Was it a little stronger?

"You promised, didn't you? You'll still love me even then? You'll still be here for me when I come home to visit."

Tap.

"Samuel," she sighed. "The reverend—my husband, soon enough—he's told us when the Day of Judgment is coming. It's only eight months away. And then we'll be with you. We'll meet. We'll see one another, won't we?"

Yes, Vern.

She heard him now, his soft voice like a spell. The sound of him could lift her, carry her through the house, through life. She thought of what Reverend Fitcher had said about sin of the flesh. She was in love with a spirit, so it must be a pure love because there could be no flesh in the bargain. She'd attained spiritual love, hadn't she, and been rewarded for it. When finally they did meet, it would be after the—

"Vernelia!" It was Kate's voice, and it brought her to her senses. She was on her feet, twirling as if in a dance in the middle of the room. The puffed sleeves of her wedding dress were pushed down off her shoulders, exposing more of her breasts. She couldn't say how she had gotten there, but she felt a sweet languor as if she'd been in his embrace. She ought to have been terrified. Remotely, she knew this, but felt nothing but pleasure.

"Vern, for the land's sake!" Kate called again, closer, as if partway up the stairs.

She called out, "I'm coming, Kate!" and hurried to the door, but paused at the threshold, looked back and said, "Thank you, dearest spirit," to the wall. Then she ran to the stairs.

Under the sound of her footsteps the wall rapped and rapped again.

Eleven

THE NEXT MORNING MR. CHAR-
ter gave his daughters money and
told them to go into town and pur-
chase whatever they needed for Vern's veil and train. She had no
shoes to go with the dress, either, but that might not be something they could help. Still, they were to look for slippers or
mules that would be appropriate.

The sky was overcast, but it wasn't raining. They dressed
warmly and walked into Jekyll's Glen.

Although she'd noticed that Van Hollander had some nice
material for a dress, Vern couldn't recall seeing anything like the
lace for a veil in his store, so she led the girls to the other store,
Eggleston's. Mrs. Eggleston helped them find suitable lace. It
didn't match the lace trimming the dress, but wouldn't clash with
it, either.

She also served up a pair of Spanish satin slippers that would
go beautifully with their mother's dress; and some black net
stockings of the kind that had been popular in Boston. They
bought those, too. Mrs. Eggleston fairly cooed over Vern's betrothal, telling the girls how excited she'd been on her own wed-

ding day, how Vern had the whole world before her—strange, romantic stuff coming from such a large and otherwise seemingly dour woman.

It was as Vern was paying for the goods that Kate pointed at a handbill on the wall and said, "Look, it's today. It's the poster you brought home before, and the demonstration of mesmerism is going to take place this noon at the home of a Mrs. Shacabac. Oh, let's go. We're here already, and it's not much longer."

"It's mesmerism, Kate," said Amy, as if that should be enough to dissuade her.

"Which is what?"

Amy had no ready answer, but Kate would certainly not have let it go if she had, so Vern weighed in. "We'll go. I want to hear what they have to say, these mesmerists. If they can speak with the other side."

"Like you do?" Amy asked.

Vern ignored her. The truth was, in Boston where mesmerists were plentiful Lavinia would have called such a meeting "a blasphemy" and forbidden them to attend. Even though Lavinia was being nice to them today, no greater motivation than to defy her was necessary. "Can you tell us, Mrs. Eggleston," she asked, "where this house would be?"

Even without directions, they would have found it. Eight people were walking on the gravel at the side of the road ahead of them, on their way toward a stately brick house near the end of the road. A semicircular drive ran past the front of it. As the girls approached, a carryall with a family of six on board pulled into the drive, and those on foot scurried to the side. At the front steps the family got down, except for the father, who drove the wagon back around and out onto the road again. He eyed the sisters with a pained expression as he drove by them.

Inside, more people milled about in the main hall and the parlor. A woman with auburn hair streaked gray, and wearing a dark green dress with a large bustle, came up to them and said, "I don't believe I know you girls."

They introduced themselves.

"Oh, my, yes," the woman exclaimed, "the Pulaski house. Why, that poor couple, that was just a terrible thing."

"Ma'am?" Kate asked.

"The way they just up and disappeared. So young, and how sweet a couple. Why, I'd spoken to Adele on the street that very day. It's a sin to Moses."

The girls nodded and muttered that, indeed, it was.

"Well, now, my name is Emma. And this is my house. You peart girls just make yourselves right at home. Have you ever seen Dr. Castleman speak before?"

"No, ma'am," replied Vern. "But in Boston, where we hail from, there were at least a hundred mesmerists this past year."

"Oh, my. A hundred? Oh, goodness. And you come from Boston? So much culture and excitement there, isn't there? I haven't been to Boston for quite so many years now. Well. There's tea and cakes in there, and then Dr. Castleman will be speaking along the hall, where we have set up a lecture room. You'll want to be sure you can see him." She glanced away from Vern, at the entrance. "Howard, my dear!" she called, and walked between the girls to greet her new guest.

"I should like some tea, I think," said Amy.

Kate sighed. "Just don't get crumbs and jam on Vern's veil. Better still, why don't you give it to me to carry?"

Amy handed her the folded material before plunging through the crowd.

"I could do with tea, too," Vern said. "Should I give you my things as well?"

For a moment Kate stared at her with feigned incomprehension. Then the two of them laughed. She wasn't being mean, Vern insisted, but Kate was right—Amy didn't want to tea half so much as she wanted to stuff herself with cakes.

They followed her into a vast and crowded dining room.

The lecture room was probably bigger than their parlor and dining room combined, and contained more chairs than they had sticks of wood for the stove, thought Vern. She and her sisters chose three seats on the far side of the room but near the front. By the time things started many people had to stand around the fringes. She wouldn't have thought there were so many people in Jekyll's Glen interested in seeing a mesmerist, and many of them looked as if they had traveled to be here. She wondered how far away the handbills had been distributed.

The woman in the green dress walked in front of the audience. A curly-headed man, his hair pasted forward in ringlets, walked after her. He wore a dark red waistcoat and held his hands just beneath the lapels as if holding his heart in. Everyone fell silent.

"Ladies and gentlemen, friends and neighbors, I thank you all for coming today. This is quite exciting, isn't it? Our dear friend Mr. Bayard has secured for us this rare opportunity to learn about a most exciting science that is going on around us right now in larger cities. Why, I was told just this day that there are over one hundred mesmerists practicing in Boston." She glanced coyly at the girls as she said it. "Our lecturer is the eminent Dr. David Castleman, a philosopher from Philadelphia. He has studied with Charles Poyen, that famous professor of animal magnetism, who toured here some five years past." Members of the audience shifted and whispered to each other at the sound of that name—it clearly meant something to them. "He tells me that he has recently spent time with Phineas Quimby as well. And I gather he is going to perform some feats of mesmerism to demonstrate this remarkable art to us. Dr. Castleman?"

Light applause followed. In a clipped and erudite voice, he thanked his hostess, then waited patiently, surveying the audience, until all was quiet.

"Each of you here today," he began, directing a finger across the room, "has a remarkable power lying within you. A power, I might add, which can find hidden meanings, cure disease, and even—if tapped deeply enough and in the right way—allow you to hear others' thoughts and see into the future, performing what will seem on the face of it to be parlor tricks. But they aren't.

There's no *magic* at work. No devils. No illusions. There is only the incredible magnetic power of the mind.

"I have spent now a decade as a student and five years as a practitioner of mesmerism. For most of that time, I've traveled quite a bit, first through England, and now to bring the knowledge I possess to communities across our young country. What I behold is a nation in chaos. Our religion is in chaos. I see a number of your pastors in the audience today, some of whom were perhaps hoping to find the devil at work here. I regret to tell you, you will not. I have no doubt some of you reverend gentlemen will concur with my . . . diagnosis of our worship. Go to any large city and you will find street-corner evangelists by the cartload, framing in their particular cant some absurd revelation upon the Gospels while they practice an artful hypocrisy that simply astonishes. These unlettered bipeds almost invariably predict the pending doom of mankind. It should take a learned man no effort at all to dismiss them. Any physician should be able to tell them that mankind is not doomed, but rather on the brink of an era of revelation of a different sort: one of unparalleled inner discovery. If physicians were not themselves without integrity—half of them peddling worthless nostrums and serving up superstitious cures—they would know this already. In the cities, physicians even pay beggars to pass out handbills announcing some fantastic elixir they've concocted, which will cure gout and whooping cough and even consumption with the very first spoonful! Travel a block farther and some other beggar working for some other fraud will be passing out news of a different curative. What is the result? It is that many have died from drinking poisons promised to them as medicines—potions for common ailments that not only don't cure but inflict suffering—dissolving teeth, burning holes in throats and stomachs. In a word, murdering. And the most alarming element of quackery is that absolutely none of it is necessary. You have within you the ability to eradicate disease by *tapping*"—and he knocked a finger twice against his temple—"tapping into this private apothecary. Disease is nothing more than a contagion of belief. You hear that someone has a cold, and soon you find yourself developing the selfsame symptoms. You catch a cold because you believe in it. Cure you of your belief, and we cure you of your cold without a drop of some unholy noxious nostrum ever passing your lips.

"Is there religion and is there medicine? Yes, of course, to both. I would never advocate you quit your church. You pastors shift uneasily without cause, I assure you. Today, right here, I shall present you with a singular demonstration of a phenomenon which encompasses, I think, both elements—faith and science— and I'll leave it to you to decide what interpretation you render. To accomplish my task, I must first ask for some assistance from you. I should like a dozen of you, men and women, to come forward."

The audience shifted again, looking at one another. A few people stood. Amy said, "Oh, Kate, you ought to go," but Kate shook her head.

The family that had preceded the girls up the driveway—the mother and her children—moved to the front of the room as a group. One of them, a young boy, was coughing into a handker- chief, and looked deathly pale, Vern noticed. The handkerchief appeared to be spotted, and she tensed with recognition. The child was coughing blood. His sunken eyes made contact with hers and she looked away.

Castleman paid the woman no mind. He was engaged in con- versation with two men who had come forward immediately. The mother called out over the noise of the crowd, "Sir."

One of the men speaking with the mesmerist directed his attention to her.

"Madam, how may I assist you?" asked Castleman. The crowd fell silent. Those standing remained on their feet, waiting to see what would happen.

"Sir, my husband brought us all this way from Norwich to hear you today. We come because of our Timmy here, who's very ill, and the doctors don't expect him to live long."

"I see. And you'd like me to use my—or rather, *his*—powers on him?" He smiled benevolently and gestured for the boy to come forward. The child shuffled past his brothers and sisters. Castleman knelt before him. He spoke gently to the boy. So soft

were his words that Vern couldn't make them out. He moved his
fingers in front of the child's eyes as he spoke, and she thought
she saw the dark eyelids flutter. Castleman stood up. "I have to
tell you in all fairness, madam," he said to the mother, "that he
is deathly ill, and that there are some things neither hope nor
skill can salvage once they've passed a critical point. He is, however, a positive subject and I will apply myself to the task." When
she remained there, he said, "You may leave him. We'll give him
a chair to sit in so as not to tire him, and I'll work with him first."
    "Thank you," she replied. Her eyes brimmed with tears.
Vern's heart went out to her.
    Castleman renewed his call for subjects. When he had a
dozen, he lined them up and walked down the row of them. He
had them grab his finger or squeeze their hands together. To
each, he spoke solemnly and softly as he had done with the boy.
Then he either directed them to stay or return to their seat. In
the end, he kept four adults—two women and two men—and
the boy. The four stood calmly, their eyes closed as if listening
intently.
    "Now, as I promised, I will work with young Timmy. But
first, let us make sure our new friends don't wander off." And he
walked down the row of the foursome once again. This time, he
stayed with each of them a little longer. Castleman then returned
to the boy. He spoke with him, and this time Vern made out the
words "sleep" and "fluid." The child coughed into his handkerchief again. The mesmerist seemed to have a different voice for
this quiet speech, much deeper and less animated than when he
spoke to his audience. She wished she had gone up there.
    After a few moments he stepped back. The child now sat,
like the adults, with his eyes closed. His hand clutching the kerchief lay limp in his lap. Castleman turned back to the audience.
"When the French Doctor Mesmer in the last century first made
his discovery of this power, he posited the notion of magical fluid
floating through the air, surrounding us. He had no idea of what
he was contacting, and so made up the best theory he could
under the circumstances. In fact, what you perceive here before
you is an altered state of *mind*. Of being. Of spirit. You are looking

upon the souls of saints, of those we know from our Bibles, who were guided by voices and forces that others around them could not hear or see. The 'magnetic state' as it's called frees the mind from the physical world and lets it visit the higher planes. As you shall see."

He turned back to the child, and Vern realized that while he'd spoken the boy hadn't coughed once. Others in the audience must have recognized this, too; people were pointing at him and whispering to each other.

"Lad," said Castleman. "Where are you now?"

A moment went by, and then the boy said, "Floating."

"Good. Do you see anything?"

"I see sun. Sunlight. I'm up in the air and I can see sun below me on green fields. I'm so close to it. It's very hot." The excitement was clear in his voice. His hands moved from his lap, to his sides, as if to steady himself.

"Hot, yes. Green fields now—do you see your house there?"

"No—I'm not sure. I don't know where it is."

"Oh, well, I tell you, it's very near and you can fly right to it. Do you see it now?"

"Yes, there 'tis. I see it."

"Now, Timmy, when I count to four I want you to fly to your own room inside your own house. But before that, I want you to leave all that heat behind you. You're going to fly down to your house and when you arrive in your bed, your fever will be gone and your lungs will be full of this sweet air that you're breathing right now, this sweet, sweet air up so high.

"One. Two. You begin to glide down now. Three. Right through the window. And four. In your bed, and asleep." He stepped forward and caught the boy as he tipped sideways. Castleman sat him back in his chair. "Now you're going to sleep deeply until I wake you. Until I address you again. You'll hear nothing and see nothing. Just sleep."

He turned away from the boy. "Let us see how our other four subjects are doing, shall we?" He approached the first in line— a towheaded man wearing a high-fastening tweed coat. He sported a stiff mustache nearly as pale as the greased hair on his head. Castleman said, "Tell me your name, young man."

"Nathan Trippet," replied the man without opening his eyes.

"Mr. Trippet. Are you suffering at this time from any ills?"

"No, sir."

"And why did you attend this lecture today?"

"I wanted to see if this mesmerizin' stuff was all flap-sauce."

"And is it?"

Trippet's brow furrowed. "I don't know yet. I haven't seen nothin'."

Castleman laughed, and the audience joined with him. "No," he told his subject, "from here you can't see very much at all. Now, Mr. Trippet, have you ever exhibited any extraordinary mental faculties?"

"You mean, am I smart?"

"Ah, well, not exactly. But I shall take that as a 'no.' Mr. Trippet, you are currently standing before an audience. Can you sense them?"

Trippet, though his eyes didn't open, turned his face toward the audience as if looking them over. "Yes, I see them."

"Do you see anyone in the audience who is ill today?"

"There's a—there's a man with gout in his right foot. He's near the back, wearing a yeller coat."

People craned their necks, stood up and looked, or pointed. Amy knelt on her chair. "I see him. He's got gray hair and a big beard," she whispered.

"I saw him when we came in," Kate remarked without looking. "He's got a big walking stick laid across his lap."

The identified man did not stand, but he waved his stick to show that he was there.

"Can you advise him on a cure?"

"Celery. Especially the seed. That will cure the gout, sure."

"Remarkable, sir," Castleman commented. "Do you have some association with medicine?"

"I took laudanum a couple times."

"You were sick?"

"Naw, I just liked it."

The audience chuckled. Castleman said, "Thank you, Mr. Trippet. You may sleep awhile now."

Trippet fell silent and his face went slack. Castleman moved to the next man in line, a thin, red-haired fellow in a seedy suit. "You are John Drench?" he asked.

"I am."

"And you live hereabouts?"

"Yes, sir."

"What prompted you to visit this lecture today?"

"The handbills."

Castleman nodded. "So, you can read."

"Well enough to get by, sir."

"Excellent. Now, Mr. Drench, I'm going to attach your left foot to the floor so that you can't move it. We have a big iron band here and we're going to screw it down over your foot so you can't move it. Do you feel that now?"

"Yes, sir."

"It shouldn't hurt."

"No, sir."

"That's fine. Mr. Drench, when I count to three you will wake up, and I will tell you to return to your seat. But that band will still be there until I tell you to sleep again. All right?"

"Fine," said Drench.

"All right. Mr. Drench, one, two, three. Wide awake."

John Drench opened his eyes. He blinked at Castleman, at the audience, looking somewhat sheepish, as if unable to recall how he'd gotten there.

"Thank you for your participation, Mr. Drench. You may return to your seat now."

Drench took one step and stopped. He glanced back at his left foot, which was still in place. He pulled at it with increasing energy but the foot, as if a spike had been pounded through it, remained in position.

Dr. Castleman asked, "Is there anything wrong?"

"Someone's put that big old steel bear trap thing on my leg. When'd that happen? Did you do that to me?"

"Why, I didn't see a thing."

People in the back had stood up, some upon their chairs, to see John Drench's feet. Nothing held him in place, but he could not make the one foot budge.

"I'm sorry that I don't have any hardware here to help you take it off, either. I didn't come prepared for bear traps."

"Well, *some*one did. They put it on me!" he answered angrily.

"Yes, it's a problem. I have a solution, though. Why don't you go to sleep now?" And John Drench's head drooped, and his body relaxed.

Castleman walked back to the podium. "Parlor tricks," he confessed. "Very simple things, but they plainly show the nature and power of mesmerism. The mind can be made to see things that are not there, and to feel what isn't present. Did Mr. Trippet notice the man with gout as he came in? It's possible. That really proves very little. And as for his curative, I've no idea if celery has any effect upon gout or not. But I would recommend it, nevertheless. It's odd how correct such diagnoses turn out to be."

He crossed to the next subject, a woman with flaming red hair, who looked to Vern to be overly dressed and made-up for this event. "Now, tell me, good lady, your name would be—"

"Louisa Hopkinson, but nobody knows me by it here."

"You changed your name in marriage?"

"Because of a marriage. I don't want him to find me."

"Louisa, you mean to say that you're still married to someone and don't wish him to learn your whereabouts?"

"He beat me before. With a strap. If I went out. When I drank." She was strangely calm in describing this. As if it mattered hardly at all.

"Where was this?" asked the mesmerist. His humor with his first subjects had evaporated.

"In Buffalo."

"You fled this Hopkinson fellow?"

"I packed what I could when he wasn't there and ran away in the middle of the night."

"What name do you go by now?"

"Ann Sawyer."

A man standing at the side of the room suddenly threw down a woman's coat and hat he was holding. "Strumpet!" he shouted at the front of the room, and shoved his way out the door. Ann Sawyer didn't move, didn't seem to be aware of what had happened.

"I am very sorry we've had to learn this, Miss Sawyer. I fear your waking will be less than joyful. Please, for now, sleep." The look of awareness drained from her face.

Amy leaned to Vern and said, "People are nothing but wax to him, aren't they?"

"That poor lady's going to have an awful time after."

"You think her beau didn't know about her past?" asked Amy.

Vern and Kate exchanged glances that said the matter was obvious. Amy folded her arms and said nothing further.

Again Castleman returned to the podium. "The unfortunate Miss Sawyer is an excellent example of the nature of mesmerism. People reveal things that they would otherwise never tell, even when disadvantageous to them. The barriers we erect to protect ourselves have melted away and we communicate with the pure and honest spirit of true Christians. We are moved nearer to God, to the essence of ourselves. Let us try one more, and see if we can get closer still."

He walked to the last woman. She was older than the sleeping Ann Sawyer, with auburn hair shot through with gray, very much like their hostess, Mrs. Shacabac. She was taller and looked as if she might not have all of her teeth.

"You are our other Anna," he told her.

"Anna Maria," she replied.

"And, ah, that would be your *real* name?" Castleman asked, as if he feared she would turn out to have a secret much like the woman beside her.

"It would."

"Thank goodness for that. Now, Anna, I want you to look upon this audience, cast your second sight over them, and tell me what you sense."

Her eyes opened, large and dark, and she slowly, unblinkingly, looked them over, back and forth like a lighthouse light.

"Someone here is getting married," she said.

Amy and Kate stared at their sister.

"She's getting married hastily," the entranced woman continued with sibylline assurance, "for the groom has urgent need of
her. The groom . . ." And here her voice failed her. She was staring now, straight at Vern with such intensity that other members
of the audience were turning in their seats to look at her, too.

"What of the groom?" Castleman prodded.

"I can't— He's in shadow, but he can *see*. He's—Mastema!"
She yelled the word as if reacting to pain, and squeezed her eyes
shut.

"What is that?"

She shook her head. She couldn't explain it.

"Is it something this bride should know, Anna Maria? Is there
something you can say to her, advice you can give?"

The woman opened her eyes again upon Vern. "Your veil is
very thin," she said. "Don't stray from the path. Take care of his
egg."

"His *egg?*" the mesmerist asked, but she didn't seem to hear
him.

"Obey his requests in all matters. Your purity—never risk it."

"Now, that's sound advice for any new bride, isn't it?" he
added, attempting to lighten the tone again. He whispered something to the woman and her eyes closed. He turned and addressed Vern then. "Is she correct, miss, are you about to marry?"

She glanced uncertainly at her sisters. Finally, with everyone
in the room hanging on, she answered, "I am. In a day's time."

"Well, there you have it, ladies and gentlemen. This
woman"—he gestured at Anna Maria as he returned to the podium—"has discovered a hidden truth through what we can only
call clairvoyance."

Mild applause followed and members of the audience spoke
to each other. A few in the rows near her congratulated Vern on
her impending wedding.

"And tell me, miss, where's this fortunate young man of
shadow?"

"He isn't here."

"Ah, that explains it. He's not in the room, hence she couldn't make him out. Was that some variant on his name that she, ah, called?"

Vern shook her head. "No, it's not. His name's Elias. Elias Fitcher."

Nearby conversation ceased. In the front rows, people craned their heads to look at her. She could feel the pressure of eyes behind and beside her, staring, squinting, sizing her up. It was the same as it had been in the Hall of Worship.

Castleman, whether or not he knew the name, did not allow the moment to linger. He drew the attention back to himself, saying, "Fine, thank you for corroborating, miss. And now, we have *one* more piece of business to resolve, and it's the *most* important one!" He gestured at the boy, Timmy, still sitting limply with his eyes closed.

The audience followed him, and Vern exhaled as if she'd been holding her breath.

"Timmy, do you hear me?" Castleman called as he approached the boy.

The boy nodded.

"I'm going to count to three, and when I do, you will awaken from your healing slumber. You'll be much improved, and able to travel home without illness. You are going to get even better once you arrive there. Do you understand that?"

The boy nodded again.

Castleman crossed to his other subjects. For a moment he whispered to the woman named Ann Sawyer. Vern assumed he was saying something to prepare her for the shock of discovering what she'd revealed. He didn't whisper to the other three. He stepped back and said loudly, "When I count to three, you will awaken refreshed and alert as from a full night's sleep. One, two, three!"

The four subjects opened their eyes. Castleman glanced back. Timmy was sitting up, alert, perhaps dismayed. He spotted his mother in the audience and smiled. She rushed forward to embrace him. Amy muttered, "It's a cure of souls, he cured that child's soul."

The audience applauded again, but Castleman waved down the noise. "Let me say this one thing in closing, please. I don't know what you expected to see here. Magic tricks, perhaps.

"It's not magic, what happened here. It's not a program of any sort. I knew no more of what we would encounter than you. Whether there was a bride in the audience or someone with gout, or a child gravely ill—it was all unknown to me. This is the new science of the mind, and we don't yet know where it's taking us. All we know for certain is that it brings us ever closer to God."

He took a bow then, and the clapping resumed, although some people were already getting up and leaving. Some clearly did not like what they'd seen, or thought it either a humbug or sinister. Castleman spoke to his foursome, shook the men's hands. Ann Sawyer lingered after the others had returned to their seats. Someone carried her coat and hat to her, but it was clear she didn't know what to do next.

The boy was surrounded by his family. His mother embraced Dr. Castleman. Vern heard him say, "I can't promise you he will improve. His state is very grave. I may have made his time easier and no more than that, madam." She didn't seem to believe him, and indeed the boy looked much improved already and still didn't seem to be coughing. Castleman caught Vern's eye and bowed slightly to her, mouthing the words "Good luck."

Emma Shacabac, their hostess, had returned to the front, too. She spoke to some of the guests. Only Ann Sawyer remained in place, her coat and hat still in her hands, her face dull, as if nothing made much impression. Castleman excused himself and went to her. He said something, and she mechanically drew on her coat and tied her hat on. She acted as if she hadn't fully awakened from her trance. Vern would have liked to remain and see how she recovered, but their hostess was ushering them out.

The sisters filed along the hall with the rest of the crowd. They thanked Emma for the lecture. She replied that they were welcome, but it was obvious she was reluctant now to speak with them.

"What's a Mastema?" asked Amy as they went out.

"I don't know," replied Vern, and neither did Kate. She

handed Vern the veil material she'd kept throughout the lecture.

The three of them walked onto the driveway, where the cold wind shattered the spell of the lecture. The sky had gone from merely gray to threatening. People moving by kept their heads down against the wind. No one spoke to them. No one congratulated Vern now on her nuptials.

The child, Timmy, and his mother and sisters climbed aboard their wagon. As it rolled past, the boy looked back at Vern as though the two of them shared some secret. His handkerchief slipped from his bony hand and floated onto the stones of the driveway in front of her, speckled with blood. Rain began to sprinkle down then.

The sisters walked home through the village again, as ignored in their passing as if they were ghosts.

Twelve

HE PREACHER'S NAME WAS FLA-
vy, a red-faced and pop-eyed little man with a nasal voice and an
unsteady hand for shaving that gave the lower half of his face the
look of a pelt inflicted with mange.

Before the ceremony, he spoke to the family in the foyer,
explaining unnecessarily that it was imperative someone other
than Reverend Fitcher conduct things. "One can't be groom and
shepherd both," he joked, and laughed at this as if there were
something clever in it.

Finally it was time, and everyone withdrew to the Hall of
Worship. Vern and her father remained in the entryway to await
their musical cue from the organist. Mr. Charter asked if she was
nervous.

"Very nervous, Papa," she replied. She fought back tears, insisting to herself that she should not be seen crying prior to the
union, only afterward.

"You look so resplendent in your mother's gown, my dear. So
lovely. She would be so very proud to know you're wearing it
this day. And in such a ceremony. I confess, just two weeks ago

I felt such terrible pain for you three girls, for surely there was
no chance of happiness, of matrimony for you, on this side of the
Advent. What hope I held out was dashed when the reverend
told us the date. How, I thought, would my girls ever know joy
when there were only months remaining to them? It's too cruel.
And then, why, out of the blue—"

"Yes, out of the blue." Her voice shook.

"Oh, but, Vernelia, you can't be anything but flowing with
happiness at the prospect today. Not merely a union, but with so
important a man as Reverend Fitcher. Why, I never dared
dream."

She almost said, "I did," but stopped herself. She *had*
dreamed, the past two nights. Dreams of the spirit lifting her
from her bed, waltzing her through the air, through space, and
always setting down inside a distorted version of this house. Always alone. She wandered through twisted halls, every door
locked. Nothing stirred. Before long, the invisible hand of the
spirit clutched her hand and began leading her along, and a dark
shape began its pursuit. The halls seemed to go nowhere, miles
of them folding back upon themselves, walls lined with doors,
every one the same, until finally one confining corridor led
straight to a solid wall, a dead end. The invisible force sped up,
dragging her after so fast that she must be crushed when she
hit, and she cried out, flung up her other hand, and averted her
face, but instead of being smashed she passed through it, across
her bedroom, and into her bed where she woke with a start.

It was all a dream. Of course it was all a dream, but what
could it mean? Was the shadow Fitcher? Was she so terrified of
marriage? Not of marriage, no, but of her readiness for it. How
would she ever explain to Elias about Henri? She'd been in love.
She'd thought it was the sort of love that lasted forever, but it
hadn't been, not in the end. Henri—the truth was she didn't
know if he would ever have married her. She'd convinced herself,
convinced Kate, but Henri had never known how close they had
come. She'd never told him, just as she hadn't given him any
reason when she broke off with him, her lover, her—oh, but the
ripples that one indiscretion caused. Here she was marrying, and

she mistrusted her worth and purity. *Never risk your purity*, that mesmerized woman had warned her. But the advice had come too late.

The organ sounded three sharp chords then—her cue to enter.

"My child," said her father. He drew her beneath the archway and onto the red runner of carpet.

She gathered up the full train of her skirt and stepped through. Mr. Charter took her arm as the music swelled.

Through the gauze of her veil, the hall and its occupants appeared not quite defined, the faces smudged and distorted, unfinished. She moved inside her own knot of awareness, the veil a shield against them, her fingertips and toes frigid, the pit of her stomach scooped hollow, depthless, a hole cored straight through her. Down the aisle she stepped, buoyed by her father, toward Elias Fitcher. He stood immobile in a black tailcoat and trousers, a gray waistcoat, white shirt, and bow tie. Beside him, the crystal skull gleamed with spectral light and, courtesy of the veil, sprayed colorful rays across the altar and her husband-to-be. At Fitcher's side stood the wagon driver, Notaro, but now in a similarly dark coat and pants, and with his hair smoothed back, his chin clean-shaved.

She saw her sisters' shapes, shades weeping for her, their faces pressed to handkerchiefs. Behind them Lavinia stood like a cutout, stiff with pride—and for a moment she acknowledged a queer sympathy with her stepmother. Over the past few days, the rancor between them had softened. Their earlier rivalry for control of the household had evaporated. Lavinia had attended to Vern as if trying to be a real mother, assisting in every preparation, sharing in the excitement of the impending marriage with almost girlish delight.

She looked again at him, at her suitor, her soon-to-be husband.

He devoured her with his eyes. He fixed upon her bodice as if counting the freckles on her skin. His gaze returned to her face slowly, and his eyes burned. It came to her that she could make him out perfectly while everyone else was a blur. As if he sensed this, he turned and faced the altar to mask his clarity. His hand slithered along the sleeve of her lace glove. His fingers intertwined with hers. They were as cold as her own. Their hands froze together.

Flavy's sermon began. " 'Love not the world, neither the things that are in the world,' " he proclaimed, and Fitcher's grip tightened: The Reverend Flavy must have been unaware that he had used the very same quotation in his sermon the day he'd proposed to her. Flavy continued, "If any man love the world, the love of the Father is not in him." Then Fitcher made a gesture with his free hand as if swiping at a fly in front of his face, and Flavy deviated from the quotation. "The things that are in the world," he repeated, as though he'd lost his way. But he was a preacher by nature, and he quickly found his direction again. "We have here today this man and this woman. Are they not in the world? If I asked you that, you would say, 'Of course, of course they are in the world. We are all of us here in the world.' What, then, can we do to clarify this passage and make sense of marriage?"

As if in reply, a baby somewhere in the back of the room burbled loudly. Vern smiled at the sound.

"First of all," Flavy continued, "we are privileged in that we—all of us here—know the end of the world approaches and soon will dissolve all that John referred to in this passage—the things that are in the world. Yet we also know that all of us here, owing to the wisdom of our prophet and our voice, will not dissolve, but will transcend the passing. We will endure. Thus are we not in the world, but separate from it. Ringed by iron, on a holy plot of ground that will be passed over come Judgment. Saved, therefore divine. Here before us have we an example of how we'll overcome—by unifying, joining together. Love, my friends, is not *of* the world. It is transcendent. Love is the provenance of God Almighty. This union is of the highest order, not the lowest. And nothing done in His name can ever be wrong or ill-considered.

"We ask then, in His name, do you, Vernelia Anne Charter, take this man, Elias Fitcher, to be your lawfully wedded husband now and forever, acknowledging no other? To love, cherish, and obey?"

Vern's heart was hammering at her breast as she answered, "Yes, I do."

Reverend Flavy beamed at her. "Do you, Elias Fitcher, take this woman, Vernelia Charter, to be your wife? To honor and cherish, protect and provide for, for as long as ye both shall live?" Fitcher glanced sidelong at her. Peripherally, she caught the gleam of his teeth. "Oh, yes," he said.

Flavy asked Notaro, "You have it, sir?"

Notaro nodded and held up a small gold band. Fitcher took it from him and fitted it on her finger.

"By powers vested in me by no less than the authority of God Himself, I pronounce you man and wife." He paused, expectantly. Fitcher lifted Vern's veil and craned his head beneath it. His lips scorched hers. She closed her eyes, tasting plum wine, feeling for an instant that her legs would not hold her. Distantly, she heard Flavy say, "Please welcome into our community the Reverend and Mrs. Elias Fitcher."

He began the applause and it spread like fire around the room.

Fitcher took Vern by the elbow and turned her, and they faced the guests together. Now she saw them all sharply. Kate and Amy both wore painful smiles—smiles of joy tempered by loss. Lavinia looked triumphant. Papa's eyes were bright with tears. The gathering applauded as though they'd been paid for it. Their faces, however, lacked any concomitant joy. Vern sought for warmth in their midst, and was little rewarded.

Fitcher led her back along the aisle while the organ pipes bellowed the opening to "Psalm 100" and the crowd sang, " 'Be thou, O God, exalted high . . .' "

Beneath the curtains covering the front windows, the shadows of feet moved, suggestive of a gathering outside the front of the house; on the side wall silhouettes moved to and fro across the stained-glass portals. It was as if all of Harbinger had collected, inside and out.

Some people singing in the pews nodded to her as she

passed, but many more regarded her coldly as her new husband escorted her, singing the psalm as if it were a rebuke to her. She supposed they must perceive her as an outsider, never mind that she was two decades younger as well; and it was possible that other women within the community had designs of their own on him, now foiled. Nevertheless, she resolved to win them to her as soon as possible. Surely, Reverend Fitcher—and shouldn't she be thinking of him as "Elias" now?—surely, Elias would help her gain their trust.

He opened the door to the foyer. People filled it all the way to the front doors, but parted like a living sea between the Hall of Worship and the dining room, opening up a corridor large enough for her and her husband. Some of the men leaned in and congratulated Fitcher as he passed; some also eyed her, and rather too salaciously, she thought.

In the dining hall, a large three-tiered cake sat in the center of the long table. It was white and covered with colored flowers. Vern was amazed by it. Someone had spent hours preparing this. Beyond it stood bottles and glasses and cups. Fitcher stopped outside, turned, and let his flock come to them.

Mr. Charter, Lavinia, and her sisters followed Vern through the throng to take their place beside her. Her father clutched her to him and kissed her. Lavinia, head tilted, said, "I'm *sure* you'll be happy." Next Amy and Kate, who hugged her tearfully. The three of them wept together. Kate in particular seemed crushed, and Vern patted her back, saying, "Don't worry, I'm not that far from you, am I. Why, soon enough, you're both going to have a husband, too. I'll tell you a secret, Kate. I know it, because Samuel told me, the same as he told me about my own suitor. He was right about me. He'll be right about you, too. So don't cry, Kate. You have no cause."

Kate wiped at her eyes in most unladylike fashion. Vern chose not to correct her. She sniffled and stepped back, searching for something in Vern's eyes, but then shook her head as if to indicate that she couldn't express what she was feeling in words. People were pressing up close, and they parted the two sisters before Kate could find anything to say.

Vern turned to accept congratulations from the next person in line, and it was the fiendish best man, Notaro. Only now the fire had left his wicked face. He refused to look at her directly, keeping his head down as if trying to show her the part in his oiled hair. He only raised his eyes once, and then to glance at her husband, who was paying him no mind, who was engaged in conversation with many others. Notaro turned aside.

After that, she was overwhelmed by a steady parade of well-wishers, hundreds of them, lining up just to go past, into the refectory. She had about decided that she'd misread their reactions to her at the ceremony, when one woman, leaning close, whispered, "You're not the first, you're not the last." The way it was said, it sounded like a riddle, and what it suggested eluded her for a moment. By then the woman had pushed into the crowd. Vern didn't even have a good idea of what she'd looked like. She'd seen so many faces by then. And they were still coming. How many had Elias told her lived here? She couldn't recall. Hundreds, though, it had to be hundreds.

Eventually, he told her, "That's enough, now. Let's go," and led her into the dining hall.

The bottles had been uncorked, glasses filled with wine. They made their own wine, naturally. She overheard her father say to her husband, "But, sir, drink—how can you condone it?" He had taken to drink after her mother died—only briefly though: He'd pulled himself out of that pit and saw all drinking now as an evil. Elias replied, "Mr. Charter, wine needs no condoning. Our Lord's blood is wine. And wine will still be with us on the other side. Are you acquainted with the Shakers? Their most famous leader, Mother Ann Lee, has communicated with them from beyond the grave—did you know that? And she grows grapes in Heaven. All sorts of grapes, for there are far more varieties there than here. And from these she makes a most holy wine, which she has in some instances shared with those in the corporeal community who still abide by her teachings. If God allows for wine, how can we do otherwise?"

Completing his lecture to her father, Elias handed her a glass of her own, then stood beside her and raised his cup to toast her:

"My bride," he bellowed, "and may she be as pure as she is beautiful." She blushed, and lowered her eyes. The crowd recited "as pure as she is beautiful" as though it were part of a litany.

Tenderly, she looked at him, only to find him brandishing a knife at her. Her shock was brief, and too ridiculous—it was the knife to cut the cake, and he was holding out his hand that she might take the knife with him and make the first cut. She closed her fingers over his. "The first cut," he said, "is always the most difficult." Together they sliced through every layer, and there was cheering all around.

The first piece was for her, the next for him, and after that, the cake was steadily dismantled, like a pyramid, brick by brick. People kept arriving to take another piece.

Across the disappearing cake, Vern watched her husband standing, speaking with her father, and thought that there couldn't be anyone finer, greater, or more true than Elias Fitcher.

Thirteen

*N*EAR SUNSET, THE REVELRY ended. It seemed to her that all of Harbinger had suspended their daily routine to join in the celebration, as people were forever flowing through the dining hall, swirling through the foyer, congealing in corners, on benches and chairs, until another group arrived to replace them. It went on for hours. The room never emptied.

Finally, though, the reverend announced that everyone should return to their duties—that he and his bride must retire. He called for "Mr. Notaro," and the young rakehell had to be sought, because he was no longer in the room. Neither, she realized, was Amy. People ran out in search of him, as if locating him constituted an urgent matter.

Notaro soon came bursting in, his demeanor disheveled, his greased hair falling in his eyes once more. It looked as if he might have stumbled and fallen on his way. Vern suspected he was drunk, but if he was, he had enough sense left to conceal it.

"Is the wagon ready to take these—my in-laws—home?"

"Yes, sir, Reverend, yes it is. Tied up around the side." He pushed the hair back on his head.

"That's good," was the response, and the way Fitcher said those two words made Vern suspect that things would not have gone well for Mr. Notaro had it been otherwise. She took brief cruel amusement at the prospect of seeing him punished.

He hurried off to bring the wagon up to the door. A moment later through the same door he'd come in, Amy entered. She wore the idiotic smile of someone lost in her cups. It appeared that, drunk or no, she hadn't loosened any of her clothing, but Vern had a sudden, horrible premonition that the spouse the spirit had promised for Amy might *be* Notaro. The matter needed clarifying, and her sister required some instruction.

And then she remembered that she wouldn't be going home with the rest of them. She would not have occasion to speak with Samuel again, nor be on hand to safeguard her fool sister.

She lived here now.

On the steps they made their farewells. Kate was weeping again as Vern embraced her. Amy hugged her, planted a sloppy kiss on her cheek, and promised in a singsong voice to visit soon. Lavinia assisted her on board the wagon, then sat beside her and quietly remonstrated against her "behavior fit for a doggery." Vern experienced a pang of loss watching the familiar scene, as if she were a spirit herself, looking upon the world she had departed.

Mr. Charter hugged her one last time before boarding. "We'll be close," he said. "We're going to see one another all the time, you know."

"Papa," she replied, the tone almost beseeching—and even she didn't know what she was expressing. *What has happened to me?* she wondered as the wagon lurched away. *Gone from betrothal to wedlock before I could draw breath. Samuel, what have you sent me to?* The wagon rolled through the wrought-iron gates. Exhaustion sank upon her as if the wagon toted her energy away with it.

Fitcher came up behind her, and his arms slid around her

waist. His legs pushed the full train of her dress against her. "My dear Mrs. Fitcher," he purred. "Beautiful creature." His hands took her shoulders and spun her lightly like a vane. He looked down into her eyes, and his eyes flared, hot as the blue tip of a flame. "All your things have been brought from that house and put upstairs. You have your own room here. Come, take my arm and I'll show you." His touch revived her, granted her energy to make her tired legs work, though her thoughts remained clouded with loss.

They went up the right-hand stairs, past the arm of the tilted cross. Vern glanced at it as she passed, noting the jagged hole in the wood near the end of the crosspiece, as if a spike had been hammered in and then torn out to add authenticity to the display.

Around the landing they went and up the center stairs to the mezzanine—a small oval balcony with a brass rail, two plush, wine-colored chairs, and a view straight into the chandelier. On the left side of the mezzanine, a few broad steps led up to a second-floor hallway, while the right side provided an enclosed staircase up to a third floor.

"You live on the second floor," said her husband. "This way." They climbed to the hallway.

The open foyer and chandelier behind them were so bright that at first the hallway seemed nearly black. As Vern's eyes grew accustomed to the dimness, she saw that the hallway was lined with doors, all of them closed, just as in her dream. The hall seemed deeper than it should have been, until she remembered that the foyer below led to an adjoining corridor and the wide porch.

Fitcher released her, strode ahead, and opened one of the doors. "Here, wife," he said. "I'm sure you'll want to acquaint yourself with your chamber awhile. Become comfortable among your own possessions. I have many duties of my own yet and there's time enough for the exchanging of gifts later." He ushered her into her apartment.

It was bigger than the room she'd shared with her sisters in their new house, and the walls had been paneled in a dark wood that made it seem larger still.

On the left, a fire burned in the small hearth behind a gilt-wood firescreen, the warm air smelling pleasantly of woodsmoke. A birch canopy bed occupied the center of the room, extending out from the far wall. White ruffles draped the bottom and the upper portion of the canopy arch. Above the headboard, the canopy seemed almost to glow. The fluted footposts were extravagantly carved with extended vases between reels. Fresh flowers had been placed upon the mattress. Her trunk, brought from home, stood beside it—open as if someone had gone through it. Her pink parasol lay across the top edge.

Along the right side wall stood a card table of satinwood. Painted green garlands graced its small drawers. Her father would have admired it. A pressed-glass candlestick in the shape of a dolphin stood at one end of it, the tail balancing the candle, which was half-burnt; a tray containing a douter and scissorlike snuffer beside it. The chair next to the table was what was called a wheelback, though the type of back always reminded Vern more of a spider's web than a wheel. The line of the narrow table directed her attention to the corner beyond it in which stood a large armoire. The doors contained panels of marquetry, much lighter than the walnut frame, and the almost black twist-turned columns on each side. One of its doors was ajar.

Vern walked past her husband to the armoire and pulled the door farther open. Her clothes hung inside. There were two drawers at the bottom, and she pulled one of them out. Her unmentionables had been placed there, neatly folded. She blushed, imagining someone like the wicked Notaro handling them. The massive cabinet dwarfed her: It must have topped eight feet, all of its bulk resting on small bun feet, which made it seem as if it must surely come crashing down. It was finer than any piece of furniture her family had ever owned. The glossy panels caught the flicker of the fire, drawing her attention across her bed to the opposite side of the room. That area contained an oval rug, a small Regency settee, a mahogany-framed cheval mirror with one candle cup, and a six-drawer commode beside a corner commode chair and chamber pot. Her hairbrushes and other toiletries had been laid out neatly on top of the commode chest.

She noticed then that the head of the bed did not in fact reach the wall, that there was space to walk around it, and that the bright glow within the canopy came through floor-length curtains behind it. She stepped into the narrow space and pushed aside the curtains. She was then looking out a slender window above one of the wings of Harbinger. If she'd pushed open the shutter and leaned out the window, she might have placed her fingertips against the roof. As she gazed out, once again her energy evaporated. She could not exert herself enough to open the window. She let the curtain drop and came out from behind the bed. Though flagging, she felt she should say something to her husband for his courtesy, for this lovely room. Mustering enthusiasm, she chirped, "Oh, Elias," but as quickly stopped as she discovered he had left her. The door to her room was closed.

"Your duties," she muttered.

She no longer needed to feign energy. She sat wearily on the edge of the bed a moment, then collapsed back onto it. The canopy was a great gauze above her. Cut flowers surrounded her head, their smell intoxicating. The light spilling in through the drapery over the bed was ethereal, and for a time she floated, dazed, content, halfway to Heaven already. There might have been a tear that trailed from the corner of her eye, or maybe it was just a tickle on her skin. She brushed at it, barely able in her torpor to raise her arm, to learn if her face was wet. Silently she insisted that she had no cause to cry except from joy. She was married now, she was Mrs. Fitcher, the mistress of a great property, the wife of a great man. She'd lost nothing in the bargain. Nothing at all.

Too exhausted to fall asleep, after lying there awhile Vern decided to undress and at least prepare for it. The light was gone behind her and the fire had burned low, but she didn't feel as if much time had passed.

She sat up, crossing her arms, fingers loosening the ribbons of her sleeves. She shrugged out of one and then the other, then undid the sash beneath her breasts. She pulled the dress up in front until she could reach one ankle. Unlacing the ribbons about it, she slid off the slipper and rubbed at her toes and the ball of her foot through her stockings—one, and then the other. She stood up, then undid the elaborate coiffure of her hair, unplaiting it, letting it fall, and shook her head.

She folded her arms down inside the loosened dress and lifted it up and over her head. Beneath it she wore three petticoats above her chemise. These she unbuttoned and stepped out of. It felt so good to be free of all the clothes.

She placed them in the armoire. Carefully folding the dress, she murmured, "Thank you, Mother." She closed the cabinet and turned back to the bed.

The door to the room hung open.

The figure of her husband stood inside. He wore a silver silk robe. He simply stared at her, as motionless as furniture. Vernelia blushed under the stare. Even from across the room it pinned her to the spot, an insect in a specimen box.

He closed the door, and when he turned back, his robe was unbelted. Underneath, he was naked. With no seeming effort or speed, he arrived before her, almost as if he had simply traded one position for another without crossing the space in between. She knew she must have closed her eyes, fainted away for a moment. She didn't want that. Not on her wedding night.

His hands, hard and hot, parted her chemise at her throat. Fingers like blades unfastened the front of it. In the firelight, his eyes looked black, the pupils huge. The smell of him was intoxicating, a sinful perfume unlike his earlier smell. She wanted to press her face against him through the opening of his gown; but he kept her away and drew the chemise from her, leaving her naked but for her stockings of black net over flesh-toned silk. She shivered, and told herself it was anticipation. Her exposed skin rose in goose bumps.

One hand touched her belly. The fingers splayed wide across it and slid up beneath, then between, her breasts. She sighed and again tried to lean against him. He pushed at her breastbone and she fell back onto the bed. She raised her arms to invite him to her. He caught an arm and rolled her over, then with both hands clutched her bottom and pulled her up onto her knees. She didn't know what he wanted but tried to comply. Her hands reached for purchase on the quilt, plunging in among the flowers. In the instant she regained her balance, he spread and penetrated her from behind with one sharp thrust. She cried out at a flare of pain as sharp as if he'd driven a knife into her. "Please!" she begged. She reached out to push him back, but he wrapped her hair around his hand and pulled her head back toward him. The pain of having her neck bent back, of her hair threatening to tear out at the roots, overwhelmed any pleasure she might have hoped for. He tugged as if at coach reins, and thrust his torso against her. She wanted to order him to stop but couldn't find the breath for more than an outraged "Sir!" His body slapped her as if to drive her across the bed. She managed finally to rake his arm and he let loose her hair, so fast that she fell face first into the flowers; heard him growl, but not with anger—more as if he enjoyed the inflicted pain. She tried to get up, twisting around. "Please, sir, let me—" His fingers hooked over the back of her head. She glimpsed his face, his eyes rolled down almost beneath the lids, his lips drawn back from his teeth—a feral face—and panic took over. She swiped her arm back at him and her fist struck his cheek. He inhaled through his teeth a hiss, then thrust himself again, crushing her face into the leaves and blossoms. The smell of her bouquet, luxuriant before, threatened to suffocate her now. She flailed, gasping, her head twisting to get air. She inhaled greedily, lay still, and let him have his way. She hoped he might think she'd given in and loosen his grip, but he maintained the hold, like a male cat biting the female's neck, pinning her while he spent himself. Her mind fled to childhood memories of cats and lions, and snarling teeth. Her mother, coughing . . .

And then it was over.

Like a storm wind Fitcher withdrew from her, from the bed, from the room.

She lay trembling in the aftermath with her knees still tucked

under her, until she was sure that he had really gone and wasn't
lurking in some shadowy recess to savage her again. She pushed
her face out of the flowers, surveyed her room. The chamber was
empty, the door closed. He'd gone, wrapped in silver, making not
a sound. He was smoke, shadow, the thing that had chased her
dream self.

The fire needed another log. She noted this, trying to pretend
that nothing had happened.

Awhile she maintained it was so: Her marriage, her fine and
noble *husband* . . . couldn't treat her like this. This was nothing
like Henri, not mutual, fumbling and tender. Nor was it anything
like the love Elias himself had promised. She was offended. Outraged. But she was mostly frightened. Discarded and unsatisfied.
Not Fitcher, though. His satisfaction chilled on the quilt beneath
her.

Turning onto her side, Vern drew up her knees and curled at
the foot of the bed. Was this the love he'd spoken of so elo-
quently in his sermon? Love beyond flesh, beyond worldly desire? Where was her ghost in the wall now with his promises of
things to come? Of husbands and suitors and happiness? This
was how he would save her? What dream was this ensnared her
now? None of her own devising. She would have dreamed far
better than this ill use.

"My duties," she moaned, then covered her head with her
arms. This time she pressed her face into the covers by choice,
to bury the sobs that began with the word "Papa."

Fourteen

VERN WOKE THE NEXT MORN-
ing to the sound of a large
bell being rung. It took her
some moments to orient herself. She unfolded her legs. Her pel-
vis ached.

She pushed back the curtain at the head of her bed, but
through the slats in the shutters could not see the source of the
alarm, though it was surely the bell behind the house.

She grabbed a simple dress and put it on without petticoats.
For a moment she considered her shoes, but as the bell ringing
didn't stop, she instead ran to the hall and down the stairs barefoot. It might have been a fire signal, and she did not want to be
trapped inside the house because she'd dawdled over what slippers to wear.

She saw no one at all until she'd passed through the rear hall
and out to the porch.

It was gray and cold outside—much too cold to be barefoot
and wearing a dress with nothing under it but a simple chemise.
Nevertheless, she braved it, ran down the steps and into the yard.
People were talking, shouting, confused, pointing this way and

that. The bell ringer—a short barrel-chested man—let go of the handle, and the bell rang once more and stopped. Vern heard the words "hanged" and "dead in there" in the snippets of conversation. No one spoke to her until she asked the man who had rung the bell what had happened.

He said, "Oh, ma'am, Mrs. Fitcher, a fellow's hung himself is what's happened. Up in the dormitory." He gestured over his shoulder at the wing opposite the chapel. "The men's side," he added.

"The men's side," she parroted, turning to look. There was a crowd gathered around a door there, and Vernelia walked across the yard. She didn't see Fitcher anywhere. Members of the crowd spied her approaching and stepped aside, seeming to signal others with their motion, so that as she approached, the group parted before her as they had done after the wedding. She couldn't tell if they recoiled in fear that she might touch them or from some idea that she was sacred and must never be touched.

Even in the doorway, they moved out of her way, allowing her to enter and climb the stairs up to the second floor. More men stood on the landing. She came up behind them. Her wet feet squeaked on the boards. One of the men heard, but identifying her, he stiffened and backed out of her way, and looked as if he might dive over the railing. The other men became aware of her and moved aside. By the time she reached the landing she had an unobstructed view of the dormitory beyond.

The room ran the length of the wing. Bunk beds had been built to either side of a center aisle—hundreds of them. The air carried a stale and unpleasant odor, as if something were slowly decomposing in there and no one had the good sense to open a window. There was no ceiling but bare beam rafters below the roof, with what looked like sharp-snouted Jenny lights hanging from them—and, near halfway along, one man. He was stark naked, dangling from a short length of rope. He had a darkened, distorted face. His tongue protruded, purple, between his lips. His eyes bulged as if at the moment of death he had seen something fearful. Three other men were attempting to lift him down.

Then one of the men beside her on the landing stepped out

and blocked the view. He said, "Ma'am, respectfully, I think you should not be seeing this."

"Who was he?" she asked. She didn't recall the dead man from the wedding reception, but there had been so many people congratulating her; and he wouldn't have looked like that.

"Please," he said, his voice tight with urgency.

"Is it because this is the men's dormitory?"

"That's so. The women live over across the way, above the chapel. No women come here. Never."

"But, are none of you married?"

"Most of us are, ma'am." The look on her face must have suggested that this explained nothing, and he added, "We're saving each other from lustful deeds. Sinful acts. The way Reverend Fitcher has instructed. With time drawing nigh, such acts must be accounted. We all have to answer to the one true God for what we've done. There's no hiding what's in your heart. We daren't lose our place, what he's secured for us. And I surely must fear for your own place if you don't leave here. It's not seemly, you seeing old Bill this way."

The man's sincerity and absolute sureness scared her more than her husband's behavior the previous night. They didn't know, these people, what lust really looked like. But there was no point in protesting, and she chose to retreat.

Even as she turned to leave, putting one foot out to step down, she saw her husband enter at the bottom—enter and look right up. For a moment neither of them moved, trapped in mid-motion, about to rise or descend. Then Elias Fitcher backed away from the newel post as if out of courtesy, offering her neutral space.

She walked down the stairs, her pink and cold feet all too visible from below, and she wished she had put on her slippers now because she could not disguise that she was barefoot any more than she could pretend she hadn't intruded here: She could see already in what ways she was objectionable.

At the bottom, however, Fitcher said nothing. He allowed her to pass on outside and started up the stairs, a shepherd more concerned with the flock than with any single sheep. Or was it the dead who mattered more? His shirt was loose and his sleeves rolled up. His left forearm bore scabbed lines like tattoos where she'd scratched him last night.

She walked back through the gauntlet, and no one said a word, as silent as conspirators caught with their daggers out. She went back beside the bell, where she'd started. The alarmist pretended he didn't see her, focusing intently upon the door. Many more people had gathered now, all across the yard, hanging back as if fearfully certain the death would be close to them.

Within a few minutes four men came out bearing the body. He was still naked. He hadn't even been covered for decency's sake; it seemed unnecessarily cruel to expose a dead man to his neighbors this way: How could her husband have allowed this to happen? The man's head hung loose over their arms, nearly dragging on the ground. His throat seemed banded by a black collar—circled by an inverted "V" where the rope had crushed it. The men laid him down on the grass. Elias Fitcher stepped out of the darkness behind them.

Behind Vern a woman began to scream, and she started to turn to see who it was. Before she could, the woman knocked into her, and Vern slipped on the wet grass and fell. The man who'd rung the bell stuck out his arms to catch her, and lucky for her he was there or she would have cracked her head against the bell. One of his hands caught her shoulder but the other glanced off and slid inside her dress, quite accidentally. Even as his cold fingers came in contact with her flesh, he was lurching away, horrified by the intimacy. She caught her balance and stepped back from him, her face hot with embarrassment. The woman ran wailing and waving her arms, but Fitcher was staring darkly and directly at Vern.

The woman collapsed on her knees. Her cries carried over them: "Oh, Bill, Bill, why go without me? Why?" She tried to kiss his face, but hesitated at his grotesquely twisted mouth. Her nervous hands hovered over him, seeking to touch him, hold him, but clearly prevented by his state. Finally she clutched at his hair and doubled so far over that her head pressed against the ground. Everyone stood around as though her display was wholly alien to them, and they didn't know how to react.

Reverend Fitcher exclaimed, "Oh, my poor sister, poor dear Alice, come look away, look away from this tragedy!" He gathered up Alice and pressed her face to his own chest. "This is not William, don't look upon him. William has gone now. William is in the other Kingdom." All at once she threw her arms around him, and bawled to the sky. As if this were a signal, other women now came forward and surrounded her. They took hold of her and pried Alice from Reverend Fitcher, then closed ranks, blocking her view of her husband, and together walked her away from the body, up onto the porch, and through one of the doors.

Fitcher knelt as she had, beside the body of William. He closed the eyes, pried the mouth open enough to stuff the tongue back inside. He took hold of one arm, and climbed to his feet. Immediately others grabbed on to the other limbs and they all lifted the body again. As they carried it off, Fitcher chided the crowd in general. "This man has damned himself as surely as if he had killed one of you. He should never have been seen in such a state as this," he said. "It's unforgivable, but it is how he chose to clothe himself for death, and so it is how he must be, here and upon the far plain. His appearance can only breed thoughts of depravity among us. Were I a harsher prophet of the Old Testament, why, your wives might have to put out their eyes for having seen him thus—such is the justice meted out in our Book. But I am not such a one. *We* are not vindictive here. Vengeance belongs to the angels.

"I shall intervene on our behalf with the Lord and beg His forgiveness for our company's inadequacy to prevent this. Let this damned soul bear the blame. He is responsible." He let go the arm suddenly and swiveled about. "But there *will* be punishment!" he shouted. Spittle flew from his lips, and his face was stretched hard and red. "There will be *reckoning*! No one is blameless. No one. And the time comes swiftly upon us. Think on that, all of you!" Then he turned back to the corpse, lifted his part of the burden, and continued hauling it away.

The people started to move off, many of them with a speed that suggested they wanted to put as much ground as possible between them and the place where the naked man had lain. Vernelia tried to thank the bell ringer for catching her. "Sir—" she started to say but he interrupted. His face was pinched with fear.

"You can advocate for me, can't you?" he asked. "Tell him they sent me down to sound the alarm? William, he was already dead, we couldn't have saved him nor stopped him none. He'd done himself while we were eating. None of us missed him right away, or we would have stopped him.

"And then you fell and I—I didn't mean to touch you that way." He clutched her hand. "Please, missus, I beg you—tell him to intercede for me. Stop the Dark Angel from coming for me next. I couldn't help—couldn't help none of what happened. Me. Stephen Ellsworth. You tell him. You speak for me—" He realized abruptly that he was touching her again and flung her hand away so hard that she stumbled. He backed up against the bell, where he turned and ran across the open yard toward the orchard.

Vern retreated from the cold and her own confusion, into the warmth and safety of the house. In her room she moved the lovely firescreen and stoked the fire, placing more logs above the embers and then pumping with the small bellows until flames ignited before her. She dragged the wheelback chair over beside the hearth and warmed her feet. Waking to the alarm bell, she'd forgotten her own fear. How odd that a stranger's death could so divert her. But death was like that bell—so loud that they must all hear and give it their attention.

Elias's presence—his nearness to her in the stairwell—seemed utterly removed from the silent intruder who had used her so coarsely the night before. Although sex was a subject not to be discussed openly, might she not entreat or entice him to express his ardor with more gentleness hereafter? He reached the same destination if he did, and she arrived, too, the sweeter for that. She soon convinced herself that so decent a man must recognize the error of his behavior. She must pick the right time to

speak of it. She could see that Elias was distressed, that he felt
responsible for the death. Of course he did—they were his flock.
He guided them. If one of them fell, he must see it as a personal
failure.

She wondered then about the bell ringer and his petition.
What was the Dark Angel? Did he think death was looking for
another victim? She must inform Elias about that, too.

She was still sitting by the new fire when he entered her
room. Once again, there was no sound to direct her attention, but
a sense of a presence, which led her for a moment to imagine
that the spirit of Samuel had arrived—it was that same preter-
natural change in the atmosphere. She looked about her expectantly, finding, just inside the closed door, the slender figure of
Elias Fitcher. He had put on his long black coat and buttoned
up his collar. He held a small package in front of him, which he
carried to the card table. Then he came across the room and Vern
stood to greet him. She had by now convinced herself that the
previous night's proceedings were merely a matter of clumsiness
on his part, of inexperience. She blushed at the thought of being
more schooled in matters of sexuality than he. She had a com-
pulsion to throw her arms around him.

"My darling," she said, "how terrible that was. I'm so sorry
you had to . . ." Her voice failed. She clasped a stone figure; fear
leeched from his body into hers and she released him and moved
back, asking, "What is the matter?"

"I can see you have no sense of it," he said gravely, "which
concerns me. You fly out of the house in an unlaced dress that
barely suits the intimacy of a bedroom, and without shoes, showing off your ankles and feet to the entire community. You—"

"I thought there might be a fire. That bell—I'd no notion of
what it meant, and I ran!"

"You conveniently fall into one of the men so as to force him
to place his hands on you—no, not merely on but inside your
undone clothing!"

"I did not fall conveniently. That woman, that poor Alice,
pushed me when she ran to her husband's body." She fought not
to show tears, but her whole being was reacting to the calumny

of his accusation. "That Mr. Ellsworth was as mortified by the incident as—"

"So you know him by name?"

"He told it to me."

"Why would he do that, eh?" he asked.

"Because of this very thing. He was afraid."

"What does he have to fear if he be honest?"

"I don't know. Something he called 'the Dark Angel.' "

He waved a dismissive hand. "Superstitious twaddle. So he's one of those, is he? It's a wonder he's stayed on if he's fallen so far from the core of our belief."

"I know nothing of any of this," she replied, wanting to find out more. He gave her no chance.

"Worst and most unforgivable of all, you actually entered the men's dormitory in that slattern's attire."

"Elias, how was I to know? I didn't know you separated husbands and wives. Not until I was at the top of the stairs, and a man there told me I shouldn't be there because of the community segregation, and naturally I turned to leave when he told me, but by then you had arrived, you saw me turning away, coming down—"

"Enough. I will not be painted the villain."

"Who is painting you a villain?" Even as she said it, she knew she would not be able to speak of the previous night with him now. It would seem to him another attack upon his character.

"By implication, you do. You know nothing of the arrangement of Harbinger, and that is because I have told you almost nothing. It's my fault, your ignorance, and so I bear the blame."

"I'm not blaming you, Elias. I'm only accounting for my own innocent actions. I ran outside for fear that the house was ablaze and I would be trapped if I delayed. I followed the crowd to the source of the alarm, and no one spoke, no one told me I couldn't go there."

"Did they not?" His eyes narrowed, but now the focus was clearly not her, but more as if he were ticking off a list of names to confront at some later time. "They should have known you had no experience with . . ." He sighed. "Yes, I see it all now.

You followed your instincts, as what woman does not?" He leaned forward and ran the back of his hand lightly across her cheek, smiled. "How can I possibly be angry with you on the very first day of our life together? Forgive me, dear Vernelia."

"Of course, of course I forgive you." She clasped his cold hand. "You must be so stricken by the event."

"Yes, I'm deeply troubled. The poor fellow had been distraught for some time it seems. I should have known that he was in peril. But there are so many here, so many hundreds, and more arriving each day." He pressed his hands together as if about to pray. "Well, then, first what we shall do is open your gifts, and then I'll instruct you in all of your duties here. You *do* want to be a part of the community?"

"Of course. I cannot sit by idly while everyone else works. I thought—I feared that the reason no one spoke to me was that they think this of me already, that I'm some lazy useless creature expecting to be pampered now that I'm the wife of the great man."

His expression softened when she called him that. "Well, we shall change their minds on that point soon enough. Now, let's see what the 'great man' has for you, shall we?"

He retrieved his package from the card table. "The card reads: 'For Mrs. Fitcher,' " he said. "I wonder who it could be from."

It was a small box in red paper that had been waxed, and tied with silk ribbon. He handed it to her and she carried it to the bed to unwrap it.

The box was of rough pine. Vern could hold it in the palm of one hand. With the other she slid the top open. Inside, it was full of sawdust. She glanced back at Elias, but he was giving nothing away. Gingerly, she moved her fingertips through the sawdust, and almost immediately touched something hard and smooth. She brushed the packing aside until a bit of it showed. It was a stone, she decided. She poked fingers around it until she had sense of its size and shape. Then she reached into the sawdust and drew the thing out.

It was an egg, an egg carved out of marble. White with dark

blue veins running through it, the egg had been polished perfectly smooth. Holding it, she recalled the sibylline words of the mesmerized woman: *Take care of his egg.*

Fitcher had come up behind her, and now his arms encircled her waist. "It is a perfect symbol of my love—like a real egg—perfect in form. Hermetic."

Once more his touch charged her. She felt as if she must explode with energy, so much that she became light-headed in his loose embrace. His words breathed into her ear, "This symbol of my love you must keep with you always, wherever you go, and so I will be with you. My little egg."

"Yes, I'll take care," she said, and tilted her head, trying to circle it back, hungry for a kiss.

Instead, he released her. But the energy, the lickerish pleasure, thrummed in her veins; she'd become a conduit, transferring energy from him to the receptacle—the egg, which, like a battery, generated the power flowing down her arms and into the pit of her stomach, where it opened like a flower, ripe and wet with dew. She didn't want to let go of it.

"And now, wife, I must impart all the rules to you in order that you may belong here. But you must dress more properly before leaving your chamber. That is the first rule: You are the mistress of Harbinger now and you have to dress properly. You must never allow people to see you barefoot or dishabille. Understood?" He stared down at her toes with obvious fascination as he said it.

"Never. I know now."

"Good. And you're not to visit the dormitories—men or women. The men, you know already how I think of that. But even the women, they will only gossip. And you occupy a station above them hereafter, so you are not to lower yourself to sharing idle gossip."

"But, Elias—"

"There are some in our company who won't be saved despite being in our company. I tell you this in private between us, but it's not to travel any further. Some are devoted. Others take pleasure in picking at the devotion, seeking its imperfections, without realizing of course that by so doing they are only revealing their own flaws. Do not fraternize with them."

Again she complied—she understood his point. Women did gossip. She'd gossiped with Kate, and even now and again with Amy, it was true. She couldn't see the evil in it, at least not in her own gossiping. She didn't think she'd ever said anything terribly wicked about anyone, or if she had she was sorry for it now.

"The next rule has to do with time here. You were left alone this morning, as it was your first here. We are up at five each morning. All of us. You'll not be an exception. There's a morning prayer before breakfast and I will expect you there each day."

"Of course," she answered. Even at home, they were all up by six.

"And again each day with the noon meal, there is prayer. The time will depend on where you are employed that day. We must find suitable work for you. I already have something in mind, which we'll discuss after you have your meal this morning." He stroked his beard a moment, then said, "Ah, yes, one more thing." He reached into his coat pocket and drew out a large ring of keys. The ring itself was brass, shiny where the rings had slid along, polishing it. He shook the keys in front of her. "When I go away, you'll be entrusted with these, as you'll have the entire house to supervise. You will have to make certain people continue to do their part." He jingled the keys again.

Vern noticed then that one of them was larger than the rest and appeared to be made of glass. Fitcher dropped the ring back in his pocket and said, "But that's for another time—when I go off to recruit. For now, please dress and we shall go down to eat together."

"Elias," she said, his name full of longing, of unfulfilled desire. But he was already walking away, out of the room.

Alone, she made herself set the egg down in its box. Her hands, she saw, were trembling.

He led her across the orchard to the village.

"Your father put the idea in my mind," Fitcher told her, "not directly of course, but he made mention of your skills, and I thought to myself then that we need those skills just now."

A cluster of children ran across their path, playing, but stopped and stared, wide-eyed, at the two of them. The oldest boy ducked his head and said, "Morning, sir." The others bowed their heads, too.

"Good morning to you, young Jeremy," Fitcher replied. "And what is our game today?"

"Sir?"

"What are you playing at?"

"Nothing, sir. Just running, is all."

"Well." Though addressing the child, he smiled at Vern. "Carry on with it then. But don't lead your little brothers and sisters into trouble."

"No, sir, I wouldn't." The child shuffled to the side, then sprinted away. The others hung back a moment, and one of them stared with big cow eyes up at Vern, before the whole pack took off in pursuit.

"Willful little tykes," Fitcher commented. "The littlest ones of course can't be expected to work. But Jeremy is old enough, he should be doing something constructive now."

"Surely, he's ten or eleven," Vern defended.

"Precisely," answered her husband, as if they had agreed upon it. He continued across the open ground, past plots of turned soil, where a few people were at work, either planting seeds or pulling weeds and dead plants from the previous year.

They walked along the lanes of the little town. As before, the adults who saw them stopped whatever they were doing and stood stiffly, respectfully, as Vern and Elias passed by; most bade them "good morning" as well.

He led her to the chandler's shop.

She understood immediately what her duties were to be. Her father must have mentioned how she helped Lavinia make candles for the family, but not how much she hated the task. Even as she comprehended what was in store, she knew she couldn't protest or complain any more than she could complain now about last night's abuse of her body.

The shop was small. On one side stood a rack containing tinned sheet iron molds—there must have been a dozen of them, and each was a twenty-four-candle mold. On the other side there was a broad low table covered in splashes of grayish wax and circular marks where the wood had been scorched by the bottom of kettles, set down between pourings. Two dirty aprons lay on the tabletop, as if tossed down just moments ago by the previous occupants. Above hung a frame like the carved spine of some mythical monster of antiquity. It comprised dozens of small rods protruding from either side of a straight pole. A few of the rods had tightly twisted wicks dangling from them, as though—again— the former chandlers had been interrupted in the midst of their work. The contraption's pole was attached to two pulleys so that it could be lowered and raised. It was quite a clever device, she thought, and would at least make the task of dipping wicks into hot wax manageable, if easier for two than for one. A large hearth took up the entire back wall, with two great hooks sticking out from which to hang the kettles and cauldrons for melting and straining the wax. Barrels and kegs stood to the side of it, and skimmers and strainers and paddles hung on the wall beside lengths of hemp cord, some of them braided and twisted. Boxes were stacked beneath these.

"Outside there is a well where you can get water. We're in sore need of these, you know, because Jekyll's Glen had not enough and we use far more candles than they can supply us and still have some left over for themselves."

"Your previous candle-makers were a couple?"

"That's right."

"They died in an accident? What happened to them?"

"Did I say that? I suppose I did, to protect your feelings. The young man took his life, is the truth of it."

"Oh."

"His wife simply disappeared. I know what you're thinking, my dear. Three people you've heard of are dead. It's both extraordinary and not surprising. The press of time weighs on all of us differently. I said when first we met that I was reluctant to announce the date of Judgment. This is precisely why. There are those who can make peace with the world and face what is to come, and there are those who refuse to do so, and in refusing, they recognize their sinfulness. They aren't accepting God's grace, they're running from it. But of course that's impossible to do. And so, in fear for their souls, or believing that arriving sooner upon the far shore will benefit them in some manner which crossing over at the date established by God, ascertained by myself, will not, they act and in doing so destroy themselves. The result is, there are those within our community who've come to believe that Death lives in our house and stalks us, one by one."

"The Dark Angel."

"That's right. The Dark Angel. Some who believe that fierce story have fled Harbinger. One of them at least, in his haste, plunged over the side of the gorge. Others—particularly women— stole away in the dead of night and were never seen again within our gates, our former chandler being one such. It's why we now keep our gates locked. From such events, otherwise unrelated, has grown the story of some Dark Angel of Death wandering the halls, hunting victims. It is one reason you will find the Harbinger House deserted more often than not. I tell you, there are no limits to human folly. Gossip is the fuel, driving a fearful engine." He clasped her hand. "It isn't worthy of your concern, my dear. And now we must return to the house. It's near lunch and time for afternoon prayer."

He led her outside, closing the door after them. He rambled on then about the topic of his sermon this afternoon—whether it should be from Luke: "Thou shalt love the Lord thy God, with all thy heart . . . and thy neighbor as thyself," or from Colossians: "Let no man beguile you of your reward in a voluntary humility and worshipping of angels." Both, he said, offered starting places to talk about members of the community who were ending their lives prematurely, and those believing in claptrap about this angel of death—how the one created an atmosphere that provoked the other and so forth.

Vern hardly heard him. The words "worshipping of angels"

had sent her into a reflection on the shadow that had pursued her in her dreams. Had the women who fled from Harbinger dreamed of that dark gliding figure? And if it visited her again, how would she escape? When the gates were now locked, what angel could protect her here?

Fifteen

VERNELIA SPENT THE AFTER-
noon alone in the chandler's
shop. She didn't begin to
make candles yet. Instead, she took inventory of what she had
and what she needed. One keg contained bayberry that had been
boiled and strained. She poked a finger at it, but the greenish
wax was hard. She sniffed its fragrance. At least the addition of
it would make for pleasantly scented work, as well as producing
candles that burned better.

A larger keg contained mutton tallow, which must be used
now while the weather was still cool. Once summer arrived, the
stuff would be unsuitable. Even the candles themselves weren't
going to be much better—she'd seen beef tallow candles puddle
on a hot summer day. Boston, at least, now had gaslights. Eventually they would replace all the candles, she thought. That is,
they would have done if the world weren't ending. She knew she
could produce better than common tallow light. She had alum
and beeswax on hand. Some camphor would be useful, too. She
would ask Elias to have Mr. Notaro get her some when he next
went to town.

Lengths of hemp and tow she cut and braided. Some of the material had been coated with saltpeter, which she braided first. For the molds, she inserted long nails through the looped ends of the wicks, so that all she would have to do was pour in the wax. The problem was, there weren't enough nails to fill even two of the large molds at a time. She would have to find more, or spikes or small sticks. Still, it was a beginning. She hung the remaining wicks off the overhead rods. Those would give her another two dozen candles, although dipping would be more time consuming, since it took at least a dozen repeated dippings before the candles would be thick enough.

By the end of the afternoon, she had everything arranged to begin making candles the following morning.

She found the portraits when she dropped one of the wicks as she was braiding it. It fell down behind the table, and reaching for it Vern touched the wood frame of a small picture. She pulled it up onto the tabletop.

The frame contained two simple black silhouettes, two profiles facing one another upon a bed of lace. It must, she decided, be the couple Elias had described, the former chandlers. The profiles looked familiar, but she'd seen so many faces the past few days, probably any cutouts would have looked familiar. She tried to imagine what they were like, imagined the woman taking flight. "Did you like the work at all?" she wondered aloud. Maybe, because they'd worked together, it had been less hateful. If so, then why did he kill himself? Why did he leave his wife alone?

We are the same, you and I, she told the woman's portrait. *The community needs us in our capacity here. It's our duty as wives. As women.* After a while, she laid the picture facedown and went back to work.

She didn't stop until she heard the bell ringing. The sun had vanished behind the shops opposite. The air was chilly, and there was no one else on the street. She set out for the house. Others were moving through the orchards ahead, going to dinner. At the top of the long rise, the lights of the house glittered in the dusk. The idea of finally sitting down among people after her day's work suddenly had great appeal. She wanted companionship, friendship. She wanted them to look at her and see that she worked the same as they did, and invite her in not because of who she'd wed but because she was one of them.

When she reached the house and entered the foyer, someone called to her. It was a woman she remembered seeing that morning in the crowd. Thick-bodied and with a blotchy complexion, the woman was shaking her head sternly as she approached.

"That was first bell," she said. "You doing the candle makin' in Harbinger village, you don't come before second or third bell. People who work in the house and fields, in the kitchens—they get first bell. They grow the food, make the meals, so they get to eat first. Those are the rules."

"I didn't know."

"Ignorance is no excuse. You bein' Missus High and Mighty, think you can come in and eat when you like, but it's not the way."

"No," Vern protested, now on the edge of tears. "I wasn't told. I'll wait my turn."

"That you will." And so saying, the woman sashayed through the doors into the dining hall from which Vern was barred.

She sat on one of the cushioned benches, hidden for the most part behind an urn and under the stairwell. Candles burned in sconces by the doors and in the chandelier, but not near her. She ached now with hunger, real and abstract; the energy that had buoyed her only moments before had evaporated. Through the wall came the murmur of a voice delivering a sermon—not her husband's voice, but someone else, haranguing, cajoling. She could have joined that congregation if only she'd had the will to rise.

She must have sat there a full half hour, because the bell rang again, heralding the second shift. People emerged from the dining hall. Others poured out from the Hall of Worship. Some of them noticed her but glanced away if she returned their look. In moments they had all vanished and she was alone again. After a few minutes more people entered the foyer. The first of these were out of breath, having run from the village. Vern didn't even glance at them now. She remained invisible as she was expected to, staring down at her image in the polished floor, a faceless ghost.

Then there was another ghost beside her, and she looked up to find a child looking at her, a girl of maybe seven or eight, with light hair and dark eyes. She looked like someone Vern knew. The girl asked, "Aren't you coming to eat?"

Vern drew a breath and it shook in her chest. She got to her feet. "Yes," she said. "Yes, I am."

The girl turned, saying, "That's good, because you know you only have a little while here."

Vern followed her into the dining hall. It was already crowded, with people shambling about, carrying bowls and cups. Vern let the child instruct her—showing her where to get a bowl of her own, and a utensil and cup. They walked down the line to where six people stood ladling a bean soup into the bowls. They sat together, but the child hesitated, her spoon in her fist, and Vern waited, too. Finally, she heard someone at the far end of the room mutter some words—she made out "bless this . . . Lord" and the final "Amen," which rolled around the room, and she said it just after the girl, who began immediately to eat. Vern followed her lead.

No words were spoken. She listened to her own chewing, to others slurping the broth. Nobody said anything, even as they passed bread to each other. They ate their meals, then got up and went through the doors at the far end of the room. Vern finished before the girl and waited for her. The girl gave her a secret smile as if they had just shared something intimate. They got up together. Vern's stomach growled. She could have consumed three more bowls of that soup easily. It was hardy fare, but there wasn't enough of it. She knew there could be no asking for seconds. At least one more shift of people had yet to partake of a meal.

In the kitchen she stood in line waiting her turn to clean her bowl and spoon and cup. These were turned over on trays that, when full, were carried back to where she'd acquired hers. She washed her bowl and, standing there above the hot soapy kettle of water, experienced a moment's contentment.

She turned to go, and found that the child had disappeared. She scanned the entire kitchen but the girl wasn't there.

She followed the main body of diners out to the yard again, and started to walk back toward the village. A thin elderly man stepped up to the bell and swung the handle back and forth, ringing it. She nodded a greeting as she passed him. He nodded back.

She walked along in the dark, and was halfway to the orchard before she realized that the child had looked so familiar because she looked just like Kate had at that age.

She paused and looked around herself, and found that she was all alone. No one else was returning to the village. The day's work was done. They had retired to the dormitories, where even now she could see the glow of candles in the windows. Candles everywhere, like stars across the horizon. Soon, she thought, it would be her light shining from the windows, bringing the vast utopia to life.

She trudged back to the house. Her legs were stumps now. Her whole body felt as if it had been dragged behind a wagon along some rutted track. All she wanted was to sleep.

She wondered what Kate was doing at the moment, and she thought, *I must find husbands for her and Amy here, and quickly.* If she could do that, they would at least be together as the sands ran out for the world. If no one wanted to talk to them, they would have each other as they always had.

It might have been a dream. His hand curving along her cheek. The smell of perfumed macassar oil, and his voice beside her ear, asking, "How is my little egg tonight?" She stirred, but could not come fully awake to tell him where she'd left it, in plain view on the card table. But then she felt it against her skin, rolling cold and smooth into the hollow of her back, and from it a current flowed into her, a thousand rivers of desire etching across her surface, so intense that when she did finally open her mouth all she could do was moan. The perfect egg slid down between her legs and opened her like light draping a flower bud. She unfolded. Pleasure broke her apart, battered her upon its rocks, swooped and swirled and spun her into the funnel of the maelstrom, down and down and down into subterranean auricles, red chambers of no expressed form, full of slithering shapes, not fire nor brimstone but hellish all the same, for all the snaking forms clambered upon her in the dark to feast upon her flesh. She grew hollow, saw her belly, and it was empty below her ribs, which stuck out like broken sticks buried in the dirt. And his hand emerged out of the writhing mass around her, reached into that void below her breasts, and pulled out the perfect egg again with a conjuror's flourish. Like her heart it came free. It glistened in the firelight, slick and wet with her. As he lofted it away, it resorbed her sensation, all sensation. The back of him, shining like metal inside the silk gown, glided to the door, where he glanced back. She saw herself from there—a skeleton covered in yellowed papyrus, flesh flaking to dust upon her bed. She knew he was gone only the moment the door clicked shut.

The sound awoke her.

She was lying facedown on her bed. Her hair made a wet tangle about her face, like a net that had been thrown over her, and as if she were a mermaid, she sprawled on this moist spot, legs become a thick fin too heavy to lift. The bedclothes had been thrown aside, lying in peaks like seafoam beside her that she could just see at the edge of her vision. Her chemise was gone, her body coated with a chilling perspiration. How long could she breathe, cast up here?

Finally, she moved, and there was a flash of pain between her legs, there and gone, as if for an instant she'd been pierced by a barb. The pain woke her completely. She rolled over and pushed herself up. The room smelled of musky sex and woodsmoke; the sheets were drenched with it. But the room was empty, the fire low, not sporting licking flames at all.

She slid from the bed, got to her feet, padded naked and unsteady to the table where the marble egg lay. She hesitated to touch it, to pick it up, glanced again at her door, still closed, at the fire and the dark corners of the room, as though he might be hiding there, watching her. She lifted the egg with thumb and forefinger. It left behind a wet circle on the wood. The pit of her stomach clenched and she set the egg down and retreated to the bed again. Where she'd lain had already gone clammy, and she crawled to the far side, under the sheets and the quilt, and wrapped her arms tight around her, because she was shivering.

The morning left her uncertain of the night's events. She'd walked in her sleep at home, and Kate had proved to her that she'd done so at the Pulaski house, too. What could she be certain of here?

Her husband was so proper, so authoritative as he climbed into the pulpit for the morning sermon. The windows were dark, the sun not up yet. Candles in sconces along the wall lit the worship hall, reminding her of the importance of her role.

Fitcher spoke of the many rooms in God's house: "Enough rooms for all who are saved, for God knows beforehand how many that shall be. He knows who is saved and who can never be. He has prepared his house for us. Heaven is the greatest utopia of all. Huge and limitless."

The sermon was brief. They must not forget that He would accept from them only perfection. The less-than-perfect had been left outside the iron gates with the less-than-perfect world. He spoke as if no suicide had occurred the day before.

The power of his voice, his words, captured Vern's thoughts, making her agree silently to try to achieve perfection. She did not want to fail her Lord.

She went to breakfast in a sort of daze. The oatmeal she was given was cold, but she ate it as if it were hot and honey sweet. She left the house and walked along the border of the orchards to the village and her job. Every question she had seemed frozen, impenetrable, and farther away all the time; so many things she could not ask.

*   *   *

The hard work began. She started a fire in the hearth, and when it was going, she filled one kettle halfway with water and hung it on one of the hooks. Into the other she scooped great gobs of tallow from one of the barrels. It sizzled and stank, but at least it hadn't turned rancid.

She scalded and skimmed the tallow alternatively, added her other ingredients, and poured the mixture off. With it still warm, she carried the vessel, a smaller kettle, to the molds with their ready wicks, and poured. Wax splashed out over the edge of the mold, but she filled all twenty-four of them. She remembered that she lacked enough nails to pour the other molds. She put the kettle back on the fire and went out in search of some.

The logical place to start seemed to be the ironsmith's. She crossed the street. Away from the fires, she felt cold, and was gathering her shawl about her, when someone said, "Good morning, missus." She jumped at the simple words, found a woman her own age smiling pleasantly at her from a doorway. She nodded an answer but skittered away.

The sound of a hammer clanging against an anvil directed her to the smith. He was hammering on a red-hot bar, but he stopped when she entered the wide door. He was smaller than she'd expected, short in stature, but his shoulders and arms were rounded and thick. He had a curly beard that split into two points, and he held a mallet in one hand and a set of tongs holding the bar in the other, looking for all the world like someone out of myth, like Vulcan in his element. He wished her a good morning.

Vern explained her need for nails or something to tie the wicks around. He pointed toward the back of the stable and told her, "I toss 'em back there, the ones that bust or get crooked. You'll find plenty in the dirt if you kick it around. If they're too bent up, I can straighten 'em well enough in a jiffy."

She walked to the back and hunted around. Some were easy to see, but she pushed her foot through the loose dirt and straw to turn up more. As he'd said, there were more than she could use.

The smith said to her, "So you're taking over the candling. That's a lot of work for just one woman. Them kettles is a heavy thing to carry when full."

"I know. Maybe if they get too heavy, I can ask you to help?"

He got shy then and tugged a little on his beard, and said, "I'd be most honored to, miss."

She collected her nails and started to leave, but then thought to ask, "What were the people like, the couple who were your chandlers before?"

"Oh, young James and Adele was a decent pair. He was as mad in love with her as you can imagine. They'd got hitched not so long before they come here, so you'd a been surprised if they didn't act like two lovebirds most of the time."

"They died?"

"Well, yes, that is, he did." He set down his mallet and rubbed his hands together, then looked at the palm of one as if to read the lines in it. "Hanged himself."

"That's how he killed himself?"

"Off the bridge across the gorge. Jumped straight into it with a noose tied to the rail."

"What happened to . . . Adele?"

"Don't know. We sent someone to the ladies' side to fetch her and she was gone. Never did find her. We thought awhile that he'd thrown her down into the pit ahead of him, but nobody found anything of her. That poor James, he was just a fresh kid. It didn't make sense, he'd do that."

"Did he—did he leave a note?"

The smith shook his head. "Didn't need one. He'd told us all, for days before. Said over and over that the Dark Angel was comin' on him. We didn't know he meant anything. You know?" He picked up his mallet again and swung it down abruptly onto the rod on top of the anvil. She assumed that meant the conversation was at an end, and turned to go. Behind her, he said, "James, he said Adele'd become the angel's bride, so that she didn't see him, her own husband, anymore even when they was together. It grieved the reverend fierce when James did it. He just doted on them two, he did."

The loud clang of hammer on metal that punctuated the statement made her jump as she emerged on the street.

With the wicks tied to crooked nails, Vern skimmed the liquid again, then took the kettle off the fire. She would do that all day long now—move the pot off and on, heating it, then cooling it and reheating it, all in the attempt to keep it at just the right consistency.

She poured the molds first, three more sets of twenty-four. The first one wasn't cool enough yet to plunge into the vat of hot water, to release the candles from the mold.

She set the kettle on the table below the rods, unlooped the rope tied round a cleat on the wall, and carefully lowered the rods until the first two wicks plunged into the kettle. After a few moments she drew them out, looped the rope around the cleat again, and moved the kettle into position beneath the next wick. Then she lowered the contraption again. She repeated this process until all thirty wicks had been dipped once. Then she began again.

It took a dozen dippings for the candles to reach the size she wanted. She had to return the kettle to the fire repeatedly to keep its contents liquid enough. She was exhausted from the repetitive process, but she was also proud of what she had made: They were all long and tapering, just the sorts of candles to line the Hall of Worship; and none of them had cracked. She had gone slowly enough and kept the tallow hot.

Now Vern took the molds and plunged them into hot water. It splashed and stung her hand, but she held on. Quickly she withdrew them and turned the mold upside down, allowing the briefly heated candles to slide out. She repeated the plunging with the other molds. She collected one of the boxes stacked up against the wall. It had compartments built into it into which she could slide the candles, once she had trimmed the excess tallow off them.

Soon she had filled the box and started on another. The boxes would go into a cold cellar room until the candles were needed. She supposed they wouldn't remain stored for very long, the way they used them here.

Only three of the mold candles cracked. She tossed the pieces back into the barrel of tallow, and hung wicks again for the next day. Her back and arms ached from all the lifting she'd done. Her feet, too. She had been standing the entire afternoon, but she was quite pleased: She had made over a hundred candles, surely enough to light the whole of Harbinger for a few days.

She ate supper as always with a roomful of people who said nothing to one another. She was beginning to recognize them now— the man with the huge gray mustache in the style of a teamster, and maybe he'd been one; the woman with the nose that had been broken and badly set; and the other one, the blotchy one who'd not let her eat with the first shift. Eventually she thought she might recognize them all. She looked for the little girl who'd been so nice to her, but didn't see her.

She retired to her room in exhaustion and dismay, too tired to be more fearful, stoked the fire, then sat on the commode chair and tried to watch the door. The egg she took from a deep pocket in her skirt and placed on the small table beside her. It had reverted to being just an egg, a smooth piece of stone, and not the sexual icon of her dreams. She closed her eyes for a moment, and reenvisioned herself on the bed, withered like a desiccated toad, and had to shake the image out of her head.

She needed to stay awake until Elias put in an appearance tonight. The things they must discuss should not be allowed to fester. But her eyes refused to stay open. They ached and wanted only to close, and finally she capitulated, closing them again.

At some point she sensed herself transported to the bed. The air took her. She floated. She opened her eyes, or dreamed that she did, to watch the ceiling pass above her, then the canopy of the bed, glanced at herself to find her body nude above the sheets; but where was he who carried her? There were only tendrils of smoke in the air from the fire. His voice whispered in her ear: "How is my little egg?" Her body settled, pressed down into the bed. She couldn't see him anywhere until she happened to glance into the mirror on her right. In the mirror she lay beneath him. He was inside her and hidden at the same time. "Vern," he said. His whisper plucked at her. She shifted her hips, laid her head back, and succumbed to pleasure. There was more of it than she could stand. It split her open.

The fire died as if doused, and blackness consumed her.

When she woke it was morning and she was on the bed again, exactly as she'd dreamed. She moved, and felt something cold between her legs. She reached down but knew already it was the egg lying there.

After his sermon that morning, Vern approached her husband. "My nights are not happy, Elias," she told him.

"My dear, I do so understand," he said, instantly conciliatory. "I've been so busy that I'm exhausted at night, I fear. I've meant to look in on you, but have dozed and then discovered that it's far too late—"

"What do you mean? Are you saying you haven't *visited* my chambers?"

"Of course. Isn't that why your evenings aren't satisfactory?"

"I—no. That's not it at all."

"Then I'm afraid I do not understand. I've been neglecting you, my dear, which is wrong of me. But you know that we're soon to leave here for a campaign to bring in more souls, and the preparations for that are so all-consuming—that and guiding my flock toward their inevitable destiny. I must come and visit you in your shop. We'll dine together at midday. Yes, let's do that." He took her hand, then remarked, "That's why I gave you the little egg, you know, so that you would have at least something of me with you when I'm not here, when you're all by yourself."

She wanted to call him a liar, make him confess the truth. Did he think to deceive her into believing she was dreaming her nocturnal encounters, that she stripped herself and aroused herself? But she remembered where she'd found the egg, and the implication made her blush. She didn't dare tell him.

He saw the color in her cheeks and asked her what it meant. She tried to think of a way to explain. Whatever she said, it would sound ridiculous or mad—either she was inventing events, or else night after night he was emerging like a vapor from that smooth white marble.

He squeezed her shoulder and said, "Never mind, we can discuss it later. For now you must go have your meal. There's not time. At noon, we'll talk about it."

By noon, she had concluded there was no possible way for her to explain, for she was already doubting herself. In any case, Reverend Fitcher diverted the conversation to other pressing matters almost the moment he arrived, and finally she said nothing and walked away.

The nocturnal pattern established itself. No matter how hard she tried to remain awake, after her day of laboring with kettles and molds, she soon fell into exhausted sleep. Elias came to her only in her dreams, which became more and more formless, until after a few weeks she could no longer distinguish them, spending her nights in charged slumbers, fueled by carnal sensation, awaking each morning to a glimmering of having been violated, but without the memory of how. She was terrified at first. She intended to petition to go home to her family, but never did. Something else was happening to Vern.

Every morning the egg lay in her bed with her, giving every evidence of having been inside her body, though she remembered nearly nothing of her night. Her hips, which had ached at first, seemed now to have no memory of being abused. Sometimes when she picked the egg up, she was overcome by desire so intense it seemed she'd burst into flame, and she lay back again, her hands coming together beneath the sheets, until she'd taken herself straight into the fire. Each day as instructed she brought the egg with her, and in her pocket it burned a little more than the previous day. She never said anything because, finally, she came to desire the touch of it more than anything else. Even had she wanted to, she couldn't have left it behind. She never knew when Elias would appear and ask to see it. Sometimes he would sit beside her at lunch, and without a word she would hand it to him and he would pass it from hand to hand before returning it to her, and then take his leave. It would be incendiary then. His touch had increased the charge.

Vern no longer cared that no one spoke to her. She forgot about her unease among her husband's worshippers, about her family, about Henri back in Boston. She worked through the day making as many candles as she could, and every aspect of her chores seemed only to heighten her stimulation while moving her into the heart of arousal. When the tallow ran out, she used spermaceti, the smell of which was salty and marine, and she half dreamed of eels and fish as she worked. She could be incited by the sight of pouring wax or of the candles themselves as they slid out of their molds. The dipped ones she made thicker, wondering would anyone notice. All the while, the egg touched her, drove her, conquered her. There seemed no longer to be a moment in the day when she wasn't thinking about sex with her husband— or more correctly, with his smoky shade. More people arrived at Harbinger, and she was introduced to the arrivals as Reverend Fitcher's wife; dutifully she attended ceremonies and services in the Hall of Worship, but all the while she was imagining the things he must do with her while she slept. How she kept herself from flying to pieces, she did not know. Lust came in waves, crashing upon her, stealing the sand of her substance little by little. Finally too much of it.

She woke one morning too ill to work. She shook with chills and ached in every joint of her body. She didn't attend the sermon, couldn't get up to go to breakfast.

One of the other women arrived finally to inquire if she was all right. Upon seeing her, the woman fled, returning with Elias. He expressed concern for her health, and promised that she would be looked after every moment of the day and night until she had recovered.

After that, she was never left alone. Two women sat with her. Their names were Emily and Margaretta. Emily had hair red as sunset, and Vern found herself fixating upon it. She may have told Emily she wanted her hair, but couldn't be certain if this was spoken or only thought.

The egg—taken from her—sat across the room on the card table, drawing her thoughts, her desire like venom. Emily often sat beside it, and maybe that was how she came to link the two things, the hair and the egg. Elias would arrive from time to time and ask after her, brush his hand through her hair, kiss her tenderly on the cheek. At one point, in a delirium, she wrapped her arms around him and tried to pull him into the bed with her, announcing everything she planned to do with him—all of it borrowed from what she thought he'd done with her already. She wanted to show him her body, tried to tear off her gown. She cried, "Get me her hair, and I can be any woman you want!" She reached for Emily, who kept her distance. Margaretta, dark and usually stern, flushed with embarrassment and looked elsewhere. Fitcher extricated himself and backed away in apparent horror.

"Why won't you come to my bed?" she demanded to know. "I want you in it. You make me like this—you and your slippery little battery. Get in with me!" Instead, Emily and Margaretta closed in and restrained her. She thrashed and snarled, demanded they let her get rid of her clothes so he could have her awake the way he used her while she slept. The women held her down until she sagged, enervated, lost in a fog again. She heard Margaretta say, "She is *teuflisch, ja.*"

When her fever broke, it shattered the looping frenzy of desire as well. She had been without the egg for four days. Separation weaned her from its power. On her bed, her head propped up, she glanced weakly across at it. Her eyes ached too much to stare. They felt as sunken as the gorge beyond the gate, but when she opened them, they always flitted back to it. Finally, hardly daring to breathe, she asked Margaretta to give it to her. No one had touched it until then.

Margaretta, whose severe face reminded her of Lavinia, regarded the egg in her hand as if it were a worm, a slug. She held it out with her head craned away. Hungrily, Vern snatched it from her palm. It was cold, however. No energy lay within. It was just a piece of marble. She could not help but wonder if it had ever been anything else. The sexual power it had manifested seemed no longer to exist and she couldn't clear her thoughts enough to recall how it had consumed her.

She curled up in a ball around the egg and fell asleep. She dreamed of a forest. Both her sisters were there, darting from tree to tree, playing hide-and-go-seek, and the harder she tried to find them, the more cleverly they hid, until she had been led into the wilderness.

Sixteen

$\mathcal{M}$R. CHARTER AND LAVINIA were driven home from the afternoon sermon they'd attended.

They had walked to Harbinger after lunch, which they sometimes did, leaving the girls in charge of the pike. The girls were expected to read their Bibles to each other while they sat, and not get into any mischief. Amy was also in charge of cooking the meal, and so left Kate from time to time on her own. The whole afternoon was uninterrupted by travelers.

The wagon rolled into view just as Amy was emerging from the house. Notaro drove it up to the pike and stopped, and Lavinia and Mr. Charter climbed down from the driver's box. Notaro gave Kate a neutral once-over, then his glance flicked to Amy but as quickly darted away. His affected disinterest in Amy did not escape Kate, but she had a more pressing issue to resolve.

As her father came around the lead horses, she asked him, "Did you see Vern?"

Before he could answer, Lavinia interjected, "Katherine, your sister is now mistress of a great estate. She's helpmate to God's chosen prophet. She isn't just sitting there in the house waiting for us to call."

"But you saw her?"

"Kate, we didn't," said Mr. Charter with more compassion. "We did not attend the sermon in the main house. The reverend instructed us to attend the meeting in the village church instead. It's his wish that we, his lieutenants, have opportunity to hear all the preachers who've come to Harbinger. He wants us to acquaint ourselves with them, make them feel welcome, make them feel their message matters to the community. You see, they aren't all death on a sermon the way Reverend Fitcher is, and having us there lends support. Sometimes he even asks us to preach the sermon ourselves."

"But she hasn't even sent us a letter, not even a note."

"Not so," replied Lavinia, and she produced a small wax-sealed envelope. "See, Katherine, you jump to conclusions." She smiled, a look more of triumph than of sympathy.

Kate took the envelope. She looked from one to the other of them. "But you didn't *see* her?"

"The reverend gave us her note," explained Mr. Charter. "You see, Katie, there are early morning sermons, and noontime ones as well. Meals are eaten in shifts, so someone is preaching before each of those. She might attend any one of them on any given day. We could go to hear a sermon there and not see hide nor hair of Vernelia for weeks at a time. Months even. Lavinia's right. She's now a very busy woman. If you heard the list of duties she has . . ."

Although their answer did not satisfy, Kate capitulated. It was more important to read the letter than to argue pointlessly. "Thank you," she told them. "Thank you for giving me this." She turned then, and caught Amy mooning at Notaro behind them. Amy saw her and quickly went to the horses, taking one by the bridle. She was going to help walk them around.

"Here, Amelia," Mr. Charter said, "let me help you." He did not notice the blush on her cheek.

Lavinia said, "You'll want to go read your sister's letter," which was her roundabout way of discharging Kate from her duties for the time being.

Kate thanked her and ran into the house.

Dearest sisters,

I hardly know where to begin. Life here is a bustle. Everything
is in a state of constant flux. One family arrives and is welcomed
and settled in, and before I can even draw a breath, another
shows up at the gates and requires my attention. I'm sure you
know this, since it's you and Papa who let them in.

Elias is such an extraordinary man. He seems to have
boundless energy. From the moment we all arise until—well,
until after I myself have retired, he tirelessly oversees everything. He works in the fields and in the village. There is no
place here you won't find him. And he asks so little of us all.
We have only to open our hearts and place our souls in his
keeping for life to be good. We *are* God's chosen. He makes us
so.

I know that you desire for me to pay a visit. Your wishes
have been conveyed by Papa and Lavinia through Elias. If time
permits, of course I will come. However, even if it does not,
you know that we shall all be together in eternity soon enough,
and afterward will never be parted again.

I am happy. Really very happy. Please do not think otherwise or worry yourselves on my behalf. Obey Papa in all things
and prepare yourselves for the time to come.

Your loving sister,

Vern

Before giving the letter to Amy, Kate read it through twice.
When she was finished, Amy set it down and said, "She's all
swelled with her position, isn't she? She'll come visit us if time
permits. As if her life is so terribly busy she can't spare even an
hour."

"Exactly," Kate replied. "It's not believable, is it?"

"No," Amy agreed, but she had arrived at a different conclusion than Kate. "She's just full of herself, is all. The same as when she told us she was a woman now because she'd been proposed to, while we were still girls."

"That wasn't what she said, Amy. She even apologized that it sounded so."

Amy would hear none of this defense. She was convinced that Vern was more than happy to have divested herself of both the family and all the chores she had, all of which Amy had inherited, or so she maintained. Papa and Lavinia had given her all Vern's chores as a punishment for her behavior at the wedding.

She'd complained of a terrible headache the day after, but that hadn't kept her father from delivering a protracted lecture about the inherent corruption of her soul and the almost certain damnation awaiting her if she didn't change her ways. Amy would have liked to have told him that she couldn't be damned if she was saved at Harbinger, but her head hurt too much to say anything at all. She just wanted to be left alone. They sent her to her room, but when she emerged, she discovered that she was now expected to do everything that Vern had been responsible for. Kate didn't have to do anything extra. At that point, Amy would have done whatever it took to get married, to get away from the family and the chores. She hated all of them, but Vern especially. She wasn't about to change her opinion of her sister's dismissal of them on Kate's say-so.

Kate dropped the subject. One thing she had learned since Vern's marriage was that, given the choice, Amy would side with Lavinia against her. It seemed to be Amy's method of punishing Kate, although Kate had no idea what she'd done to deserve it. After all, she hadn't gotten drunk at the wedding and she hadn't chosen who did which of Vern's chores. In fact, given who *had* made those choices, it seemed truly perverse that Amy sided with Lavinia on anything. Kate protected herself now by defusing arguments, by walking away from them, by keeping her opinions more to herself. Part of the reason she missed Vern so much was because she missed having someone to share her thoughts with.

The problem with Vern's letter was that it rang so falsely. Vern's proclamations of her happiness seemed too conspicuous,

more as if Vern didn't believe any of it herself but knew she had
to say so. It might have been different if Papa had received the
letter directly from Vern, but since he hadn't, Kate was disin-
clined to believe its contents. Of course Papa's explanation of
why they didn't see her made perfect sense in its way, and should
have set her mind at ease; but it was all somehow too tidy. She
had no more time to dwell upon it then because Lavinia called
them to dinner.

After the meal, Amy went out by herself. Kate had the responsibility of cleaning up, while Mr. Charter and Lavinia retired
to the parlor.

Amy went out to commune with God. She took her Bible and
left the house.

Almost as soon as they'd settled in after Vern's wedding, Amy
had begun to ask permission to go out and "walk with God."
Sometimes it was in the afternoon, sometimes the evening. It
wasn't every day, but she was almost always gone for an hour or
more. Mr. Charter of course approved of her private retreats,
pouncing on them as an indication that his daughter was trying
to make up for her ungoverned behavior at the wedding.

By the time her chores were finished, Kate had no idea where
Amy had gone. Her father and Lavinia were seated in the parlor,
discoursing on the sermon they'd listened to in the village and
on Fitcher's preparations for a crusade to Pittsburgh. "The place
is a locus for many people who are setting forth into the wilderness," explained Mr. Charter. "Many people who are dissatisfied
with their lives. They haven't found fulfillment. They're looking
for something and they hope to find it out in the world where
society has yet to go. It is these minds, these seeking people
whom Reverend Fitcher hopes to persuade. He can offer them
the truth they hunger for. That we all hunger for."

"You'll be going with him?" Kate asked.

"Yes, both of us. You and your sister will be in charge of the
house."

"And Vern, is it likely she'll accompany him, too?"

Mr. Charter puzzled for a moment. "I don't know." He looked
to Lavinia for an answer, and she said, "It's as likely she will as

that she'd stay behind and look after Harbinger while he's gone."

Kate looked out the window. The sun was setting. She wondered suddenly how Amy could read her Bible in the dark. She arose and bid them a good night.

In her room, she sat awhile in the twilight. She held Vern's letter, although she could barely see the writing. Her doubts continued, but were formless, leading her nowhere. Why, she asked the shadows, was she the only one in the house who considered Vern's absence peculiar? Was she simply being willful and impatient, as Lavinia always told her? Yes, she was obstinate, but things that were wrong *ought* to be challenged. Though she didn't wish to admit it, perhaps Vern really was dismissing them in some fashion. Certainly, she knew how to put on airs.

Unhappy with her conclusions, Kate finally removed most of her clothes and lay down in the warm night air.

When Amy returned, the room was dark. She had a candle with her and set it on the dresser. She placed her Bible beside it. Kate's eyes were closed, and Amy quietly took off her shoes, then started to undress. When she drew off her chemise, pine needles and leaves sprinkled out. Amy knelt to sweep them up. When she looked up again, Kate was staring right at her. Guiltily, Amy said, "I was staring at the stars and I tripped over a root. I was with our Lord."

Kate said, "You mean, our Lord the holy wagon driver."

Amy blushed and lowered her head. She gathered up all the debris that had sprinkled out and carried it to the window where she threw it outside.

"What have you been doing, Amy?" Kate's question was too simple to get around, and it implied that Kate already knew what she'd been doing.

Amy had no good story to offer in place of the truth. She finally went to Kate's bed and sat. "You can't tell," she pleaded. "You have to promise you won't. I love him, you can't tell anybody."

"Notaro?" Kate asked. "You love *him?*"

Amy nodded. "He isn't like you think," she said.

"Tell me."

                    *   *   *

It had begun the evening he'd driven them home from Vern's
wedding. He'd helped everybody out of the wagon except for
Amy. Her head still spun from the champagne she'd drunk. She
had one foot on the edge of the wagon but she couldn't figure
out how to navigate from there. Notaro had caught her around
the waist with both hands and lifted her safely to the ground.
Then he'd nuzzled her neck and kissed her. Everyone else was
walking away in the dark, not paying the slightest attention. The
two of them had been kissing at the wedding, too, behind some
bushes, and she hadn't minded at all. Amy had told herself she
was going to discover what Vern bragged about, and really it was
pretty fine. She liked kissing.

At the wagon, however, he only kissed her a little, then he
whispered that he would come calling later on, as soon as things
got back to normal "out at the place."

Afterward, between her fierce hangover and her father's
scolding, she convinced herself that she'd seen the last of him,
that she had been nothing but a quick bit of fun to him.

About three days later, she went out to the privy and he
jumped out of the woods and nearly scared her to death. He had
stood out there for over an hour, hoping to see her. He'd swept
her up in his arms and, laughing, had kissed her again. She wasn't
drunk that time, and she decided that she liked him.

His duties for Harbinger took him into town nearly every
other day for supplies of some kind. Nobody paid much mind to
how long he was gone.

He was rough and uncouth and far too interested in what lay
beneath her clothes, which interest she rebuffed. If that was all
she'd meant to him, he could have driven off right then the way
she half expected he would. But he didn't. He was genuinely
eager for her company, which no one else in the house seemed
to be. Papa was still angry at her, and Lavinia had piled on all
her new chores.

At that first meeting, she and Notaro made a pact to keep an
eye out for each other. She would watch for the wagon, and he

would try to signal her as he went by, so that she'd know whether he would be stopping or not. Usually, he met her on the way back, before he'd reached the pike. That gave her ample time to finish up chores or make herself scarce without anyone noticing where she'd gone. That was when she'd come up with the idea of going off to commune with God.

The next time they met, he told her his first name, which was Michael. She told him they had a spirit living in their walls called Samuel. His arm about her, Notaro snorted and replied, "He can't be of as much use to you as *I* am."

A few times he brought liquor with him, a jug purchased in town just for the two of them. She'd developed a strong fondness for it. She liked the way the world grew softer when she was drinking with Michael Notaro, and she didn't mind the way his hands roamed her body then. She could close her eyes and forget everything else, and lose herself in sensation, in the crinkling of the leaves under her head, in the warmth of his breath, the way his fingers kneaded her.

He had more interest than that in her or she would have spurned him. In any case she wasn't about to let him have his way completely. Vern had told her to always keep something back if she wanted to keep a man interested in her. Of course, Vern had said a lot of things, only some of which were to be believed. The French boy, Henri, hadn't really been the won-derful lover Vern made out—Amy knew it, even though her sisters had hidden the affair from her. But he'd lived just up the street, and she had seen him plenty of times. He hadn't even looked as old as Vern; and Amy had suspected he was in-terested in her, too, though for once she was smart enough not to say so. About not being free with her favors, however, Vern seemed to be right.

Notaro talked about how things were inside Harbinger, es-pecially how strict Fitcher was with the people. Was he mean? she asked. No, that wasn't it. It was just that he expected them to stick to a rigid structure of his devising. One of the most in-flexible requirements was the segregating of the sexes, men from

women. As a result, almost all mixing between them was orga-
nized by Fitcher and under his scrutiny.

Notaro had said, "He knows everything everyone is doing,
even before they do it. Sometimes before they know they're
goin' to do it. Like he can guess at what's in their mind. He come
to my town down south winter before last. My pa's a drunk an'
my ma's no good, and they got no sense of things, 'cept maybe
to kill each other, and me as well. I didn't have nothing and
wasn't going to have nothing later on. Then there comes Elias
Fitcher, telling us all that there ain't gonna be no later on. That
we's all doomed to an eternity in the lives we've made unless we
change our ways. He roped me in with that picture—I sure didn't
want to go through forever with my ma and pa tearing at each
other and me in between. I needed saving more 'n most, and it
was like he could see that. Like he could tell.

"So I followed him here and he puts me to work straightaway.
Hard work, too. I helped the cooper and the 'smith, and even
gutted some steers, but mostly I listened to when he needed
something done, and I always stepped up and did it. And a'fore
long I got kind of important. Like how I got to hold the ring for
your sister. He gives me things to occupy myself. Fill my time,
'cause he knows if I have things to do, I won't think so much
and I won't get into trouble. Idle hands make trouble. So now I
got a place and I don't need nothing else. He says so, he says,
boy, you're better off here than in perdition. We's your family
now and will be forever more. No need to worry about that. This
family forgives, too, he says, but you ain't gonna give people
cause to have to forgive you, are you? Of course, I says no. I
know if I say yes, I'm gonna get chucked right out that gate
before the forgiving starts. Now he forgives me when I do wrong.
Guess I do it plenty, too. He's always forgiving me. He could
forgive Judas. So everyone, they love him, you know, even
though he's a hard man. He has to be, to save us all. To get us
all through the gates.

"And then I seen *you*."

At that moment, Amy had melted. It wasn't just the secret

pleasure of the assignations anymore. It was love, pure and simple.

Elias Fitcher had taught Michael Notaro how to interact, how to be around people, which he hadn't known how to do on his own. Fitcher had prepared him, but he hadn't known what he was being prepared for until Amy had appeared.

The good thing was, she lived outside the community. Inside, too many eyes were watching. Secret meetings were nearly impossible to arrange when everybody was kept so well apart.

If they were careful how they went, there would be no repercussions out here; no one would discover them. And before the end time arrived, Notaro swore, he would get Fitcher's blessing to marry her. They would arrive at "them shinin' gates of Heaven together." Finally, then, he had confessed his love for her, too. There was no one in the world for him except Amy.

"Samuel told Vern that you and I would both have suitors before the time was up," Amy explained. "He was right about Vern, and look, he's right about me. Kate, he's going to be right about you, too. I just know it."

Kate was too astonished by the elaborate deception Amy had orchestrated to dispute it. Whether or not she believed the prophecies of the fugitive ghost, she believed that Amy had found love. Nevertheless, her response to the confession was to take her sister's hands and say, "Please, be very careful, Amelia."

"I will, of course I will, Kate. I have been."

"But *I've* found you out. You mustn't let any others."

"I know." Amy didn't want to dwell on the dangers. She had pretended they didn't exist for too long to confront them now; in the same way, she didn't want to think about how blasphemous it probably was to use God as an excuse this way. But she couldn't help it, she couldn't give up Michael Notaro now.

She got up to finish undressing.

Kate asked, "Amy, has he—has he said anything about Vern? Anything at all?"

Amy felt a slight spark of anger that Kate could still be worried about Vern after what she had just revealed about herself; but she bit it off and instead only replied, "No, he hasn't." She didn't add that she hadn't asked him anything, and had no plans to do so. Vern was the princess in the tower, the one who'd gotten the "happily ever after," and Amy was not going to risk any of her own happiness in order to worry about her.

Seventeen

*V*ERN HAD BARELY RECOV-
ered from her illness when
Fitcher announced he would
be traveling to Pittsburgh on his new campaign. He came to her
with this news as she lay upon her bed, still too weak to be about,
and tended to by the same two women. The white marble egg
lay in the bedclothes beside her. Its powers lost, it had become
a strange source of security for her. Keeping it in sight proved to
her that events that otherwise might have been imaginary had
happened. Its perfect hardness was something she could hold on
to. She could enclose it, hide it in her cupped hands, cling to it
in the sea of sheets. She feared, if she lost the egg now, she would
lose her mind as well.

"Your father goes with me as I asked him to," Fitcher told
her, "and I expect you to run things here at Harbinger while I
and my crusaders are gone." It was a lot to ask of her, he admitted. He wasn't expecting her to conduct sermons or occupy his
duties as the pastor of their church—which, really, he couldn't
have countenanced since she was a woman. She must help the
new arrivals. There were sure to be many; all in need of lodging,

of some job to do. She was to introduce them to other members of the community. "It will occupy your time as well. You must strive to deny these feelings of lust that poured from you while you were ill."

Vern stared accusingly at him. Did he think she was a fool? Did he think the fever had confused her to such an extent that she didn't know what he had done to her before it had struck? She'd had time to work out how she'd been manipulated, maneuvered, blocked at every turn. She vowed then never to let him touch her again, even if she had to stick a pin in herself all night to keep awake. With him gone, she would have time to build a bulwark against him. When he returned, he would find her as obdurate as his egg.

He noted, "Emily and Margaretta both heard the terrible things you said, and I fear they've reported what they heard to others—as I warned you once, the dormitories are nothing but dens of gossip. Of course, everyone knows you were not responsible for the delusions. It was the fever. I delivered a sermon just the other morning on when we are and are not accountable for our actions, and who has any right to cast blame. It's understood that you were *not* accountable. Still, I want you to be aware—some will talk about you, dearest Vern, regardless of my remonstrations." He stepped forward to touch her hair, and she shrank back.

Fitcher lowered his hand, studied his fingers. "I see. You believe even as you recover that I am the fiend you dreamed up in your sickness. I see that distance will be a tonic. When I've been gone a few weeks, I hope you'll recover your reason, and try to see me in a better light. There was a point, I must tell you, when we were all gravely concerned that you had succumbed to the fires of your illness and would have to be sent away, to a hospital for the insane. It was not a happy prospect, for any of us, least of all me." He smiled but his brow was furrowed to show her how grave her situation had been, how close she'd come to being committed.

Her purpose stumbled with that revelation. He was reminding her how easily he could dispense with her. He would only have to say she'd gone mad and let the witnesses do the rest.

"I hope, when I return, you will be able to embrace me with open arms, and then perhaps we can consummate our holy marriage properly."

"Consummate?" What did he mean? Did he think she could forget the first night? She hadn't been asleep on *that* occasion.

"Why, yes. Again, I bear the blame. I was so busy that I postponed and postponed until, really, it was past forgiving. I confess that I suspected you of consorting with others in our flock—oh, yes, the jealousy of a weak man, but I *am* a weak man, and there you were in dishabille in the men's dormitory where no woman is ever to set foot, and my thoughts ran to such dark misgivings of your character for which I entreat you to forgive me. We do not know one another, you and I, though we're married. Truly, I feared to lose you before the appointed day of the Lord's arrival. And then, finally, you fell ill. I hold myself responsible entirely for my early inattentiveness. If only I'd come to you and performed as a proper husband should, perhaps you wouldn't have become so obsessed with coupling that it manifested in your illness in so—so unspeakable a manner. It's my fault, Vernelia. I'm a man who lost sight of what was close to him while so focused upon the well-being of the larger group, acting for the greater good but not for his own. Please, can you forgive me for my blindness?"

She sat still a moment, but finally, slowly nodded her head, more as if to say "We'll see" than in accord. Oh, he spoke cleverly, his words looped around and around her, one story fitting so neatly upon another that she should go dizzy and comply. Assuage his guilt. Promise to be the wife he implied she was not.

Part of her did want everything he had done to become a dream, a nightmare she could dismiss and elude. She desired a normal life, which made her want him to provide one. Him, the villain. She would not be persuaded otherwise.

"Well," he said. "When I come back, we'll begin again, just like the newlyweds we are." He smiled. "I *will* make it up to you, dear Vern. After all, we shall enter the Kingdom together, and after that, everything will be changed. Now, however, I must take my leave of you, and you must suffer a few more rules." He stood and withdrew from his coat the ring of keys he'd shown her once before.

"These are the keys to every door in this house and across our utopia. You can go anywhere, open up any room as is necessitated by circumstance, for who can say what you'll need to do while in charge? But"—he slid his fingers around the one key that was unlike any of the others, the glass one she had noticed the first time he showed her the keys—"this one opens a room that's completely private, a sanctum sanctorum belonging only to me. I tell you, go wherever you like across Harbinger save for this one room. Do not use *this* key." And then he held the ring out to her in such a way that to grab it she had to take hold of the queer and forbidden glass key itself. When she grabbed hold of it, he did not immediately release his grip. For a moment longer the ring bound them.

He said, "There now. And do take care of my little egg while I'm gone." Glancing at her hand wrapped around the blade of the key, he smiled thoughtfully. "You will keep it with you wherever you go?"

"Of course," she said.

"Good. Do these things, and I shall be the happiest of husbands upon my return."

He leaned down and kissed her tenderly on the cheek. She twitched at the smell of him, the scent of that pomade she'd come to know even in slumber, the smell forever a part of her violation. He pressed her hand between his own and stepped back, drawing her arm up until her fingers slid from between his and dropped again to the bed. His teeth flashed within the blue-blackness of his beard. He stepped out the door.

Only then did she realize that she was gripping the glass key so hard it had left an imprint in her palm. The key must have been carved by the same person who'd created the glass skull of Christ on the altar, because the bow of the key was a miniature of that skull. This led her to conclude that it must open something on the altar—possibly some hidden compartment inside the pulpit. She determined she would investigate first thing after he'd gone. Not use the key? How could she not when he had forced it upon her? She tucked the keys beside the egg, curled up, and went back to sleep. It would be weeks before Elias Fitcher returned. The National Road didn't go as far as Pittsburgh. He would have to travel over rough land. Before he came back, she swore, she would find a way out of his utopia, and she would know the truth about him.

She woke and was all alone. It was late afternoon and sunlight made the curtains beyond her head glow molten gold. She lay still and listened to the silence of her room, the distant asymmetrical roar of wind outside, the little creaks of the house; but no voices. No echoes of people. She supposed she had been left unattended quite a bit while she was ill—she certainly would never have noticed—and now they all thought she had recovered. Even Elias had more or less said so.

He would have put me in an asylum.

The thought shouted in the silence. Married—how long now, a month, possibly two? Or was it longer? She didn't know, and realized she'd lost all track of time even before the fever had struck her down. She tried to sort it out, make sense of it, but everything melted together. The days of working, sweating in the tiny shop as she poured candles, dipped candles, twisted wicks and more wicks, emptied one barrel of collected grease and opened another, till her back and arms ached and she no longer knew how many she'd made, if it was dinner or supper's bell she heard. The days seemed to stretch backward into infinity, as if she'd never done anything else. There must have been Sundays, days of rest, but she couldn't recall any. Her life before Harbinger had become a memory borrowed from some other person's past. She'd fallen into the work to hide from herself and from the sense of being kept apart from everything, ostracized by the community, though they hadn't done so openly. Now it all rushed in upon her again. She had set out to lose herself and had accomplished it well. It might be May or June, even July. She had no idea at all.

She sat up and looked past the foot of the bed. There was no fire in the hearth nor evidence of embers, and she couldn't remember the last time there had been one. She could not say with any surety that there'd been fires during or after her illness . . . it *was* after now, wasn't it?

She assured herself that it was. She was herself again and no longer the puppet of a supernatural force, some incubus.

"Incubus." She spoke the word aloud without realizing. The sound of her voice startled her.

Despite the obviousness of the idea, it hadn't occurred to her. What if Elias was telling the truth that he'd never visited her? What if some demon—but no, his words were intended to deceive her, another knot he hoped she wouldn't master. She remembered him, after that first horrible night, remembered his arm as he leaned on the newel post in the dormitory, remembered the scratches on his arm that she'd made. It had been he and no other demon. No one would believe her. If Emily and Margaretta had gossiped, they would think her mad.

She was not mad. She would show them they were wrong.

Vern threw back the covers to climb out of bed, and saw the egg lying upon the mattress, shiny and white. Beside it were the keys to Harbinger.

She picked up the egg and cupped it in her palm. It was nothing extraordinary any longer, just white marble shot with blue veins like a deformed eye. It held no power over her, if it ever had.

Standing, she clutched the nearest pillar of the bed frame; her head spun. The room threatened to tip, but didn't quite. She waited for the sensation to pass before she dressed.

Her clothes felt loose, as though she'd shrunk. Her ribs showed. Between working and the fever, she must have lost a good deal of weight. Her waist was tight and narrow. Her unmentionables could have rotated around her hips.

The light blue dress she picked had a pocket sewn into the frilled bodice, between her breasts, designed for keeping a fan or handkerchief. She took the egg and put it in there; she would keep it with her as he'd requested. The last thing she would have was someone reporting back to him that she had not done as he ordered, had not kept the egg on her at every moment.

She put on her white slippers, the ones they'd bought for her wedding, and after tying the ribbons around her ankles, she took her keys and went out.

In the hallway she stood awhile, listening. The house was so quiet that if she strained hard to hear, she could imagine catching the slightest wisps of whispering. She walked down to the landing and surveyed the foyer, as empty as the day she'd first set eyes on Harbinger. She glanced at the chandelier, at candles no doubt of her own making. She descended.

Like the foyer, the Hall of Worship was empty. Vern cautiously closed the door and crept along to the arch. She peered in. The Christ skull leered upon the altar. The dried gourds and cornstalks had been removed; now the altar was covered in a mantle of crimson velvet. Deep red filled the orbits and recesses of the skull.

She walked down the aisle. Prismatic beams of afternoon light reached from the small stained-glass windows to the dais. Vern circled it. The rear of the pulpit revealed two steps up to the platform on which Elias stood as he preached. A shelf near the top held a silver chamber candlestick and douter. She climbed up the steps, crouching and peering over every inch of the ornately turned wood, the embedded bone crosses and ornaments. She could identify where he placed his hands while he preached, by the smoothness of the wood. There was no hidden door, nor a keyhole of any sort. Her glass key did not fit anything here.

She stood upright in the pulpit and overlooked the room, imagining what it must be like to stand before a roomful of people, commanding their attention, directing them, having them hang upon your every word. But she could think of nothing to say to the vacant pews and got down.

Walking back up the aisle, she glanced at the windows, recalling how on the day of her wedding she could see the silhouettes of people milling about outside the chapel. Now no one stood there.

The dining hall was deserted, as well. She wondered how many people could have gone off with him? Surely not everyone. And in fact she could smell food being prepared in the kitchen beyond. She ought to go and help out, as kitchen duties must now be shared by fewer people, and so each dinner shift must change. It wasn't near dinnertime yet—the clock on the landing had shown the time at half past three. Nevertheless she left convinced that everyone was hiding from her.

It's like a dream, she thought, *where you search and search but never find what you want, and something always seems to be moving where you aren't looking.*

Vern exited to the back porch. She faced the house, keys in her hand. One of them must lock up the outside doors. She looked at the lock in front of her and tried to find a key that looked as if it matched. It took her a while to find the one that fit that door. She walked the length of the porch then, locking and unlocking the doors—the same key fit all of them.

Elias hadn't said directly, but she supposed she was responsible for locking up the house at night. But did he lock it? Was the house *ever* locked up? Just because there was a key to a door didn't mean it should be locked. Who would it be locked against?

She left off pondering and stood awhile against the rail. Out across a landscape burnt orange by the sun, she could see people at work on the far side of the orchard. They might have been tilling. Just the sight of them put her heart at ease: She had not been abandoned.

She climbed down and set off for Harbinger village.

Her path was indirect—she wanted to see someone else up close, and there was a cluster of people standing about the newly turned fields. She wandered over to them and bid them all a good afternoon. They smiled and welcomed her in the usual, traditional manner. Beyond the greeting no one had anything to say. Their attention returned to the tilling and planting as if they anticipated something exciting was about to happen in the soil at any moment. Vern watched them until she understood that none of it included her. She continued on her way. Those nearest bid her farewell, as if she were about to travel far from them.

The candle shop stood in the shadows of the buildings across the lane. There were no lights within—no one else had taken over her duties. She could not remember in what state she'd left it. What she found stunned her. The shop was stacked full of boxes, and each of them contained dozens of candles packed in straw. There might have been a thousand candles in the boxes in that room. Half-finished candles still dangled by their looped wicks from the ceiling rack. She touched one of them, her fingers sliding down the greasiness of it. Grease had pooled on the table below, and the candle was too spindly to be useful. The kettle, half full of congealed spermaceti, stood at one end of the table. She must have abandoned the work after only a few dippings.

The molds were all full. She hadn't put away the last batch she'd made. Maybe she'd been unable to find a box. She couldn't remember where she'd found all of the others stacked here. Had the cooper made them for her? She didn't remember asking him, although she remembered a face that she thought was his.

She had thought until then that she would return to her duties; now she saw how unnecessary that was. There were months and months worth of candles here—enough to last the summer. No wonder she'd caught a fever. She had exhausted herself.

The bell sounded at the house, calling the community to dinner. How many shifts would there be now? Even if she couldn't eat during the first shift, she wanted to see how many people were on hand. She left the shop and the duties of candle-making behind.

Tomorrow, she would explore Harbinger itself. The utopia was huge. Vast. Elias had said as much. She closed her hand around the ring of keys. She intended to go everywhere.

Eighteen

*V*ERN TOOK HER MEAL IN A
half-filled dining hall. The
shifts, it seemed, were run-
ning as always, only with fewer people. The system had been
determined without her participation, despite Elias's assertion
that she was in charge. The emptiness of the refectory suggested
that a hundred or more must have accompanied him. During the
meal she knew better than to ask—no one would have answered
her.

Afterward, she assisted in the kitchen, washing dishes and
utensils in a large tin sink filled with water that had been heated
to near-boiling on the stove. A slight, older woman named Sarah
worked beside her. When she asked how many had gone, Sarah
answered that she didn't know, because they'd been gathered
from all over the whole of Harbinger and she hadn't been on
hand to see them leave. "Took my Daniel, though," she added
proudly. "It's a rare and special thing to go with the reverend.
Rare and special." By implication neither she nor Vern could consider themselves special. One of the men, overhearing, told her
it had been " 'bout a hundred," but he was contradicted by both

Sarah and another woman, Sarah insisting it hadn't been more
than half that—"no, *only* the very special, like my Daniel"—and
the other woman saying it was at least two hundred.

Sarah patted her shoulder and, in apparent misunderstanding
of her frustration, advised her, "Try not to worry yourself, dear.
It's your first time separated, and that's hard for any woman to
bear. I been without my Daniel twice before. But you both gonna
be together for eternity soon enough, and there's nothing can
stand in the way of that, 'cause that's God's will, that is."

Vern made herself smile, and thanked Sarah for her consideration. She turned back to scrubbing at the plates, but Sarah
wasn't finished. She said, "You'll want to rest up, girl, get your
strength back so that when he returns, you can greet him proper."
The statement might have been innocuous, but Sarah seemed to
leer as she said it.

Vern stood at the sink, almost afraid to look at the faces of
the others for fear they would all be grinning in the same grotesque way. Did they somehow know the intimate details of her
life with Elias? She glanced sidelong at Sarah, but the older
woman was stacking up plates with innocent efficiency, seemingly thoughtless and content, as if that look of depravity had
only been in Vern's mind. Riddled as she was with self-doubt,
she thought it just might. No one was going to accuse this petite
old woman of lewdness.

Vern quit the kitchen at the first opportunity and retreated
to her room. As always, the second floor was deserted. Without
women attending to her, the sense of isolation was complete.
Comforted at first by the distance, she soon became uneasy. The
solitude became oppressive, not as if she were alone but rather
as if she were surrounded by a population already become ethereal. The whole house hovered in between moments of time;
even the dark clock on the landing held silent, the hands motionless, until she arrived at the top of the stairs and set everything in motion again. The community waited for her and never
blinked.

She got up and opened the window at the head of her bed,

and let the evening breeze in. It billowed the gauzy curtains. She lit a candle and tried to read from her Bible: "And when he was come to the other side of the country of the Ger-ge-senes, there met him two possessed with devils, coming out of the tombs . . ." Devils and tombs—her mind could not focus on the words. She read whole pages of Matthew without any sense of what they were about. Without realizing, she was straining to hear something.

The breeze carried the hint of distant voices, brief laughter. Absurdly, she imagined that someone somewhere was laughing about her, despite which she wanted to fly there, to take part in the conversation, even laugh at herself, making light of her situation: "Oh, yes, I was quite out of my head when I said those things. Do you know, I actually thought my husband was some sort of nocturnal demon himself."

She needed the company of others. There were so many unanswered questions that someone in the community must have answers to. What was the fearsome Dark Angel? How many people had taken their own lives here? Was it only the end of the world that frightened them? The idea remained so abstract to her.

She closed her Bible. The last question surprised her, but as soon as she'd thought it, she knew it was true. Everyone *was* afraid. Now her picture of them changed—from clockwork mechanisms to quivering rabbits, so terror-struck that they rushed to judgment, condemned too quickly, took their own lives out of fright.

The end of the world was coming and they couldn't do anything about it, couldn't stop it or change it. Couldn't be certain if they were saved or not.

They were like Amy, weren't they? So sure of their evil core and damned for it despite anything good they'd ever done. Amy hadn't always been like that. Vern could recall how her father had come back that first time from the tent meeting on the commons. The Reverend Fitcher had preached a sermon that persuaded him, and in turn he had explained it to all three girls. Perdition awaited them, it should be expected sooner than anyone imagined, but they might yet save themselves if they followed Fitcher's precepts. Amy had responded as if she'd believed all along that she was corrupt and was free at last to admit it. Maybe the kind of people who enlisted in Elias Fitcher's cause despised themselves the way Amy did. But Vern didn't want to hate herself. What she did hate was what this calling of the world's end had stolen from her.

Abandoned in the midst of hundreds of people who resented her insertion between them and their intermediary to God, she had been *wed* to the harbinger. She was the bride of death, his concubine, his victim. She had no friends here, nor ever would, before or after the world's end. They must all hate her, like that woman who wouldn't let her eat.

For an hour perhaps she lay upon her bed in the throes of self-absorbed despair. Then at some point, out of the darkness spilled music.

Like the earlier voices it ebbed and flowed with the breeze, distant, tantalizing. She had forgotten how music could sound.

She sat up, perched, listened. There—voices whooped in with the instruments. There—a fiddle most certainly, and a piano, and another sound that brayed beneath them.

She picked up the keys, then stopped; turned and placed them on the bed. She removed the marble egg from the pocket between her breasts and set it down there, too. She knew this defied her promise to Elias, but she felt these things did not belong with her when she didn't know where she was going. Surely they would be safer here.

Once outside, Vern had no trouble following the sound. It came from down in the village, from the big barn on the far side of the ironsmith's. There were people hollering, joyous.

The barn was open. There must have been fifty or more people dancing, and another fifty milling about. Candles and lamps were lit not just in the barn but in places along the street. The light and the noise spread an exuberance through the night.

People looked Vern's way. They saw her and stopped talking. But she went to them, full of a brand-new resolve, and said, "Hello," and "Please don't spurn me, don't shun me, I'm no different than you. I'm alone here." She would *not* be the wife of death. She would be herself, vital and young and kind. She couldn't tell what effect her words were having—she kept trying different ones, hoping to see someone break out in a smile that would tell her she'd made them understand her plight. At least they didn't flee from her, and the music and dancing didn't stop on account of her. Fiddle and piano, and someone cranking the handle of a stringed hurdy-gurdy—*that* was the exotic whine.

She entered the barn, and a young man sitting on a bale of hay by the door jumped up and said, "Here, sit here, Mrs. Fitcher." Vern gawked at him—he couldn't have been any older than she was. The name he called her felt as if it belonged to someone else. How old she must be to be thought of as "Mrs. Fitcher." It was the way she didn't want anyone to think of her, but she accepted his offer and sat on the bale. She took in the crowd, many of them staring back. Even some of the dancers as they spun by cast her a glance. She felt tears welling up but refused to give in. She made a brave face, wanting them to see how happy she was to be in their company. She glanced aside to find that the young man had left her, but when she turned back it was as if she'd passed some test, or a cloud had rolled out from behind the moon and banished the doubtful shadows. Dancers had stopped paying her any mind. Others met her gaze with a smile, a true welcome.

The young man came back shortly. He offered her an earthenware cup. "It's only hard cider," he said, "left from the winter." She took it and thanked him. He nodded and remained standing beside her. There was plenty of room on the hay, she thought, and moved over, then gestured for him to sit. He performed a slight bow before seating himself. She almost giggled at his formality.

"I'm Lanny," he said. "It's really Orlando, Orlando Gibbons. I got named after a musical composer, though most nobody's heard of him. Everybody calls me Lanny." He was a little taller than she. His hair, she saw up close, was actually a brown that had been burned lighter by the sun. His thin beard was a little darker.

"Then I shall, too. You must call me Vern, then."

"Vern," he repeated, nodding.

She sipped the cider, which was cool and sharp. "I didn't know anyone danced here," she said. "I wasn't sure . . . how we felt about dancing."

"We didn't dance in the winter much, on account of it's too cold," he explained. "But now it's warmer, we'll dance on Friday nights sure enough."

"You sound like you've been here awhile."

"Since the groundbreaking of the house," Lanny said proudly. "I was fifteen. Come here with my family." He pointed at the dancers as if all of them might be his family—she couldn't identify who he meant. "The reverend, your husband, he says dancing is God's pleasure."

"Does he? I didn't know."

"He told us about Sister Anne of the Shakers and how she allowed them dancing even though about everything else they might have done was forbidden. And how after she died, they still went right on dancing, in order to communicate with her spirit. So dancing, he said, moved them up closer to Heaven."

She surveyed the crowd again, looking for the kind of ecstasy he described. "And do you move closer to Heaven?"

He blushed and lowered his eyes. "Sometimes, ma'am. When I have the chance."

She set down her cup. "Well, I've never done. Would you show me how?"

"You don't know how to dance?" he asked, incredulous.

"Oh, I know how to *dance*, but I've never flown to Heaven on account of it." She tried to keep a serious face, but her mouth trembled. He laughed, realizing that he'd been teased, and the moment made her nearly burst into tears. The burden of her doubts, so heavy an hour ago, was lifted for the first time since she'd arrived.

Standing, he offered her his hand. "I hope you know how to contredanse and galop."

She replied, "I think I can do those," with some bravado. "Contredanse" could mean just about anything here. She would have to watch closely.

They moved through the crowd to the last position just as a new sequence was beginning. The beat of the dance was easy to find, and Vern watched and followed only a fraction of a second behind the woman in the line beside her. She hadn't done a quadrille in a while but it came back almost immediately. Lanny crossed the floor and she passed him, and then turned, switching places. Then he took her hand and they half promenaded, turned, and separated.

The second figure of the set began with them approaching and retreating. People were laughing, enjoying themselves however they went. The energy filled her. Lanny caught her hand and passed her to the next gentleman. He was grinning at her as he did.

They proceeded on through the third and fourth, returning to their partners, falling in line beside one another with faces turned away, promenading once more. Then she moved into the ladies' chain and from there into the step called the great round, which this time ended in a galop, as Lanny had implied. It caught Vern by surprise—she recovered almost immediately, but the surprise was a delight, and she burst out laughing. After that she lost herself in the dance, counting her steps, minding her position as the top of the line became the bottom and the first figure of steps began again.

She danced and whirled, and everyone who took her hand was friendly and as carefree as she felt.

When the tune stopped, everyone applauded the musicians; Lanny led her over to a middle-aged couple. The man was heavy

and half bald. He was flushed from dancing. His lady had sparkling eyes and the same beaked nose as her son. Her teeth were
bad, though, and she smiled with her lips pressed together.
Lanny introduced them as his parents. When they heard who she
was, their receptive expressions stiffened for an instant, barely
noticeable, but enough to bring Vern back to herself.

She said, "Your son is very kind to dance with me. And I see
how he has come to know the dance so well."

"You did not travel with your husband," said the father.

He was stating the obvious, and she knew some explanation
was expected. "I was ill for some days, Mr. Gibbons—weeks actually, I think—and he didn't want to risk my falling ill again
while traveling."

"It is hard on the road," he agreed.

"But you aren't ill now," said the mother, her tone identical
to her husband's. Without asking, without truly intimating anything, they were questioning her behavior, doubting her inten-
tions. Did they think she'd come here to tempt their son?

"No, I am much mended—I didn't know how well until I
took a few turns upon the floor."

The music began again.

"It is good to open oneself up to the beauty of God this way,"
said the mother.

"Yes," answered Vern, "it brings us all closer to Heaven." She
glanced at Lanny as she said it.

"That's right," the mother replied. "That's just so right."

Her husband said, "The reverend has attended the dances
from time to time, but he so rarely dances himself."

She couldn't fathom what criticism this implied; perhaps the
man meant simply that Elias had no partner before her. Was he
inviting her to change that? "I cannot say, sir, how he goes," Vern
replied. "It was my own opinion of dancing I expressed, not my
husband's."

"Oh."

"We have not—he and I—had much time together since I
arrived, and dancing has not even been discussed. He's had so
much planning to do. The date and all—"

Lanny's mother pressed her hands together and bowed her head a little. Father and son followed. "The end time is nearer every hour, isn't it?"

"Sometimes," Vern said, "that's very hard to forget."

The couple exchanged perplexed glances, as if unable to decide what she could mean by that.

Then the father took his wife's hands and asking, "One more dance, Mother?" led her toward the middle of the barn.

"And for you, Mrs. Fitcher?" Lanny asked. "It's going to be a Virginia Reel this time."

"Please, Lanny, I'd like that very much." They moved to take their places as the dancing began anew.

As the night wore on, the Gibbons family introduced Vern to others in the barn, most of whom were happy to have her in their company. Some spoke of Judgment Day with an implicit understanding that she was on intimate terms with Fitcher about it and so might tell them things. They talked about what they hoped to find afterward or, whether they felt themselves prepared to face God. Most seemed to feel they had banished their sins and cleansed themselves. They owed their cleansing to her husband. It was Reverend Fitcher who had shown them the path they must follow. Everyone knew far more about the end of time than she did, as they all seemed to know more about her husband. The former they shared, but whatever they knew about Elias Fitcher as a person, they kept to themselves. Certainly the dance was not the place for confrontation, and she didn't want to confront anyone for fear that she would lose the friendliness she'd just gained. There would be plenty of time to winnow his secrets. After all, he must be gone for weeks yet.

Having danced herself to near-exhaustion, Vern finally wandered back to the house and her room. Though her legs ached, she felt wonderful.

The room was dark. The candle she'd left burning beside her Bible must have guttered—it was too new to have burned away.

She fumbled her way to the mantel and found the container of matches, then knelt and sparked one, putting the flame to a bit of kindling in the hearth. From that she lit a spunk, which she used to light the oil lamp on the mantel and the candles around the room. Afterward, she removed her dress.

From the bed she scooped up the keys. She stopped, paralyzed. The egg wasn't there.

She knew she'd placed it beside the keys. It could not possibly have rolled off. She carefully patted the covers all around, as if the egg might have sunk through them. She got on her knees and peered under the bed. There were clumps of dust there but no egg. She stood, turning, glancing at every surface, none of which supported the egg. She thought: *What will I say? How can I tell him I lost it?* He would not understand—after all she'd sworn to keep it with her every moment everywhere. She'd been so careful with it, how could it not be here? Someone had come into her room while she was gone. She realized now that she should have taken the keys, if only to lock her door. Of course Elias had entrusted someone to keep an eye on her—maybe that Notaro fellow. She hadn't seen him since before she'd taken ill, but maybe that was because he was spying on her.

He would tell Elias what she'd done—how she'd gone out for an evening of pleasure and left the egg and keys in her room for anyone to take. She felt shamed, though she'd done nothing to be ashamed of. Why did she feel as if she'd betrayed him by enjoying herself?

Finally, overcome with a sense of doom, she tucked one foot beneath her and sat on the bed in her chemise. She knew she would never be able to sleep now. She lifted her pillow to hug.

The marble egg rolled out from beneath it.

"Oh, God, oh, thank God," she sighed. She clutched it in both hands and pressed it to herself. It was safe. She was safe. Yet its appearance did not answer the question of how it had come to *be* under the pillow. She vividly recollected the bed as she'd left it; the egg could not have rolled there on its own. She looked across at the door. From now on she must be more careful.

There were agents at work here, whoever they were, whatever their purpose.

In the morning, after closing her door, she fumbled through the ring of keys until she found the one that locked it. The glass key attracted her attention again, and she wondered again what lock it could possibly fit. Somewhere in the house lay the answer, but she did not want to be in the house today.

Outside, the air smelled as if it had been washed of its sins. Today she would explore the boundaries of Harbinger.

The dining hall was half-filled again. Some of the people she had met last night were there and she greeted them with a formal nod. She took a plate of buckwheat cakes and apple butter, sat silent and ate. Afterward, she assisted in grilling cakes for the next shift of diners, then in cleaning. Where she'd felt ostracized in their company only last night, the dance had changed her. Vern now thought of herself as an integral part of a larger process. She greeted Sarah, who told her, "You look better today, dear. It's good you rested." Rather than contradict or explain herself, she agreed. "I'm very good today, Sarah, thank you." She decided she had misapprehended a clumsy smile from Sarah for something coarse and troubling—that was the degree to which she'd been confused. She'd give them all benefit of doubt now. They were all parts of God's plan, these people. They only wanted to be saved.

Later, when no one was looking, she took a Johnnycake that had been made for the afternoon meal and folded it up in some paper and put it in her pocket with the keys. Then she ventured out onto the back porch. People were wandering across the open lawn, back to the fields or the village or the orchards. Whoever remained in the house, she still hadn't discovered. Someone must, as things were always dusted, always polished.

With her hands in her pockets, she went down the steps and across the yard herself. She clutched the egg and the keys. She would not leave them behind again.

*   *   *

She walked past her shop, past the ironsmith's and to the barn where she'd danced last night. Rather than continue past it to the church, where there might easily be a swarm of people, she turned, walking between the livestock pens and henhouses that lay beyond. Chickens clucked and strutted around a narrow yard dusted with a scattering of feathers. A smokehouse stood apart from the livestock. Thin bluish smoke rose from it.

A man in a dirty apron was standing just beyond the smoke-house. He was rolling a cigarette, his hands dark with charcoal. He glanced up in surprise at the sound of her approach. Over the little paper as he rolled it, his eyes followed her. Otherwise he might not have noticed her at all. Vern wondered if he would report her whereabouts to Elias. Whatever she did, wherever she went, it seemed that someone was sure to see her; but the way through the village was labyrinthine, and with luck it would disguise her destination, too. Even if the smoker reported that he'd seen her, he wouldn't be able to swear where she was heading. The next lane took her past an abattoir, which stank of blood and offal. Beyond it stood an empty corral. The far side of the corral consisted of a six-foot-high board fence, and Vern turned there. The fence hid her until she had topped a low rise, and the lane had become a ragged path.

The path led down to a series of rolling rises—too small to be called hills—of cleared pasture. Soon enough she encountered grazing cattle. Farther away there were sheep, though she didn't spy a shepherd.

Eventually the pasture gave way to woods. At the edge of it, Vern paused to look back. Only the church steeple and the top of the barn located the village beyond the grazing sheep. Harbinger House seemed too tiny to be threatening. The pyramid at the top shone like a spike of silver.

Once in the trees, she had no trouble following the path. It was more of a cart path, rutted by wheels. She soon heard a kind of roaring as well as a metronomic metal squeal. The source of both appeared soon enough—a stone mill set on the banks of a nearby stream. Its wheel produced the rhythmic noise. Elias had said they had their own mills for flour and flax. As she approached the mill, the path divided. The left-hand fork looked as if it wound back in the direction of the village. The right fork led past the mill and deeper into the woods, and she followed that one. When she could no longer hear the squeaky wheel, she stopped and listened to the sound of the woods—the calls of birds, the buzz of insects, and overhead the occasional creak of a branch, the shush of leaves in the breeze. It was cooler in the woods, but it was also pleasant. The woods smelled alive.

She contemplated the possibility of finding a way out of the enclosure, an escape from Harbinger and back home, but with less urgency now than before.

The path narrowed to a trail, still identifiable, but obviously not used for carts or anything with wheels. She didn't even see horse's prints in the soil. Off to her left, she caught occasional flashes of sunlight on the surface of the stream.

She felt as if she walked for miles. The path snaked around outcroppings of rock, and the ground was never smooth, always broken with stones and roots. She tripped a few times, and wished she'd worn something other than soft slippers. She needed boots for this. After a while she unwrapped the sweet cornmeal Johnnycake and ate it.

By now she had lost sight of the stream, so she was surprised by the sound of distant splashing. The ground grew more rocky underfoot. She had to be careful of how she went.

The path split again. She followed it to the left, toward the noise. Beneath the splashing, another noise grew, a kind of hollow roaring.

Within a minute she had climbed up a rocky rise and was stepping out onto a broad promontory. The view if not the climb robbed her of breath.

She stood above a sheer drop hundreds of feet to the floor of a canyon. The stream she had glimpsed emerged from the rocks off to the left of the promontory. It was much larger than it had appeared through the woods. The falling water created a spectacular waterfall down to a wide pool, and another stream, which snaked along the floor of the gorge below. Where the cascade fell it made a rainbow, a great banded sheet of color hovering in the air.

This had to be the same gorge they had crossed on the way to Harbinger. Somewhere around the bend would be the bridge itself. She must be beyond the wrought-iron fence, but there was no point in fencing this off. Nobody could have climbed up or down from here.

She stood on the promontory a long time. The waterfall to her felt like God, like something huge and beautiful—more like God than anything at the house; even the Hall of Worship with its windows and great ceiling, its skull and pulpit, was dwarfed by the grandeur of this.

She wondered how God could choose to destroy a world so beautiful. It saddened her to imagine all this, outside the perimeter of Harbinger, being obliterated. The sadness made her long to see her family again. She felt then that she must get home. She must see Kate and Amy, Papa. Even Lavinia. Yes, even the gorgon.

Vern turned and clambered back down the rough slope too fast. Her foot slipped and she fell, scraping her hands. Sharp rock jabbed her hip. She scrambled up immediately, angry with herself for being so stupid, in such a panic. Exercising more caution, she made her way back to the path and went on. Her palm had a stone in it that she pried out, then licked the blood away to see the puncture. It wasn't too terrible.

The path seemed to parallel the gorge. She hoped it would take her outside the fence by the time she'd reached the bridge. But already the distance between path and gorge was widening. The path, weaving around natural obstacles, was leading her away from it. Worried, she tried to make her way through the woods, but the bushes snagged at her clothing. Her wide skirt wasn't intended for wildernesses. Thorns pricked her legs, snagged her stockings. She tried to avoid them, but they grew everywhere. Off the path, the woods seemed to be full of them, blending into the underbrush, a cunning barrier.

She tried to make her way so as to avoid them, but kept the edge of the cliff always in sight.

Ahead were stripes of darkness, trees behind trees, receding into dim distance, but Vern's attention remained fixed upon the location of the gorge. She would not stray too far from it.

Then suddenly the dark stripes had marched up before her and she raised a hand protectively and stopped. She had nearly collided with the fence.

It had been built right up to the edge. She clutched the bars and pushed her face into the space between them. There was the bridge, five hundred yards distant beyond the bend, a cruel glimpse of freedom and impossible to reach. Where the wrought iron ended, a person might have been able to swing out and around to the other side, but they would have to be willing to dangle in space with nothing below them and nothing to hold on to but the black uprights. The cliff offered no purchase. She could picture herself falling to her death.

She had also inadvertently rejoined the path. Narrower now, it ran along the inside of the fence. At least she wouldn't have to navigate more thorns to get back. She would simply follow the fence.

It brought her out of the woods between the orchard and the house, and just on the edge of a cemetery. There were dozens of small headstones. One grave looked newer than the others, and she supposed it must have been that of Bill, the man who'd hanged himself, although that surely happened months ago. The rest didn't look very old, either: A lot of people had died in just the few years Harbinger had existed.

People were working in the fields; others in the orchard were wrapping something around the smaller trees, probably to keep deer away. The afternoon meal had surely come and gone. There was nothing to do but return to the house.

She glanced up. Sunlight flared off the glass of the pyramid at the top, creating a spectrum, reminding her of the waterfall in the gorge. Behind the colors, something moved. There was someone up there, someone inside the pyramid.

Vern stood awhile, watching. Her hand moved into her pocket and curled around the keys. Her fingers identified the larger glass one. Her mouth set in determination. She was going to get up there.

It was time to learn Harbinger's secrets.

Nineteen

*T*HE FOYER WAS DESERTED WHEN she entered it, but she encountered Margaretta on the stairs. The dark-haired Margaretta said, "Ah, I vas looking for you to see if you vere *wohl*. When you did not come for the meal."

Vern made a smile. "I'm fine, thank you. I went for a walk in the woods."

"So," was Margaretta's reply, as if that summed everything up. She patted Vern's shoulder and continued down the steps. If she had noticed the condition of Vern's clothing, she gave no indication.

Vern reached her room, locking the door after her. Setting the keys and the egg on top of the commode, she took off her dress, now stained and torn. Her hands were dirty, her calves scratched, hosiery all but ruined. She poured water in the basin and rinsed her hands and face. She stuffed the ruined dress inside the armoire, and put on the blue dress she'd worn the previous night. It wasn't fresh, but at least it wasn't in need of stitching.

She picked up the keys again, but stood before the commode

awhile, staring at the egg, debating whether to take it or not; but remembering how it had disappeared beneath the pillows the night before, she finally slipped the egg into the small kerchief pocket between her breasts again before going out.

The hallway was dark and silent. While she intended to find the stairs up to the pyramid, she wanted most to find Elias's rooms. She wasn't forbidden to seek out those, unless the glass key turned out to be the key that opened them. Even if it was, she was half determined to use it.

She crossed to the first door on the opposite side. Although it was identical to hers, it didn't take the same key. There were six keys on the ring that looked identical. On her third try she chose the one that fit the door.

The room inside was a near-mirror image of her own, with a single bed and sparse furniture. It was musty, and heavy drapes hung over the window, letting in only a glow of daylight, but enough for her to make out cobwebs and dust. It was a room for ghosts. Clearly, no one lived here, and hadn't from the time the house had been constructed.

She closed and locked the door, then tried the next. The same key opened it, and she supposed the keys and locks might be identical on different sides of the hall. This second room was like the one beside it and hers, save that the bed had no canopy but was low with black iron rails, and the walls were painted some greenish color. The drape had slipped from the rod above the window, letting in much more light, which gave the room a sub-marine essence. It was not as dusty as the first, but just as empty.

Guest rooms, she thought as she closed the door. He'd said as much, hadn't he? But aside from Reverend Fitcher and herself, what guests were expected? If everyone else lived in dormitories, then who were these rooms meant for? Probably because she occupied one, she thought the rooms seemed inherently femi-nine, although admittedly there was nothing in their composition to indicate it, save perhaps for the canopy beds.

Methodically she opened every door on the second floor, first down one side and then down the other. Most of the rooms were the same. Disused. Vacant. Had they not seemed so utterly lifeless, she might have thought they belonged to Elias's inner circle—to those who had accompanied him. However, a few—those farther back on her side of the hall—suggested some more recent use. In the one next to hers there were dead flowers in a vase, a locked wardrobe, tortoiseshell brushes, and a pair of small boots. The boots were dusty, but not terribly so. *Some*one had lived there not so long ago.

She passed her own room again, but didn't open it, admitting to an absurd fear that if she did, she would find it as dusty and barren as the rest.

When she'd opened every room on the second floor, she knew Elias's quarters weren't there. More than that, she knew she was the only person living on the floor. Her earlier sense of isolation had proved true.

She descended the steps to the landing, where she chose the alternate staircase, the one that led to the third floor. All this time she'd known it was there, but not once had she looked up at the long steep climb or considered how odd this arrangement of stairways was.

Unlike the stairs below, these had no runner. They were plain pine coated with a yellowish varnish and reminded her of the stairwell in her house, the one to the attic. The enclosed stairwell was narrow and claustrophobic, offering little headroom. She held on to the railing and went up. At the top hung a drapery, parted in the middle. Beyond it was a hallway like the one below if significantly darker. Doors lined both walls. She wished she'd brought a candle, and had to fumble through the keys, holding them up against the brighter patch of light between the drapes to identify them.

Despite this handicap, it took her only two tries to find one that fit the first door. The handle rattled loosely in its collar as she turned it. The door creaked on its hinges. The room was in better shape than those below. It wasn't dusty at all, although it was curtained, with only a little sunlight spilling through the slit between. It smelled, not of mustiness, but of sweat, of recent habitation. The narrow foyer opened onto a larger room, and someone could easily have been hiding out of sight there. She

didn't think so—the room didn't feel occupied—but she was reluctant to enter. She backed out and closed and locked the door
again.

When she put the key to the next door, it opened. It had
been hanging on the latch, unlocked. This one smelled worse,
giving off the reek of a chamber pot that needed changing. Vern
thought, as the door swung open, that in the dim recesses something shifted; but the odor was like a barrier, and she didn't even
want to call out. Whoever could exist in that atmosphere was not
someone she wanted close by. She withdrew, and closed the door
firmly after her. For a moment she hesitated, then locked the
door. If someone *was* lurking in there, she would not give them
the chance to surprise her.

At the third door, Vern thought to knock. There was no reply,
but the door was also unlocked. Inside, the remains of a candle
was burning on a small dresser, with wax pooled around it. It
might have been burning for hours. The little flame threw
enough light upon the wall above it for her to see that someone
had written something there. She crept inside, leaned her head
around the corner far enough to see the rest of the room. It was
empty. In fact, except for the small desk, there wasn't even any
furniture. She turned her attention to the writing above the candle. The words had been written in a spiraling circle, beginning
in the center and whirling outward. They read: "And I saw the
dead, small and great, stand before God. And the books were
opened."

Almost the instant she finished reading it, she was overwhelmed by the sensation of someone behind her. She turned
quickly. The doorway was empty. No one was there, but now the
sensation enveloped her again—someone was behind her in
the *room*. She swung around, her arm out to ward anyone off.
The room was barren. Quickly she retreated, slammed the door,
and locked it.

It took her a moment to cast off the terror she'd conjured.
She put her hand to her breast, felt the lump of the egg there.
"Stupid," she muttered, "you're acting like Amy." Amy could
scare herself to death if left alone for two minutes; and Vern

smiled, thinking about her. She had to go home after this. She had to get away from Harbinger. For now, however, she stiffened her resolve to finish what she'd started.

She crossed the hall and tried the first three doors on that side. The same key didn't work those, and she spent time finding the one that did: as with the second floor, one key for each side of the hall.

The rooms were mirror images of each other. One stank of cigars, another of a fire that had been doused, perhaps upon her approach, she couldn't say, but the room was smoky. Where the almost abandoned second floor had borne an unmistakable feminine aspect, this one was utterly male. The dwellers in the dark here were men, she was certain of it.

Dark angels. Dark angels, the way the spirit of Samuel in her house was a dark angel. He hadn't harmed her. Yet in her dreams, in the dark warped halls not so unlike this house, something malefic had pursued her.

Vern looked at the other doors and decided that she didn't need to open any more of them. Elias did not live here, either. She wasn't going to find his room, not on this floor, either. She was certain of it.

The last one on the right was a smaller door than the rest, as to a cupboard. This end of the hall was too dark, however, for her to make out anything distinct. She tried the key she'd used for the other doors along that side, and it was too large to fit.

Once again, she held the keys up one at a time against the brightness emerging from between the now distant drapes; but even that didn't help her much. It was certainly not the lock for the glass key. It would, she suspected, prove to be a cupboard.

She stepped back, leaning to steady herself against what she thought was solid wall, and nearly toppled backward. Quickly she caught herself, stumbling.

She squinted into the gloom. The hall's end was not a wall. A vertical line of casing was just visible as a stripe that wasn't quite as dark as that which lay in the center. She reached out, touching it, touching stone. And in that black center, what seemed like blank wall was in fact a recess. She dared to stick her hand into the darkness, touching nothing. The air was much colder, though, as if a draft flowed up through the floorboards. She edged forward, hand extended, until she touched the door.

It had to be black, because she could see nothing of it. Her fingers felt inset panels slick with a rime of ice, the spade shape of a large hinge, and across from it the lock stile and handle and keyhole. When her hand passed before the keyhole something flashed. She moved her hand back, watching a point of light flow across her palm. Crouching down, she peered into a keyhole.

It was a large hole, but afforded her nothing more than a nondescript view of something bright with reflected color—the lip of something, a bathtub perhaps.

She took hold of the handle to stand. It was thin and elegant, knurled, and icy cold. She snatched back her hand, placed it against her breast, and felt the lump of the egg there. The air seemed to come alive with a tiny whispering voice that she knew was only in her head—an interior voice compelling her, urging her.

Would this give her the access to the pyramid or let her into the secret rooms her husband kept? Instinct told her which key to use. It was obvious. It had to be *that* key.

She remembered what her husband had said. She knew he didn't want her to enter his private domain: the chamber of Elias Fitcher. The truth of him. But all the admonishments in the world couldn't have kept Vern from fitting the shaft of that key into that hole. It slid in as if the one fluidly embraced the other. Turned and pushed the mechanism with such lubricated slyness that she hardly felt the bolt release. Standing in that cold spot, as the door inched inward she sighed, and it seemed the door was hissing at her, releasing a kept atmosphere around her, drawing her in, her hand upon the handle as if frozen to the metal, unable to release it, unable any longer to escape her fate.

Light spilled down just inside the doorway, a wedge of brightness casting everything behind it into murkiness. The air from the hall collided with the chill in the chamber and produced a mist, a sparkling, smoky membrane before her.

The colors and light came from a large stained-glass panel

fitted into the ceiling. It showed Adam and Eve standing on either side of the tree of knowledge, with the serpent, as large as either of them, entwined around its trunk. The heads of the figures were almost directly above hers. Eve's eyes were cast down. Adam stared across at her in judgment. The serpent, its head bowed, eyed her sidelong with heavy-lidded mockery. The tip of its tail was curled around her ankle.

What Vern had seen through the keyhole was the lip of a large bronze cauldron. Raised figures decorated the side of it, but she couldn't make them out too well and drew closer.

Peripherally, she noticed on the far wall shapes like canvas sacks or animal carcasses. Now she could see the cauldron better. Along the side of it, human forms in bas-relief wrapped around each other. Large heads with long snouts and round eyes, more animal than human, pushed out from between the figures. There seemed to be lines of text here and there as well but in a language she couldn't identify. Grabbing the lip, she knelt and looked at them closely. The figures might have been intertwined sexually except that many looked to be in agony. Heads were thrown back, mouths gaped in silent cries, and the bodies were contorted. She pulled herself up. The mist had thinned. Vern looked straight across the room at the shapes hanging on the wall.

There were four of them. They were women's torsos.

The heads and limbs had been hacked off. Two hung upside down, robbed of context, dehumanized into things so abstract that at first she could not comprehend what she was seeing; her revulsion grew slowly, and then it became too awful, too horrible to see, and she had to look away.

She looked down. Into the cauldron.

It was half full of liquid, a red-stained solution. In the center, four hands stuck out like little trees planted in a circle. Something like moss was tangled in the decaying finger branches. It was hair—hair strung from beneath the surface of the solution, strung from the most terrible sight of all. From severed heads.

There were four of them, too, all women. Hair of gold and red and black waved like seaweed below the surface. Through the strands the stare of milky eyes met hers. The eyes were all pale marbles, dead as stones. The mouth of the nearest was open as if to say "Oh," as if death had come as a tiny surprise.

Vern dropped the key ring.

The instant she let go she knew it. The keys fell and she lunged to grab them, catching them just above the bloody surface. Only the glass key, longer than the rest, dipped for an instant into the imbruement. Ripples raced away from it. The marble egg slid from the pocket between her breasts. She sensed it happening, collapsed her arm, and bent almost double to trap it. Cold fingers poked at her cheek. She trapped the egg in the crook of her elbow, curled her hand, and clutched it to her breasts. The contents of the jostled cauldron splashed against the side. One single sanguinary drop spattered the egg.

Vern flung herself away from the cauldron and out of the chamber, across a floor soaked in blood. She realized it would be on the bottoms of her slippers. She stumbled out, keys in one hand, egg in the other, then leaned against the thick jamb and trembled. Her teeth began to chatter, from cold or terror or both. She had to close the door but couldn't make herself set down either of her possessions.

Eventually she made herself turn back, reach back into the room, and hook her fingers over the handle without letting go the keys. They rattled against the black surface as she pulled the door closed. With palsied hands she scraped the key over the stile again and again until she thought the hole must have closed up, disappeared—she would never be able to find the lock. Then the key inserted. She turned it and shot the bolt.

She tore it free and backed into the hall a few steps. She wanted to run, but knew she mustn't.

Placing the egg on the floor, she carefully undid the ribbons on her ankles and kicked off one slipper and then the other. She collected the shoes and the egg once more. Then, in her torn stockings she ran.

She only glimpsed the doors as she flew by them. The pounding of her feet must have thundered into every room, but no door opened. No one leaped out to stop her.

Down the precarious stairwell, she pressed against the rail. At every moment she might have fallen.

The second floor remained deserted. Outside her own room she took an eternity finding the right key. One-handed, she kept trying to flip them around the ring to try another, but either the lock had changed shape or she was frantically trying the same key over and over, and finally she had to drop the egg into the pocket between her breasts and use both hands. She quickly found the right one. By then she was whining with fear.

She opened the door and all but fell inside, slammed and locked it after her, then stood pressed against it as if she might melt into the wood.

Twenty

*I*N THE AFTERMATH OF DISCOV-
ery, her terror grew steel wings,
lifting her above her fear. She
looked down on all she had to do to protect herself.

The first thing was to clean up. She dropped the key and the
egg in her basin and poured water over them. Blood leaked in
tendrils off the key, turning the water pinkish. She wiped off the
keys and egg and set them on her commode table.

Then armed with menstrual rags and a candle, she carried
the basin to the third floor. Barefoot now, she hunted down the
traces of her transgression. She found footprints outside the room
and scrubbed them away, being careful not to kneel in others as
she worked. She made sure she missed nothing. A part of her
had broken free from the terrified girl at her core. Most important
of all, she must feign complete innocence and give neither the
community nor her husband cause to suspect that she knew the
enormity of his secret. She wondered, did any others know?
Those men who lived on the third floor—they must know. His
inner circle, surely, acted as guardians of his crimes.

She rinsed the rags in her basin, emptied the water into her chamber pot, and carried that to the outhouse, where she poured the evidence into the pit. That the rags might bear traces of blood wouldn't matter. It was expected.

The key had cleaned up well. Only the tip of it had submerged. Nevertheless, she obsessively went through the entire ring key by key to make sure she hadn't missed anything.

The egg had only one spot on it—a pink circle no larger than the nail of her little finger where blood had spattered; but even with soaking this blemish would not come out. It was as if the stone had absorbed the color. All the rubbing and polishing she did failed to remove it entirely.

She stole a boar's bristle brush from the kitchen and scrubbed the egg to no avail. The spot remained. She resolved finally that nothing could be done about it, and she must simply be careful how she showed it to Fitcher. He was bound to ask her for it. If she held it right, he might never notice. And if he did see it, she would say it was her own blood.

After that, she remained in her room, awake through the night, unable to do more than doze in the chair. The keys and egg stayed in her pockets. The candle at her side finally exhausted, but by then the grayness of dawn was bleeding into the chamber.

She went down to breakfast, nodding to those who greeted her, trying for all the world to seem unperturbed. For once she was glad they didn't speak during the meal. Surreptitiously, she glanced at them to make sure no one was observing her oddly, no one acting as if anything out of the ordinary might be going on; some of them did seem to be eyeing her askance, and quickly looking away if she noticed. One little girl stared straight at her. It was the child who'd led her to dinner on her first day. They shared a smile; her own surely looked strained; but seeing the girl caused Vern's face to flush with heat as if she were about to cry.

Scanning all their faces, she tried to identify who she could trust, and who looked as if they knew his secret. It was impossible. Would anyone know? She thought if she could find Lanny Gibbons, he might help her; but she'd no idea where he was, what his job was here in the community. She must find a way to get out of here before Fitcher returned. She must have days if not weeks left. If her father came to a sermon—but no, he'd gone with Fitcher, hadn't he? He wouldn't come. Kate, though—mightn't Kate come to a Sunday sermon? Or even Amy. God, let them bring the wagon. She would hide in the back of it. But could she wait for them? How many nights could she go without any sleep?

All through the meal her mind whirled through escapes. Then afterward, in the kitchen, Sarah came up to her, saying, "Child, you look peaked this morning. But your hair—why, how did *that* happen?"

"I'm sorry?" She put a hand to her hair—she hadn't even thought to arrange it. She'd been too absorbed in all the other details.

"Were you struck by lightning?"

When it was clear that Vern didn't understand, Sarah hauled her over in front of a glass cabinet door where she could see herself reflected. Sarah pointed: On the right side of Vern's head, a shock of hair had turned absolutely white.

"What did that to you, child?" Sarah asked.

She couldn't think of any good explanation, but had to say something—it couldn't be dismissed. *He* would ask, too. She answered, "Oh, Sarah, I had a dream, an ugly, awful dream. Can dreams do such a thing?"

Sarah took the bait, nodding emphatically. "Oh, my dear, anything can do it if you git scared enough. Why, being alone in this big old house must prey on you something awful." She squeezed her hand. "But he'll be home soon now. You needn't fear. And there's nothing in this place to harm you. Nobody here would do that."

"No, nobody here now," Vern agreed. Sarah patted her arm and turned away. Vern reached out to stop her, but hesitated. Her hand trembled. Could she trust Sarah? Could she show her what she'd found? No, she didn't dare. If she was wrong . . . Nevertheless, she took advantage of Sarah's explanation for the streak in her hair and used the nightmare as an excuse to withdraw.

Sarah would surely spread the tale, and that should help. People would cluck their tongues, shake their heads for the poor dear girl, and maybe chalk it up to her recent illness. "She's had the worst luck, that poor girl." Elias wouldn't know how she'd fared after he left, whether she'd made a complete recovery or not. Better to let him think she hadn't—except of course that people had seen her dancing, and they would tell him. She devised then to pretend that she'd had a relapse. Feeling too healthy, she had exercised her frail system prematurely and worn herself out.

She retired to her room, sat on the bed, her brain alight with machinations. She could not wait for Kate, for rescue to come on its own. She must effect her own escape.

If she could find an excuse to loiter about on the front lawn, then she might wait until someone was going out. When did Notaro go to town for supplies? Was he even around? She couldn't remember when she'd last seen him. She could hide on the wagon before he left, or run through the gates when they were opened, run all the way home. She would have to befriend whoever was in charge of the gate, engage them in idle conversation until the opportunity arose. Or she might insist she needed spermaceti or more alum for her candle-making. Yes, *she* must ride in with Notaro on the wagon. *She* must go to town. Fitcher had put her in charge and she would use that to her advantage.

There was time, plenty of time. First she must get her energy back. In everything hereafter she must go cautiously and draw no attention to herself until she'd gotten outside the fence. Lanny would help her. Surely he must be innocent in all this, and his parents. Then Kate—Kate would believe her. They could come back together with the keys and show everyone what Elias Fitcher had done.

She lay back, scheming, certain she would seize her opportunity before he returned. A day—two at the outside—and she would get away. She would sleep during the heat of the day, and stay awake at night. No one would miss her at the noon meal one or two days in a row. She closed her hand against the egg resting between her breasts, looked up at the sweep of the canopy, but her sight traveled beyond it, up through the ceiling and out of the house, through the air and over the fence to home, to her sisters and safety. Her terror had exhausted her, and she finally fell asleep.

When she awoke, Fitcher was standing beside her.

She closed her eyes and opened them again. It had to be a dream. She was feverish, hallucinating, because he could not be back already. Above her head the light pouring in was golden and unreal. A dream, and she would wake up now.

He sat beside her. "My dear Vernelia," he said. "How are you?" He reached his bony hand to her cheek and she flinched just as he touched her. She didn't mean to, but she couldn't help it. Her body knew what his hands had done.

The change in Fitcher's demeanor was slight, but significant, and she saw it. The bearded smile tightened, the eyelids dropped like guillotine blades, and he glanced away from her and down, at her hand. She was lying on the bed, clutching the keys tightly. When she saw his look, she made herself relax her grip.

He extended his hand, palm up, and she gave him the keys. He flipped them around one by one with his thumb while he asked, "Did you enjoy your exploration? Did you go everywhere?"

She thought of the glass pyramid that she'd never reached, and held that in her mind, to answer truthfully, "No, not everywhere. The grounds—"

"And my little egg, did you keep it warm and safe for me?" He ran his fingertips up her arm.

Vern wanted to get up. Trapped on the bed wasn't how she'd wanted to confront him. She said, "Yes, of course. I took it everywhere."

"Oh, not *every*where," he replied slyly. Did he know about the dance then? How many people would he have talked to before entering the room? She mustn't deny, mustn't answer directly in any way that he might catch her out.

"I meant, everywhere I went."

"Yes. Where might it be then?"

"I have it here." She pressed her hand against her breastbone. The egg was not in the pocket. She sat upright, glancing around on the covers.

Fitcher said, "What's happened? Have you lost it so carelessly?"

"No. No, it was in my pocket when I fell asleep. It's here."

"Yes, I know it is." He brought his other hand into view. The egg floated upon his palm. "I found it when I came in." She tried to take it from him, but he snatched his hand away at the last moment, and held the egg up between his thumb and forefinger. "How remarkable," he said, inspecting it closely, "that I never noticed this slight imperfection before. Did you see this?" He turned his wrist to show her the ghostly pink circle. But the veins in the marble were no longer blue. They had become a deep crimson.

It must be the light, she told herself.

"And look here," he said. He flipped the keys around until he was holding the glass one. "Isn't this remarkable as well?" He held the key toward her. The key, like a phial, had filled with color; glass had transformed into ruby. It was impossible: She'd cleaned it herself, inspected it a dozen times.

"Such a shame," said Fitcher. "I asked of you one thing only. One small good thing. To protect you. I asked you not to eat the fruit, didn't I, but you could not deny your hunger. You insist upon knowing that which is denied you. Do you think we deny it for no good reason?"

"Elias, what—"

"There are secrets that women should *never* be party to, but you all insist, every one of you. You inquire, you inveigle. You use your wiles, your charms, your sex. That courtesan Sherazade should have had her head cut off the moment she opened her mouth. She tricked her caliph. Wore him down with words. You've all been the same forever. You all were trained by Eve. 'Cursed shall be the fruit of thy body.' "

"Please stop, Elias, please." She grasped his sleeve.

"All of you the same, and so must I be with you all." He dropped the egg and as she instinctively tried to catch it, he grabbed her by the hair and jerked her to her feet. "Every time the same," he repeated.

His strength defied her. He was so slight, so slender. Where did he get such strength?

She screamed—his name, for forgiveness, in pain. She screamed. He kept her upright, stumbling along beside her until they reached the stairs up to the third floor. Then she refused to stand, thinking that her dead weight would be impossible to haul up that steep incline.

Fitcher did not even hesitate. He climbed the stairs, dragging her behind him. He'd fallen silent. She struck steps with her shoulder, her head, her knees. Out of the stairwell, thrown forward, she hit the floor with her knees, and tumbled. The wood burned her skin. She grabbed at his hand in her hair, digging into it.

The doors to the rooms she'd explored stood open. She saw three men standing in the shadows, each silent, deformed, gray as ash. The other doors opened as they passed but seemingly without human agent. As if the power of Fitcher's passing blew them wide.

She scrabbled to get her footing, and managed to pull herself up along his sleeve. He drew her into the cold dark, and she knew she was outside the chamber. Panic seized her. She fought, clawed, kicked at him. "Elias," she cried, "Elias, what are you doing?" She shrieked—didn't anyone in the house hear her?

He remained grimly silent. The keys rattled. Then the bright colors splashed over her. The floor beneath her glistened red. Her bare feet slid in it. She twisted in his grip, turning to plead: "Husband, stop, please, stop!"

Instead he drew her up straight. Something flashed, like a bright dove bursting out of the shadows to surprise her; she opened her mouth to scream and the sound of it filled her brain, but it wasn't her scream, it was the screaming whine of all creation as it was crushed; the shriek of a rabbit, too high to be heard. The room spun round and round and she saw him, with each pass, circle her like the world around her frenzied calliope, his arm outstretched, over her head; and spinning, she saw below a

body clothed in her dancing dress, falling, collapsing away, sink-
ing down, as if the body were deflating inside it, which it must
have been for there was no head, and the blood of the room was
pouring out over the neck of the dress, and down her face, into
her eyes, blood going dark, dark, black.

Twenty-one

SHE PROBABLY THINKS SHE'S TOO important for us now," argued Amy.

Kate was complaining again about Vern's absence. She must have said something every single day for the past month—ever since Papa and Lavinia had gone off to Pittsburgh—and Amy was sick of it. Vern's absence was all her sister dwelt on anymore: Where was Vern and what kind of life might she be having inside Harbinger, and why didn't she ever come for a visit? And what had happened to the spirit guide in the wall?

The two girls were sitting by the roadside on this sunny afternoon, barefoot and wearing light cotton dresses and nearly nothing else. It was too hot these days for corsets and crinolines.

Vern hadn't traveled with the Fitcherites (as Kate called them—and Amy had picked up the habit). The girls had stood in the yard beside Mr. Charter and Lavinia and watched the crusade go by, wagon after wagon, and some on foot. There must have been a hundred or more. Fitcher rode in a Concord coach drawn by four horses, and with four people on the roof above him. He shared the interior with one other man, who was skinny and dark. They didn't recognize him. Fitcher had the coach stop at the Charter house, and he got out to welcome Mr. Charter and Lavinia on board. While they climbed inside, he went to Amy and Kate. "I know I can count on you both," he said, "to discharge your duties." He hugged each of them in avuncular fashion, then got back aboard the coach, which rolled ahead before the door was even closed.

Kate complained that she should have confronted him about Vern's absence. That subsequently Vern still hadn't paid them a visit bothered her more than the initial lack of communication. Amy had the same ready answer she'd been promoting since the letter had arrived earlier in the summer.

The two girls spent their whole days working the pike. When someone came by, they had to determine whether to ask for money, which was to say they had to identify those who were already members of Harbinger. Anyone could have said they were in the community and been let in for free, but folks who'd traveled so long to get there didn't have the presence of mind to lie about it; plus, Amy thought, you could just tell.

Insects buzzed about and birds called from deeper in the woods. Amy had to get up and move every so often, because there were ants and they were attracted to her. She'd eaten a Johnnycake with honey on it earlier, which the ants found appetizing. Wherever she moved, within ten minutes the ants caught up. She'd licked her hands clean, but there was a drop of it on her dress that she couldn't get out, and that was enough for the ants. She could have gone back to the pump and cleaned up, but didn't want to be absent should someone come by—especially because it might be Michael Notaro. Even though Kate knew all about it, Amy remained protective of her relationship with him. Kate continued to pester her to ask him about Vern. In fact she had asked him, not so long after they'd gotten Vern's letter. He had hardly seen her himself, but he knew that Vern had been given the job of making candles for the community— a piece of information that Amy found particularly delicious. He also claimed that Vern had taken sick, but that didn't make any sense to Amy, seeing as how the letter made no mention of it.

She decided that Vern was pretending she was sick in order to avoid having to make candles and pretending to them that her life was wonderful because she didn't dare say anything else. It was just like the way she'd inflated her relationship with Henri back in Boston. In any case, Amy did not share what she'd learned with Kate.

Notaro would willingly have reported Vern's circumstances to her daily, but Amy made it clear she didn't really want to hear about her sister anymore.

Kate wanted to go to Harbinger herself. Amy argued that she couldn't handle the raising and lowering of the pike alone. She wasn't strong enough. Kate insisted she could, even going so far as to push the thing up on her own, though it took all her strength. Amy's response then was to say, "Kate, she'll come visit us if she can, you know she will. I know you don't want to think so, but maybe she doesn't want us to see her. Or maybe she wants to surprise us with our own place there. Or maybe even, she's finding you a suitor—after all, the spirit promised you'd have one, too."

If all other arguments failed, then Amy pleaded with her not to go because it would stir up trouble for her and Michael, and if that happened, it would destroy the only thing Amy had. She didn't think that Kate believed anything she said, but Kate did hold off walking to Harbinger. At least in some small part Kate must have believed as she did that Vern had spurned them.

A few times, after she'd been with Michael Notaro, Amy tried to communicate again with the spirit of Samuel. She wanted to let the spirit know that she'd met someone just as it had sworn she would, but there was never a response to her raps or her quiet calls. The walls never snapped. She never heard a voice. She wanted to believe the spirit had been real, simply as reinforcement of her belief in the relationship she was having. However, the ghost's coincidental disappearance with Vern's departure left Amy convinced that Vern had manufactured the whole thing. She simply ignored the way the ghost had terrified her the very first night, excising from memory what she couldn't explain.

Kate disregarded Amy's theory of the ghost. She felt that the ghost must have traveled to Harbinger with Vern, or maybe been a part of Harbinger all along. Ghosts didn't just leave, did they? Haunted houses couldn't pass their ghosts on to other houses. So if Samuel was gone now, then he'd either come in the first place specifically to advise them, or he was Vern's guardian, attached to her rather than the house. Kate refused even to consider that Vern might have invented him. She acted as if Vern was some sort of saint: Vern hadn't deceived anybody; and Vern wouldn't have forgotten about her sisters.

Amy knew better.

Their conversations were invariably about her eldest sister unless she managed to focus it upon herself. She would ask, "What if he wants to marry me, Kate, what then? Should I say yes?" and Kate would ask her to describe what she thought her life would be like, married to Michael Notaro. It was almost as if Kate didn't think the Next Life was going to happen after all. Kate petitioned Amy to invite Notaro to dinner, too. She was, Amy thought sourly, acting like the elder of them: like a stepmother who wanted to meet the suitor to decide if he was a good match for her daughter.

Amy would never have let him grace their dinner table. She knew that all Kate wanted was to ask him about Vern. She made up the excuse that he could not have explained his absence from Harbinger long enough to share a meal with them—which wasn't entirely a lie. Even though he had keys to the main gate, if someone were to spy him leaving except on his way to get supplies, they might report him. As he'd told her, "I got to keep myself looking right so that nobody starts to wondering about me."

It only dawned on Amy after weeks and weeks of repeated suasion that there might be something wrong after all—that Kate might have legitimate cause for worry; but it was a fear in which she did not wish to share: She had convinced herself that inquiring after Vern could only bring trouble for her and Michael. Underneath it all, she resented that Vern had talked to a spirit who would have nothing to do with her.

That was how things remained until a night shortly before the crusaders of the Next Life returned from their Pittsburgh campaign.

A wagon came through very late. Kate heard it and got up, leaving Amy asleep. She put a shawl on over her nightdress, lit a candle in a lantern, and went downstairs and outside.

There was a breeze. It blew her hair into her face until she batted it aside. Crossing the yard she stepped on acorns and twigs, jumping at each stab in the bottom of her foot.

She could smell the vinegary lather of their horses, hear the chime of the bridles, the creak of boards upon axles well before she could make out anything at all of the travelers, and that just lumpish shapes. Their guiding lantern hung off the driver's side, casting its wan light down at the side of the road. She held up her own lamp as she neared.

The wagon contained a family of five who had obviously been driving all day to get here. The woman was driving the team, her husband beside her. She wore gloves and a slouch hat, the front of which stood up against her forehead. The wind had probably fixed it there permanently. The woman cast a tired glance her way across her shoulder and the man beside her. Kate said, "Welcome to you. Harbinger's just up the road a little farther."

"That's good," said the woman. "I know, 'cause they told us, that we's to pay you here to go on in."

"Then you're coming from the Reverend Fitcher's group itself?"

"Yes'm," the husband answered. "We saw the light of the Next Life when we heard him speak. Knew we wanted to be saved, wanted our little girls saved, too."

Kate moved the lantern to see three small girls in the back of the wagon, none of them older than five. The child in the middle was awake, sucking her thumb. She looked back at Kate fearlessly. For a moment Kate felt as if she were looking upon herself, and experienced a strange sense of displacement, as though she'd stepped into some hole in time itself, even though there was no such episode in her past. Yet the sensation remained, even when she moved back to the couple.

The man was already holding out his hand with the coin in it. She accepted it, then set down the lantern and pushed on the pike. It was difficult by herself, but she'd pushed it up for Amy, and she would do it for this family. The pike rose, but not high enough. It bounced back down. She was tired and her arms ached. She could have asked the man to help, but Kate insisted to herself she could do this. She doubled over the end of the pike, dropping every bit of her weight and strength upon it, and the pike rose high enough to let them pass. Her feet came off the ground.

The man said, "Much obliged," as the wagon lurched slowly forward. The tiny light on its side shrank to nothing in the night. The wind billowed up inside her nightdress and blew it above her naked legs. She jumped off the pole and it thwacked against the post opposite, bouncing once. Pushing the dress down, she looked around herself at the complete darkness that would have drunk her up without the small lantern. The sensation of being watched was unmistakable.

She picked her lantern up and walked back across the yard, managing not to step on anything sharp this time. She hoped no one else would be coming tonight.

In the doorway she glanced back, but the dark was as solid as cast iron.

Inside, she spent a few moments rubbing her feet before continuing back up the stairs to their room. Wind was blowing the curtains up at the landing, but she didn't smell any rain in the air. The cool breeze felt good, although she thought she'd never get back to sleep.

Approaching her bed, she saw the shape in the sheets. It was Amy.

Kate stopped still. Why had Amy gotten into *her* bed? She called her sister's name.

Amy was lying on her side, eyes closed, facing the wall. She was muttering in her sleep. Kate distinctly caught the words, "Yes, I hear." An instant later, something snapped inside the wall.

Kate stepped away from the bed.

Amy whispered something else, and the snap repeated. Kate backed to Vern's bed, where she sat and listened to the knocks and the breathy hints of her sister's voice replying.

The spirit had returned.

Kate knew that Amy had tried for weeks to communicate with it without luck. While she maintained that it had traveled with Vern to Harbinger, to guard her, that was a hopeful explanation of the spirit's absence, turning it into a guardian angel because the alternative seemed to be an admission that it wasn't at all what it pretended. But, ghost or angel, if Samuel *had* returned, then he had abandoned Vern to do so.

Something terrible had happened to Vern.

She knew it now more surely than ever.

The remainder of the night she sat propped up on her sister's bed, staring at the wall and at her sister prone below it, listening for the knocks as whatever lurked invisibly inside it spoke words she couldn't hear, but that Amy clearly now did, just as Vern had before her. Eventually, sitting, Kate dozed. If the conversation ever stopped, she didn't know.

When she woke next the faintest light of a cloudy wet morning was bleeding into the room. Amy was back in her own bed as if nothing had happened and Kate had dreamed everything. The lantern stood on the floor by her dirty feet. The candle in it had melted to a puddle.

Mr. Charter and Lavinia returned a few days later. A steady rain had been falling for hours.

The girls were standing in the sentry box when the swarm appeared. Next Life converts came marching up the road like an infestation. They filled the road from side to side. They clogged the length of it as far away as the bend where Michael Notaro liked to hide his wagon while he paid his visits.

Somehow word of the converts' arrival reached Harbinger, because Notaro came driving out before long in search of Fitcher. Passing through the turnpike he pretended not even to see the sisters, which nettled Amy a little even though she knew he was doing so to protect her. She and Kate stood the pole upright by running a rope around it to the tree beside them. There would be no toll asked from this crowd. It would have been impossible to collect. Still, some of the converts seemed to recognize that they were obliged to pay at a turnpike station, and came over and handed coins to the girls. One man on the far side of the congestion flung up a handful, and for a moment it rained money. Each time someone came forward with their toll, one of the girls had to leave the protection of the box and step out into the rain. They'd taken turns but were both wet and uncomfortable long before the bulk of the crowd had passed.

Some of the people looked to have walked all the way from Pittsburgh. Some must have walked there and back, too, but it was impossible to tell them apart. Their clothes were filthy, their feet dragged. They just wanted to see Harbinger and now were close enough that their exhaustion was leaking out around their will. They were an army of corpses.

Notaro came back up the road. The crowd parted for the wagon, turned, and faced it. Fitcher stood in the back of it, shouting hoarse encouragement to them. "You're nearly through the gates, my friends, nearly to your last resting place here in this world. Lift up your spirits, your hearts, good people, for God has walked this way with you. Wait on the Lord: Be of good courage and He shall strengthen thine heart. Wait, I say, upon the *Lord*!"

The words galvanized them. Those depleted people rallied— waved their hats at Fitcher, cheered him, jostled to reach him. Fitcher bent over the sides and touched their outstretched hands. "Give unto the Lord the glory due unto His name," he recited, and people in the crowd replied with *his* name: "Fitcher." Fitcher smiled but waved them to stop, then pointed at the sky as he said, "*He* is the saving strength of His anointed."

Mr. Charter and Lavinia rode in the back of the wagon. Notaro drew up and let them off before continuing. Lavinia had to help her husband down.

The Reverend Fitcher cast his gaze down upon the sisters, from Amy to Kate, and the fire of evangelism seemed to blaze in his eyes with new life. "Soon," he promised. "Be thou my help-mates."

Then the wagon lurched forward again and Fitcher returned to hailing his crusaders and converts. Mr. Charter shuffled like a drowned scarecrow across the yard. "Girls," he said to his daughters, a world of weariness bound up in that one word. He lifted his head in their direction and winced a smile before going on to the house.

Lavinia lingered, her bonnet protecting her. "Your father is weak," she told them, leaving the statement open to interpretation awhile before she clarified: "He became peaked on the road till I thought at one point he might make a die of it, but he's recovered somewhat. We'll have to give him care now he's home again. I expect you girls to continue with your duties here as if we had not returned. I don't wish to see him out here—and we all know he will stubbornly protest and insist on working the pole himself if he isn't prevented."

"Yes'm," Kate replied. "Amy, you go on with Lavinia and make them both some tea now. I'll stay here and gather what coin is paid."

Amy was about to protest that she ought to stay and Kate go in, when Lavinia said, "That's most thoughtful of you, Katherine. Come along, Amelia. And bring those bundles with you." She turned. Amy made a sour face but picked up the luggage and followed. The adults weren't back ten minutes and already she'd been relegated to taking orders from everyone again. She wished then that they hadn't come back, that they'd been killed on the road so that she and Kate could keep living in the house unsupervised right up to the end. Or until Michael Notaro took her away, took her to Harbinger to live with him. She expected him to come for her soon, now that everyone had returned. The spirit, the knocking thing in the wall, had told her that her suitor was close by. Vern's archangel was *her* guardian now. Who else could he have meant but Michael Notaro?

"Once the crusaders return," Samuel had prophesied in her dream, "then shall your suitor come for you."

"And will I go with him?" her dream self had asked.

"Of course. It can be no other way."

She couldn't wait. She hoped it would be tomorrow.

Lavinia said, "Stop dawdling, girl, you haven't sense enough to get out of the rain."

Amy sidled inside with her bundles. *Tomorrow*, she thought, *please let him come tomorrow*.

As it happened, no one came the following day except more converts. There were three sleeping beside the road when the sisters went out in the morning before breakfast, and all steadfastly insisted they pay the toll, though they were on foot and could easily have walked around the pole barring their way. Amy thought they were ridiculous to have stopped, and they smelled bad.

A dozen more arrived throughout the day. Notaro never appeared.

Two wagons did come from Harbinger on the way to buy supplies in Jekyll's Glen, but Notaro wasn't driving. The second wagon, tied behind the first, was a small buckboard for Mr. Charter. The driver explained that it was a gift from Reverend Fitcher to allow Mr. Charter to attend the daily sermons hereafter. A single tired old horse pulled it. Lavinia commented that the girls would have to add tending the horse to their daily chores. They didn't have a stable, so he would have to be tethered in the yard.

When Notaro hadn't shown up by dinner, Amy told herself he was too busy with the newly arrived. As Reverend Fitcher's right-hand man, he had to help settle everyone. She clung to the phantom promise that her suitor would come.

Mr. Charter remained in bed through the day, wheezing, shivering with chills. The girls and Lavinia brought him broth, and emptied his slops and wiped his brow with hot wet towels. He gazed up through sunken eyes, never quite seeming to focus. Amy thought he was looking past her, at something above her. He muttered under his breath but she couldn't make it out.

The next day he was better and came down to breakfast, although clothed only in his nightshirt and obviously weak, and with the stink of illness on him. He drank tea and ate eggs, and said almost nothing. He still didn't seem to occupy the same space as they, as if his mind were elsewhere and his eyes could see a different place.

"What is it, Papa?" Amy asked, but Lavinia shushed her.

Mr. Charter, slow to respond, focused on her and replied, "It's God's will."

She wasn't sure he even knew he'd spoken. He returned to bed and slept through the morning, and by afternoon was much revived. He cleaned himself up, shaved, dressed, and came downstairs. He would have gone out to the turnpike if the three women hadn't insisted he must not. It was misty and humid out, and they didn't want him to lose his newfound strength. They didn't inform him of his new wagon.

Late in the afternoon that second day, the supply wagon appeared again. Amy saw it far down the road and came out of the box. She leaned expectantly on the pole. Instead of pulling up at the barrier, the wagon turned and rolled up into their yard beside the stumps. Michael Notaro was driving but he wasn't alone. The reverend was with him. Fitcher climbed out. He wore a long dark canvas coat and a wide-brimmed, low-crowned hat against the mist. He looked Amy over and smiled, although she found no humor in the curl of his lips. Notaro sat with his head bowed, his eyes hidden beneath his hat brim as though sleeping. He didn't glance her way once.

The reverend said, "I expect you ladies might want to come inside for a time. Mr. Notaro will watch your pike for you."

Then he turned and started for the house, with his walking stick under his arm.

Lavinia opened the door at his approach, almost as if she'd been expecting him. He made a slight bow before entering.

She led him into the parlor, where Mr. Charter was already seated, and Fitcher bade him remain so. Amy and Kate followed behind him, and their father's glance fell upon each of them in turn with a mounting anxiousness as though conspirators were gathered around him, about to plunge their daggers into his heart. The look was all the more terrible to the girls because they had no more idea than he what was happening.

"I shall come directly to the point," Fitcher said. "Vernelia has left Harbinger."

Mr. Charter's brow knitted. "I'm not sure I understand this. Left it how?"

"Some days before our return, it appears she ran off. To Boston." He reached inside his coat and produced a folded note, which he handed to Mr. Charter. It had been stamped with a wax seal, which was broken.

Mr. Charter read it silently. His face darkened and grew taut with anger. Abruptly he flung the piece of paper away and said, "The willful child. I disown her on this spot. May she know the fires of hell and the tortures of the damned for this!"

Lavinia picked up the note. She held it in such a way as she read that the girls could see it, too. It began with an apology to all who were injured by this action. It claimed that Vernelia could not continue her false and loveless existence at Harbinger. She cared nothing for her husband, nor wished to try. She was leaving to be with her lover in Boston, with whom she'd already been intimate.

Reverend Fitcher spoke as they were reading: "I cannot keep you from your ire, sir, but I must share in the responsibility for her disappointment. You see, in all the business I had to oversee at Harbinger, I'm afraid I much neglected Vernelia. We'd not yet even consummated our vows."

"But it's been months," said Mr. Charter.

"Yes, it has, and the fault for this is entirely mine. I feel as if I drove her away, creating as I did this chasm between us."

"You mustn't blame yourself, Reverend."

"I can hardly blame anyone else for my inattentiveness, Mr. Charter."

"No, sir. It is the *girl*," he replied, and stared at his remaining two daughters. "She has disgraced us. Disgraced *me*. After all your kindnesses, after granting me this position so close by and bringing us into your flock—no, she has reduced me to I don't know what."

Fitcher stepped forward and raised a hand to stop him.

"Please. I've already taken steps to have the marriage annulled. It will be as if it never happened."

"Why, if I were healthier, I'd go to Boston and find her and drag her back here, the trollop."

"Papa!" Kate exclaimed.

Fitcher said, "Yes, comfort thee, sayeth your God. You mustn't say such things about your daughter, Mr. Charter."

"But look at the *shame* she's brought upon me." He seemed ready to burst into tears over his sullied name. Lavinia handed him back the letter, and took her place beside him, her hands upon his shoulders. Like the girls, she remained standing.

The reverend sat then, pulling his chair close beside Mr. Charter. "I may have a remedy to our mutual embarrassment," he said. "You have lost a daughter and I a wife, as if neither ever existed. I propose to you then that I take a wife as if for the first time, and you once more give your blessing to it."

Mr. Charter looked confused, but Amy took a step back. She brushed up against Kate, and gripped her hand.

Fitcher reacted to her movement by looking directly at her and smiling. "Your eldest girl must marry first, as you told me the first time I came to you. As you sit here, you have but two daughters remaining. Give me your eldest in marriage now, and it will be as if nothing had happened between us to tarnish our good relationship." He took Mr. Charter's hands between his own. "We must rebuild the bridge between us as God intended when He blessed our first union."

Mr. Charter's gaze flicked from daughter to daughter. They clutched hands as if meaning to block access to the doorway behind them. Neither girl, so far as he knew, had any prospects nor any hope of finding a husband; and so little time remained.

Amy knew what his answer would be. She knew the ghost in her dreams hadn't lied about her suitor, and now she understood why Michael Notaro had arrived with his face hidden, unable to look at her. The reverend must have voiced his plan while they drove here. Michael didn't dare object. How could he? As how could she, unless she wished to be cast out like Vern? To confess now would doom her, doom them both. A lifetime lived in subservience, in routine capitulation to her father's wishes, shaped Amy for the answer and her response. Her father said, "Yes, of course, you'll marry Amelia," and she let go Kate's hand and took a step forward again. *His will be done*, she thought. Her older sister had ruined her father's good name. She, with one simple act of sacrifice, could erase that blemish and make everything right.

She looked out the window, where she could see her lover walking back and forth beside the pike. She would still have Notaro close by her, in fact closer than they had been. Somehow they would find a way . . . She stopped herself. She mustn't think like that.

Fitcher came to her and held out his hands. She took them. "I promise," he said, "I will not treat you as I did Vernelia." He let go with one hand and collected his walking stick. The Medusa head glared at Amy. "I assure you, dear Amelia, I will not make the same mistake with you."

Twenty-two

*A*MY'S WEDDING WAS A SUB-
dued and quiet affair, in part
because it occurred a mere
twenty-four hours following the proposal, in part because no one
felt much like celebrating on the cusp of Vern's banishment, but
mostly because there were now at least a hundred new converts
to accommodate, and most of the community was engaged in
helping store their belongings, in piling belongings deemed unnecessary onto a bonfire out by the fields, or in pitching tents
down by the orchard, a bivouac progressing up the back lawn.

Once more, the Reverend Flavy presided. He'd had no more
luck with his razor than before, his face as scratched as it was
shaved; and despite a proper, bespectacled demeanor, he seemed
unwashed to Amy. His collar was yellow around the edge. When
he patted her hand, she saw that his fingernails were broken and
dirty, as if he were a mole dressed up for the occasion. He told
her quietly, "Poor dear girl, let me wish you well here," before
mounting the pulpit. The altar before it was piled with flowers—
blue columbine, purple lilac, and white lilies—all atop red velvet
pushed into folds and cascades, with the thorn-spiked milky skull

situated in the center, tilted back as if frozen in the act of laughing.

Amy wore a plain creamy dress purchased from Van Hollander's. Her mother's wedding dress would never have fit her and there was no time to have another one made. This dress, with its vertical line of rose buttons, was too large, but Kate and Lavinia had done a reasonable job of stitching pleats into it to fit her. The nice slippers they'd bought for the first wedding were unavailable—Vern had taken them with her in her flight to Boston. Again her stepmother and younger sister came to her rescue and, just hours before the ceremony, hurried into Jekyll's Glen and bought new ones for her. The only thing she shared with her elder sister on this wedding day was the veil she wore; that, and of course her husband.

No throng filled the hall this time. Other than her family barely a dozen people occupied the pews, and they were a solemn lot. A man not much larger than a dwarf played hymns on the pipe organ in the corner. She couldn't remember if he had played for Vern's wedding. He performed as if unaware of the proceedings, as if he were practicing alone, and never looked up as she was led down the aisle on her father's arm. Mr. Charter trembled against her so much that she almost forgot her own terror in supporting him and muttering reassurances to him as they walked; each stride was a beat of her heart.

Fitcher wore his black tailcoat as before. To Fitcher's right, Michael Notaro wore a dark brown coat and black trousers. He'd plastered down his wild hair and shaved his chin, revealing the dimple in it that she liked to press her index finger into just before she kissed him. She banished their familiarity, drove the image from her mind. This must never happen again.

Notaro stared at her as if at an approaching ghost. Even with the veil softening the effect, she almost couldn't bear to look at him. That he had to act as ring bearer seemed the cruelest of tortures. Surely someone else could have done it? Why hadn't he said he was sick? Was he punishing himself? *He gives me things to occupy myself*, he'd once said about Fitcher. But not this, surely not this. *He knows*, she told herself, *he knows about us.*

Flavy proclaimed, "We come here today to unite this man and woman. The world outside our happy clime is even now in turmoil, a violent and uncaring place, despite which we've lost a sister to it." He smiled with pained sympathy upon Amy. "It is most regrettable, for she has abandoned not merely those who loved her here among us, but also the new life which was promised her. Nevertheless, this is no funeral we gather to witness, but a happy union resulting from that unfortunate event, necessitated even by it." Flavy glanced down at Elias Fitcher, and twitched. He cleared his throat and quickly opened his Bible, and recited, " 'Be merciful unto me, O God, be merciful unto me; for my soul trusteth in thee; yea, in the shadow of thy wings will I make my refuge, until these calamities be overpast.' This psalm is our guide today. These two find their refuge in the Lord through holy marriage, and so will be protected from these approaching calamities we know."

He closed his Bible and came down the steps of the pulpit and around the altar. He bumped it as he went past, and the crystal skull rocked from side to side, then fell over upon the red velvet cloth beneath it. Flavy turned to grab it and Fitcher said sharply, "Don't."

Flavy turned uncertainly back to him. Fitcher disengaged from Amy. He lifted the skull and set it down again. Then he backed around Flavy and slipped his arm around Amy. "Continue," he ordered.

Flavy stuck a finger inside his collar is if it were choking him. He cleared his throat again. "Ahm, well, then. Do you, Elias Fitcher, take this woman, Amelia Chelone Charter, to be your lawfully wedded wife, to have no other wife but she, to honor, love, cherish, and . . . protect as long as ye both shall live?"

"I do," Fitcher answered.

"And, Amelia, do you take Elias Fitcher as your lawfully wedded husband, to have no other before him, to love and honor and obey him in all things, for as long as ye both shall live?"

Amy thought her head would spin off. She remembered Flavy's questions to Vern. He hadn't asked Vern not to have any other person before her husband. Why did she have to answer that? She hesitated, sure now that they all knew about her and Michael. Reverend Flavy asked, "My dear?"

Through her veil, Amy looked at the dark figure of Fitcher beside her, and the thought swept through her that he wasn't real, wasn't human, couldn't know her secrets unless he was something diabolical. She threw off a shiver and thought, *Too late.* Her mouth formed the words: "I do." She couldn't help it. Standing here in the Hall of Worship, what else could she have said?

"You have the ring, sir?"

Michael Notaro edged forward. She watched his hand appear, the ring upon his palm. The hand was shaking, and she prayed that he wouldn't give them both away. Fitcher took the ring, at the same time asking softly, "Mr. Notaro, are you ill?"

Notaro opened his mouth to speak. His jaw worked and he finally just shook his downcast head. Amy could see his profile. Tears were flooding her eyes. She hardly noticed Fitcher sliding the ring onto her finger, hardly heard Flavy's words. Then suddenly the veil was thrown back, and she had one last clear glimpse of the man she loved before the Reverend Fitcher leaned in close and pressed his lips to hers. "My dear wife," he said. She stared into his eyes and beyond them, as if she might possibly see through him.

When he drew away, there was no one standing beside him. Notaro had vanished. She dared not look around for him. Fitcher's hand on her elbow turned her and she walked beside her husband into the new world of Harbinger.

Like the wedding, the reception was small and hastily assembled. The newlyweds stood in the foyer outside the refectory and received the well-wishers, many of whom seemed to have come directly from the fields to welcome her. Notaro was not among them and Amy didn't know whether she was relieved or stung by his absence.

One elderly woman hugged her and whispered into her ear, "I'm so sorry for your loss." Amy watched her move away, daz-

edly trying to make sense of the sentiment and concluding that
the woman somehow knew she was Vern's sister.

A cake had been hastily prepared—a single layer cake, badly
mixed, riddled with dry lumps of flour. There was wine, and the
attendees toasted the bride and groom as if there was all the time
in the world; as if the world weren't five months away from ending, as if there had never been another Mrs. Fitcher. Amy drank
as much of it as she could, downing her glass at every toast,
quickly reaching inebriation. The fog of drink blocked her longing and shut down her instinct for flight. She hugged Fitcher
enthusiastically, hugged the members of her family. If Notaro had
appeared then, she might have burst into tears, but he spared
her. Perhaps he had taken to his bed. She wished she were with
him. She wished she'd given in to him at least once while they
lay in the leaves. Now she never could.

The rest of the day was a smear of events. People left, her
family left, but Notaro didn't drive them now because they had
their own wagon. She was led by her husband up to her room.
She recollected his giving her a lecture about the rules of the
house. Her memory was foggy, but it must have been important.
She would need to ask him to repeat them, although to do so
would reveal how drunk she had been.

She found all of her belongings were in her room, which surprised her. She looked at her bed and thought of being in it with
Notaro. She tried to undress, but it was too difficult to make her
fingers work, easier just to fall back on the bed and sleep. At
least she'd removed her shoes and stockings.

How long it was before Fitcher entered, Amy had no idea.
She opened her eyes, turned her head, and there he was, drifting
across the floor toward her. He seemed to float. She giggled and
held out her arms.

What happened after that she either could not or did not want
to remember.

The following morning at first light she awoke alone on top
of her bedding with a dreadful headache and no clothes. It had
rained in the night, and the morning air was thick with moisture,
already steamy hot. When she rolled over and her back touched

the sheets, she hissed and flopped quickly onto her stomach again. She reached around and touched her back. It stung to the touch.

She got to her feet, but too quickly. Her head throbbed and she squeezed her eyes tight until it subsided. She hadn't felt this awful since Vern's wedding.

There was a revolving mirror on the dresser and she moved in front of it, tilted it, then turned her back to it and looked over her shoulder.

Rows of welts ran from her shoulders all the way to the middle of her thighs. They weren't deep slashes but they were angry and raised. She'd been whipped. She'd also had sex. Something cold trickled along the inside of her thigh, and a small bloodstain spotted the sheet.

Amy returned to the bed, perching on it cautiously. She recollected Elias Fitcher entering her room—or at least she remembered a kind of candlelit, drunkard's dream in which he appeared. She couldn't be sure any of it had been real. But the welts across her backside were real. Someone had whipped her during the night. The welts were less terrifying than the absence of any memory of how they'd appeared. Even drunk, she couldn't imagine enduring such a beating unawares.

She looked about for the clothes she'd been wearing, but they were nowhere to be seen. The armoire hung slightly ajar. Someone had stripped her and then taken the time to put her clothes away. Nothing about that made sense to her. She got up—more carefully this time to let her thunderous headache subside. She opened the armoire.

There was a hook on the inside of the door. Her petticoat and dress dangled from it, and over the dress hung a braided leather cat with a wooden handle—the instrument of her punishment. It looked newly made, the leather strips dark and oiled.

She had been punished, and surely by no one other than her husband. He had punished her for her corruption. She'd gotten drunk at her wedding, she'd been intimate with another man, had lied to her family, and still here she was on the inside of Harbinger, where she would meet the end and the new beginning in the company of the blessed. That could not occur until some just punishment was meted out. She couldn't expect to stand with the pure ones unless she herself had been purified, could she?

The justification for her whipping hung like an odor in the air, waiting for her to inhale. If the Reverend Fitcher had whipped her, didn't she deserve it, and more? Hadn't she humiliated him by getting drunk at the wedding? She was weak, tragically so, a puppet to her vices; and he was divine purity himself. She could not rail at him. He had simply seen into her soul, that she'd always known to be depraved. She might disguise it from her family, even from Kate, but not from Fitcher. Finally, Amy had found someone who recognized her sinfulness and responded to it.

It was, she decided, nothing less than she deserved.

She would get up now, dress and go to him, show him that she understood his message and would obey. He would guide her from her wickedness back onto the path she must walk if she was to regain Heaven in the company of the Fitcherites.

" ' . . . and straightaway many were gathered together, insomuch that there was no room to receive them, no not so much as about the door: and he preached the *word* unto them.' " Fitcher paused, glancing up at the assembly. He stared over them at Amy, his wife, who had entered in the middle of his quotation.

He continued to look at her as he said, "So it will be here. Many will be gathered, more than we have room to receive. Even now they are on the road to us. The lame, the blind, the sick. Those hopeful of salvation, those certain they won't receive it. All of them are coming to us."

The pulpit that yesterday had towered over her as her bondage was proclaimed now seemed small and distant. She moved to the last pew and sat. Her husband continued to sermonize about the new arrivals. He talked about the people he had met on the road, the people who had come to the tent to hear him—as many here had done once—how worried they were. "Yes, my friends, now that time is running out, more and more souls will sense the approach of the Next Life. They know they must face their God and He will not hear their excuses for the lives they've led, for the repentance they have left undone—any more than I shall listen to it. Harbinger had best be peopled by those who truly repent their sinful ways. As more of them come to us, each of you must look to yourselves and determine if you are so devoted to salvation as they. If your spirit is not set upon the path, now is the time to admit it. You may give voice to your feelings, but the Angel of Death knows what you've placed in the locket of your heart and he will act upon the secrets you keep there. Keep them from me if you so desire, but you keep them at your peril. For when the angel confronts you, he will *not* ask. He will not care for the excuses that ring you like a wall. He will slaughter the deceitful and corrupt among us just as surely as he will smite all those outside our fold.

"It is time to know your *heart*!"

The last word echoed around the hall. Amy jumped at the sound of it. It had been nothing like when her father tried to preach. While he often persuaded her, his words were flat and stumbling. Fitcher was speaking to her and about her. No one else. He described what she knew about herself. The question— the fearful dilemma that he had expressed so well—was how to purify the heart before the angel looked upon and judged you. It was fine to announce your wish to shed your sin, but quite another to succeed. His sermon was an extension of the cleansing he had begun last night, that she had discovered only this morning. She would be shriven. He must shrive her. She could not do it alone.

Nevertheless, she dreaded the act of contrition, for she must—if she confessed all—admit to her relationship with Notaro. She might admit it to an angel (for an angel would know already), but not to Fitcher. Not to her husband; and surely not on the first day of their own new life.

The others left for breakfast until only she and her husband remained in the hall. When Fitcher came up the aisle, he halted beside her. His face expressed no emotion, as if he were waiting for her to assign it one.

Amy reached for his hand and clutched it with both of hers. She looked up into his ice-blue eyes and said, "Thank you, sir, for reminding me of my sinfulness. My behavior of yesterday— I admit that I love your wine too much. It was—it was only right that you punished me for my wickedness."

His towering look softened. "Then you recognize this condign punishment?"

"I do."

"You were insufficiently punished in your former existence?"

"I was, yes. Papa, he—they didn't know." She tried not to let her voice quiver as her lip did, but it was difficult. "I mean, they knew nothing of what runs so deep inside me. The secrets of my heart are as you describe them."

He drew his hand away. "Then I shall make it my duty to purify you here. I can forgive much, but not sullage. My wife must be pristine and unblemished come the day we meet our Lord."

"I want to be."

"Good. Good." That seemed to resolve the matter for him. He said, "Now, dear Amy, *dear* bride, I have gifts for you that I couldn't present you with last night." He paused to let that statement prod her once more on the matter. "I'll bring them to your chamber after breakfast. You must go and eat with the others. The shifts don't last very long. When you're done with your meal, I'll join you in your room."

Holding out both his hands, he raised her to her feet and then walked with her through the doors and across the foyer.

After a meal that was bland and unsatisfying, Amy tried to help with kitchen duties, but didn't know what she was supposed to do. She looked for someone to give her orders, but no one did. They moved around her like ants around a piece of wood, their routines already established without her. She didn't know whether she could ask—no one spoke during the meal, and silence reigned in the kitchen as well. Confused and frustrated, she withdrew to her room.

She walked silently along the hall. The door to her chamber was open and Elias Fitcher was already inside. He'd thrown open the window and curtains, and light like a fireball blazed now through the gauzy canopy at the head of it. Fitcher stood beside her bed, holding her stockings like a bouquet beneath his nose. He must have sensed her presence, because all at once he dropped the stockings. His smile was already in place by the time he faced her.

She walked into the room.

She saw on the bed a large garland of flowers, possibly the same ones that had bedecked the altar the previous day. In the center of them sat a white box tied in pink ribbons. Fitcher stepped back and gestured toward it.

Someone had made the bed—the covers were straightened and folded, pillows arranged decorously.

Amy knelt on the bed to retrieve the box. She turned then, with one knee tucked under her, and faced him as she undid the ribbons.

"This is a little something, a trifle," he said.

She opened the box and pushed aside the tissue within. She took out the marble egg between her thumb and forefinger.

"Careful not to drop it," he warned.

"I would never." The egg was milky white and shot through with blue mineral veins. She rolled it across her other palm. The smooth surface was polished and unblemished. The tiny veins sparkled.

"Now," he murmured, "I hope that you will carry it with you wherever you go. It joins me to you, knowing you have that in your hand, or in your pocket, or somewhere about your person. Its properties are, I think, quite soothing."

She agreed. Even as she stood there, its coolness in her hand seemed to insulate her from the humid heat of the room.

"Here," said Fitcher, and he took the egg from her. "Unlace your gown and lie upon your stomach."

She glanced warily from him to the armoire and back again, but she obeyed. She unbuttoned the front of her dress, then shrugged it down to her waist and pushed down her undergarment. She climbed upon the bed then and lay facedown.

At the first touch of the egg to her back, she made a little gasp. As lightly as a feather Fitcher rolled it over the welts. The first time, the sensation stung ever so slightly, like nettles brushing her skin; but afterward only the coldness of the marble remained, and she felt comforted. She looked from where she lay at the mirror on the dresser. She saw herself in shadow, and the Reverend Fitcher glowing in the light coming through the window. The imperfect mirror warped the image, made his figure twist, cut hers in two with a shard of light. An instant later the sun passed behind a cloud and they both were cloaked in shadow. She moaned, and the sound surprised her. She luxuriated in the sensation rolling down her back. The egg dipped down to her buttocks and rolled up again, like a blanket to cover her, to let her sleep.

He withdrew the egg. The room was warm again, and he stood, waiting for her. She got off the bed, her hands covering her small breasts. She couldn't feel the welts on her back now. She glanced over her shoulder at the mirror. Her back appeared smooth, free of any marks.

Seeing her confusion, Fitcher lifted the leather cat from the cupboard door. "This," he said, "is for punishment. This"—he held out the egg—"for palliation. It does not cure, but makes the punishment bearable, just as punishment makes our sins themselves bearable."

He dropped the egg so that she had to catch it, thus uncovering herself. She pressed it to her breast. Blushing, she stood exposed, and for a moment thought of Michael Notaro—the look on his face when she'd first let him see her breasts—and remembering it, knew she needed more punishment yet.

"I must attend now to my duties," he said. "You'll have yours, too, which I'll show you. This evening, we'll take up the matter of purification." He started to turn away, but hesitated. "Oh, and I will lead at least one more crusade between now and the new life. To Boston, to Providence. When I'm gone, you will be the person in charge here." He hoisted a ring of keys out of his jacket. "These will give you access to everything in Harbinger—with a single exception." He held out the clear glass key. "This one is not to be used. What it unlocks is not to be opened. Do you understand?"

"Not to be opened, yes. I understand."

He smiled, "Of course you do, my dear," he said. "All of you do." It struck her as an odd thing for him to say. He must mean everyone in the community.

He put the keys back inside his jacket and left Amy in her room, with the cold marble egg like a stone heart between her breasts.

Twenty-three

*A*MY HAD NO WAY OF KNOW-
ing that she was living her
sister's life.

Fitcher directed her to make candles, but this proved to be
next to impossible in the summer heat. Tallow refused to maintain a shape. It dripped off the hung wicks like blood from sac-
rificial lambs. It stayed in the molds, but when she flipped them
over in the cold water and took out the candles, the bottoms went
soft and they began almost immediately to bend.

Vern was the one acquainted with the chandler's art—not she.
She had only watched and couldn't have told the difference between tallow and spermaceti except for how it smelled.

Rooting around for a solution, she went into the cellar of the
shop and found boxes of candles her sister had made. The cool
cellar kept them intact: There were dozens of boxes containing
hundreds of candles lying in straw. Vern had prepared enough
light to repel an army of darkness. Amy picked one up and looked
at it. It was hard, not melting. Somehow Vern—and it had to be
Vern's handiwork, didn't it?—had fashioned ideal candles, candles that could stand up to anything short of a direct attack of

sunlight, candles like vampires asleep in their boxes. Amy was both amazed and thankful. She swore never to speak ill of her sister again.

She brought out a box. By herself she lugged it up to the house and left it in the foyer, where people could see it and take candles as they passed by after their meals. The first box lasted three days. She added up what she had stored and speculated that they might last until cold weather returned, and she could make tallow ones. After that would come October, and then she wouldn't have to worry about making candles anymore. In the Next Life, divine light would accompany them wherever they went.

In the afternoons she returned to the house to listen to her husband's sermon before her meal. He spoke with such passion, such fire, that she couldn't help but be persuaded by him. Often now she found her father and Lavinia in attendance at the sermons. Sometimes she spoke with them afterward. Her father had never been one for small talk, and always seemed itching to return home, where Kate manned the turnpike alone. He would ask how Amy was, but not how the reverend treated her. Not that she would have told him about her fearful course of purgation. She wished he would have let Kate come in his place, but never seemed to get the opportunity to say so. Lavinia was always there, always ready to interrupt, as if clairvoyant of what Amy wanted.

At night she waited in her room for Fitcher to come. The nights were warm now, and Amy wore only the lightest cotton chemise to bed. She sat in front of the window, holding the egg in her hands. If there was a breeze, she let it blow her dark hair and cool her skin.

He always came in quietly. She almost never heard him arrive. Sometimes he was right upon her before she realized it, and she jumped in terror at the sight of him. Their meeting became a ritual. He would hold out his hand, and, trembling, she would lay in it the marble egg. She would go to her place beside the bed, draw off her clothing, and kneel. The first lash was always a shock. He seemed to withhold it almost as a taunt, infusing the final moments before he struck with terror. She bowed her head and prayed: "Our Father, who art in Heaven, hal-*lowed*"—the whip would fall—"be thy *name*."

Fitcher would ask her to list her sins as he whipped her. She described a lifetime's worth—secret things, words spoken to her sisters in anger, an episode where she'd touched herself, pretending it was a man, the ways she had manipulated situations to get Vern or Kate into trouble, instances when she'd said aloud she wanted to kill one of them—the list could be made endless. What siblings didn't, sooner or later, wish one another ill? She withheld only Notaro's name. That large, final secret sin she would not admit to. She loved him. She would not betray him.

One night as the leather cat snapped across her skin, Fitcher asked her, "Are you like your sister? Have you known any men before you came here?"

"No," she said at once. She wasn't like Vern. Vern with Henri was not like her with Michael Notaro, and she chose to interpret "before you came here" as here to Jekyll's Glen with her father and Lavinia. She hadn't known anyone. Hadn't wanted to know anyone before then. She couldn't be made responsible. "No," she repeated, reaffirming, settling it in her mind.

Each whipping seemed more brutal than the one before. One night the intense pain pushed her beyond tears, beyond agony. It was as though she moved outside her body and floated over him, where she could watch the knotted strips bite into her back, the welts rise up beneath them, red lines slashed like ribbons from her shoulders to her bottom. Her bare feet protruded beneath her, and he resorted to whipping her soles. She felt none of it. Someone approached her, and a voice whispered in her ear, "You are free now." The sound gathered her on invisible wings. Her spirit soared. She turned her face to the sky and said, "Thank you," and Fitcher, his arm raised, stopped. She could see him even though he was behind her.

He dropped the whip, then bent down and lifted her. From her vantage, she looked frail and tiny, no bigger than a child in his arms. He placed her upon the bed, stretched her out. Then, with the egg, he smoothed her skin. The poison of perdition leached out of her and into the egg. Held by some angel, she hovered overhead and watched. His hand let go of the egg, left it lying in the small of her back while his fingers brushed gently over her backside, and down into the crevice between her thighs. Her body on the bed moaned and her spirit floating above dissolved.

She lay upon the bed, dreaming of his exploring hand, wanting him to delve deeper. She turned over to embrace him.

There was no one there. The room was dark. The cold marble egg lay upon the mattress. It had been that touching between her legs, that sensation casting her dream.

She cupped the egg in her hands and curled childlike around it. The rest of the night she didn't dream at all.

At the end of the week, as she was walking to the house from the village, she overheard someone outside one of the camp tents speaking of a dance that night. It was a dark-skinned boy no older than she, and he was describing the dance to whoever lay inside the mildew-darkened tent. He said they danced in the barn at the far end of the village. He didn't seem to be aware of who Amy was. She asked if the Reverend Fitcher attended. The boy rose up and replied, "Sometimes, but he don't dance. He just watches."

After the meal, she located Fitcher on the back porch of the house and asked him about the dancing. "It is a healing thing they do," he said, as if describing the behavior of a different species. "A release of energy, a way to overcome their exhaustion, to free themselves in a way from earthly bounds. You would like to join in, I take it."

"If I might be allowed."

"If you feel the need, then most certainly you may. I myself will be on hand to safeguard them. For while it is a harmless, even beneficial pastime, there are always some who would warp it like a bad piece of lumber into some unnatural shape. Rather than allow that, I will enter the dance myself and lead it. I must stand vigilant always for signs of depravity. Of course, not from you, my dear Amelia. You've come far through your penance."

"Yes," she agreed. She did not mention—barely even acknowledging herself—that she hoped to see Michael Notaro there. It had been weeks since she'd even laid eyes on him.

The dancing began before Amy and Fitcher arrived. They strode through the orchard, and past the dark shops. He spoke of the stars in the heavens, of God's purpose in creating the lights of the sky—"to entice us, to give us mysteries to solve in our lives."

Amy said nothing. She was listening to the music, watching for the light spilling from the barn, which glowed from behind the buildings like a hidden fire. Like a lowly earthbound star.

Then ahead, in the gleam of lamps and candles, the dancers sashayed across the floor, back and forth in a formation she recognized from years gone by, when Vern had shown her how to dance. She had only danced with Vern and Kate, never with a man.

The people were strangers to her. Some of them interrupted their pleasure to acknowledge her husband. They bowed or nodded, just as they'd done to her the time he'd taken her family on his tour. She'd thought the welcome was meant only for strangers, newcomers.

Off to the side, Michael Notaro stood against a post watching the dancers. He had one knee bent, and held a cup of something. His look was dark and brooding. He seemed thinner, and his hair unkempt. Secretly, she delighted to see him so; not that she was cruel, but she wanted to know that he truly cared, that their separation had been difficult for him, too. She saw him and knew that he missed her.

She and Fitcher entered the barn. At once two people jumped up and offered him the bale of hay on which they'd been perched. He thanked them and sat down upon it. Amy took his hand and tried to draw him back onto his feet. "Won't you dance with me, Elias?" she asked. Despite everything, she thought she could coerce him.

He replied, "Not just now, my dear. You must find someone

else to entertain you awhile." His glance flicked from her to
something across the room. Even before she turned, following his
gaze, she knew. He'd looked at Notaro, as if he knew what was
in her mind.

By now word of Fitcher's arrival had spread through the barn.
Notaro glared their way resentfully through the rows of dancers,
as though angry and frustrated that they should rob him even of
this small retreat. He pushed off from the post and walked over
to a group of women. A moment later, one of them stepped out
with him into the center of the room. They joined the dance in
progress, and once they'd fallen in step, Notaro looked straight
at Amy once and thereafter pretended she didn't exist.

Fitcher called, "You there, come over here." She turned back,
fearful that he'd called to Notaro, but he was gesturing to a
blond-haired boy who was standing off to the side of the dancers
and who might not have been any older than she.

He came forward with obvious reluctance, giving her a troubled look. "Reverend?" he said.

"My wife needs to dance, Mr. Gibbons, and I would greatly
appreciate it if you'd be so kind as to accommodate her. You don't
have a partner, do you?"

"No, sir."

"Then it's settled. Amelia, this is Orlando Gibbons, who has
been here almost since we laid the first stone at Harbinger."

The boy bowed and offered his arm, but his eyes met hers
with worry, almost fear. She accepted his arm and together they
walked toward the dancers. The dance was just ending, and so
they waited while some dancers left. Amy looked for Notaro, saw
him walk away from his partner and out of the barn.

Orlando Gibbons leaned close to Amy and said, "I'm most
sorry about your sister. I did like her very much."

"My—you knew her?"

"She came to this dance one time, when your husband was
away. And I met her and danced with her just like now. She'd
been ill, too ill to go with the reverend upon his crusade."

The fiddler played introductory notes and they moved up the
floor and took their places among the two rows of dancers. Amy

picked up the steps quickly. It was a reel of the sort she'd done with Vern a few times in the parlor back in Boston. She thought of Vern back there right now. "Ill or not, she should never have deserted him, Mr. Gibbons."

"No, I suppose not," he said, then danced away from her. Upon his return, he said, "The reverend has pretty terrible luck that way. I think God tests him to see if he's worthy to lead."

She wanted to ask what he meant by "that way," but now the dance led her to another partner, and she cast her eye about for Notaro as she promenaded back to the center line. If he had returned, he was hiding from her. Fitcher, on the other hand, seated prominently, was engaged in a discussion with a red-headed woman whom Amy hadn't seen before—or was she the same one who had danced with Notaro? Yes, she thought, it was. Fitcher glanced her way, then said something sharp to the woman. She lowered her head, took his hand and kissed it, then moved off through the crowd and out of the barn.

Amy changed partners again. She had to pay too much attention to the dance, which distracted her from what was going on around her, the little puzzle pieces of larger events. She stepped to the edge of the dance area and turned to step back to her partner. He had gone, and in his place, dancing opposite her now, was her husband. His hands were on his hips and he grinned at her surprise. As they closed, he commented, "I do so love a good fiddle tune." The look of glee on his face surprised her.

They danced around each other, and it seemed to her that the music changed, its tempo picked up although she continued to step in time and felt no faster herself. She sensed movement outside the line of dancers and found that everyone was standing up. They moved apart, in pairs, in groups. Like a fire the dancing spread across the barn. Fitcher clapped his hands, and others picked it up. The pattern changed, no longer a reel. People were whirling in place, spinning around each other, a living astrolabe of wheeling bodies. The forces gathered her up and spun her in her own orbit, around Fitcher, around the floor. She slid past Orlando Gibbons. He didn't even notice her. His eyes were rolled to the ceiling as if focused on Heaven. A palpable wave of ecstasy washed over her. Her body tingled. She shuddered divinely, linked arms with someone, and they flung each other into new orbits, remarkably never crashing into anyone else. She had no idea where she was going but her every step seemed choreographed.

She rolled against someone, laughed, and found that she'd linked arms with Michael Notaro. Where had he come from? She ought to have been shocked, embarrassed. She should have pushed away, but she couldn't release him. The wide-eyed look he gave her might have been terror, as if he also didn't know how he'd come to be there, but he didn't let go either. He said, "Amy, I love you."

Then something cut between them—a shadow, a swift blur like a storm cloud scudding through the room—and the link broke and she spun away, into the middle of the maelstrom, up against Fitcher again. He anchored her while the crowd, young and old alike, whirled about them, heads thrown back, faces turned to Heaven, beaming, joyous; a few shaking, eyes either closed or rolled back in their sockets. A woman nearby cried out, an animal sound. She fell into the crowd.

The music wound down, slowed, slid into the simple reel it had been before. Dancers stumbled and walked this way and that, some with their arms out as if blind. Many of them headed for the outdoors. People collapsed on the floor, others upon the hay bales. One woman had her head thrown over the end of the bale, her tongue protruding, her hands stretched up for the ceiling. She made noises that might have been demented utterances, words in some alien language. Those outside the barn walked in circles or away down the lanes, into darkness. A wind was blowing now, as if their spinning had set the sky in motion. At the very edge of the light Amy saw Michael Notaro glance back once, straight at her, then turn and break into a run. The night swallowed him.

The original row of eight dancers and the five-piece orchestra remained. They continued the reel as if nothing had happened, though they were visibly shaken, as disheveled and confused as anyone else—as much as she was.

Fitcher's hands touched her shoulders. He moved behind her, guiding her in a sidestep. He said, "I hope you enjoyed the dance. It's all the purifying we'll do this night."

The music concluded. Moving beside her, Fitcher took her arm and walked with her out of the barn. The remaining Fitcherites beamed at them as if every earthly care had been swept away. Most bid the reverend a good night. A few thanked him for dancing. She saw one couple embracing, kissing, off in the shadows between two buildings. She thought of Notaro, imagined it was herself there, and felt a stab of loss, a twist of desire in her belly. Amy saw the hands of the man, whoever he was, slide up under the woman's skirts. Her head craned around to watch but she couldn't slow down: She was floating on Fitcher's touch and he impelled her on, down the twisting lanes and toward the house on the hill that glowed with candles like a spray of stars.

Twenty-four

*A*MY WANDERED DOWN TO the village after dinner the next night in the hope there would be another dance.

She found the barn closed up, and the village lanes oddly deserted, as if everyone had left. She wondered if they had all stayed at the house, maybe gathered in the Hall of Worship. How could she have missed them? Even to herself, she pretended that she was looking for everyone, and not just Michael Notaro.

After walking through the maze of lanes, she meandered back across the edge of the fields and into the ripe groves. She hadn't come out the other side when the alarm bell sounded.

Amy had heard it rung for meals, but this was nothing like the leisurely clanging that called the devout to dinner. Someone was pulling the clapper back and forth in a fury. She ducked under the branches to where she could see the rear of the house.

People in and around the tents had sprung up and were walking or running toward the noise. At the house, lights appeared—lanterns or torches being lit at the back porch. These clustered around the bell. Then, like a swarm of lightning bugs, they headed across the yard and toward the woods.

A compelling sense of urgency overtook Amy. She lifted the skirt of her dress and broke into a run. She dodged through the treacherous tents with their ropes and pegs, and then between the markers of the cemetery.

At the edge of the woods a man was waving his arms. She reached him at the same time as the crowd did. He turned grimly and led them all into the woods. The lanterns revealed the path, and she fell in among the others moving one or two at a time along it. The path soon ran up against the towering iron fence. The man stopped there.

"A couple a boys playing Indians found him," he told everyone, and gestured up with the light. Up the black iron verticals, almost the height of two people, up to where the body hung. In the dusk she couldn't quite tell what had happened: It looked as if someone were balancing on the top of the fence. The light dwindled before it reached that high. Farther back a torch was being passed along, hand to hand above them. At the same time the crowd parted and Elias Fitcher came marching through. He overtook the passing torch, snatched and carried it with him to the fence.

He asked what had happened. The man who'd led them repeated his explanation about playing children, and pointed. Fitcher raised the torch high overhead.

The face, twisted sideways, stared down as if in terror at the torch itself. It was Michael Notaro.

The body hung impaled upon two of the uprights: One had pierced his belly, the other his throat. The body had sunk on the spikes all the way to the top rail. His arms dangled, one inside and one outside the fence. Blood from his wounds had run down them. Drops hung from the splayed fingertips of the hand above Fitcher, extended as if offering to pull someone up.

The crowd evaporated for Amy. The woods around her own house folded around her. She saw places where she'd lain with him, kissed him, laughed with him, in the dark, in the underbrush, once in the back of his wagon. She combed leaves from her hair. She touched his dimpled chin, felt his stiff whiskers, smelled his hair. Then someone spoke, and she stood among them again.

"He was trying to climb out, looks like," said the man who'd led them there. "Trying to run away. He must'a shimmied up one of the poles, but slipped and fell back'ard."

"Yes, poor fellow," Fitcher concurred. "We must get him down from there. Someone bring us ropes. We must be very careful how we go about it. I don't want to lose someone else on the prongs of this slippery fence."

The call carried through the crowd for ropes.

Fitcher turned suddenly to Amy. "I think you should not be here for this," he told her, then to the others, "nor any other woman or child should witness this. It's too grisly a thing. Please now, some of you men stay and assist us. But no one else."

But Amy couldn't move. She had fixed upon Notaro's open eyes. The flickering torch made it seem that they shifted, that some life was left in him. Fitcher finally stepped between her and the horrible accusatory face. He turned her firmly until her back was to the fence. "Go on now. This is nothing for you to dwell on."

The majority of the crowd were moving away, following lights back to the house, and she fell in with them. She trudged along silently, unable to react to the death of her lover—even to acknowledge that was what he had been. Now she would never tell Fitcher about him. *Don't speak ill of the dead.*

Someone ahead of her said, "It was the Angel of Death got him, sure as I'm alive." She glanced up sharply but couldn't make out more than the shape of a head, a shaggy silhouette in the darkness. Out of the woods, they wove a path around the grave markers. The silhouette beside him replied, "I seen something moving about in the woods just afore supper. Tall and thin it was."

"You probably saw *him*."

"Naw, was nothing like him. I knew Notaro well enough, and he was a short fella, though he'd got a mite skinny of late. This thing was like smoke outen a chimney."

"Probably all it was. Chimney smoke clings in them trees all the time."

"No, 'twasn't the same."

"Well, what was it like, then?"

"Like a shadow turned side-on—more that than smoke. I come near as the cemetery to look on it. Didn't have a face, far as I could tell. Like maybe there was a cloak over its head. I wasn't going to get no closer. Notaro—I bet it was hunting him, sure as I'm here. You saw his eyes. Dear Jesus, I'm tellin' Emma not to go into these woods on no account. Someone should warn them young boys to stay off, too."

"Children play in there all the time. You can't keep 'em off. Anyhow, *he* was trying to run away."

"Maybe so. Or maybe he saw it, too, maybe he saw it close up. If that thing cornered me, I'd a' climbed to the moon to get away."

"Maybe it was just his time."

"It's all our times soon enough, but if the creek don't flood and the sky don't fall, I'm for waiting till the day itself."

Another man behind them muttered, "Vengeance is mine, saith the Lord."

The two others twisted their heads around. One replied, "That's for outside here, Benjamin. We're supposed to be spared from all that. Fitcher's said. Besides, vengeance for what? Notaro hadn't done nothin'."

She barely caught Benjamin's reply: "Unless the angel ain't *from* the Lord," he muttered.

The men walked on awhile in silence as if pondering that. Amy followed, although they seemed to have stopped talking and the rest of the crowd had gone. She fixed upon the image, remembering a moment at the dance the night before when something gray and cold had swept between her and Michael. She'd thought it was just her imagination then, a dizzy moment in the dance.

As they reached the back of the dormitory wing, one of the men added, "If you're right, we got the devil in among us then."

"Always been so," said the other. "Since the day Adam bit into the apple."

In her room, Amy lit a candle, then sat and tried to understand why Michael Notaro had been running away. She could only conclude with heavy guilt that he'd been running from her—from having to watch her with Fitcher. He'd lost weight, the man had said. He'd been escaping from his own desire for her.

From there it was a short step to convincing herself that she had killed him. She hadn't meant to, but that hardly mattered. Her marriage had put him in an impossible situation, where he had to look upon her every day in the possession of another man, and he had finally fled from it. Possibly it had driven him out of his mind. Nothing else really explained his trying to climb out of Harbinger. For Jesus' sake, he held the keys to the gate! He could have walked out.

He'd told her about it—it had only been weeks but seemed a lifetime ago. Fitcher had entrusted him with his own set of keys so he could bring in supplies. He could open any of the gates in any of the fences. He could open the village shops, the mills, most of the rooms in the house and dormitories. Why, if he had the keys, would he have felt compelled to *climb* out?

Perhaps Fitcher had taken them away from him. She wanted to ask, but couldn't think of a way to broach the subject that wouldn't sound suspicious.

But Fitcher hadn't taken the keys.

The discovery of their whereabouts occurred on the second day after the death of Michael Notaro, and in a manner she could never have anticipated.

Amy had finished her kitchen duties. She wanted to change into fresh clothing before she walked to the village. The humid heat of the morning had made the kitchen an oven, and already what she wore was drenched with sweat.

Upon reaching the second-floor landing, however, she encountered her husband with one foot on the second step up. He put a finger to his lips and gestured for her to proceed quietly. She stepped up and peered over his shoulder to her floor.

A child of no more than six years stood halfway down the hall. He was at one of the doors on her side of the hall, but beyond her own room. At first she couldn't tell what he was doing. The sound of clinking metal came to her, and his movements—even in shadow—made it abruptly clear. "He's opening the door," she whispered.

Reverend Fitcher glanced back at her and smiled wickedly. "Indeed he is." The door opened, throwing a wan light upon the boy and across the darkness of the hall. Fitcher said, "And I think that's probably enough."

He climbed up the last few steps and walked boldly into the hall. Amy hurried after him.

The child became aware of them almost at once. He frantically looked about, but finally just withdrew a couple of steps from the doorway and waited. There was nowhere to run. He put his hands behind his back.

Fitcher began to laugh. "Look at this boy," he cried, glancing back to her. "This *boy*. Why, if he found one plank on a beach, he would hunt until he found the whole ship!" He barked another laugh.

He and Amy reached the child, who looked guilty of the worst crime in the world despite Fitcher's good humor. "What is your name, lad?" Fitcher asked.

"Jonathan, sir," the boy replied. "Jonathan Hollings." He had short blond hair, and smeared red lines across his cheeks and forehead: war paint.

"Ah, yes, I know your family. And what have you been up to, Jonathan?" He was looking past the boy as he asked. Amy came up behind him, and peered around him into the opened room. It was dimly lit, and virtually identical to her own. The light came from a window beyond the bed. A chest of clothing stood half-opened to one side, in front of an armoire. A dressing table stood opposite the bed. Fitcher stepped into the recess to close the door, but as he did, Amy saw, lying across the table, a folded parasol.

Fitcher shut the door, then held out his hand. "You'd best give those to me now," he insisted.

Jonathan sighed and brought his hands into view. He was holding a ring of keys that Amy recognized immediately as Michael Notaro's. He'd shown them to her while bragging about his position at Harbinger. Fitcher knew them, too. He nodded to himself as he asked, "And you found these where?"

"In the woods, sir. We were playing, and I was being the Mohawk and hiding out. I got down behind a big log by the fence, and my foot kicked 'em."

"I see. And so you had to find out what you could do with them. No, don't worry, it's nothing at all. I'd been looking for these awhile, and you've recovered them. So you're owed a reward." He fished in his pocket and came up with a gold half-dollar. The boy's eyes grew the size of saucers. "There, now. You find anything else in the woods, you will tell me right away, won't you?"

"Oh, yes, sir." The boy stared at the coin in his palm.

"One more thing. This was not good, what you did. You snooped in other people's rooms, and that's wrong. Your Lord doesn't like nosy meddlers, Jonathan. To stay in good with God, you must stay in good with me. You understand?"

"I do, sir, yes, I'm sorry, sir. I didn't—"

"Yes, I know. You found something exciting. A treasure hunt you were on. But we'll have no more of those, will we?"

"No, sir."

"Good. Now run along." He pushed the boy out of the doorway, closing the door after him.

Jonathan ran down the hall and leaped the stairs to the landing. Fitcher laughed again and said, "That boy!"

Carefully, Amy ventured, "You'd lost your keys, husband?"

"I? No, no. These belonged to our late Mr. Notaro." He turned and dangled them before her. "He and I shared access to so many things. They surely fell from his pocket as he attempted to scale the fence and no one noticed them in the leaves—we came upon him at night, after all. Frankly, I was of the opinion that we'd buried them with him. I'd quite forgotten them." He pocketed the keys. "Now it's time to go to work. I have a field to inspect and you must have some candles to dip."

"I wanted to change first. It was so terribly hot in the kitchen."

"The midsummer heat is like a blast from Satan's furnace, isn't it?" He patted her shoulder, then walked off down the hall. She heard him say again, "That boy."

Amy stood in place. She listened to his footsteps descending, heard them cross the foyer floor. A door closed, and then there was silence. She crept back to the room the boy had opened. Fitcher had closed the door, but her question had sidetracked him before he could lock it.

She opened the door and carefully sneaked inside and shut it behind her. She stood in the dimness a moment before crossing to the dressing table. The parasol was pink with a few dangling tassels, and a white handle. Its identity could not be mistaken: Vern had carried it with her almost like a talisman when she went out. Likewise, the hairbrush lying there was too familiar. She pulled a few strands of her sister's hair out of the bristles, then set it down.

She walked around the bed to the armoire and pulled open one of the doors. Clothes hung inside, and she could identify most of them, one dress in particular: her mother's wedding dress, the one Vern had worn. None of the Charter girls owned many outfits. Amy knew Vern's wardrobe. There might have been one or two dresses missing, but surely Vernelia would never have run off to Henri in Boston without her clothes or her hairbrush, and never ever without her parasol.

Amy looked through the bottom drawers for anything to explain this. There was nothing. Vern had left no writing behind, no diary or journal—it hadn't been her nature to record things.

Finally, fearful that Fitcher would remember he'd left the door unlocked, Amy crept out of the room and back to her own.

She changed her clothes hastily and then set out for Harbinger village; all the while her mind tumbled with the elements of what she had learned. If Vern hadn't run off to Boston, then where had she gone?

Twenty-five

THE BOY HAD OPENED ALL THE rooms.

Amy didn't realize it until the next evening, when she took a candle and crept to Vern's room again to see if it had been locked in the interim. The door opened at her touch. She closed it again, pausing to glance the length of the hall. She pattered to the next room along and tried that door, and was surprised when it opened, too.

She pushed only a little, enough to peer around the frame.

The room looked more uninhabited than Vern's, if identically furnished. The armoire was closed and the smell was musty. She entered and closed the door carefully behind her.

A layer of dust coated the top of the small table against the wall, but there was a lopsided candle in a pewter holder there and it spat and took the flame from her own, casting enough yellowish light that she could see about her.

Cobwebs stretched across the bedposts. It wasn't a canopy bed like hers and Vern's, and it was off to the side rather than under the window. A scar in the floorboards suggested that at some point the bed had been dragged closer to the hearth. She snooped in the armoire, where as in Vern's room clothes were hung—a dark poke bonnet, a blue Princess dress, a whalebone corset, and a burnouse above the unmentionables and stockings. In the drawers at the bottom she found, folded in lace, a silver cameo with a woman's hand-painted portrait and a name, "Adele," written beneath it. She put it in her pocket to take it, but her fingers brushed the egg there, which reminded her that she must delve into the pocket each night for Fitcher. She knew sooner or later she would inadvertently grab the cameo by accident, and he would know where she'd been. Better to leave everything undisturbed. She folded the lace back up around the cameo and replaced it in the drawer, closed up the armoire, then blew out the crooked table candle. It had dripped onto the wood but there was nothing for it. If she tried to wipe up the grease, she would only clear the dust and make her intrusion the more obvious.

She left the room. Awhile she stood outside the door, glancing toward the stairs, debating what to do next. It was too early for Fitcher to arrive. He came to her at the same hour each night. She had time to look at a few more rooms, provided they were open, which they were. She made a cursory inspection of the next two, then hastily looked in upon the rest.

Five rooms proved to be identical to hers, the dressers and armoires containing women's apparel and belongings. Of the others, two were empty, unused, the bed frames bare; and two others had been converted into storage, full of trunks, boxes, and additional furnishings piled up, no doubt from the latest arrivals to Harbinger.

One small door at the very back of the hallway opened onto a narrow stairwell. But where, she wondered, was her husband's room? It appeared that they didn't even share the same *floor*.

She'd just determined that the last room was open when she heard her husband's voice below in the foyer. He laughed once, then spoke softly. Amy hurried across the hall to her own room and slipped inside.

Fitcher did not arrive for another quarter hour. He had gone to his chambers, wherever they were, and changed out of his

clothes and into his silver dressing gown. He entered her room
noiselessly as always. Amy was lying on her bed, pretending to
be engrossed in reading her Bible, and wearing only her chemise
as if she had been waiting for him since supper. The marble egg
lay beside her on the bed. He always wanted to see it first.

Fitcher strode to the armoire and retrieved the whip. Amy
closed her Bible and stood to remove her last item of clothing.
As she knelt, she spoke from the psalm she'd just read: " 'It is a
good thing to give thanks unto the Lord, and to sing praises unto
thy name, O Most High.' " The nightly ritual of the mortification
of her flesh began.

When he was finished, and the whip's venom had been drawn
out of her back through the magical, ecstasy-producing touch of
the egg, she lay in a transported dreaminess, her thoughts flying
like a released spirit through the rooms she'd penetrated, the
strange dusty sanctums she'd violated. She felt neither guilty nor
sinful for what she'd done, only confused by the complexity of
the mystery of five women's chambers containing no women.
Had they all, like Vern, "run away"? And where was *his* room?
The question threaded its way in. Where did Fitcher himself
stay? In her lucid dream, she saw him flip through his ring of
keys until he came to the strange glass one. That key must surely
answer the mystery for her. There was no such key on Notaro's
key ring. She could think of only one reason why that should be
the case. She couldn't very well ask for the keys, but she had the
scent now. She would find out, and when she did, she would . . .

What would she do?

Finally, her dream spirit settled back into her body. As it did,
the answer came to her: "I shall tell Kate."

After the morning sermon and breakfast, Amy tracked Fitcher's
movements. He'd worked the past few days in the fields, and as
she'd hoped, he set out for them again. She stood on the porch
and watched until he disappeared into the orchard. The hot,

steamy morning gave her an excuse to freshen up before going to the village, but no one was paying much attention. Like her, they had tasks to perform.

For perhaps ten minutes she stood in the doorway of her room, listening to the sounds of the house. She heard people walk in and out of the foyer; then a door closed and all was silent.

Amy hurried to the far end of the hall. The narrow door was still unlocked, and she climbed into the stairwell. The stairs curved around the wall as if inside a turret. Over the railing she peered into darkness below.

She reached a landing that contained a door. She pressed her ear to the door, but could hear nothing on the other side. Nevertheless, she took great care in turning the handle—all for nothing. The door wouldn't open. The little boy hadn't made it this far with his stolen keys. It hardly mattered, since she didn't need to creep onto the third floor—she could just walk up the main staircase some other time.

The source of light in the stairwell came from somewhere above her. Amy crept up the circling stairs one entire circuit of the spiral to reach another landing and small archway. On the far side of it was a straight, steep flight of steps gleaming in the light. Amy ducked beneath the arch and, at the bottom of the steps, found herself peering up into the glass pyramid at the top of the house. She had reached the roof.

The pyramid threw a spray of colors across the space. The glass doubled as a prismatic surface, and the sunlight pouring in split into crisscrossing rays. Amy climbed through splashes of violet, blue, green, and red. There was a railing at the top, and she crouched against it, reluctant to stand at first for fear someone in the yard or the orchards would be able to see her. She crept to the side and looked out over the rooftop.

On either side chimneys shielded the pyramid, impeding anyone's view. Amy could see only the last few windows at the ends of the dormitories. Surely no one could see her within the intersecting colors.

She rose and stepped into the center of the room, with her back to the rail. She could see the forests on every side. To the north she could make out the shimmer of the lake on which they'd steamed to Jekyll's Glen, the cleared land on the hillsides, orderly rows of planted crops, and the town itself. She thought of her home, and there it was, clearly visible, right down to the pole across the road and her father in his box, awaiting the next pilgrim. Then the impossible displacement swept over her like a wave of vertigo so intense that she had to cling to the rail and close her eyes.

When she opened them, she was looking straight down upon her house. She muttered, "Papa," and he appeared in the glass before her, seated idly in the sentry box, passing the time by reading his Bible. She was close enough to see the stubble on his cheek. Now her view hovered just above the pole. She said, "Kate," and it was as if she had become a bird. She flew from the sentry box, straight at the house, the vision so overwhelming that she recoiled as it penetrated the wall, sped up the stairs and into her room, where Kate was sweeping around the furniture. Kate was barefoot and dressed only in her chemise; but of course she wasn't expecting company, no one was going to see her, and it was enervatingly hot. Amy walked to the canted glass, pressing her hand to it as if she could simply pass through it and into the room. Distantly, she seemed to hear the whisk of the broom. "Kate," she called. Her sister went right on sweeping. "Katie, can you hear me?"

It was as if she were a ghost, a spirit hovering beside her sister. Amy wanted to grab the broom out of Kate's hands—that would shake her to her soul. Before she could, she saw the wall above Kate's bed. A shadow was etched in it, a slender faceless shade, like smoke made solid. Amy recalled what the men in the crowd had said after Notaro's impalement, and she knew she was looking at the Angel of Death. Even as she watched it, the shadow withdrew into the wall again. Had it been observing Kate or herself?

Amy closed her eyes and said, "Vernelia."

When she opened them the pyramid had gone dark. It was not black, but a deep red, the color of the molten belly of the earth. The color seemed to ripple and run, making the side of the pyramid look as if it were in motion, flexing; yet at the same time the rippling imparted a sense of peacefulness. At some distance were two luminous shapes. They might have been human but the color acted like some mercurial membrane stretched across her vision and kept her from distinguishing any features. Where was Vern in all this? Amy couldn't tell. But then she thought: *Unless*—she almost dared not think of it—*unless Vern was dead and the two glowing shapes were angels.* That would mean that she, Amy, was gazing upon Heaven itself. "Oh, my sister," she whispered.

She considered then what this pyramid at the top of the house might be. Fitcher communed with God, he spoke with Him. It was what pastors and preachers always said, but what if Fitcher spoke of a literal communion? This room, that let him look everywhere, upon everyone, could it allow him to look to Heaven? If so, would the Almighty deign to speak to her?

Without thinking, she recited, "Our Father, who art in Heaven." The glass sides of the pyramid erupted with searing light. Amy shielded her eyes, but even closed, they burned red. The brightness dimmed and she dared to peek between her fingers.

The outside was gone and she was whirling down a dark hallway, down stairs. She glimpsed the chandelier in the foyer of Harbinger spin past, then her view burst out into daylight. Her stomach threatened to disgorge. She clutched the railing at her back like a sailor clinging to a storm-tossed ship. The world whirled around her. *This isn't Heaven*, she thought. Her view dove into the orchard, sliding through branches, leaves, and fruit, then out across the field, through rows of shoulder-high corn, and out the far side. There, among dozens of others laboring in the sun, in shirtsleeves and a wide-brimmed hat, Elias Fitcher stepped one foot on a spade, turning over soil. Even as her vision rushed right at him, he straightened and whipped about, his face filling the glass before her, his crystal-blue eyes piercing the distance, locking upon hers. She shrieked and flung herself into the stairwell. Only at the last did she glimpse that there was a design, figures, set in the floor on the far side of the railing. It caught her eye beyond the flashing colors. She couldn't stop to look, however. He'd seen her.

She ran under the arch and back down the steps, down and down to the second floor, out into the hall. She took the front stairs to the foyer and dashed out the back. Instinct compelled her to guard herself. On the porch she drew up, collected herself a moment, then went down the steps. On the lawn she tried to hurry without seeming to be in a panic. The encampment was full of people, many of them sleeping in the heat, others chatting. She didn't want them to pay attention to her, didn't want them to report her. Yet she had to put as much distance as possible between herself and the house. The village might as well have been miles away.

Amy strode as fast as she could and watched the orchard for any hint of him. She saw his legs before anything else, saw him burst through the trees like a hell-bent juggernaut. She dropped to the ground behind a tent. When she dared another look, Fitcher was speeding across the lawn to the house without even acknowledging the greetings of people who climbed to their feet at his passing. Some of those working in the orchard emerged to watch him go. They traded worrisome looks as if they knew what his purposeful gait meant—as if they had witnessed this before.

Amy got up and dashed into the orchard. Panic overcame caution, and she ran the rest of the way to the village. She entered her shop, closed the door, and collapsed, gasping. She trembled, began to whimper, but forced herself to stop, to gather her wits. It wasn't over and she had little time.

The shop was hot and confining. Soaked from her run from the house, Amy looked as if she'd been at work for hours. She grabbed matches to start a fire in the hearth, took the lid from a keg and fanned the flames. At the same time she scooped spermaceti out of the keg and into one of the kettles. It melted rapidly. She added bayberry wax, mixing it in as she took the kettle off the fire. She didn't care whether the mixture ever made candles or not. The sharp scent filled the shop, and she opened the windows front and back then to let it and some of the heat escape. That was the moment Fitcher burst in upon her.

His sleeves were rolled up, his pant legs stained and dirty. Dirt smudged his brow and clung to his forearms. At first his eyes were narrow, calculating, darting all around the shop. Then he gave her a disaccording smile as if he were just making a routine visit and nothing about it were out of the ordinary. He inquired, "My dear, how is your day going?"

Amy answered just as casually: "It's very hot work, husband. Candles should be made in the cooler parts of the year, I think." She had no idea where the steel in her spine came from, how she managed not to quake and collapse with those crystal eyes boring into her. It was fear that anchored her—fear of what, she wasn't sure. It wasn't Fitcher alone. It was of something huge. Something that would destroy her if she slipped up in the slightest.

"So they should," he agreed. He walked to the hearth, looked in the kettles hanging there. "However, that observation will not take us forward very far now that we're so close to our new life. The cooler part of the year will be with us only briefly." He faced her. "Before we are gathered up."

"Of course."

"And surely it's no hotter work than baking—and dare I submit you would never suggest that we should bake no bread in summer."

"No, I shouldn't do that."

"Well, then. I did want to tell you that in a week, I will mount another crusade to go out and bring back new converts. We'll go to Providence most certainly, and New Haven. This will be our final push, our last crusade. Those who heard us in Pennsylvania are still arriving. They've transmitted the message between there and here. It's spreading on its own now, south of us. But in a week's time, you will be mistress of Harbinger while I go north. I must discuss some matters of the house with you. Tonight. Tonight, we'll talk." He passed by her, and touched his fingers to her brow. His fingertips were cool. She realized that despite the heat and the speed with which he must have raced to arrive here, he was not sweating, nor breathing hard. "Do you have my little egg?"

"Always," she replied, and brought it out of her pocket.

He nodded. "I'm so glad, my dearest Amelia. And your back, it doesn't pain you?"

"Why, no, sir."

"Then I shall leave you to your work and return to mine. I'll meet you at evening prayer." He swept through the door like a gust of wind and was gone.

That evening, as he whipped her, Fitcher demanded that she ask forgiveness of God for her many sins. He played upon her certainty of her befouled soul. With each slash of the whip, he demanded, "Confess!" She bit her lip and drowned in the pain, accepted it, welcomed it because she deserved it more than he knew. She was addicted to it, but she refused to confess anything about her visit to the roof.

Later, as he rolled the egg across her skin, he spoke tenderly to her, promising her such glory as she could barely imagine if she unburdened her soul. "God," he told her as he had many times before, "will know all. When you account finally, you'll want no blemish left upon your soul. He will find it out." The sound of his voice was hypnotic, enveloped in the ecstasy of the egg upon her skin. His words threatened to steal her spirit away. She could feel her will dissolving before the sound and sensation, but she remembered that she'd seen Vern in Heaven and clung to that vision to give her the strength to deny him.

Eventually he set down the egg beside her and left the room. When the door closed, Amy roused herself. Normally she would have let the opiate egg pull her down into sleep, but now she must act. She listened at the door, then stole naked out into the hall. It was empty. She would have little time: He must be climbing up to the pyramid even now. She hurried to Vern's room. The door didn't open. It had been locked. She ran to the one beside it just to satisfy herself that there was no mistake. She didn't need to try the others to know they would all be locked. He had corrected his mistake.

Then she raced back into her room, closed the door, and returned to the bed and lay down.

If he gazed down upon her now, she would be in her bed, where she belonged, where he expected her to be.

She was safe. For a while.

Twenty-six

THE NEXT DAY AFTER THE MORN-
ing sermon, Amy asked for a day
to visit her family. Fitcher re-
fused. "There's too much to do now. So many people arriving
daily—just step out on the back porch and behold the tent city
being erected. They spill into our orchards. Our stables overflow
with their animals. We've turned so many horses out to pasture
that they compete with our cattle. The mill can't produce enough
flour for us. The crops can't grow any faster. Even supplies from
Jekyll's Glen are in short supply. Mr. Van Hollander can hardly
keep up. Soon I'll have to be sending wagons to Trumansburg to
keep us fed. I could not let you go off even for a day, Amelia.
You must assist me in maintaining some semblance of order here.
If you're satisfied we have enough candles now, there are other
things you can do. Critical things." It was the first he'd said anything about her involvement or about the condition of Harbinger
being less than utopian.

The tents *had* spread across the lawn. Maybe half of it remained open. People crammed the Hall of Worship at each sermon. They stood in the back, lined the walls. They strained

forward when he spoke; they lowered their gaze when he walked
by. She'd seen it for weeks, but only now did she begin to realize
the scope of the problem. "If space is restricted, why not clear
more forest, erect more buildings? There must be enough people
in those tents for a log-rolling?"

If he realized she was challenging him, he didn't take the
bait. Rather, he agreed with her and suggested she consider mar-
shalling the community to this endeavor while he was gone to
Providence and New Haven. "We'll be bringing even more back
with us—a flood of converts as the end nears. They also will need
space. Yes, you're wise, my dear, this is a good notion. And you
can have more corrals assembled for the animals."

Amy grimaced. All she had done was trap herself.

He added, "Besides, if you need time with your family, why,
your father and Lavinia come almost daily to hear my midday
sermon; you can speak with them here. You needn't go outside
our community for that."

"It isn't my father I wish to see," she protested.

He pursed his lips. "No, I understand. Amelia, soon enough,
you'll be bound together, and the Next Life will be forever. You
and your sisters."

"What, even Vernelia?"

He lowered his gaze as if mentally upbraiding himself for the
slip. "I may—that is, I am in a position to intercede on her behalf
with our Lord. You may well find yourself in her company. I
believe I can make that happen. Only a short time remains—a
few months. Can you not wait that long?"

"I—" she began, then broke off. "Of course, Mr. Fitcher, of
course I can."

He brushed his cool hand across her cheek. "Good."

As he walked away, she was thinking that this was how he
had kept Vern from visiting them, too. She understood, finally,
that Kate's fears for her sister had been all too well founded.

The matter was settled. Amy could think of no way to circumvent
him. Worse, now he'd assigned her new duties, new tasks to an-

chor her. She went to the noon sermon with no hope; walked into the crowded Hall of Worship, and there found her sister waiting for her.

The instant Amy saw Kate, she cried out. She ran down the red carpet to embrace her. Kate reached out to her, kissed and hugged her. Amy was in tears. The nearest worshippers stared at this display of affection as if at two pillars of salt. In Amy's ear, Kate whispered, "I asked Papa to let me come hear a sermon in his place. He agreed because he wants me to experience the joy he's found with Fitcher's words. I didn't tell him the truth." She stepped back and looked her sister in the eye. "I didn't tell him you called to me."

Amy gaped. "You heard?"

"Not exactly. More as if I felt it beneath my skin. But I knew it was you."

"Oh, Kate. There's so much to tell, but it's so awful—" She stopped. Kate's gaze had shifted somewhere behind her. Amy turned. Reverend Fitcher stood at the door behind her. He was too far away to have heard anything they said, but the lids of his eyes were lowered with suspicion.

"Why, Miss Katherine," he said. "An unexpected visitation." He came forward, the crowd parting as if afraid to touch him. "Your sister and I were speaking of you only this morning. She wanted to visit you at your home."

"Then I've saved her the journey, sir. I wished to see her as well, but also to hear you preach, which my father promises shall fill me with the glory of God."

"I should very much like to see you filled, Miss Charter, and I'll try to live up to the promise." He raised his hands as if giving benediction and squeezed past them down the aisle.

Amy said, "We must talk while he's speaking." She took Kate's hand and led her out of the hall before Fitcher had reached the pulpit. She looked back once to see him place his hand upon the glass skull as he navigated the altar.

People pushed past them in the entryway. They entered the foyer, Amy bowing and nodding to people who were still arriving to hear the sermon. If they wondered at her being out there, they were too concerned about getting inside themselves to say anything.

Finally the foyer was empty. Amy said, "Michael Notaro's dead."

"My God, Amy, you didn't—"

"No, I didn't do anything. We didn't even speak after I arrived. I saw him at a dance only once. He couldn't stand to look at me. And then he was dead."

"I'm sorry."

"The Angel of Death took him, Kate. It pursued him into the woods and it killed him." Kate looked at her as if trying to make out how literally to take the statement. Amy continued, "They talk about it here all the time, like it's some monster roaming the grounds. But I've seen it. When I called to you, I saw it in the wall, where we thought we were talking to Samuel, I saw it watching you. And then I tried to find Vern, too, and, oh, Kate, I think she's dead, I think I saw Heaven and maybe God and angels. They glowed."

"Amy."

"No, I know how it sounds. But, look." She fished the marble egg out of her pocket. "He gave this to me on my wedding night. I have to keep it with me all the time, because I never know when he'll ask me for it." She dropped it onto Kate's palm. "And there are rooms next to mine. A little boy found Michael's keys. He had the keys to all the buildings and the gates. The little boy opened all the rooms, and I went into some of them, and one was Vern's. It was hers, Kate, and it had everything of hers in it. Her parasol was lying there. And her dresses, mother's wedding dress, everything."

"I don't understand. If Vern ran away—"

"*Yes.*" Amy grabbed her arm. "If she ran away, why are her belongings still here? There were other rooms, too. Other women's rooms, just like hers and mine, but older, dustier. I looked all around but I couldn't find his room anywhere. I don't even know where he stays in this house. And where I called you—it's the pyramid on the roof. It has some kind of magical power I don't understand. I said your name and it took me to you. I saw you sweeping the floor, and I saw the angel."

"Vern's Sam Verity is the Angel of Death?"

"I don't know. I don't know—maybe it killed him, too. Kate, it hovered over you like it was waiting for you to walk beneath it. Didn't you feel it there?" But it was obvious she hadn't. Amy shook her head. "It doesn't matter. I believe Elias can talk to God, I believe he can see into death and everywhere he likes."

Kate considered before she spoke. "But if that's so, Amy, then he is what Papa says—he's the true prophet. He *can* lead us to the other side."

"No, I mean, yes, he has that power. But there's something hidden, there's something we aren't told, any of us. His room— where's his room in the house? Everything feels all wrong. And I'm so afraid of him now."

Kate placed her free hand over Amy's, as much to loosen the grip on her wrist as to comfort her sister. "Afraid? Does he hurt you?" she asked. She tried to sound as if everything her sister was saying made sense to her. She was still holding the egg. Amy let go of her wrist and closed the fingers of both hands around it and Kate's hand. Her laugh sounded brittle. "He punishes me for my sins. He takes them away, then puts them back."

"What do you mean, he puts them back?"

"It's hard." Amy tried to make sense of it so she could tell it. She had to make Kate understand, convince her that she wasn't raving. Her eyes started to fill with tears. "He has a whip, a leather cat. But then he has the egg, and when he touches it to me, it undoes everything that the whip has done, so that every night my penance begins again, as if it never happened. It never ends. I'm never shriven. Kate, I'm so terrible. I've lied, I've deceived him, I broke my promises to him. I loved Michael. I don't *want* to go to Heaven. I can't—I'll be thrown down with Vern, only he's going to get Vern in, he told me he can, and I'll be the only one cast out." She wailed the last few words.

"Oh, Amy dear." Kate wrapped her arms around her sister and held her while she cried. In the background, the voice of Elias Fitcher rolled like thunder.

*   *   *

Amy knew she hadn't convinced Kate of anything. They'd gone back into the dark entry hall and listened in the shadows to the last of the sermon.

"To enter Heaven," he proclaimed, "you must let your many and horrid sins come forth. Let God see them in order that He may forgive them, and cleanse you of all sin. We're all of us just poor sinners, and cannot work out for ourselves how Righteousness must unfold, or how the blemishes of our sins may be wiped away. When Christ asks you 'What will ye that I shall do unto you?' you must answer that you come seeking instruction. You must welcome it, and let the word of God guide you. Now, let us pray together . . ."

After the prayer, the sermon ended. Fitcher strode through the crowd, eventually reaching Kate. She told him how his voice had rung like a bell and how his words had banished her doubt. He asked if she had been filled by the sermon and she responded, "Oh, completely." There was something going on in their dialogue that Amy couldn't grasp—some embedded code being exchanged, but one that seemed to have nothing to do with her. Kate never so much as inquired about how Fitcher treated his wife. Nothing the two of them said involved Amy at all.

Kate hugged her before leaving, and whispered again in her ear, "Do nothing to provoke him, sweetheart." Amy saw this as Kate's way of telling her that she hadn't been believed and must endure her state. Kate must think her hysterical. She had been, yes, she *was* hysterical, but with cause. With such cause!

She heeded the advice, although it took no effort to do so. He was busy planning his crusade, gathering up the soldiers of God who were to accompany him.

His whipping of her in the evening was only cursory, as if the process of scourging her now bored him. His mind was elsewhere. She didn't care. She went to the whipping post willingly, half convinced now that she was insane, and it would just be one more obstacle to her entering the gates of Heaven when the time came.

Her days she spent doing whatever was asked of her in the kitchens, leading new arrivals from the gate into the encampment, guiding them to where the horses were being released to pasture, to where the wagons were being abandoned. She didn't so much throw herself into her duties as try to lose herself in them. Let Amy vanish in servility, she thought. Maybe through compliance, she could enter Heaven.

Then one night, after Fitcher had whipped and cleansed her, he sat beside her on the bed. She had her eyes closed, luxuriating in the sensations still vibrating through her from the touch of that cold marble anodyne. Beside her head something tinkled. She opened one eye.

Fitcher had placed his keys on the bed beside her. Her other eye opened. She stared at them, at the light glinting on them. At the one key unlike all the others.

He said, "Now you are in charge, my dear. Of everything." He rolled the egg up and set it in the center of the keys. "Keep this with you always so I'll always know that you're safe."

Such kind words. Such tenderness. In her narcosis her terror seemed a distant memory, unattached and floating far from her. Now she trusted him and had so misjudged him, when all he wanted was to protect her. She could imagine almost anything. She asked, "Who will scourge me if you're not here?"

He patted her rump. "Ah, that's important to you now. You can't be without it."

"It can never end."

"Forgiveness is a steep climb. One does not return to Heaven without effort."

"Return?"

"Yes," he said slowly, drawing the syllable out. "You were in Heaven before you were born, and you'll return to it very soon."

"With you?"

"I shall enter, triumphant, with so many souls in my keeping." He rattled the keys. "You know about these because I've instructed you. Go where you like."

"Except for the one place."

"That's right." He leaned over and kissed her cheek. She

could not remember him having kissed her since the wedding.

The keys seemed to hiss; or was it the trees outside her open window?

"Elias?" she asked, rolling over, wanting to pull him down on top of her.

The room was empty.

Amy lay back and tried to sleep. It was a hot late August night, and she lay lethargically atop the sheets.

Whenever she closed her eyes, the light of the lamp or the candles flickered, as though something had passed through the room. The first time she thought Elias had returned, but he wasn't there. No one was. It must have been a breeze from the window, although none was blowing upon her.

She finally rolled onto her side with her back to the egg and the ring of keys. Out of sight, the keys seemed to exert an even stronger pull on her imagination. She told herself she must be good, she wanted to be good, and good meant not prying, not looking where she'd been told never to look. She was the dutiful, obedient daughter. Even Kate had said not to look, hadn't she? Why, then, could Amy not help but dwell on that glass key, on her husband's secret rooms that no one was to visit? *Where does he live?* she'd asked her sister.

Amy tossed and turned. She got up and blew out the lights. She stood and looked out upon the camp, drained of color by the moon. Could any of them see her up here, naked in her window? Would they have understood all the knots and twists in her soul? How could she want to be good and still wish to defy his imposed restrictions? She picked up the keys and the egg from the bed and placed them on the table before lying down again.

She never did find sleep.

In the morning, exhausted, she sat in the rear of the Hall of Worship and listened to him exhort the community to behave like perfect Christians while he was gone. They were to listen to Reverend Flavy, attend to his vision. He said nothing whatsoever about her or her plans for Harbinger. Nothing about raising new buildings for all the latecomers. Nothing at all.

He bid them farewell, strode down the aisle and out of the

room as if he didn't even see her. The hall emptied as the devout followed him through the foyer and onto the front lawn. They cheered him and his legion as they set out: dozens of wagons, fifty or more horses, men, women, and children. There must have been twice as many as on his previous crusade.

Amy felt in her pocket for the egg and the keys. She turned away from the cheering throng and went up the stairs to the third floor.

He didn't live on her floor, she knew that. She'd seen every room there. His quarters had to be here, somewhere.

The hallway was darker than on the second floor. She walked along, looking at each door, looking for some indication that one of them might lead where the others didn't. The end of the hall was as dark as night, but her eyes adjusted until she could make out the thin reddish line of light spilling from under a door there, a door set back in its own alcove, unlike any other door in the house. She sorted through the keys by feel. The glass key was slick as ice. She transferred the egg to her other hand.

She entered the alcove. The wall of chill air inside it surprised her. She looked back down the hall, which remained empty. Her breath misted before her. Then she fit the key into the hole and turned it. It clicked and the door swung open in invitation. She saw the skylight first—the stained-glass panel of Adam and Eve. Something about it looked familiar, and she wandered in until she was directly beneath it. She couldn't quite place where she had seen it before, but knew she had. Then her belly bumped up against something, and she gave up trying to identify the stained glass and looked down.

Her sister stared up at her from inside a huge tub, from underwater.

Vern's eyes had gone milky and soft, the lips were slightly parted, showing the hint of her lower teeth. Her neck was pressed up against the side of the tub. There was no body, only more heads, forming a ring in the middle of which five arms had been planted like small trees. Some of the fingertips were rotted to bone.

They were dead; Vern was dead.

Amy almost swooned, but caught herself. She forgot that she held his egg. It slipped out of her grasp and plunged into the cauldron.

She thrust her hand in to retrieve it. Her fingers found the egg, but also Vern's lips. Her knuckles slid down her sister's teeth. She screamed and, clutching the egg, yanked her hand out. The egg had turned bright red.

She saw everything around her now. There were dismembered torsos hung upon the wall beside tongs and scythes and other strange devices; she looked away, and found feet and more hands sticking out of a barrel across the room. Aghast, she turned, and there was his ax propped against the wall beside the door. She saw it all.

Nowhere she looked shielded her from what she'd seen, only compounded the horror until it all boiled over. Amy fled out of the room, back through the icy air, back into the hall.

She picked up speed—faster as she saw that the doors on either side now hung open, faster to get away before whatever lurked there could emerge. Down the steps and down her own hall, the keys thrust ahead of her as if drawing her to her room, ready to unlock the door, but it was open already, thank God! And she ran straight inside, straight into him, into his arms, already open to catch her. She shrieked and jumped back.

Her brain flew apart at the collision, but not before she'd hidden the dripping egg behind her. She sought for words, but there were none she could assemble. She could only gawk at him.

Fitcher, with half-lidded eyes, held up a leather-bound book, and said as if nothing were odd, "I forgot my Bible and had to come back for it. I'd forgotten you, too, in my haste—to say goodbye." Snail-like, he seemed only to notice her quaking terror sluggishly, and then, brows knit, he looked her up and down. Staring at her feet, he ticked his tongue against his teeth. "Oh, dear," he said.

Amy followed his gaze to her feet. Her slippers, her pale blue
slippers, were now dark and wetly red. They smeared the floor
where she stood, the blood as thick as syrup. His walking stick,
tucked beneath his arm, pointed at them as though in accusation.
She twisted her head to see the smeary prints she'd left in the
hall—just the ball of her foot and her toes. She'd been running.
She closed her eyes in search of an explanation. There was none.
She let go the egg. It thumped on the floor, then rolled around
her. He lowered his stick to the floor and stopped the egg against
its tip—the egg incarnadine, as if alive.

"My poor apostate Amelia, all of our efforts and still you
failed me. Not even was I gone from the road." He pocketed the
small Bible in his long black coat. "Now, what shall I do?" he
asked himself almost idly, then closed his hand around her neck
and pushed her into the hall.

His fingers were talons, his arm a plank. She had no time to
struggle, she could barely keep her footing, forced backward. He
drove her up the stairs and to the third floor, following the trail
she had left. She half twisted in his grip to make the climb.

The doors along the hall were open. Gray and silent men
stared out from the rooms. One of them, his hair as wild as ever
it had been in life, was Michael Notaro, but torn by the fence.
She shrieked then, but it came out through his clutch no more
than a bleat. She bucked, twisting and turning her torso but her
head was fixed. They flew now, down the hall, straight for the
door she'd left open. She imagined she saw herself impelled toward it. *I'm not here*, she shouted in her head, *I'm far away. My
soul is far away!*

And so it seemed that her body swept into the room so fast
that her spirit separated from it, lagged behind and hung safely
in the dark alcove, barred by the chill wall between her world
and his. The door slammed, cutting off her view. Her spirit didn't
need to watch him raise the ax nor hear her screaming stop.

Twenty-seven

KATE HAD READ IN HER BIble: "Narrow is the way which leadeth unto life and Few there be that Find it"; but as the time of Fitcher's apocalypse approached, the number of those seeking the way increased a hundredfold at least—and that was just along her road.

Most of the travelers were sent ahead of his crusaders. They all called themselves "Fitcherites" now. The derisive sting had been stripped from the word. They worshipped the man and were proud to be named after him. There were some who had used the epithet to slur others but now counted themselves among his staunchest defenders. Many of these individuals publicly proclaimed their change of heart at the various local tent meetings. Such public expiation persuaded many who lurked on the fringes to "come into the light."

Jekyll's Glen was evolving into a canvas city. The new structures weren't really tents so much as huge awnings on poles, but there were dozens of them. The first was raised for one afternoon and evening of preaching, and had captured perhaps ten people—

a mix of locals and a family who were passing through on their
way to Harbinger.

Kate happened to go to town the same afternoon to buy supplies, encountering not only the tent meeting but also the first
squatters settled along the Gorge Road.

Under the tent, a short, pop-eyed preacher had been proclaiming that "We spend our lives exposed to peril—and of our
own making—just as anyone who walks along a slippery precipice
is sooner or later going to fall. Well, my friends, as the psalm says,
we've been set in slippery places and will surely be cast down
into destruction!" Returning home, she mentioned the tent
preacher to her father. Within the hour, he'd gone off to town
himself to take part, leaving her in charge of the tolls. He didn't
come home until late.

Within the week, awnings flanked the main road in and out
of Jekyll's Glen like a transported Middle Eastern bazaar. Awnings stood in vacant lots, in front of houses, and even on the lawns
of the two churches. The sermonizing went on round the clock.

The latest converts counted among them many preachers of
the traveling sort, who went normally from town to town on one
circuit or another, but found themselves united in the service of
the greater preacher, Fitcher. Either they realized this was the
way the divine wind was blowing, or they had sense enough to
hedge their bets. Here they only had to stand along the street
and proclaim loudly to draw an ample crowd. Harbinger fed them
a growing audience by closing its gates to anyone lacking the
specific consent of Reverend Fitcher, and he was still on the road
amassing legions. The crusaders included Lavinia but not Mr.
Charter. He had stayed home on orders from Fitcher, who expressed concern about his general frailty. Better for everyone that
Mr. Charter stay home to act as gatekeeper. Afterward, he would
be brought up to the house—before the end, naturally. Accepting
his exile with stoic resolve, Mr. Charter had insisted that Lavinia
go without him. One of them at least should be there to assist
their commander. Fitcher depended upon his lieutenants.

With Lavinia gone, Mr. Charter seemed to change shape. The
guise of adamant authoritarian was shed like a skin. Although he

still maintained his rightness as passionately as ever, he withered: His diminished role robbed him of the zealot's essence. While he would have denied it had Kate confronted him, Mr. Charter was humiliated. Not only had he been refused his rightful place, but he was seeing finally that his wife's affections were not his to command and never had been. Lavinia desired only Fitcher. So long as Mr. Charter shared her view, her enthusiasm, with equal passion, he had a place with her. Zeal had forged their union. In being forced to accept a reduced and distanced position, Mr. Charter gained a less happy perspective of how things were.

It transformed his relationship to his youngest daughter: Kate became the surrogate wife and mother—a role she recognized from Vern's having occupied it before her.

She and he ate their meals together and read their Bibles together; sometimes her father would lie back on his bed, utterly drained, and she would read to him by candlelight.

One night she came to read and was settling herself upon her chair when Mr. Charter, lying upon his bed and with an arm thrown over his eyes, confessed, "I do miss her so." Kate nodded but didn't ask for clarification. He must have sensed her perplexity, however, because he continued, "Your mother. I've had no compass since she left us. I try to sight upon her but she's nowhere. Sometimes I remember something she said—I can almost hear her voice the way it was, and my heart fills with her, as if she's within me. And then I don't know where to look. I cast about, and she isn't there. I'm so lost, Katie."

She put down her book and did not read, but let him drift to sleep while she sat by his side and held his hand.

During the day, when she wasn't preparing meals or tending to other quotidian tasks, she assisted him at the pike, where she soothed the ire of those who objected to having to pay a toll before going on. Even when it was explained to them who the pike belonged to and that the money was used for the upkeep of Harbinger, they often raged: What did Harbinger need in the way of maintaining, when the whole world was only weeks away from complete annihilation? Kate would answer, reasonably, that for the few remaining weeks, people still had to eat, and animals had to be tended. Did they wish to die of starvation before their appointed time because no one wished to contribute?

Her reasoning usually settled them down, although she didn't believe any of it. In truth much of the collected money was languishing in bags in their cellar. No one had bothered to come and retrieve it since August, from which she concluded that things must be just as chaotic behind the iron fence.

And then Harbinger closed its gates.

Those who walked there only to find themselves turned away until Fitcher returned came wandering dejectedly back down the road. They would stop and talk with Kate or her father, mostly to despair that they'd come all this way only to be told they must wait a little longer. One man, as he returned, proclaimed: "Hitherto shalt thou come, but no farther." He explained the situation and many who heard him turned back toward Jekyll's Glen. Most of those denied entrance wanted to make sure that they would be remembered later on when they had to trudge up the road again, and not asked for another toll. Kate's response was to give them back their coins. She suspected that once Fitcher did return, the collection of tolls would be suspended, in which case they all would have been clamoring for a refund if she kept the money. She could not help but wonder why a pike had ever been set up on this road at this spot. Turnpike roads were nearly a thing of the past. Why not collect the fees at the front gate? Yes, Mr. Jasper had claimed that Fitcher didn't want his people soiled by the touch of money, but Fitcher himself had never intimated this was the case. If people were delivering their entire fortunes to Fitcher, why bother to separate a meager toll from them first? She could not work it out. It seemed only cruel.

When she wasn't busy with some task, she thought about Amy. She was terribly worried about her sister, especially after her last visit to Harbinger. Amy had behaved so strangely, and told such unlikely stories, that Kate couldn't help but think she'd lost her senses. Amy had always been so inclined to believe in her own damnation, very little effort would have been required to send her spiraling into millennarian frenzy.

So, on her seventeenth birthday, Kate asked her father if she could go to Harbinger to hear a sermon. It meant that he had to give up his daily visit to the tent preachers in town, but he willingly acceded, and let her take the buckboard and drive there— his gift to her.

She found the road dotted with small encampments, tents and people who were now living beneath their wagons, who had not come back after being denied entry. What they were eating, how they were subsisting, she didn't know, but she supposed they must be dodging the pike and going into town for supplies. The number of campfires concerned her, but the cooler weather had brought with it storms, and the forest would be wet enough not to ignite easily.

It occurred to Kate as her wagon rumbled across the gorge that she might not be allowed in, either. However, the two men at the gate knew her—or at least knew that her father was in charge of the pike and that her sister had married the reverend. They couldn't tell her where her sister was but they let her pass.

Harbinger looked more like a displaced temple than the last time she'd seen it. Previously, the front lawn had been devoid of people. Now it teemed with life. People were camped everywhere on the grounds, all the way to the fence. Children ran around the clusters of barrels, boxes, and tents, squealing the way playing children invariably did when they were running away from a harmless threat. She thought that more trees had been cut down outside the fence than the last time she'd been here—and that only a month or so back.

She left the buckboard in front of the house, tying the reins to a hitching post even as a boy came down off the portico and said he would watch it for her. She thanked him and went up the steps and inside the house.

She could hear the noise of the crowd before she even opened the door.

The foyer was packed with people. Half were pressing toward the door of the refectory, the rest pushing into the doorway to the Hall of Worship. Kate joined the latter group. She had come here to see Amy, but she felt some obligation to attend a sermon. And Amy might be there, too.

The pews were filled. Some of those in attendance appeared to have converted their space into a temporary residence. Blankets were draped over the backs of some pews, and clothing. People jostled one another. She witnessed anger and what might have been drunkenness. In the center of this tumult, Reverend Flavy upon the pulpit waved his arms like a little mad doll to which no one gave their attention. He was shouting but his words didn't reach the back of the hall. On the altar below him, the translucent skull absorbed the color of the drapery below it, seeming to burn red in furious judgment of these so-called Christians.

Finally the noise subsided enough that Flavy could be heard. The audience turned and observed him, an army of ants diverted by a leaf that had settled in their path.

"Please, dear friends, we must begin the sermon," he cried. "Settle yourselves."

A few catcalls answered, but mostly people took their seats or else stood still, waiting to hear the rest.

"I've taken for my text today the words 'Who knows the power of God's anger?' Many of us here today think we know this power, think we've met it. We've all had tribulations with our triumphs. You have. I have. But is that the power of God's anger? Can any of us here say we've ever felt that fearsome power?" He made the mistake of looking at them all, of saying nothing long enough for someone to think of a response: "I can. He's put me in here to listen to *you*!"

The crowd roared.

Flavy, although he might have a solid text prepared, lacked the skill to command. Fitcher spoke and people stopped breathing. Even when he was out of the pulpit, there was something in his manner, his speech, that held attention rapt. Poor Flavy might have answered the same call but not with any particular gifts.

Now as he clung to the sides of the pulpit people came in from behind it to drag him down. He cried out to them, "Don't cast yourselves down by this act. You defy the voice of God!" Few seemed to think so. He was pulled from his perch, and immediately another man climbed into his place and held up a Bible to silence them.

The moment the noise subsided, he asked, " 'What benefits a man to gain the world and lose his soul?' " Wisely he filled in his own answer. "No one here should have to know this, for we've rejected the world and *kept* our souls. We have chosen salvation over iniquity because we *are* here." The new preacher, though he looked to Kate as if he'd slept many days in his clothes, and not in a bed, had enough sense to make his case more softly, forcing people to pay attention, drawing them to a more intimate position, where they would have to listen too hard to ridicule. He knew what he was doing.

Meanwhile, Flavy was hauled to the side, where he wrestled himself free of his captors and marched past the stained-glass portals. Kate withdrew from the hall ahead of him, then waited in the foyer. Some of the crowd there had dispersed, although people occupied every bench, and a few sat on the bottom stairs.

When Flavy pushed through the door, she called his name. She said, "I hope you'll remember me, Reverend. You married my sister."

He looked confounded.

"You married her to Reverend Fitcher?"

"Ah, yes, of course." He nodded vigorously. "You're—"

"Katherine Charter."

"Katherine. Miss Charter." He ran a finger inside his soiled collar. "What might I do for you, child?"

"I was hoping to find my sister here, but no one can tell me her whereabouts."

He looked toward the ceiling as if the answer might be written there, but shook his head. "I'm not sure I can help. The community is in terrible shape. Just look at it—ruffians, scabrous jackals, all pouring in, and not half of them deserving of anything like salvation. We've had robbery, a murder, and two rapes here in the past week alone. Here, on the holiest of grounds.

"It's an abomination, which is why we're turning 'em all away now. We caught the murderer and hung him, naturally, but I expect he won't be the last the way it's going. People think because they've got inside the fence, onto the plot of land, that they're automatically worth saving. I tell you, when Fitcher gets back, I'm going to hand him a list of people who need to be tossed outen here. People who'd lay hands upon a man of the *cloth*."

"It does not sound anything like God's estate, sir. All the more reason for me to be concerned that my sister is here in the midst of it, because she did not accompany her husband on his crusade."

He scratched the stubble on his chin. "Well, that's peculiar, isn't it? She should have. I can't see why he would have refused her. Or else should have put her in charge—Lord, someone oughta be. An abomination," he repeated. "If she's here, she could well be down to the village. I think she made the candles, didn't she? Like the one before her. I think so. You could look there. Someone might tell you something."

"She had a friend who was close to Reverend Fitcher, who also did not go on this crusade. His name was Notaro, I believe."

Flavy winced at the name. "Oh. Horrible thing. Impaled trying to scale the fence out in the woods." He closed his eyes and made a little shake with his head. "And that was before it got bad. People used to talk about the Angel of Death taking lives in here. Talked of it like something evil lived in among us good, God-fearin' folk and singled out the sinners at its discretion. Some here attributed Notaro's death to it. I tell you, if that annihilating angel is about, it's not doing its job anymore."

Kate could think of nothing more to say to Flavy. She thanked him and headed out the back doors to the rear porch.

This view had also changed since she'd seen it last—the rear lawn was now lost beneath the tents, wagons, belongings, and people. Cookfires smoldered, imbuing the air with a greasy haze. More than cooked meat, the air smelled of too much unwashed humanity, of unwholesome effluence in a hundred uncovered pits. It was a barnyard smell—pigs rolled in dung.

Against the dormitory wing on her right a row of little shacks and cages stood—feather-strewn coops for chickens that even now scratched and strutted around and under the porch. Feathers floated on the breeze.

She overlooked Harbinger's converts and thought, *No promised afterlife was ever shaped or stank like this.*

To get to the village, Kate had to make her way through the camp. Nothing had been erected to any plan, no straight lines, just tents any old where. She zigged and zagged through them, climbing over bundles, logs, tin pots, and the occasional sleeping Fitcherite. Dogs wandered past her, people glanced up, some so filthy that by comparison Kate was a fairy-tale princess in their midst. One man made a rude, grasping overture to her as she passed by, but was too drunk to stand and pursue her. She realized that anything could happen here, and in broad daylight. No one would stop it.

She passed into the orchard. The trees were heavy with apples, and there were people on ladders picking them, as there were people in the fields. The corn had been harvested and the stalks bundled up or cut down. Elsewhere, people were gathering squashes and pumpkins. Even in the face of chaos, she thought, there remained people who didn't let their lives unravel.

She remembered the chandler's shop. Fitcher had pointed it out to them the day the family first toured Harbinger. The door of it was open and the smell of melted spermaceti leaked from within. She called her sister's name even as she entered.

Three men looked up. One wore an apron. All three made their slight bows and said, "Welcome," the way everyone had done on the first morning she'd visited. She answered in kind, then asked if they had seen her sister—that she understood Amy had been put in charge of making candles for the community.

"True, she was," said the man with the apron, who identified himself as John Marsden. "And we'd have been fine if it weren't for all the new ones here. So we been making more of them. Lots of people knowed how. I thought your sister'd gone with the good reverend out to spread the word."

"No, she stayed behind."

"If 'n' that's so, I can't recollect as I've seen her in a while. You fellas?"

The other two shook their heads. Kate had the impression the other two wouldn't have recognized her. She thanked them, then turned to go. She saw a small framed picture on the wall behind the candle rods. It was a silhouette cutout of two people in profile—a man and a woman. She wasn't sure at first what was familiar about them. John Marsden said, "We found that lying on the floor under the table. Looked like it'd fallen down, so we hung it up. I seem to recall it's a couple what used to be the chandlers way back a year or two."

"They died," said one of the other men. "Angel o' Death took 'em."

"Aw, Harley, you an' your Angel of Death. Sorry, Miss Charter, but—"

"That's quite all right. I've already heard about the angel." As she left the shop, she muttered beneath her breath, "I believe, in fact, we've spoken." She couldn't be absolutely sure, but she thought the silhouettes in the picture resembled the young man Pulaski and his runaway bride. If so, it answered the mystery of where they'd gone if not what had become of them. Where Amy had gone, however, remained a mystery she did not solve.

Twenty-eight

TWO NIGHTS AFTER HER FAILED attempt to find Amy, the spirit of Samuel Verity began appearing to Kate. She was not entirely surprised that he did.

As is often the case in dreams, she and the spirit seemed to be in her house, but at the same time she was aware that the dream interior wasn't her house, that the doors lining the walls were nothing like her doors, the halls were all wrong, and that she trailed the spirit through endless, winding corridors that would have required a castle or a fortress to contain them.

She'd never seen the ghost before. Vern had described him to her once as a dark-haired man who had no mouth, but the man who led Kate through the labyrinth had both mouth and a beard. He was dressed elegantly, as if for a gala event, and he held her hands, which she saw were gloved. She must be attending the event with him. Music played somewhere. A waltz.

He smiled and said, "Your turn is coming."

"My turn upon the floor?" she asked.

"Upon the stage of the world."

"But the world is ending."

He shook his head. "Yours is about to begin. You are next to be courted, next to be asked."

"No," she argued, "there's no one for me. My sisters had suitors, both of them, and even so they married someone else."

"You will be asked before the end time arrives. You will wed."

The news troubled her. She almost answered that she didn't wish to wed, but that wasn't entirely true. She had convinced herself it couldn't happen with time so short. She had accepted that life would not offer her anyone. She didn't want just a mate. She wanted a kindred, and was realistic enough to know that few people ever met their kindred, even without the final grains of sand pouring out of the world's hourglass.

She couldn't hope. It was too ridiculous, and she might have disagreed with him, except that he chose that moment to vanish completely, leaving her in the strange corridors alone, lost in a maze. She wandered along, calling out, receiving no answer, hearing now and then little scrapes and shuffles as if something trailed her just out of sight; but there were no shadows that could hide anyone, no hidden recesses. Finally, she simply tried one of the many doors. Opened it, and woke up.

She sat up and looked around herself. The two stripped beds across the room were holes torn in the fabric of her existence. Mr. Charter was all that remained of her family—even Lavinia was absent. She thought of the dream, of the promises being made. "It's nonsense, my girl," she told herself.

The wall sounded with two sharp raps. Kate stared at it, wanting to say "No, you aren't real," but holding her tongue and thinking, beneath her fear, that this was part of the pattern—she ought to have expected it. The focus bore upon her now. Her sisters had run the pattern and disappeared. Now she was the fox, with the hound close upon her heels.

Dressing, she was careful to make no other comment to attract the wall.

No further dreams of the strange house and the ghost troubled her—at least none she remembered—until the night before the crusade made its triumphant return. Only three nights remained until the world's end. The crowded road had been in an uproar all day. People had begun to fear that Fitcher wasn't going to return, that he'd abandoned them and they were doomed, damned, or otherwise cast adrift. It had been late in the night before they'd quieted down and dispersed to their respective encampments. Kate might have been more anxious of the end time's approach herself, if dealing with them hadn't exhausted her utterly.

Deep in the bowels of the night she awoke to find herself standing in the parlor. Her nightdress was gone and she was wandering naked through her house. The chill in the air raised goose bumps on her skin immediately she awoke. She could recall no dream, only the vaguest impression of a voice, a presence—something that had spoken to her, told her things she could not hear when awake. Apparently, it had undressed her as well.

Outside, the night was pitch-dark. There should have been a half-moon shining down, so the sky must have been overcast. She rubbed her arms. Something was leading her into the same trap where Amy and Vern had gone before her. She was terrified, maybe even more than she might have been if this hadn't happened to them first; but she was also furious at the ease with which this force manipulated her. She checked her thighs for blood, but found none.

She started to leave the parlor, but stopped in the doorway. A gray figure was descending the stairs. Noises came from it— murmured breathy words. For a few moments she stood paralyzed as the figure approached. Then through her fright she realized it was her father. She stepped back to hide herself from him.

Mr. Charter still wore his nightshirt and a cap upon his head. He muttered as though in conversation with someone, "Yes, I understand, I'll honor my promise. She's to . . . to wed, and shall be. Certainly she shall be." He walked past the parlor, threw open the front door, and strode out into the night as if he could see perfectly. Kate dashed back up the stairs. She found her gown in the hallway and put it on before chasing after him.

From the front door, she tried to see anything. If he was out there, he'd wandered too far away for her to make him out. She was about to go back for a lamp, when she heard the dull *thock* of the pole across the road bouncing against its support. A few moments later the sound came again. Kate crept across the yard. She stepped cautiously to avoid the blanket of acorns.

Soon she could perceive the shape of the sentry box and the white of Mr. Charter's gown. He was raising the pike as if to let a wagon pass under, then tilting his head as if following its progress up the road. As soon as the phantom wagon had passed, he released the pole and let it drop, which he would normally not have done; and the pole loudly struck the stump across the way. Then he began again. He reached out as if collecting a fee, and proceeded to raise the pole. She was surprised no one else had come to see what the noise meant. Perhaps they were too scared.

Kate came up behind him and placed her hands on his shoulders. "Papa," she said. "Papa, wake up."

He let go of the pole and it hit with a loud whack. He jumped at the sound, looked about himself, then turned around, facing his daughter. "What am I—"

"You walked in your sleep, Papa."

"Did I?" He seemed completely disoriented, and had to regard the pike again. "I must have. I was walking with God, Katie. God was at my side. We were walking through a beautiful meadow and the sky was full of rainbows. It was Heaven, surely."

"Yes, Papa." She took his hand and drew him toward the house. He stumbled along willingly, but no longer strong in his stride. In his sleep he had been as steady as the father she remembered from childhood.

"God's been speaking with me awhile now. It's because time is short. All that divides this world from the next now is vapor."

"Then you've seen Mother?"

He stopped walking. "Your mother, Katherine? No, I haven't seen her. That—that's odd, isn't it? I haven't seen her at all." Trembling, he allowed himself to be led back inside, and up to his room. Kate lit a candle and used it to light the Betty lamp that hung near his bed. She tucked him in, then sat beside him. He was like a child in that bed, a little boy wearing the expression of someone much older who'd forgotten something critical and now, having been shown it, knew that their faculties were crumbling.

By candlelight Kate read to him from a book of Washington Irving's stories, a piece called "The Wife."

" 'Those disasters which break down the spirit of a man, and prostrate him in the dust, seem to call forth all the energies of the softer sex, and give such intrepidity and elevation to their character, that at times it approaches to sublimity.' "

In many aspects this brief essay about the surprising strength that a friend of the author's, having fallen on hard times, discovered in his wife, was all about her own mother. Kate would have selected any other of the stories by the fictitious Geoffrey Crayon, Esq., but Mr. Charter—as he had often done before—petitioned her to read that seemingly cruel and painful piece.

Near the end, the wife in the story linked her arm into her husband's and told him, "Oh, we shall be so happy!" More than once, her father had listened to this passage with tears upon his cheeks. This night, though, he dozed after only the first page.

Kate closed the book. Instead of returning to her room, she rocked awhile in the chair, staring into the greasy black smoke of the Betty lamp and speculating that whatever had accompanied her father down the stairs, it certainly wasn't God. She couldn't help but recall Amy's suspect Angel of Death, and how she had been able to make herself known to Kate from far away. From the heights of that damned house.

The crusade of the Next Life returned early the next afternoon. A handful of people preceded the main body up the road, announcing the imminent arrival of "the most holy reverend." They grinned with a kind of fanatical madness, a joy that did not belong to the earth.

It was October the thirteenth. No one had ever thought they would return so late.

The road was soon occluded by squatters. Word somehow spread even to the far side of the turnpike, so that people came walking back from the direction of Harbinger and crowded around the pole, their eyes wide with desperate hope, asking Kate and her father if Fitcher had yet been spied. Even as she told them he had not, a great roar came from farther down the road, and as everyone looked in that direction, he appeared above the crowd.

Fitcher sat a horse this time, like a commanding general awash in his victorious troops. He greeted everyone as he passed, waving his walking stick. He leaned down and touched their outstretched hands. People parted for him, but stayed close, trying to touch him, his stick, his boots, even the tired horse. They squealed, they cried. Some reacted to the touch violently, flinging their arms up, twitching like Shakers. They had to be dragged aside, set down in the grass. Foam bubbled on their lips, and some babbled insanely in foreign or improvised tongues. A plump woman began to spin about in circles and slapped those nearest before they scrambled back out of her windmilling way. The tension had cracked like the wall of a dike, and pent-up frothing fanaticism burst out.

Fitcher rode through like an avatar. His smile was benign eminence. At the pole, he reined in but did not dismount. For a moment he stared down at Kate with cold consideration, as if contemplating a meal, and she felt herself flush in response. Her cheeks burned and she stepped aside, behind her father.

Mr. Charter reached up to shake Fitcher's hand and welcome him back. On the horse behind him, visibly transformed, rode Lavinia. Kate did not immediately recognize her. Lavinia had let her hair down, and she wore men's riding clothes—breeches and a boiled white shirt. The severity and darkness of her had vanished. Her sharp features had filled and softened. Kate found herself thinking that her stepmother was surprisingly lovely. Lavinia turned her horse and rode onto the lawn.

Behind her flowed a multitude. If the last crusade had dou-

bled the population of Harbinger, the takings of this one threatened to quadruple it. The mass of people extended as far as could
be seen back down the road. They moved forward slowly, turning
the confines of the road into a warren enclosed by trees. They
spilled out onto the lawn of the house. They circled Fitcher now
that he had stopped. One of them held Lavinia's horse as she
dismounted. She seemed to move with the fluidity of someone
half her age. Kate noticed, and observed that her father noticed,
too.

"It is a great success," Fitcher proclaimed. "A triumph. We've
collected hundreds more on this campaign. Our new world will
thrive with new life." He twisted around to overlook his flock,
and called out, " 'Believe in the Lord Jesus Christ, and thou shalt
be saved, and thy house!' " The mob cheered, and the sound
rolled like a huge wave down the road, echoing back from farther
than could be seen.

"Now, we must go on, only a little farther. We will charge
them nothing here," he said to Mr. Charter. "We've all their
goods, their monies, and it will all come to us in Harbinger. Their
dedication is not in question. Now, *you* must come to the house,
too. Move in. It's time, you know, only mere days remain to us
and I do not want you to find yourselves outside the fence when
all around is obliterated. We can't lose our gatekeeper, or his
family." His gaze flicked to Kate, then to Lavinia. Then he
straightened in his saddle and shouted, "Onward!" They cheered
him again.

As he rode under the upraised pike, he began to sing the new
words Mr. Isaac Watts had written to the tune of "Antioch,"
which Kate had heard only a few times in church: " 'Joy to the
world! The Lord is come! Let earth receive her King; Let ev'ry
heart prepare Him room . . .' " Unlike Kate, the crowd seemed
to know the song well. They picked up the words and sang along.
Their song roared past. It was, thought Kate, a beautiful song,
but it sounded like a martial chant to her now. In the sky to the
west, the front of a storm was rolling in.

*   *   *

"You have allowed conditions to deteriorate, Katherine," said Lavinia. "I'm disappointed with you."

"Lavinia," Mr. Charter interjected, "it has been difficult for her, for us both. Without you."

No doubt he hoped that would placate her, but Lavinia would not be misdirected from her chosen target. "It's scandalous, what if the Reverend Fitcher had wished to come in? Why, I couldn't have stopped him, and the conditions here would not have been to *my* detriment, I can assure you." She brushed crumbs off the tablecloth, which was itself stained here and there from recent meals.

No, thought Kate, *you're now queen of all you survey. We're only here to serve.* What she said was: "Ma'am, I fear that with my father's weakness at the forefront of my thoughts, I have not attended to household matters that didn't directly impinge upon our day-to-day lives."

"And insolent." Now she turned on Mr. Charter. "Do you see? While I was gone, you did nothing to curb her habit of insolence. If anything, it has increased. Insolence like a weed."

Mr. Charter listened, his head lowered, but his eyes following Lavinia as she circled the room. She ran her finger across various surfaces, staring sourly at the result each time, passing judgment upon them both with a look.

She said, "Two days remain. We must close up this house and take ourselves to the next estate, and here she isn't even in an appropriate state of mind to walk through the very gates."

Mr. Charter snapped, "In the name of God, woman, shut up!"

Both Kate and Lavinia turned to him, disbelieving. He still sat hunched, but trembled with a rage he could not contain. "She has done exactly what needed doing. She has looked after me as I wished. If this house is in some way dissatisfactory, it is because I cared nothing for the dust on a mantel or the crumbs on a table—and I *still don't*." He strode from the dining room, and went outside. The wind had blown up. A throng with no end continued to push along the road toward Harbinger.

Lavinia stood stiff, her cheeks flushed, her eyes flashing like lightning. Kate had to walk by her to leave. She tried to hold her tongue, but her own anger overwhelmed her common sense.

"I believe," she said softly, "your reign is over."

The wind whirled about the house. It pulled up tiny cyclones of dirt and leaves. One gust caught the tied-up turnpike pole, wrenching it free from the rope that held it upright. Mr. Charter and Kate, busy gathering up stray items and tethering horses, saw it slip loose but couldn't reach it. The pike crashed down on the stump and splintered in two. It was sheer good fortune that no one was beneath it when it fell.

People on the road scrambled to tie down their belongings as wind billowed tarps and worked tent pegs loose. There was thunder in the west keeping its distance; and sheets of lightning flared beyond the trees; but no rain had yet fallen when Elias Fitcher rode into view like some dark apocalyptic horseman from up the road. The wind flapped the ends of his long coat, but seemed reluctant to assault him as it had everyone else.

He dismounted and left his horse tethered to the broken pike. He walked with solemnity to the house, gesturing on the way for Mr. Charter and his daughter to leave off assisting others and follow him.

He led them into the parlor. Kate noticed that Lavinia was already there, reading her Bible by lamplight; she had changed from her riding gear into a print dress, and twisted her hair into its usual severe bun. Seeing the reverend, she closed the book, placing it upon her lap. Her hand went to her hair, as if to let it down again. She had eyes only for Fitcher. It was as if neither her husband nor her stepdaughter existed.

"How fares Harbinger?" asked Mr. Charter.

Fitcher turned away from Lavinia. "We're drowning in people at the moment," he replied. "We're having to hold them at the gates until we can find space for them to occupy. People are doubling up. The dormitories now have people lying in the aisles and between and under each bunk. It will all work out. We will get them all in. We must accommodate everyone, leave no one behind who truly wishes to join me." He hesitated a moment before continuing: "I have tragic news."

Kate said, "Amy." It was like a gasp.

The three adults glanced at her. "Indeed," Fitcher replied. "Your sister has succumbed to illness. I suspect malaria, but can't be certain. There is sickness in the encampment—not surprising when so many are forced to share space, and conditions are not hygienic. Believers they may be, but many of these people are less than tidy about themselves. Of course I wasn't on hand to maintain order, with the result that people sprawled about."

"I saw them, I was at Harbinger last week."

"So I've been told."

"No one knew where Amy was. No one could tell me."

"That is because she had stopped appearing at meals. Some-one should have investigated, of course, but in the chaos of all the new arrivals and the concomitant problems they brought, she was simply overlooked. Many thought she had gone off with me and I hadn't assigned anyone to watch after her. There was no cause, she seemed so sanguine when I left."

"Amy's dead?" Mr. Charter asked.

"Regrettably. She must have taken to her bed, and never got out. I—I found her. She'd been dead for weeks. That room . . . the heat. It's too awful to describe."

Mr. Charter had sunk down upon a chair. "There must be a funeral—"

"Mr. Charter, there will certainly be a memorial service, but I've had the body buried already. Her illness is likely commu-nicable, and the state of the corpse prevented me from keeping it above ground for even an hour. The smell in that room . . . With all of these new arrivals, dear Lord, the last thing we can afford is a plague in the final hours before we would be saved."

Her father looked lost, cast adrift. His head swayed between Kate and Lavinia. Finally he faced Fitcher. "All my girls," he said.

"Not quite all, sir," Fitcher answered. His blue eyes cut the distance to Kate. "I find myself once more bereaved, once more without a mate for the Day of Judgment at hand."

Lavinia squinted at Kate with rancor.

Mr. Charter sighed deeply. His head hung down below his shoulders. "You must take Katherine, then," he said.

"Papa!" she cried, but he didn't respond. He didn't seem to know she was there. When he raised his head, he was looking at Fitcher and his face had gone slack, as if the man within had absented himself. It was the expression he'd worn when she'd spied him descending the stairs the previous night, talking to the unseen companion—to God, he claimed—promising to *honor his promise to wed her.* She'd thought it was a memory, that in his despair he was recalling her mother. Now she recognized the look: the expression that the mesmerist's subjects had all worn while under his command.

"She will go with you. There's no time left, is there? She's young but strong." His head bobbed, puppetlike.

"Headstrong," corrected Lavinia. Fitcher gave her a glance, and she stiffened up and looked away.

"That is what I was hoping you'd say, Mr. Charter. Fallen though I am, I know that I am saved. I must have a wife pure and strong enough to stand with me when we face God."

Kate considered pointing out to him that he had literally hundreds of women to pick from now. There was no reason to choose her, except that it had been his goal from the start, from at least the moment he had encountered them aboard the steamer. " 'And the king made her queen instead of Vashti,' " she quoted, and Lavinia's eyes blazed. She knew then how much lay between Fitcher and her stepmother. She hadn't suspected until then that there might have been a much greater plot at work than any of them had imagined; it would never have occurred to her or her sisters that he might have been collecting them. Collecting them all.

*T*wenty-nine

*T*HUS WITH THE FIRST OF THE rain lashing them, the Charter family rode in their wagon behind Elias Fitcher to Harbinger House.

Beyond the turnpike, people clogged the road and only moved aside reluctantly when it was clear the wagon would not stop. In the dark of the storm, whipped by rain, they kept their heads down, and snarled like beasts as they shuffled aside. Lightning flashed again and again, capturing the human nightmare in a series of still pictures for Kate: a dark woman at the side of the road, wailing and tearing at her hair; two men staring out from the open flaps of a rotting tent; three bodies hanging like pale fruit from the trees, the nearest bearing a sign with the word SUCCUBUS painted on it. All of this they passed before they'd even reached the bridge.

Someone must have been camping at the bottom of the gorge; the flickering glow of a bonfire outlined the bridge in hellish hues. The crowd upon it was a huge, many-headed thing, a shape in constant flux. Seated on the wagon, Kate was reminded of the Geneva wharf as she'd viewed it from the gangplank of

the *Fidelio*. Fitcher's horse cut through them, the wagon rumbling
after, both forcing people to push against the rails. Someone
dropped a bundle off the side. The fires below lit it for the instant
it was in view—at least Kate hoped it was a bundle. It could so
easily have been . . . but she would not think something so awful.
What she did think was that this could not be the pathway to
Heaven, that these could not be the chosen and the saved. Was
that why they had been kept from entering Harbinger? Perhaps,
yet she found herself wondering how Elias Fitcher, as she was
coming to understand him, could open the gates to eternal life.

Their wagon trundled on to the gates. The house appeared
through the trees as a quilt of lighted panels against the night.
The torches on the exterior had been put out by the storm.

She looked up but could not see the pyramid at the top.

A mob hung on the gates. They swiped at the guards inside,
who were refusing them entry. When Fitcher rode up, most of
the mob moved aside, but a few clung to the bars despite his
instructions to get out of the way. They held on until the gates
parted, then sprinted through, only to be met by men wielding
clubs. Scuttling back, they fell against Fitcher's horse and against
the gates, where they were beaten and flung back out like
squashed rats, all of this occurring before Mr. Charter had even
driven inside. Kate wondered if he saw the barbarity, or if he was
even conscious of what was happening around him.

Fitcher dismounted and came to her, lifted her out of the
wagon. "My dearest Katherine," he said. "Finally." From beneath
her hood she spied Lavinia looking darkly over her shoulder at
them. Fitcher closed his hands around hers in their lace gloves.
"I confess to you, I was smitten by you most of all from the very
first."

"You did not much disguise it, sir."

"As much as I sealed up my heart, the plain truth leaked out,
did it?"

"Through your eyes. Their color hides nothing. Your intent
is clear."

He smiled and offered her his arm. "We go directly to the
chapel, for there's no time for preparing, no time for the cere-

mony Vernelia knew, or even for the ghost of that accorded Amelia. You understand."

"I don't stand upon ceremony," she said.

"Excellent." They strode up the steps and into the house. Mr. Charter and Lavinia followed, though not together, not presenting anything like a united front any longer. Lavinia walked with fury, Mr. Charter in his trance.

The Hall of Worship had become a makeshift encampment. Bundles and belongings crammed the aisles; clothes were draped over the pews. The red runner had turned black with dirt. The candles along the walls were all lit, as well as a few scattered lamps and pewter lanterns. The air stank of oily sweat.

Fitcher seemed as surprised as anyone by the entrenched trespass. Letting go of Kate's hand, he went forward, his head swinging from side to side. In his long coat, he was like some enormous wasp with folded wings stalking through their midst. His long legs surmounted the debris clogging the aisle, but he kicked aside those who reclined in his way. Most didn't move far, but huddled between pews as if hoping they might be overlooked, forgotten.

When he reached the front, Fitcher leaned over the bloodred altar. When he came about he was holding at chest level the milky crystal skull. One hand rested on the crown, fingertips on the sculpted thorns; the other cupped the jaw. He rotated the skull as if providing it a view of them all. He said, "What do you think you're about? Do you not know what place this is? *Whose hall?*" He pushed the skull at them. "Do you think it brings you closer to your Lord that you establish yourselves in this chapel? You followed my voice and it brought you *here?*" He shouted the last word. Then, almost in a whisper, he looked down upon the skull and said, " 'Surely, thou didst set them in slippery places.' They fall faster than angels."

At that moment Reverend Flavy burst in. He stopped when he saw the condition of the hall, and Fitcher at the front of it. By comparison with the others around him, his disheveled collar and shadbelly coat were sartorial perfection. "Oh, my," he said. "Someone's made a grave error." His eyes swept the squatters, and he smiled disdainfully as he identified many who'd mistreated him. Now would they be sorry.

"An error indeed, Mr. Flavy, and it shall be answered," replied Fitcher. He set down the skull as he gestured Flavy to come forward. Then he circled the altar and took the pulpit for a moment. "There is to be a ceremony here momentarily. Those of you who wish to participate may do so, silently. Your host is about to marry in preparation for the opening of the gates. Stay or go, but choose now. Whether or not you stay, your *belongings* will leave before morning."

A baby began to cry as he spoke. Its mother whisked it out of the hall.

"Reverend," he said to Flavy.

They traded places. Fitcher handed him a torn piece of paper, then removed his long coat. Flavy stuck the paper in his Bible. Kate took off her shawl. Mr. Charter stood beside her. Lavinia moved to the far side of Fitcher as if to fill the position of best man.

From one of the pews, someone said, "I'm an organist, if you should wish one."

Flavy exchanged a glance with Fitcher, then said, "Please."

They waited for the fellow to settle himself. He began with a few tentative chords, then began playing the tune for "The Tyrolese Evening Hymn," a verse and chorus, after which he stopped.

With the music dying away, Reverend Flavy cleared his throat and said, "We welcome this great man and this woman before us to join in holy wedlock before God, and to approach Him as one. Be there anyone who opposes this union, let them speak now or forever hold their peace." He looked up nervously as if actually anticipating an interjection, then hurried on: "Do you, Elias Fitcher, take this woman as wife—as your ring girdles her finger, so you shall bind her to you always?"

"I do."

"Do you, Ame . . . that is"—he quickly glanced at the paper Fitcher had given him—"Katherine Proserpina Charter, take this man, Elias Fitcher, as your lawfully wedded husband, to honor,

and follow in strictest obedience, to love and cherish, both now
and in the life to come?"

Kate gave no answer, and the silence became uncomfortable.
Lavinia leaned forward and glared at her around Fitcher. He
watched her uncertainly. Kate addressed Flavy, "Why is it that
our ties are not equal, Reverend? He has only to bind me, to
harness me with his ring, while I must honor and grant him sway
in all things, as well as love and cherish, never mind that this
must continue both here and in life everlasting. You require me
to make a gift of my will, and that I shall not do."

Flavy looked for some direction from the groom. Fitcher
stared openmouthed at Kate. She refused to shrink from his um-
brage. Facing him, she said, "Find better vows, sir."

Lavinia, had she been standing beside her, would surely have
strangled Kate. Her father squeezed her shoulder, though
whether as a warning or a precursor to shaking her sensible, she
couldn't tell. Fitcher began to chuckle, quietly at first, but it rose
to a guffaw. "Better vows!" he exclaimed. He dabbed at one eye.
To Flavy, he said, "You heard her."

Flavy opened and closed his mouth, fishlike. He looked at
his prepared text, at the scrap of paper with nothing but her name
on it. He was completely at sea. "What—what should they be?"

"Oh, come, man, tit for tat. If I bind her to me with my ring,
then so the reverse must be true and no more, else I must give
her all that is required of her in turn. So . . ."

"Ahm, Mistress Katherine. As your—your ring circles the finger of Elias Fitcher, do you thus bind him to yourself?"

She smiled sweetly. "I do."

Flavy nodded in relief. "The rings, then?" Lavinia handed
one to Fitcher. Kate's father provided hers, a simple band that
she placed on Fitcher's hand. Her ring was more elaborately
crafted and Kate wondered where it had come from in such short
order. It fit her perfectly. Flavy said, "I, by the powers vested in
me, do pronounce you both husband and wife. Go with Go—"

But Fitcher was already leaning across her for his kiss, and
the crowd broke into cheers and clapping, though with uncertain
enthusiasm and less comprehension.

*   *   *

There was no cake, no reception at all. Some of the dwellers in the chapel approached Kate as she was led past them—some expressed their congratulations, others reached out to touch her, their heads bowed; she heard herself called "the Virgin." The rest hung back, wary of Fitcher's ire. Some of them began gathering up their clothing and paraphernalia, making ready to leave. In the foyer, her new husband apologized to her for duties that he now had to perform "because someone has let the wolves in with the sheep." He bid her father a good night, then marched off with Flavy to find whoever was responsible for settling people in the chapel.

Lavinia fumed at her then for her insolence: How dare she presume to instruct the Reverend Fitcher. It promised to be a long-winded diatribe, but quickly ran out of steam when she was ignored by both father and daughter.

A minute later, an elderly woman holding a bull's-eye lantern entered from the rear doors. She spotted Kate and came to her. "I'm Louise," she said. "Reverend Fitcher's told me to take you up to your room." She jangled a ring of keys at Kate.

"You have your things?"

"No, we didn't have time to bring them."

"I'll gather up your belongings, Katie," her father said, "and bring them along tomorrow." He seemed to be waking from his spell. He added, "We're all coming here tomorrow," as if there were a multitude accompanying him and Lavinia.

"You shouldn't drive back," Kate told him. "Not in this downpour. Not when there are rooms. And you," she said to Louise, "needn't walk up those stairs. If you'll give me the keys and tell me where my room lies, I'll go."

"Oh, but he said—"

"Yes, but he had other things weighing on him." She held out her hand, not defiantly, but as a gentle request. Louise gave her the lantern.

"It's the very first room on the second floor, on the left side of the hall."

"Do you know where my father might stay the night?"

Louise thought for a moment but shook her head. "I've little acquaintance with the upper floors. None of us has much doing with them."

"But why, if there are empty rooms above, are people being crammed into the chapel and keeping room?"

Louise tilted her head as if the idea had never occurred to her. "I don't know, missus. It's not for me to say." She handed over the keys then as if happy to be rid of them. The largest, made of glass, seemed to drink the light from the lantern, transmuting in reflection into gold.

"Papa, you must wait here. And you, Lavinia."

She went up the stairs, and into the second-floor hallway. It was dark. No candles had been lighted there, but with the lantern Kate had no trouble finding her room. She had to set it down to try the keys and open the door.

Inside, she moved to a small dressing table. There was a small lard-oil lamp on it, and a stick of punk beside it. She lit the punk from the candle in her lantern, then touched it to the wick of the lamp. The window beyond her bed was open. The curtains swelled like ship's sails with the storm. She closed the window against the chill. Lightning flashed at her, capturing the landscape below in an instant—bent trees, and people scattered everywhere. She closed the curtains but the afterimage burned on in the darkness.

The bed was surrounded by wine-colored drapes hung from the canopy frame. Inside, it was a secret place, smelling faintly, she thought, of lilac. A box tied with ribbon lay atop the pillow.

There was a writing desk, some logs for a fire, and an open armoire. She drew back the armoire doors, thinking it at first completely empty until she saw, hung in the back, what looked at first like a snake but proved instead to be a long slender crop. She recalled Amy's seemingly mad claim that Fitcher whipped her nightly. She ran her fingers over the braid of the crop as if convincing herself by feel that it wasn't her imagination. Then she closed the armoire.

This room, she thought, if it were exemplary of the rest of

the chambers on this floor, could easily house a handful of people. It was absurd that she should have such quarters and they in their final hours be turned out into the storm. What would God think of them if they failed to help one another now? What sort of Christian refused to afford even so little kindness?

She thought again of what Amy had told her about the rooms—about her own and Vern's and the others on this floor—and she went out into the hall and to the next room.

She unlocked it and went inside. It was very like her own. It had been lived in recently, too. There were clothes draped over the armoire doors, and familiar clothes at that. Sticking out from under them was a small leather cat with six leather strands to it, exactly as Amy had described it. On the dresser, beneath a hinged mirror, there was a small box tied with ribbon identical to the one on her bed. She knew what it would contain.

Kate hastily withdrew and locked the door on Amy's room again. Even as she did so, she realized she hadn't smelled anything like what Fitcher had described. No doubt the room had been aired out afterward . . . still, she must assume it was unhealthy. She could not house her father there.

The next room along proved to have been Vern's. She recognized the items laid out in it—the parasol especially. There could be no mistaking that. After sorting through the wardrobe, she had to agree with Amy's assessment: If Vern had run away from Harbinger, she had left behind some of her most precious belongings.

Kate returned to the hall again and locked the door. Some sense of the danger they presented convinced her to mention neither of these rooms, not even to admit she had entered them. Did he keep them as shrines to his lost wives? She was reluctant to grant him that much humanity or to allow that he had in fact lost anything. If her suspicions were correct, and he was a collector, then no one had been lost, merely acquired. The overarching question was what form acquisition took. If she went into the rooms beyond them, would she find items belonging to other women? How many had preceded her sisters into this house and never come out again? What sort of God granted him such power

over women? It might be the end of this world but if God was
truly just it could not be the beginning of the next, not with Elias
Fitcher in the lead. She wondered if he was merely mad or if
some plan greater than she could imagine had yet to unfold.

As much as she wanted to know more, she could not now
enter the rooms beyond Vern's. Instead, she crossed the hall.

Here she had some luck. The first door hung open. The room
had been turned into storage. Trunks and satchels had been piled
inside every which way, but a path could be made to the bed.
For tonight it would offer her father shelter. Tomorrow they could
retrieve his belongings as well as hers, and move some of the
stored things elsewhere. Why, she wondered, did they bother
storing belongings when everyone had only tonight and tomorrow
left to live in these material bodies, in this world? Unless it was
Fitcher's notion that after the Advent they would all be returned
to Earth in the same physical state, in this hallowed place, and
would need their things again. It occurred to her that while she
had heard endlessly of the Day of Judgment and of how their
souls must be readied for it, the nature of life beyond that day
had never been fully detailed. Did the dead receive new bodies?
Did anyone know?

She was speculating on the matter when she exited the room,
and ran right into Fitcher himself.

She jumped, startled. He didn't so much as flinch. He held
a bottle of champagne and two slender glasses. "*That* isn't your
room," he said. "Where is Louise?"

"No, I know. I was looking for someplace for my father to
rest. And I dismissed Louise."

"Unnecessary. I've already had Mr. Charter driven home."

"But why, sir, in this storm? He'll have to come back tomorrow. There is adequate space here behind the trunks."

With a glance around the corridor, he asked, "Have you gone
into any other rooms?"

"My own."

"Ah. And did you see the gift I'd left for you?"

"I saw its container. I felt I shouldn't open it alone."

"Well, we'll open it together now, shall we?" The topic of

her father had been dismissed, removed from play. She recognized how she'd been maneuvered.

Kate followed him across the hall to her room. He set the champagne on the writing desk, then parted the canopy and offered her the beribboned box. "It's a small thing," he said, "but mine own. A trifle, but it means everything to me and I hope it shall come to mean as much to you."

Kate gave him the lantern and opened the box. The egg looked identical to the one Amy had shown her—bright white stone shot through with cobalt. It might have been the same one, she couldn't tell, but if it were, then what was in the box next door? She rested the egg upon her palm, and even through the lace of her glove she could sense the arcane power of it.

He stood behind her, placing his hands upon her shoulders. "The house has a few rules. Despite its size, there are no servants, for it would be improper to make others serve us. Everyone takes part in the duties—all of them, whatever they might be, whatever must be done.

"This little egg is the embodiment of my affection for you— perfect and pure. I expect you to keep it with you at all times, that I might be close to you wherever you go. Will you do that for me?"

"If that is what you desire."

"Swear it."

"You doubt me, sir, already?"

His hands slipped. "Why, no. No, why should I doubt you? You are as reliable as *all* your sisterhood."

She wet her lips, listening to the meaning that flowed like a subterranean stream beneath his words. His voice was powerful, intoxicating. She could do nothing to protect herself from the allure of him, but unlike her sisters before her, Kate had come equipped with some knowledge of him and his methods, and with greater self-possession. Stepping within his spell, she refused to be robbed of her own percipience. It might be divorced from the simmering emotions his beguiling voice put the flame to, but she would not disregard or doubt it any more than she would disregard the artfulness of his application.

He bent his head and kissed her neck. A spiderweb of pleasure, crisp and cold as ice, ran through her from the touch of his lips. She rolled her shoulders and tilted back her head.

He unbuttoned her blouse and his hands reached inside her garments, stirring her further. With him behind her and the egg in her palm, she could do little more than absorb it all. She was his instrument, his fiddle, vibrating as he drew his bow across her. She thought, *He knows me.*

He made a sound then, a low animal snarl, and his hands spread wide, separating her clothes, pushing them down, rending them if they didn't comply. He propelled her forward, against the bed.

She caught hold of the drapery. The errant thought wormed its way into her pleasure that there was a whip in the armoire next door because he'd known Amy's soul just as perfectly—known that she would respond most to punishment—and no doubt fathomed Vern as well. However he'd taken her, she had opened to him willingly. He knew them all. And so, a riding crop for her? Was she to canter for him?

Instead of going down onto the bed as he tugged her garments to her knees, Kate spun about to push at him with the egg in her fist. A carnal face, fanged with lust, met her. She caught only a glimpse. It vanished even as she turned—peripheral phantom of his true nature, so brief that anyone else would have denied they'd seen anything at all.

Already in her mind the image had congealed of how she was supposed to go down upon the bed, open and willing; and she wanted it, wanted the passion he instilled, wanted it as desperately as anything in life, but she knew he'd planted this yearning in her brain to direct her. How he did this, she didn't know and couldn't say, just as Amy hadn't been able to explain how she was being consumed. Her flesh trembled with the urge to surrender to him, even to know the sting of the crop. He would have her beg for that.

His hands reached around her fist, their heat about to melt her, and she drew the drape between them, warding off his ungovernable touch. He darkened angrily. It took every ounce of will she could muster to say firmly, "Sir, we are husband and wife, not dog and bitch."

He bent his head, lowered at her through his brows. His breath rasped in his nostrils. For a moment she didn't know what would happen. He seemed arrested between his own lust and his awareness that she'd discovered the truth of him. He was like some chrysalid unable to take form. If he chose to strike, she would not be able to fight him. Sex with him would obliterate her as it had done her sisters. She was certain of it.

Then the moment passed, and he brushed back his hair. He looked at her with gentle, half-closed eyes and replied, "Yes, forgive me, I am too much in your thrall, madam, for reason to hold sway."

"You would blame me for your iniquity?"

"Blame? No, I don't blame, merely account for myself. I've waited a long time for you."

She ignored all that this implied. "As we've all waited for this new life in God to begin," she answered. "And so let's you and I make a pact that we will give in to our passion only when we reach Him. Then we should know the truth of it, whether this is animal lust or the passion of love as God intended, beyond the flesh."

"That is your bargain?" asked Fitcher.

"My . . . offer."

"Your soul, tomorrow night, as the world outside ends? You'll face Him in my arms?"

"You make it sound like a dare."

"Oh, much more than a dare, my dear Kate. Much more than that. It is the world itself." He took the keys she'd carried, hefted them a moment, and then tossed them on the bed at her side. "You are the mistress of Harbinger till the end of time. You may go about as you please, put your father in whatever room you like, and pack in the rest of the stragglers as they crawl through my gates for their salvation. I care not, save that you don't go into one particular room, which that glass key opens. If you find *that* doorway, shun it for your life, just as you carry my little egg with you wherever you go."

"For my life."

He looked away, as if something elsewhere had caught his attention. "You're the youngest but the cleverest, aren't you?"

"How many of us have you judged?"

"Enough to know," he said, and faced her again, smiling. "Enough." He straightened his coat. "You'll want a fire. It's turning cold at night now. You'll find some lucifers on the mantel. Loco-focos they call them hereabout."

"You could light it for me."

He hesitated, then nodded and walked around to the far side of the bed. Once he was out of sight, Kate's legs failed her. She sat on the edge of the bed, listening to him collect the wood, open the damper. She pushed her clothes the rest of the way off, drawing her legs free. She wore only stockings now. Before he finished with the fire, she'd dragged the covers down on the bed and wrapped a sheet around herself. She set the egg beside her.

When Fitcher came into view again, she gestured at the bottle on the table. "We should still have our celebration," she suggested.

"You think so?" He studied her oddly, as if unable to make up his mind about her. "Why not?" he said at last. He wrestled the cork out of the bottle. It made a dull *pop* and a thin smoke emerged. He poured the glasses, offered hers to her. Kate took it, and raised it to him. Then, letting the sheet drop, she patted the bed beside her.

Fitcher's gaze slithered from her own eyes to her lips, down around her neck and to her now exposed breasts. His nostrils flared, she thought, exactly like a horse's. He stepped up beside her to sit. The glasses clinked together. Kate drew the sheet up again and, with it, reeled him closer. She said, "Tell me about the pyramid."

"Pyramid?"

"Atop the house. I've seen mansions with widow's walks, and signal towers from the days of the Indian wars, but none with a pyramid at its apex."

" 'Tis a symbol of power. Know you of the great pyramids of Egypt?"

"Nothing save that they exist, sir."

"They have magical properties—mathematical relationships, combinations of special numbers."

"Special numbers?"

"Twenty-five, fifty, three hundred sixty-six. And of course nine."

She considered, then shook her head. "No, I see nothing special in those numbers that might conjure magic."

"No? Alas, it's impossible to explain to one uninitiated in the mathematical aspects of God. They are found in Revelation, these numbers, and they prove God to be the architect. I should give you Mr. Taylor's book on the subject, but he won't be publishing it for a while yet. As for why it's there, I wished for it to be. I included it in the plans for our utopia. We have neither Indians to fight nor widows to watch for lost sailors here."

She sipped her champagne. "No, only widowers," she commented, then added, "I'm still wondering about the mathematical aspects of God."

"Revelation, full of mathematical clues to the resurrection, to the millennium that now rises before us, brims with aspects. Most seekers cannot parse the secrets. The Book of David, wherein lie the numbers which provided the date of the Second Coming, is another such. I've spent a great deal of time with numbers—I daresay as much as I've spent with believers."

"It's too much to take in."

He slid his hand across and covered hers around the stem of her glass. "You shouldn't try. You need not know every grain of sand to realize a beach, nor every raindrop to know a thunderstorm engulfs you. Thinking is often the pursuit of insecurity. Why unbalance yourself, when I have already counted the numbers and established the answer for you?"

"I am by nature curious, I suppose."

His demeanor stiffened. "I would advise against giving in to your nature here. All the mysteries will be solved tomorrow night. Trust in that. And in me, dear Kate." He drank his glass and refilled it. "Some things in life should be accepted without question, because they are too great to be questioned. That is the definition of faith."

Kate handed him her glass. "On the contrary, Mr. Fitcher, I believe the greater the promise, the more closely it must be scrutinized. The largest promises govern our lives. I'm unwilling to embrace blindly that which I've not considered to the fullest."

He assayed her, and a small smile twitched at his lips. "You have never heard me preach, have you, Mrs. Fitcher?"

"Briefly, I have, sir, that time I visited my sister. And my father has described and even reenacted some of your more dynamic proclamations. I know he is persuaded, as is my stepmother. I have not had *that* privilege."

He stood and carried the glasses to the writing desk, setting hers down. "Then tomorrow morning, you shall have it—the culmination of all my sermons on the final day. I predict I will persuade even you, madam."

"I look forward to my lesson," she replied.

He chuckled, and lifted his glass in a toast to her. "The cleverest by far, oh, yes. I was right to save you for last. You are the purest and most steadfast."

"As you said, sir, when you asked for my hand."

He waited a moment longer, as if in final hope that she would invite him to her bed, let go the sheet and shift the battle from words to sensations, where he would easily triumph. When she said nothing, he turned smartly and strode away with the bottle and the glass. "In the morning, then," he called back over his shoulder.

She didn't see how he managed it, but the door to her room swung closed after him as if on command.

Then Kate sank back upon her pillows and allowed herself the luxury of terror.

Thirty

I SAY UNTO YOU, 'GIVE EAR, O YE heavens, and I will speak: and hear, O earth, the words of my mouth. My doctrine shall drop as the rain, my speech shall distill as the dew, as the small rain upon the tender herb, and as the showers upon the grass.' Thus begins Deuteronomy thirty-two."

Fitcher stood upon the back porch of Harbinger. His audience had swollen beyond the confines of the Hall of Worship. They filled the yard as far as Kate could see. She sat off to one side, along with the small group of his inner circle. Thirteen chairs had been set up, three on a side and one in the center for the new bride. Kate was surprised to find herself enclosed by women as well as men—not just her father, but Lavinia sat there, both of them in the chairs ahead of her.

Kate looked at the faces of those to either side of her, faces that regarded her husband with pure adoration, even before he began to speak; and once his voice split the dark and threatening morning, so did virtually everyone within hearing turn their attention to him with expressions of adulation.

"The Lord says here, 'To me belongeth vengeance, and rec-

ompense; their foot shall slide in due time: for the day of their
calamity is at hand!' We know who is spoken of here. They are
the people outside our blessed utopia, those people who have
ignored the signs, who care nothing for our message, who will
not come in. Calamity *is* at hand! And their reluctance can but
consign them to damnation.

"Some of them are dear ones, close to us, who would not be
entreated to join us. Others are what they are—unyielding ob-
jects deaf to words they haven't themselves formed.

"They as we have always stood upon the brink of destruction.
God placed all mankind on the blade of that sword which Solo-
mon raised. We've been there since Eden. One foot stands in
peril, the other in peace. The likelihood of tumbling into the pit
has always been with us, and many before this day have slipped,
their fates already sealed. We cannot change their fate. Others
think they can wait and see how the sword will fall, and make
their choices afterward. Not so, for does it not also say, 'The Lord
shall judge His people'? Who, other than God, decides when His
children shall plunge into hell? No one else has this power. He
may allow the wicked to persist in their ways, knowing that each
act they perform only further secures their damnation; He may
place temptation in their path, but He does not make them embrace it.

"God grants you all free will. You can choose. Today you are
here before me because you have heard and you have chosen."

Many in the crowd answered this, shouting in the affirmative,
or just shouting.

" 'See now that I, even *I*, am he, and there is no god with
me: I kill, and I make alive; I wound, and I heal; neither is there
any that can deliver out of my hand. For I lift up my hand to
Heaven, and say, *I live forever!* ' "

Fitcher's fist was raised to the sky. Thousands of other fists
joined his in the air. Thousands of voices chanted: "I live forever!" Kate found her own arm hovering, but folded her hands
together tightly in her lap. The group around her had their fists
raised, every one of them. The power of the speech swept her
up, but the sudden movement of the crowd in response had bro-

ken the spell. She glanced aside, saw the crowd as far back as
the orchards extending their arms like clockwork creatures. His
words still rang, the last quotation from Deuteronomy resounded.
It must have been the three walls of the building that kept his
voice spinning around them.

"I speak for you. I have called the people far and wide unto
this mountain, and you have answered that call, you have come.
You have made your sacrifices to me, given up the goods of the
world, cast off that which burdened you, which tied you to the
sensual life. Those who have *not* answered, let them be cast
down. They are condemned already by their very disregard. He
that believeth, he is not condemned.

"Tell me, then, that you believe!"

The multitude shouted out their belief.

"Tell me that you know there is nothing between you and
hell itself but the air. Nothing protects you from everlasting
flames. Hell is an open maw beneath you. The flames lick at the
soles of your feet. The demons dance within, awaiting your arrival, the arrival of all mankind. The slope on which you stand
will tumble you into their cruel care for all eternity. They will
flay the skin from you. Terrible torture awaits those who lack the
necessary faith, who question the truth even when it stands before them." He glanced, as he paused, at Kate.

"Nothing can save you from the pit of hell except faith. You
have journeyed far to be here, you have shunned the false prophets and the false churches, but you still stand upon that fearful
blade and you can still fall even at the last moment, even as God
makes the cut which severs us from them. Those outside our
gates would kill you if they knew you would be granted a special
place at God's side while they plunge into the fiery pit. They
would slaughter you in their anger and their jealousy. But *I* protect you from them. I know who you should fear. Fear he who,
having slain you, can throw your soul down into hell. I say, fear
him above all others. Let *me* protect you from the wrath of God.
I deal in fury. *I* deal in judgment. Place your souls in *my* keeping!"

They cried out with answers—swearing allegiance, commit-

ting their souls every one to his keeping. In the front rows of the
multitude, some people collapsed. They twitched and kicked in
spasms. Their eyes rolled up. A man foamed at the mouth. Some
babbled incoherently and clawed at the sky. Those nearest
caught them, laid them down, but got up quickly again, not wanting to miss anything. White feathers burst into the air as people
in the throes of ecstasy crashed into the makeshift henhouses on
either side.

The gathered lieutenants had risen around Kate to shout
along with the others, and Kate found herself on her feet in their
midst, though she had no sense of rising with them. She felt the
words of allegiance in her throat but fought them down with
urgent fear. He hadn't lied to her about the power of his preaching—if anything, he had understated it; but she had glimpsed
his true self, and she made that memory burn like a jack-o'-
lantern behind his enchantment. She listened and dissected his
words more carefully than his loyal followers. The promise of the
pit might be real enough, but the path by which one fell was not
so obvious as he would make it. She had always maintained that
those quickest to condemn were most in peril themselves, because they pointed the finger with a piousness formed of hubris,
of haughty superiority by which they could eclipse their own
shortcomings; and Fitcher's proposal for dividing the saved from
the damned began with just such an imperious pose.

Her father, she guessed, would not believe her. She couldn't
make him admit that the casuistry of this salvation had misled
him. Even if she could find proof, she doubted she could persuade him. Fitcher was too skillful, too clever by half, to reveal
himself in a casual way. She might trip him up with words, but
only by verbal thrusts and parries as subtle as those he employed
to twist his proclamation of redemption. His keys and the marble
egg burned in her apron pocket, symbols of his control, of the
limits he'd already established. It was all a matter of limits. *Torture awaits those who question the truth*, he'd said, but he didn't mean
that. She could question truth all she liked. What she wasn't
allowed to question was *him*. None of them was. As he spoke
again, she closed herself off from the intoxication of his voice.

"We read the words of God in Isaiah:'I will tread them in mine anger, and will trample them in my fury. For the day of vengeance is in *mine* heart, and the year of my redeemed is come.' Tonight at midnight that day of vengeance shall commence. But I, holding your souls in my care, will act between you and your Lord, and together we will realize these promises that God has spoken. Together will we face *our God*!" His arms stretched up and out as if to embrace them all.

Their cheer must have been heard as far away as Jekyll's Glen. It filled the air, and each time the front gave out, from the back it rolled in again, wave upon wave of ululation like the roar of a huge cataract—like the waterfall in the great gorge that ringed them off from the rest of the world.

The shouting mob was where Kate placed her hope. They would need his close attention more and more as the time drew nigh. Sooner or later, he would have to leave her alone to attend to them.

She did not yet appreciate that leaving her alone had always been his intention, or that her two sisters had already stood upon the same arranged and fatal brink as she contemplated even now.

By late afternoon, the number of those come to salvation had redoubled. Inside the fence, people moved into the woods. They cleared spaces for themselves and their families in the underbrush, content just to be inside, knowing they were both safe and saved. According to her father and the other lieutenants, their numbers had reached twenty thousand, and at least as many more were on the road.

Jekyll's Glen was a town trapped in the path of a flood. Converts covered the streets, the yards, the sidewalks. They jammed the taverns. They clustered beneath canvas awnings to hear other preachers, who extolled the virtues of Elias Fitcher and painted their own descriptions of the fate awaiting the unsaved.

Ministers of the two traditional churches had gathered their flocks together inside the buildings out of fear that the faithful might fall prey to this millennial fever, but also out of a keener fear that they, preaching against the end of the world, might be accused as false prophets by the chaos of converts and strung up if not protected by their congregation.

The steamboat *Fidelio* chugged wearily down the lake with hundreds more packed upon its decks—people who had converted only at the last, or who had bothered to set their secular accounts in order before coming. All across New England, banks were suffering as a result of the massive cash withdrawals by converts who were bringing their wealth with them, either to bribe their way across impasses or in the misapprehension that they would be able to keep their money in the Next Life. So many people with ready cash did not go unnoticed, either. Some had been waylaid as they left their banks, others upon the roads, beaten and robbed of their entire fortunes by individuals interested more in immediate than in eternal reward. The steamboat provided a safer mode of travel than coach or horse, but only because it offered no escape for the thief. The town of Jekyll's Glen, on the other hand, now entertained a network of pickpockets and cutpurses with easy pickings and little likelihood of consequences, although one such had been caught and clubbed to death, and his body, hung with a sign marking him as a thief, now dangled from a tree on the road into town as a warning.

On the Gorge Road, the turnpike and sentry box in front of the Charter house had been demolished, broken up during the night and used for firewood. Squatters exhausted from the crush of people on the road currently occupied the house. They ate off the family's plates, slept on the sofas, slouched in the chairs. They were filthy and tired and not much given to concern themselves with treating someone else's property respectfully. If the spirit of Sam Verity was still about (or ever had been), it kept its own counsel now. No one among the squatters was treated to a session of spirit rapping.

Then, in the hour before sunset, the bridge across Jekyll's Gorge collapsed.

The bridge had not been built to support the weight of the two hundred people who were on it at the time. The braces gave out.

With an explosive crack the center split and both halves tipped the screaming, wailing crowd into the widening gap in the middle. Finally the whole structure gave way. The push from the back continued, and another three score were forced over the side before the mob realized what had happened and could stop their momentum. The bridge hit the bottom of the gorge with an explosion as loud as a volley of cannons. A few souls instinctively sprang after their tumbling loved ones, committing themselves to the same sure fate. The rest began racing like frantic ants along the edge of the gorge in search of a path to the bottom—some to give aid, but most in a desperate hope of finding another way to the opposite side. They couldn't have come this far just to be damned by a collapsing bridge. It wasn't fair!

People clinging to the debris of the bridge were hauled up. From below came cries for help. It was impossible to tell if these were from people who'd been camped below or from survivors of the fall—the smoke from the fires at the bottom obscured the view. Calls went up for rope. Some people wanted to climb down for a rescue, others to make a new bridge across while there was still time. But no one had any rope—most everyone had divested themselves of practical items on this, the last day of the world— and so a handful of reluctant converts began to fight their way through the teeming crush of crowd back toward Jekyll's Glen, where they might buy enough hemp to get across the divide.

The thunder of the bridge landing in the basin of the gorge made the ground shake at Harbinger House and, because of the nature of sound in the gorge, seemed to come from all sides at once. Random panic followed, fueled by the belief that the explosion was a first sign of the end. People who'd only just settled themselves in the woods came flying out, wild-eyed, terrified. Others wailed and fell to their knees, hands clasped to the sky as they begged for their salvation.

It was another half an hour before the first of the injured was carried to the front gate and the story of the disaster made its way through the community. The call went out for aid. Someone hitched horses to a wagon and drove around to the gate only to find the road so congested that they couldn't go any farther. At Harbinger there was plenty of rope, and coils of it were rushed out to the gates, tossed into the wagons. As the gates parted, many who hung on the outside tried again to push through, and a battle raged until some had been hammered unconscious or dead and the rest pushed back to let the rope bearers and wagons out.

At the lip of the gorge, the arrival of the rope was cheered at first. The men tied their ropes to the remaining struts, then threw them over the side. Those who were alive and unharmed at the bottom secured the ropes to those in need of aid. The laborious process of hauling up the injured began. It became complicated, as those with broken ribs had to be hauled up by being tied by the ankles and pulled up upside down. No one could think how else to get them safely to the top. Meanwhile, on the far side, the cheers had turned into angry demands that the ropes be thrown across the gorge so they could get to Harbinger. Their demands were absurd—no one could have thrown a rope that far—but they were frantic to reach their safe haven.

The bodies were carried along a thin lane through the midst of the crowd. Some who were light and not so injured were passed overhead like participants in a grotesque festive game.

Word reached Fitcher as he was sitting down to his meal. He got up and apologized to his flock that he would not be able to share a final supper with them. He raised his eyes to the ceiling and said, "Lord, I should have closed the gates before but for my concern for the many who might not join me. It's I who'll answer for their having fallen into the pit." Then he went out. Some of those at the tables—Mr. Charter and Lavinia among them—got up and followed him. Kate, closest to the door, led them.

People had already been laid out on the floor of the crowded foyer, attended to by others she didn't recognize—most of whom had been all too happy to carry the wounded into Harbinger in order to gain swift entrance for themselves. Fitcher and the rest of his entourage filed out the front door.

Attending to the group, Kate said, "Bring them upstairs." She took a man who was hobbling on one foot, put his arm over her shoulder, and helped him to the stairs. They led the way up. On the second floor she helped him sit against the wall, then pulled out her keys.

It took her a few moments to unlock the first door, but once she had identified the right key, the other rooms were easy to open. Those following behind her had to set down their fellow travelers and drag trunks and crates aside to gain access to the beds and sofas in the rooms. More people were coming up the stairs, bringing more wounded. Some they placed on top of the crates. The bedding was stripped and brought into the hall, and mattresses laid on the floor. Community members arrived— three men, who announced that they were surgeons and immediately fell to performing as such. They barked orders down to the first floor, calling for bandages and splints. Someone began ripping up the bedsheets.

Kate came back along the far side of the hall, unlocking the last of the doors. She returned to the main group of the wounded just as one child, lying on his back upon a crate, was pronounced dead.

She asked one of the surgeons if she should open more rooms on the next floor.

"No," he told her. "We'll make them comfortable with what's here. Don't want to spread 'em out too far anyway. Better we can attend to them all in close proximity. We won't be sawing at anyone. Bandage 'em up is all we're going to do." He patted her shoulder, smiling. "They only have to hold up till midnight, after all." He thanked her for opening the rooms and added, "Best let us work now. Some of these broken bones do have to be set."

Kate withdrew then. She stood awhile at the rail, overlooking the foyer. It seemed that the first wave of wounded had all arrived. No one else was bursting in. She noticed then the blood on her skirt from the wounded man she'd helped. In some way she couldn't explain, the sight of it cemented her will to act.

She ran to her room. She was going to change the skirt, and removed the egg from its pocket, placing it on the bed. She

374 GREGORY FROST

stopped. There wasn't time to change. She didn't know how long
he would be gone or how much she would have to search for the
evidence she wanted. She pushed the egg beneath her pillow,
then hurried out.

The top floor of the house was deserted. This would have
seemed stranger were it not for the atmosphere there: It was
almost impenetrably dark and uninviting. The drapery at the top
of the stairs barred even the low light of the sun from entering.
Amy had asked rhetorically where Fitcher lived, and Kate could
only speculate that he must have a room here at the top, unless
he truly lived in that pyramid of his, that construct of magic numbers and powers. It was glass, and she suspected that the glass
key opened it. She wanted that answer, but she also wanted to
know what lay behind all of these doors. Why, as she had wondered before, was there an entire floor of the house empty when
the people below could not find enough room to sit?

At the first door, she fumbled in the dark with the keys until
she thought she would never find the right one. When finally the
door unlatched, she thought it must be a trick, because she'd
hardly turned the key. Charily, she pushed open the door.

The room lay all in shadow. Unlike her room and those of
the floor below, there was an alcove inside here, a narrow hall
leading to the main part of the room. She could make out shapes
of the furnishings, of a table sporting a tin candelabrum, of a bed
and a dresser. It smelled as ancient as a tomb, though. As she
moved into the main part of the room, she heard something scut-
tle into the corner. She could just make out the shape of a man
squatting, with his arms crossed over his head as if to hide from
her. "I'm sorry," she said, and was going to withdraw, but changed
her mind. What if the man was someone she knew? Immediately
she thought of Pulaski.

She crossed to a window that was heavily draped and shuttered. She pushed back the drapes and opened the shutters. Low
red light poured in, and she turned around to discover who it was
crouching there.

In the light she saw clearly. Every shape, every piece of furniture, every suggested detail of the room, had vanished. There

were no furnishings—no chairs or tables, no bed. It was a cadaverous room. The walls were chalky and cracked. The floorboards looked to have rotted in places. A spider bounced on its web in the corner beside her.

The crouching man in the corner had also vanished.

A ruddy glow came from the narrow alcove leading to the door, as if a fire burned out in the hall. It was, she thought, as if the room had been transported to another place. She sensed instinctively that these were the rooms of her dreams, the places where the spirit had brought her. The hall outside was the dark hallway down which she'd been propelled.

Kate closed the shutters and pulled the drapes together again. When she turned, all the shapes that had been there before were back. She retraced her steps, dragged her fingers through the dust on top of the table, touched the cold metal of the candelabrum, her senses recording the details of things that were not there, or only formed in the umbra of dreams. She closed the door, locked it. What were these rooms then? Repositories for ghosts? How did he make this happen?

Her heart was hammering in her breast. She would not open the other rooms beside this one. She did not need to meet the rest of his dead men.

She felt for the glass key and walked into the depths of the gloom. There must be *some* lock it matched. She had nearly reached the end of the hall before she made out the recessed doorway there. This was a different sort of door from the rest. She took a step into the entryway. Her skin rose in gooseflesh from a sudden blast of arctic air.

The keyhole emitted an incongruously molten glow. Its light struck her keys, and they glittered. The keyhole was large, easily identifiable as the match for the glass key, and she fit it into the lock. The air seemed to breathe around her, to sigh. The door latch clicked as it released, such a small sound for so black and immense a door.

Kate pushed the slender handle and opened the door a crack to peer into the smoky red room. The first narrow glimpse revealed strange devices of torture on the far wall—pincers and tongs, a flaying knife, and a cage to fit over someone's head with a locking band around the neck. A mist swirled around them, pushed by the air leaking into the chamber. A smell emerged, a salty, coppery stink at once familiar and foreign.

When she pushed the door wider she saw the first torso, and then the second. Beneath them stood a black wrought-iron candelabrum bearing six thick candles. "My God," she said. The words simply escaped her.

The door swung back until she could see the whole monstrous abattoir, and she had to hold on to the jamb for fear she would collapse in the face of it.

The torsos were all female, in various states of decomposition.

The weird light filtered down through a stained-glass window in the middle of the ceiling, a portrayal of Adam and Eve and the Snake of Eden. A bronze cauldron stood beneath it, splashed by the reds and greens of the glass. Tendrils of hair like strands of moss hung off the side, bony fingertips protruded just above the rim. She knew without even crossing the room what the cauldron contained, knew it as if her soul flew ahead of her body on the icy steam of her breath and peered down into the bloody depths at the six blind faces. Beside it, assorted hands and feet jutted like the handles of freakish walking sticks out of a squat barrel. An ax leaned against the barrel as if it had just been set down. The floor all around was sticky-wet with blood and gore.

Kate grabbed the handle and pulled the door closed. She locked it, then backed carefully out through the layer of cold air and down the hall. She held the keys rigid at her side. Her mind whirled like clockwork gearing, adding up the facts, insulating her from the grip of terror by seeking a solution: six torsos, Vern and Amy and four more besides. Wives, they must all be wives. How easy it was for him, with his power of persuasion, his position as emissary, messenger, angel of the Lord. Who wouldn't wish their daughter allied with one so exalted? Who could have refused his compassionate advances? Escaped his treacherous traps?

One day the ax just fell.

This house where no one and everyone lived, where rooms could vanish in the light of day, where Christ was a glass ornament—what was this place if not hell?

Kate knew she'd been gone dangerously long and hurried back to her room. The surgeons were still at work, though most of the injured had gone. She stood beside her bed while her brain spun.

When had he begun to take his brides? Would there be others in other places, the landscape of proselytizing sprinkled with the blood of more women? How many had he sampled? She'd asked and he had eluded her question. "Enough" was all he said. More than Vern and Amy—at least five or six here, and he meant for her to join them. She might survive awhile, but his goal was clear. She doubted his promises of any next life, doubted his predictions, yet knew he had powers beyond those of other men. He was mad, yes, but he was much more as well. What she had to do was shake her father's belief in the madman until it cracked, show *him* the truth before the hour—

She sensed rather than heard the presence behind her. As she turned, she pocketed the keys in her skirt.

Fitcher looked her over, a predator sniffing his prey. "My dear, where have you been?"

"Why, I attended to some of the injured across the hall while you went out to the bridge." She saw him looking at her skirt, at the blood on the hem. His gaze, rising to meet hers, was vulpine. Kate said, "I helped a man with a broken leg up to this floor, where the surgeons set his break. He was bleeding. I didn't notice it at the time, and when I did, I returned here to change." She undid the sash of the skirt, and reached behind her to unfasten the buttons; as she did, she sat on the bed, and let one hand stray beneath the pillow.

"Ah, I see. Well, I shouldn't trouble you after such a shock. But I wonder might I see my keys and my little marble egg?"

"Of course," she replied, as if it were the most natural request in the world. She drew the keys from her pocket and produced the egg in her other hand.

Fitcher looked at them both. He took the egg and rolled it

over in his palm before placing it again in hers. He held up the glass key as if to admire it. A look of wonder shaped his features. "I'm so glad, dearest Kate, to finally be wedded to you. You alone, untarnished by Eve's rashness. The perfect flower. We have but a few hours remaining, so dress as you might for a ball, for some gala event, for it certainly shall be so. I probably won't be with you now much before the end. There are so many yet whose good souls I must reap. This tragedy at the bridge makes me keenly aware that I do not wish to lose many more. We have thousands upon thousands here, you know. You will be all right?"

"I will."

"I did not doubt it. You are worth them all, my dear." He leaned forward and gave her a kiss before he left. She never flinched, even as she tasted his deceit.

Thirty-one

*T*HE TIME ROLLED ON INTO THE last night of the world, and the community of Harbinger came unhinged. Contemplation of impending Rapture seemed more than most minds could bear, and a kind of diabolical hysteria swept through the gathered thousands. By torchlight, candlelight, and lamplight they took to dancing, pockets of the faithful leaping and whirling in ecstatic freedom, while their fellows played tunes that went faster and faster. Some people collapsed from the dancing, but it didn't deter the rest from continuing. Exhaustion kept the brain from thinking, from having to acknowledge the terror of the heart.

Others who didn't join in the dancing spent their time clustered, kneeling, reading and praying, making their spirits pure for the Parousia of the Son of Man. Families gathered together to pray and await the end. Preachers in the community took their cues from Fitcher's sermon of that morning, and berated the listeners for their innate sinfulness, particularly the women, who were tarred as "Jezebels" or "harlots," and none of whom ob-

jected. The air throbbed with music, sermonizing, and wild rhap-
sodizing voices.

A group wearing thin cotton nightshirts and carrying long
birch switches took over the Hall of Worship, where they set to
flogging one another upon the altar. One of the squatters they
displaced from his pew stole the glass skull of Christ, which he
carried into a corner of the foyer. He sat beside it, engaged with
it in a secretive dialogue.

Kate found her husband and asked where her father was.
Fitcher replied that he'd sent Mr. Charter out to preach to those
people camped in the pastures and fields. He was a lieutenant—
he had duties. As did she. "Those such as ourselves are charged
with obligations that transcend our own corporal desires. You shall
have eternity with your family, after today." She did not reply
that she understood the truths encoded in his words, the tricks
he was playing. She let it stand. What mattered was that her
father was safe for now inside the gates.

Late in the evening a small boy fell from the landing of the
main staircase inside the house. Kate heard cries of alarm, and
rushed into the foyer to find the parents kneeling over his body
as they wailed and clutched one another. When she looked up,
she saw Fitcher leaning over the rail of the landing. From there
he descended almost casually, as though nothing that happened
from now on could surprise or affect him. The crowd parted for
him. He consoled the couple with the promise that their boy had
gone ahead of them by hardly an hour—he pointed to the tall
clock on the landing. It showed the time as five minutes before
eleven. The parents and the body of their child were taken into
the keeping room. Seeing Kate, Fitcher shook his head and muttered to her, "Oh, that *boy*," as if the child had done something
mischievous rather than fatal. He took a step, then paused to
consider her approvingly. She had, as he'd requested, dressed as
for a ball, in a silk dress with a tiered skirt and an off-the-shoulder
neckline. Fitcher purred, "One hour, dear Kate," then walked
after the parents.

Kate rounded the wide staircase, away from Fitcher. It was
then she came upon the caretaker of the glass skull. He had his

knees up, his feet hooked over the edge of his chair. He held
out his coat flap to try to hide the skull on the chair beside him.
Kate caught a gleam of light off one of the thorns in its crown
and came closer. The squatter looked around at her approach,
inadvertently lowering his coat. When he saw that he'd revealed
the skull, he slid his feet to the floor and sat upright, turning his
body away from her as if unaware of the skull's presence. He
gave a cringing slantendicular glance her way. Their eyes met
and his face went taut with fear. He got up guiltily, handed the
skull to her, then fled through the crowd into the refectory.

Fitcher and the family were gone, so she went to return the
skull to the Hall of Worship. People sat along the dark entryway.
She stumbled over someone. Hands brushed her, possibly grop-
ing. The one or two hands that clutched, she struck away with
the skull. Shortly she emerged into the rear of the hall and found
herself at the edge of an orgy. The whippings taking place there
on the pretext of self-loathing had excited other desires in the
penitents. Lying naked on the altar had given way to coupling
naked in the pews. Kate backed away and retreated before someone noticed and tried to force her to join their mad assemblage.
She held the skull before her in the dark corridor again, but no
one tried to grab her this time.

She took it with her upstairs, intending to place it for safe-
keeping in her room.

She found that the open rooms where the injured had earlier
been cared for had subsequently been looted. Trunks and crates
lay pried or smashed open, their contents spilled out across floors,
dragged into the hallway—clothing, pillows and sheets, neck-
laces, pots and pans, even a miner's pickax, lay incongruously
beside the bloodstained mattresses, shredded sheets, and makeshift stretchers of canvas and tree branches.

Downstairs, the clock chimed eleven times, and a cacophony
of voices bawled back with beseeching prayers, fortifying quo-
tations: "I have faith in Lord Jesus Christ, the Only Savior!"

"He that believeth shall be saved!"

"By Grace are we saved, through Faith and not of ourselves
is the Gift of God!"

Kate heard the mortal dread in their words. She returned to the landing to scan the crowd below. Fitcher had gone. She must act now. Whatever happened after midnight—however many angels appeared and hallelujahs were sung—she would see the monster exposed. Whether or not she would be reunited with them in the next life, Kate's sisters had been murdered in this one. Her only defense in Fitcher's new world lay in the evidence of his evil.

Her bull's-eye lantern had been left on the floor there. She set the skull down beside it, then ran to her room and grabbed the lucifers from the mantel. She lit the lantern with one and put the rest in her pocket.

She picked up the skull—if she left it here, it would just be stolen again—and climbed to the top floor.

The floor was as dark and seemingly lifeless as before, but now the doors to all the rooms along the hall stood open. Walking past them, she was startled to see figures lurking just inside. When she stopped, they shuffled back from the doorways and haunted the shadows. This time, when she shone the light of her lamp into the doorways, the men did not vanish, as if their presence had grown stronger. Their faces were gray as ash. All were solemn, their eyes sunken, heads down as if afraid to meet her gaze. She saw that they all bore wounds, some disfiguring. She knew that she was looking at shades, men who now existed only in the dark, condemned to these rooms like souls condemned to purgatory. In the third one along, before he backed out of view, Kate saw a face with a wide mustache with waxed ends. It was the man in the daguerreotype, James Pulaski.

Then, in the fourth doorway, Michael Notaro stood. She could not mistake him, nor the black wounds in his belly and his throat. Slowly, he raised his head and looked into her eyes. He made a gentle smile then—a look she'd never seen on his face in life. Was this the face Amy had seen? He backed away into the shadows. Kate stepped toward him and shone her lantern through the doorway. Its light fell upon an empty foyer. She nodded as though understanding that his shade could not speak to her, and went on.

At the rear of the hall, one door to the side remained closed. She hadn't noticed it before. It was smaller than the others. She found the key for it after only one try. The door opened onto a small stairwell—servant's stairs. Going down they no doubt exited at the back of the house, near the kitchen. Going up, she could guess where they would take her. That might make things easier for her, but later. Afterward.

She steeled herself for what she must do next, then unlocked the door to the bloody chamber and went inside. She locked the door behind her. Now she was sealed in with all of his wives.

The room was cold as winter. Kate set the skull down beside the cauldron, and carried the lantern to the rear wall. She had to look closely at the horrible torsos to identify her sisters' bodies. They hung side by side on hooks, the least decayed of the six.

She set the lantern behind her on the candelabrum. Then with a silent prayer to God to give her strength, she took hold of Amy's torso and pushed it up off the hook.

It was like lifting a great dead fish. The skin was cold and rubbery, horrid to the touch, but she refused to give in to her repulsion. She laid it on the floor. She had to shove aside some leg irons and move the candelabrum up against the barrel to place Vernelia's torso beside it. The arms and legs were hard to judge. She pictured Amy's feet, against the wall of the bedroom, as she cracked her toe joints. It seemed as if that had been years ago.

Through trial and error, she matched the arms and legs to the bodies, placing them like the parts of enormous bloodless dolls. One arm from each body had been stuck in the cauldron for display, and it had to be for his own amusement, for who else was meant to see it?

Now came the worst of all. She picked up the lantern again and held it out above the cauldron as she leaned over and made herself look into the dead faces of Fitcher's brides. So many heads. She recognized Vern and Amy—and, she thought, the head of Mrs. Pulaski. Of course it was there. It had to be.

Into the red depths, she plunged her hand to grab hold of Amy's hair and lift the head out. The water swirled. The heads shifted and rocked.

Cringing, keeping it at arm's length, she placed Amy's head at the top of its body, then went back for Vern's.

In taking hold of Vern, she caught strands from another, more decayed head as well, and it came up with Vern's, like a submerged monster aroused by Kate's intrusion into its domain. She dropped Vern's, and both heads fell with a splash. Kate had to leap aside as a bloody plume sprayed out of the cauldron. She knocked over the wrought-iron candelabrum; the candles tumbled and rolled across the floor.

Kate hesitated. "Again," she ordered herself. "Only once more. Dear Lord, only once." She leaned over the cauldron again and grabbed hold of Vern's head. Quickly, she raised it. Watery blood splashed over her silk dress, but she didn't care, didn't stop. Blood was on her hands and forearms, her feet, her knees and petticoats where she'd knelt. It couldn't be covered up now. She wanted the blood there. She wanted her father to see it, the blood of his girls.

She left them lying there, unlocked the door, and went out, locking it once more to disguise her handiwork. She realized that she'd locked the skull in with them, then decided that was as it should be. What was the skull if not a demonic distortion of Christ, stripped of meaning, of truth? One more cruel jape of Fitcher's. It belonged to that hellish room, too.

How much time did she have now? Probably only a quarter hour, not much more than that. Yet she knew with unshakable certainty that no one here was Heaven-bound. No man as monstrous as Elias Fitcher would ever enter Heaven. He might inveigle all of humanity with his arcane gifts, but what deity would let him in? Did he think that Satan had gained control of the celestial city? And with that thought came a flash of insight too outrageous to put into words, but which—if it *was* true—meant that eternal damnation lived inside and not beyond the iron rails that bordered Harbinger.

She returned to the door to the servant stairs. There couldn't be much time left. She had to find her father now, and if he was in the fields, away from the house, he might be anywhere. And there was the possibility as well that Fitcher had lied about that,

too. She would use the pyramid. She only hoped Amy's claims
of its magical properties were true.

Holding the lantern ahead of her, Kate climbed the circling
stairs. Even before she saw the pyramid, she could hear the howl
like a great storm above her.

From the view she'd had of it on the ground, the pyramid
had looked clear, but the light of her lamp reflected off its surfaces as if off mirrors. Yet it wasn't a simple reflection. As she
watched, the brightest part of the light moved and took on
shapes, which crystallized into images of the people below. Each
of the panes showed her some portion of the thousands surrounding the house. There were people mutilating themselves, tearing
out their hair, gouging out their own eyes, then reaching with
blood-drenched fingers for the sky in agonized supplication for
God to come and take them now. She realized she could hear as
well as see them—what had seemed the howl of the wind was
the wailing of so many souls in torment. At the chained front
gates, hundreds pushed against the iron to get in. Some attempted to scale the bars. At the top, many had lost their hold
and been impaled on the points, but more crazed converts
climbed and crawled over them to get to the other side. They
dangled from the bodies, jumped to the lawn. Some succeeded
and ran off. Others hurt themselves in the jump and couldn't
move. The guards beat anyone within reach the moment they
landed.

Then Fitcher arrived. He approached the bars and those outside reached between them. Children stuck their heads through.
Fitcher strode along the fence as though he walked down an aisle
in a church, seemingly unaware of the carnage and cruelty around
him. He touched their hands, promising them salvation if they
entrusted their souls to him—or, no, she realized, he was quoting
from Proverbs: "Confesseth and forsaketh and you shall find my
mercy!" Yes, *his* mercy. His mercy dripped from her hands.

Remembering what Amy had said about the properties of this
place, she called out her father's name. The image blackened,
was replaced by that of her father on his knees, his elbows
propped on a bale of hay. A dozen others knelt with him, all deep

in prayer. It was the village barn. Somehow Mr. Charter had found a pocket of sanity and sanctity in the midst of the horrors below. She heard his whispered prayer as if she were beside him: "Oh, Lord, forgive me for in my weakness I gave myself to him. I am damned forever but spare my girls, please, they entered here as innocents, lambs for his slaughtering, O Merciful God, spare them, let them join their mother, who I know is with you. Elizabeth, my darling, I shall never see you again."

Kate glanced away from the view, her eyes brimming with tears. So he knew, he already knew. The spell upon him must have lifted. Her poor father had been deluded in his grief by the persuasion of Fitcher. And by Lavinia. Turning back to the glass, she said her stepmother's name.

Abruptly there was darkness. Trees in tidy rows stood on either side of her. It was the orchard. In the distance were the lights of the village, but no sign of Lavinia. Then she burst into view between the trees, turned, and ran straight at Kate. She was dressed again in her riding clothes, her hair unfurled, fanning blackly behind her. Her face taut with terror, she sobbed between ragged breaths. She looked over her shoulder, as if watching for pursuit, as a gray veil appeared between Kate's view and Lavinia. It fluttered and settled in her path, flexed into an anthropomorphic form like smoke trapped in a human-shaped bottle. Kate cried out, "Lavinia, no, go back!"

As if hearing her, Lavinia faced forward and saw it. She shrieked and tried to run the other way, but the grayness swept right up and embraced her. Lavinia wailed, "Please, Elias, no, let me stay! I'll find you more, I'll find you *new ones!*" Her feet rose off the ground. She was held in the air, and slowly, inexorably, she began to wither. Her scream of agony thinned, became a shrill whistle, her skin wrinkled and collapsed as if everything inside were desiccating. Her bones cracked like kindling taking a flame. Under the crackling sound, the thing whispered to her soothingly, "There, now, give unto me your life, there can be no resurrection for you, my servant, slave. You were judged so long ago." Kate shivered at the awful slyness of a voice she'd only heard in dreams till now. This was the thing he'd sent to their room, the shade in the wall that had enticed each sister in her turn. It was no spirit, no angel as she imagined angels, no matter what they called it here.

When finally the thing set her down, Lavinia was nothing but a dry skin in a boiled shirt. The skin crumpled into the grass, vanishing as if the earth had absorbed her. The murdering shade slid away between the trees.

Lavinia had been Fitcher's lieutenant, his lover, his jealous procurer. She had delivered his wives—at least, thought Kate, the last three of them. Kate made a silent prayer that God would forgive Lavinia what she had done: She couldn't hate another victim of Fitcher, not even her stepmother. In a few minutes, he would claim Kate's soul as well. That was the plan, of course, and always had been. Lavinia's task had been to find him his perfect flower. No doubt she worshipped him as Kate's sisters and the multitude did—worshipped him and desired him. Now he didn't need her any longer. He had everything he wanted.

On the first floor, the clock struck the first toll of midnight. A roar reached Kate from the yard far below. She'd been absorbed too long. She had to get to her father.

She turned to run but in her haste lurched against a small rail she hadn't seen. She hit it with such force that she nearly tumbled over it headfirst. Her lantern rang against it like a bell. The egg spun out of her pocket. She clutched the rail to keep from going over, and found herself hanging above the stained-glass panel over the slaughter room, over the cauldron. The egg fell straight through the glass, sending cracks in every direction, puncturing the image of Eve. For an instant the window sagged around the hole. Then like the bridge in the gorge, it collapsed. It crashed down as the clock struck its fourth chime. "Vern! Amy!" Kate cried. She raced down the stairs to the room.

Most of the window had landed in the cauldron. The bodies she'd laid out at the side were untouched. The skull was rolling around in the sticky blood on the floor, and Kate picked it up. She stood up the overturned candelabrum and set the skull on top of it, between the prongs.

It was then that she witnessed the unfolding miracle.

The bodies she had assembled were knitting together. Where Fitcher had hacked them apart, skin and bones were rejoining, the awful seams were closing up.

The clock tolled again.

Kate looked up at the refulgent point of the pyramid above her and thought, *Not a Day of Judgment, but one of Resurrection.* Whose power, whose magic, was this? Surely not his, not Fitcher's. His powers delivered only death.

As she watched, dumbfounded, her healed sisters opened their eyes and sat up. Vern looked at herself in wonder. Amy began to cry. Kate knelt and hugged them both. The skull, perched above, seemed to gaze imperiously upon the reunion.

From the floors below came the din of the congregation, sounding more animal than human.

"It's the end of the world," Amy cried.

"Not for us, not if I can help it," said Kate. "But it will be if we walk out through the front of this house—he'd recognize us and have us torn to pieces. He's out there now with his Angel of Death. And you two, you're drenched in more blood than the angel."

She paused a moment then, thinking of what she'd seen in the magic glass above. The clock sounded one final time. The fifteenth had arrived. Kate rose and began to undress.

"What are you doing?" Vern asked.

"I'll show you soon enough. Help me now. We have to get to Papa and take him with us." She undressed quickly, and draped her fancy clothes over the candelabrum. The matches in her pockets spilled across the floor, but she ignored them. She didn't need them now. She began to smear herself with the blood from the floor. They saw what she was doing and joined in. They smeared her and then themselves with it, until all three of them were covered from head to foot in blood.

"Follow me now," she said, and took them by the hand, leading them out of the chamber and down the back circling stairwell. She emerged on the second floor. It was empty, although the crowd sounded as if they stood on the stairs below. Vandalized belongings were still strewn across the hall. She wanted the mattresses where the surgeons had worked, in particular the expensive ones. Kate grabbed the pickax beside them and used it to rip a mattress down the middle. She stuck her hands into the cavity and flung the contents into the air. Feathers flew around them, settled, and stuck. "They're all expecting signs," she said as she shook out more feathers. "Demons or angels. They'll let us through, they're too terrified to reason it out."

Vern nodded, uncertainly but gamely reached into the mattress and threw more feathers at Kate. In a few minutes they were all covered in a layer of feathers, unrecognizable as Fitcher's brides, almost as anything human.

People were milling about on the second floor now. Kate led her sisters to the back stairs and quickly descended.

At the bottom, one door opened to the kitchen and another to the back porch. They went outside. As Kate had hoped, most of the crowd had surged to the front of the house at the stroke of midnight to be close to Fitcher, their savior, and abandoned the makeshift encampment. Many of the tents had been trampled flat. There were bodies lying strewn through the debris. Kate said, "Listen to me, now, Papa is in the village barn. We have to go and bring him."

"What about Lavinia?" Amy asked.

She replied, "She's gone."

Vern said, "All right, sister."

The three girls crept down the steps into the yard, but they hadn't gone more than a few steps when a cluster of people barreled out of a dormitory door and saw them. "My Lord, it's the angels!" They pointed and clung to one another. "The angels are come for us!" The group sprang apart, scrambling in every direction with their announcement. Kate said, "Go, hurry, get Papa. I'll stay here and divert them." Vern and Amy bolted for the village, running through the night like fabled monsters out of a bestiary.

Shortly, more people came crowding around the sides of the house, rushing to see the angels. Kate reasoned that if they thought she was an angel, she would be an angel. Rather than trying to flee, she stepped boldly to the alarm bell and swung

the clapper back and forth. Now no one would pay attention to
Vern and Amy.

More people crowded around her. They pressed in, some
quivering with terror, some crying, so many that she could not
bear their collective misery. They wanted salvation so much that
they had lost their wits.

"Listen to me, good people," she said. "The world has not
ended. It was never going to end the way you've been told. You
were lied to, deceived."

"Who?" they cried. "Who deceived us?"

"You deceived yourselves. You let one man promise he could
save you, one villain—"

She was grabbed from behind and spun around. Fitcher
loomed over her in his black coat, his face blackly furious.

Kate twisted out of his grip and shouted, "Look for yourselves, look at First Corinthians, fifteen-two. You are saved—"

Fitcher hauled her around again. "Where is *He*? Why has He
sent you instead? Behold you, and tell Him"—he turned her
about again and swept his arm across the gathering—"here they
all are, his most ardent worshippers, but they're all mine now,
they've given *me* their souls, every one, even the most virginal—"
He stopped suddenly and craned his head. "Where is my wife?
I want Him to see her especially. She's the purest, the most perfect, but I have her, too. She promised me her soul tonight and
I'll have it. Where is she?"

She replied, "I know where she is. I'll show you, devil."

He grinned. Then he followed her up onto the porch and
inside. The crowd moved to the porch but hesitated to go farther.
They tried to fathom what the angel had been saying, tried to
recall her verse.

Crossing the foyer, Kate watched Fitcher as he followed her.
Clearly he did not recognize her. She dismissed it as more proof
of his madness, until they passed the large girandole mirror on
the side wall and she caught a glimpse of herself and her husband. Her reflection glowed. Her feathers looked more like a

gown, and nothing like how she saw herself. To him and to the Fitcherites, she had been transformed.

Kate led him up the main stairs. People on the staircase fled before them and scurried onto the second floor as they continued to climb. Fitcher jabbered insanely behind her, "He makes me walk among them, these bovine golems of His. How easily I could collect them, every one, and He'd have nothing. He must let me in now, or I'll smash His little world."

At the top floor she stopped and pointed down the hall. "There she is. She's waiting for you."

Fitcher saw his wife in the bloody chamber. The door was thrown open and candles set on the floor burned all around her. She faced him, fearless it seemed, standing her ground. Her hands gestured, waved him forward, invited him in. His eyes narrowed. "So, Katherine, you, too. Daughter of Eve. You lie like all the others, you're all the same, every *one of you!*" He strode hard, faster and faster down the hall. Kate ran after him. The doors of the rooms had closed. The silent men were gone.

Fitcher burst into the bloody room and swiped at the enticing figure. His fingers caught the dress. It tore away from the frame of the candelabrum. The skull spun into the air and struck him. One of the glass thorns gashed his forehead. Underfoot, glass crunched, and he looked down at it, then up to where stained glass leading hung empty and contorted. His mouth opened—it seemed to Kate in fear. For the first time, he was afraid.

Decayed fingers crawled wormlike out of the cauldron and grabbed on to him.

"What is this?" he cried. He realized he'd been tricked and struggled to fight off the clawing hands, but more hands reached out from beneath the cauldron and took hold of his ankles. He faced Kate.

In the doorway she replied, "Behold, thou art wiser than Daniel, and there is no secret we can hide from thee!"

The hands drew shards of broken glass, shattered pieces of Eve and Adam, and drove them through his feet and his hands. The cauldron trembled and frothed. One disembodied skeletal

GREGORY FROST

hand pushed a long thin blade of crimson glass through the back of his neck and out between his teeth. Mouth pushed wide, Fitcher howled inhumanly and stretched out his impaled hands to the sky. His fingers writhed like snakes, curling, uncurling, grasping for power.

Kate slammed the door on him. The keys were still in the lock where she'd left them. She turned the latch, then broke the glass key in half. With a loud *crack* it snapped off in the lock.

She raced for the stairs. As she ran down them she yelled at everyone ahead of her to get out of the house. Before the charging, feathered avatar, the Fitcherites fled shrieking. She could see the glow of herself reflecting on every polished surface.

They stumbled, crawled, and ran out the front doors ahead of her. She stopped upon the portico and surveyed the melee below. The crowd became aware of her. They turned, pointed, and fell silent, both inside and beyond the fence. Torches were raised. Perhaps three dozen smaller lights glowed among the crowd—candles, lit so that they might not meet their maker in darkness.

As they beheld Kate, there was movement at the side of the house. The throng parted and Vern and Amy appeared, like creatures woven of light themselves, leading Mr. Charter and the group who'd been with him in the barn.

"Open those gates," Kate cried. "Let everyone *out*." She went down the steps and snatched a torch from one of the men nearby. She carried it back to the front door and threw the torch inside, against the stairwell. It broke apart, scattering flames into the green drapery. Flames caught the dried flowers between the stairs and climbed angrily up the huge wooden cross.

The crowd was bewildered—ordering them to be let out suggested that they'd been locked in and not the other way around. They looked at the sky, at the stars scattered above them, and at all the people pressed against the outside of the fence: people who had not perished. Midnight had come, and no one had perished.

A man with one of the large tallow candles approached the front of the house. He sidled past Kate, then threw his candle into one of the tall windows. The glass shattered and the curtains burst into flame. Someone yelled, and as if it were a signal, a horde rushed the building. Candles, lamps, and torches sailed into the air, through the windows, into the parlors. Within minutes, the fire spread to the upper floors. Flames danced at the windows and caught the siding.

The shades upstairs—would they be released? she wondered. Would the fire grant them escape? Cleansing? Would the dead wives know peace now? She prayed it would be so.

Kate crossed to her father and sisters. Mr. Charter looked at her with no less amazement than did those around him, but he seemed to recognize her. He wrapped his arms around her and hugged her close. "At times it approaches to sublimity, oh, my dear," he whispered in her ear before he released her.

The glowing angels went forward, and the multitude, in its awe of them, parted to let them walk through the gates. Mr. Charter and those who'd prayed with him followed close behind, and the others, with a trembling Reverend Flavy in the lead, fell in step after him.

A woman, as Kate passed her, reached through the bars and asked, "Will we be saved then?"

Kate looked into her desperate eyes and answered, "There's no one here can tell you that."

Epilogue

S HE IS SEATED BESIDE HER FA-
ther. It's the first time she has
seen him since moving away. He
lived, she thinks, not as long a life as she might have wished for
him, but now he's where he wanted to be for most of it—with
her mother.

Looking at his face, so composed in the coffin, she knows
he's found peace. The last part of his life he spent as a Quaker.
She attended some of the meetings with him and knows that he
found great resolve there, as well as the guidance he'd sought
mistakenly from Elias Fitcher to help him navigate a life without
the person he held dearest.

The Pulaski house (does anyone call it that now?) is as she
remembers it. Her sisters haven't done much beyond the general
upkeep to take care of it, despite still having bags of money in
the root cellar from all those travelers who once came down this
dead-end road in the hope of finding salvation. Gaslight has arrived in Jekyll's Glen, but it won't be coming here anytime soon.
They still use lamps and candles, but at least they don't have to
make their own.

Her daughter is in the other room right now talking to the two of them, everybody giving her time alone with the body. With her thoughts.

So much changed after that night. So much of what happened remains untold. She finds she prefers it that way.

Newspaper accounts across New England and as far south as Virginia reported the events of that night as "the False Rapture." So many people were tarred and feathered, beaten or hanged for having lied about the end of the world. It's so strange, she thinks, that so many people were furious because their world *hadn't* ended.

The destruction of Harbinger House and the presumed death of its charismatic leader proved to be nothing but footnotes to the main event. All that remained of the house afterward were foundation and chimney stones, thrusting like deformed fingers out of the rise on which it had sat.

The aspect of the story that has remained alive afterward is the account of the three glowing angels who led the way out of the fire. At least, that's how people remember it—people who weren't there.

She still comes across references to "the night of the angels" in articles as far away as Boston. Nowadays they're usually in spiritualist pamphlets, which she throws away whenever she receives one.

As if knowing her thoughts, her daughter suddenly races into the darkened room and asks, "Mama, have you ever seen angels?"

She knows exactly where this has come from, who has put this question in her child's head. A moment later, her husband comes quietly in and lifts their daughter up into his arms, saying softly, "This isn't the time, darling. Your mother's having some time alone right now with your grandfather's memory. You come outside with me and we'll play in the snow." He trades an apologetic smile with her. She mouths the words "Thank you" to him.

Those two witches, she thinks. They won't dare come out

here now from the kitchen. They'll hide back there like the two mad harpies they are.

There's so much the newspapers never reported. So much no one else knew. For instance, no report ever mentioned those members of the community who escaped the conflagration by fleeing into the fields, and who claimed to have seen the glass pyramid explode like a volcano on top of the house, hurling a fireball into the night sky, which ascended until it was lost from sight, and never came down. She didn't see it herself, but she believes it.

For the first few days after the failed Advent, the family was too busy to discuss what had happened. There was no time to mourn Lavinia at all. When day broke on October 15, a rope bridge was strung across the gorge, and many of those who'd escaped from the Harbinger side stayed on to help with the dead and dying below.

She and her sisters, all scrubbed clean and pink as newborns, worked through the whole day. They ripped sheets into strips for bandages, helped carry the wounded back to the house, made splints and tied tourniquets. If anyone recognized them as brides of Fitcher, they didn't let on, but the vast majority had probably only seen Kate and then only at the turnpike. Over the next few days the sisters did encounter faces they recognized. The ones she didn't know, like Sarah, who seemed to have lost her wits, the other two pointed out to her. There was Reverend Flavy, presiding ineffectually over the sorting of the dead in the gorge; and the man with the teamster mustache, who oversaw the clearing of a cart track from Mill Creek Road to the path leading into the gorge, and whose name they never learned; and also the slight, bearded stranger she'd seen once in Jekyll's Glen, who wasn't even part of the community but without hesitation pitched in and helped carry the bodies out of the gorge to the cleared track. The stevedores, too, all brought their wagons down the track and solemnly piled the many unidentified bodies on board, then took them back to town. Their procession through the woods looked peculiarly medieval to her. She has a mental picture of them rolling through the trees like a train of men carting off plague victims.

It was in the woods between the path and her house that she encountered the young man. He'd been struck upon the head a great, bleeding gash, but had no memory of how, or where he was. His parents were somewhere in the area but he didn't know where. She took him home and ministered to him along with the many others. At least he remembered his name, which was Orlando, and she felt as if she'd rescued a knight out of legend. For her, that was the best thing to come out of it all.

It was a few days before the injured and exhausted former Fitcherites cleared out of their house. Some would only go as far as Jekyll's Glen before settling down. Orlando and his folks numbered among those.

She remembers the night she and her sisters rested together again for the first time since Fitcher had entered their lives. She asked them what it had felt like to be dead. The two exchanged an odd, nervous glance and then denied having any memory of death at all. She knew they were lying. She knows it still. She knows that they could tell her right this minute, but that they won't. Something in their relationship was changed forever by those events. Although she rescued them, she isn't allowed to know what she rescued them from.

Those two became inseparable afterward.

Once when she was just finished sweeping their father's room, she caught the two of them seated together on what had originally been her bed. They were whispering and rapping on the wall. Nothing seemed to be answering. She watched awhile from the doorway, then very deliberately she broke the broom handle across her knee with a loud *Crack!* that made them both leap to their feet. They were furious and resentful, but they never tried talking to the wall again while she was around.

They probably do now, she thinks. She doesn't really want to know.

They still have never married, and she knows they never will. She suspects that they are probably both mad, but not dangerously so.

Outside there are black gum, basswood, elm, and maple trees where the road used to wind on to Harbinger. The cart track that was cut to Mill Creek Road became Falls Road, the only access to the gorge now. No one goes to the far side of it anyway, because of the stories of the haunted ghost town lost somewhere back in the woods there. It, like the angels, has become part of the local lore, like Mr. Irving's headless horseman elsewhere in New England.

In a few days, after they've buried her father, they will go out and cut down a tree for Christmas. Her husband will handle the ax, and they'll be more than happy to let him, she's sure. Her sisters will bring out the decorations for it—all the ornaments with the trio of angels painted on them, that match the quilts on the beds, the needlepoints on the walls. The two of them sell the quilts, which act alone keeps the tale of the angels alive, she supposes.

No one ever gets the real story, however. Kate's heard the tales her sisters tell, and they're nothing like what happened at the gorge, nothing like the real way the three of them were transported across it. She may be the only living soul in her right mind who knows. The two of them either have no memory of that night's final miracle or have suppressed it as they've done their other disquieting recollections.

Just as she, estranged by their collusion, will never share with them how she climbed across the rope bridge to Harbinger that first winter and sowed the grounds with salt.